CELIA'S SHADOW

SANDY LEVY KIRSCHENBAUM

PUBLISHED BY FASTPENCIL PUBLISHING

Lisa.
Hope you laugh a little
while you read Celia's
Shadow
Happy Reading
Sandy ♡

Celia's Shadow

First Edition

Print edition ISBN: 9781499904611

http://www.fastpencil.com

Printed in the United States of America

TABLE OF CONTENTS

"I would rather walk with a friend in the dark, than alone in the light."

Helen Keller

❧

ACKNOWLEDGMENTS

I started this fictional novel so far back in time that I think the first chapters were stored on eight-inch floppy discs. Celia was my maternal grandmother's name—she used to sneak food under the table to my dog Heidi. I didn't know where this story would go, but I did know the title would be Celia's Shadow.

William Charles was my father's (Leonard Levy) photography studio in Salem, Massachusetts. I miss him every day.

There are many people who encouraged, supported, doubted, and laughed at me. I'd like to thank those who encouraged and supported me.

My wonderful husband Howard, your love and support inspired me throughout this entire writing adventure. Thank you for allowing me to read chapters to you and for saying you liked them—I used many of your funny suggestions. You make me laugh. I love you more and more each day.

My twin sister Susan Schale, thank you for everything you did to help make this book happen—creating the perfect cover to depict Celia and her dog (it is exactly the way I dreamed it would be), taking my photograph, reading every word, and providing me with your wonderful feedback. Oh, and thank you for taking those science tests for me in high school.

My niece Alison Levy (might be Alison Thompson by the time this book is published) and Winnie, thank you for giving up your Saturday to pose for the cover image and for your positive feedback on the chapters.

Lenna Kutner, thank you for reading this book (some chapters repeatedly) from cover to cover and word for word. Your sharp eye, as a fellow author, found key and important points throughout the pages. You helped to make the storyline flow smoothly and to keep it chronologically correct. Thank you for being my friend.

Stephanie Levy, my sister (in-law), thank you for being one of the first to read and comment on the chapters. I loved the notes you wrote in the margins—your words of reassurance kept me going.

Peggy O'Connor, thank you for reading Celia's Shadow so quickly and for your honesty. Your friendship means the world to me, and

I'm happy I could share Celia with you. You are an inspiration in so many ways.

Jane Krakauer, Judy Sharoff, and Peggy Simmons, thank you for your enthusiasm about Celia's Shadow. You continually toasted my accomplishment and supported me along the way. You believed in me, when I doubted myself. You have been a great pep squad during our travels and your excitement for my success was contagious.

Rick Bettencourt, your honesty during our writing group made an incredible difference. You encouraged me to take chances and make Celia jump into scenes. It's amazing how helpful you were.

Wendy Leavitt, thank you for your positive words and the time you took to read this book.

Mary Elliot, Lisa Burke, Alison Doris, Nancy Dyer, Janet Kazmierczak, Michael and Donna Greenburg, you most likely have no idea how your encouragement and praise helped me find the confidence to write the final chapters for this book.

And to my mom Rose Levy and the rest of my family—thank you for your love and support.

Part 1

Celia

Outside, heavy dark clouds intensified the isolation of her room. A soft glow from the ceiling lights illuminated over her bed. Unaware of all that surrounded her, Celia remained motionless under the thin green blanket. With quiet, barely noticeable breaths, her chest moved softly up and down. Her skin was pale. Her long auburn hair lay tangled and clumped on the hard pillow beneath her bruised head. From a shiny metal pole, tubes delivered fluids to her veins.

"Celia?" The light-haired friend's anxiety was apparent in her voice. A tingle generated into her wrist, as she banged her index finger against the cold bedframe. She held Celia's hand gently.

"Celia, can you hear me?" She waited for a response. "Celia, if you can hear me, squeeze my hand. Blink. Do something–anything." She never expected to say these words to her dear friend. Celia lay silently in the sterile hospital room.

The friend rested back against the torn leather chair–the chair she had pulled close to the bed over two hours ago. Tensely, she watched Celia breathe. The intravenous drip trickled slowly down the plastic tube. She stared at the bruises on Celia's face and arms and she sighed.

Desperately, she prayed for Celia to respond. Except for the slow breaths that moved her chest up and down, Celia was motionless.

In stillness, she continued to hold Celia's hand. The doctor entered the room and interrupted her private vigil.

"Does she know yet?" She clenched Celia's limp hand tightly. "Does she remember anything?"

"No, she doesn't know. We won't tell her until she is fully aware. She's been in and out of consciousness. That's all."

"Did she wake up before?"

"Yes, she was awake for a very short while. She's heavily sedated right now. She needs her rest. Perhaps you do as well. Why don't you go home and come back later? She won't wake up any time soon." He placed his hand on the shoulder of Celia's blonde friend.

They watched Celia breathe.

Part 2

Three Years Earlier

The Birthday Girl

It was after eight o'clock. How much after, she had no idea, but Celia knew it was enough past the hour that her Sunday *Globe* would be gone. She imagined the paper bandit set their alarm clock for 7:59 a.m. to snatch it before its rightful reader arrived. When she opened the door seconds before eight o'clock, the paper was hers; a minute later, the paper was off on its journey to someone else's breakfast table.

Celia resigned herself to the fact that a walk to the corner store, for another *Globe*, would be part of her morning schedule.

Celia had been awake for half an hour. She promised herself she would stay in bed and not look at the clock until she heard the bells ring. She propped her pillows against the iron spindles of the headboard.

Her antique bed was one of the few items she took when she moved back from Connecticut. Years before, when she had first moved to Connecticut, she had discovered it in a neighbor's trash. The iron had been painted bright pink with purple round knobs at the top of each post. She wedged it in the back of her little green Volkswagen Rabbit. A third of the headboard hung out of the hatch as she drove home slowly. She stripped the pink away and spray-painted it charcoal gray. The brass knobs, no longer purple, were the only parts not made from iron.

Except for some personal belongings, Celia left mostly everything else back in Connecticut. The bed was her treasure, and she was pleased to have saved it from abandonment.

She relaxed and enjoyed the warm morning air. From her opened windows, she heard the sounds in the neighborhood start to escalate. A soft breeze drifted in and brought with it the faint smell of freshly baked bread from a nearby bakery. Brilliantly colored marionettes, which hung by the window, swayed together as if dancing to a finely choreographed performance. Occasionally they gently clinked together.

Celia observed a layer of pollen on the mantel above the fireplace. The fireplace, situated between two windows, was the focal point of the room. Whoever had lived there previously had dramatically different taste from Celia. The pollen-coated fireplace had been painted with a medley of colors. The outer molding was colonial blue, the middle was mustard yellow, and the inside was a barnyard red. The colors contrasted with the brick surround. The walls around were dark yellow on the bottom and pastel yellow on the top. A golden chair rail surrounded the entire room. Months after she moved in, Celia had abandoned her plan to paint the room a soft creamy white. Now, three years later, she was oblivious of the eclectic array of colors.

She reached to the little round table alongside her bed and lifted the pale lace tablecloth. She pulled out a cigarette from the package taped underneath the tabletop. She used to hide the packs in the freezer, but Kate had once discovered them between the ice cream and frozen corn, and then flushed them down the toilet. Currently, Kate had not caught on to the fact that there was always a fresh pack neatly secured in the little hideaway beneath the table. Celia stretched to the nightstand on the opposite side of her bed. She fumbled for matches, which were stored in a small porcelain box. It was 8:47 a.m.

"Damn!" Out of habit, she glanced at the clock. She wanted to wait for the bells to ring before she knew the time. It had been years since she stayed in bed this late. She lit the match and slowly drew it up to the stick of tobacco that extended from the center of her lips. Leisurely and deliberately, she inhaled to light it and then just as gradually and deliciously, she exhaled a soft swirl of smoke. A cloud puffed out of her mouth, while the rest of it filtered through her nostrils. She rested back against her pillows and enjoyed her moment. The strap to her silky nightgown slipped from her shoulder. She left it down and dramatically savored her habit.

Celia used the first cigarette to light the second. As she enjoyed the second as much as the first, the bells rang. Initially, they rang beautifully and musically and then they chimed nine times. She stared out beyond her puppets, where she could see the top of the old church steeple through her window. She loved the sound from those bells.

From the kitchen counter, her cell phone rang and interrupted her peaceful moment. She threw the covers back, adjusted the straps on her nightgown, and got out of bed. She didn't check the caller ID when she answered the call.

"Hello?" She crushed the butt in the ashtray.

"Hey, Celia, it's me. Are you interested in a Mexican brunch at Tequila Maria's?"

"Kate, how can you think of eating that stuff this early in the morning?" Celia walked to the sink, took a large glass from the strainer, and filled it with water. The small kitchen table sat below a large window, where a rectangular flower box was attached to the outside sill. Celia lifted the screen and poured water into the soil that held pink and white begonias. The strap of her nightgown again fell from her shoulder.

"I like it there. Please come with me. Don't forget, I'm the birthday girl."

"Yesterday! Yesterday you were the birthday girl. Not today." Celia lifted the strap of her nightgown back up to her shoulder. Again, it fell off her shoulder, where it remained.

"It's still my birthday weekend. Come on, my treat."

"I can't be ready for a while. I haven't even had a cup of coffee yet."

"I'm not ready either. Tom's on call and left a little while ago to see a couple kids at the hospital. How's 11:30? Could you be ready by then?"

"I'll be ready." Celia emptied the glass and placed it in the strainer. "I'll pick you up. You drove last night."

"It's quite all right, Celia, I'll drive. I want to get there."

She ignored Kate's comment about getting there. "I'll be ready at 11:00."

"I said 11:30!"

"Oh, yeah, sorry, 11:30. I need to go down to Pete's to get a paper and a coffee first. See you at 11:30."

She stepped over her clothes that had spent the night on the floor by her bed and went into the bathroom. She pulled out a plastic tray from below the sink and picked out a brown-coated hair band.

Celia stared in the mirror and sighed. Her sleepy eyes, surrounded by smudged and flaky mascara, stared back. Her hair was flattened to the back of her head and tangled by her temples.

She gathered it in one big clump and pulled the band around it. The ponytail, which held most of her hair, was high on the top of her head. A few snarled strands didn't make it into the clustered mane. She didn't notice how her big green eyes sparkled like sun-drenched sea glass or her beautiful high cheekbones. She saw the bump on the bridge of her nose.

She lowered the straps of her nightgown and let it fall from her tall, thin body. She walked naked to her closet and found her favorite light-gray sweats. In her tattered sweats, she walked to Pete's for her morning coffee and a *Globe*.

Pete's Market was next to the bell-ringing church at the bottom of the hill at the end of her street. The store was famous for its freshly brewed coffee and homemade muffins. For Celia, Pete's was the only place to shop. It didn't matter their prices were higher than other markets. She didn't need a big superstore for her staples of lottery tickets, eggs, cheese, chicken, potatoes, onions, garlic, bananas, ice cream, and cigarettes.

Celia was surprised when she found several Sunday papers still stacked by the cash register. She took a paper and walked to the back of the small store. She ordered a large coffee with cream and three packets of sugar. With the paper tucked under her arm, she took a quick gulp of the coffee. The paper was too large to be handled this way; it slid down to her hip. As she reached to stop it from falling further, she bumped into someone standing to her right. In front of her stood a well-built handsome man with deep, dark eyes. She glanced down and saw a massive brown coffee stain on the front of her sweat shirt. She felt the heat from the coffee seep through her shirt and the hot blush of embarrassment on her face. She had never seen this man at Pete's before; she would have remembered if she had.

"You okay?" He reached around to the counter, grasped a cluster of napkins, and then handed them to her.

"Yes, I'm so sorry. Did I spill any on you?" The flush intensified on her face.

"I'm all set. I think you got the worst of it."

"Thank you." She turned and walked toward the cash register. She left the store as fast as humanly possible.

Celia walked up the three flights of stairs to her apartment. She took the last few sips of her coffee, tossed the empty cup into a brown paper bag by the stove, and pulled the damp sweat shirt off. She filled the sink with cold water and liquid soap and threw in the shirt to soak out the fresh stain.

She walked into the bathroom and gasped out loud at her reflection. *Never go to sleep without taking your makeup off. No mascara is better than these dark circles.*

Vigorously, she rubbed her eyes and further smudged the mascara. She turned on the water and stepped into the shower.

ORANGE MARGARITA

"Good morning, ladies." The waitress seated Celia and Kate at a sun-drenched table on the outside deck. "How would you enjoy starting the day off with a delicious orange margarita? Or how's a Bloody Mary sound?" She handed them menus.

"No thank you," Celia and Kate said at the exact same time.

"Rough night, ladies?"

"Yeah, we celebrated my birthday. Let's just say we stayed out past curfew." Kate adjusted the belt on her black cotton shorts. She wore a purple sleeveless top, which severely contrasted with her bright-red shoulder-length hair. A mass of freckles covered her from head to toe. She had thick, pouty lips; beautiful, big, white teeth; and, in Celia's opinion, the perfect nose. "We'll have the usual huevos rancheros and iced coffee."

The server took their order and walked inside.

"I'm exhausted. I hope she comes back soon with our coffee. How come you don't seem exhausted?" Celia picked up her glass and poured a small amount of water into the palms of her hands. She splashed it on her cheeks.

"I should, because I am. If Tom hadn't left as early as he did, I'd still be sleeping. I'll take a nap later."

"Thank God for coffee. I've already had half a cup. I started with a full cup, but I spilled most of it all over me when I literally bumped into a guy at Pete's. He was kind of cute."

"And?"

"And nothing. I got a paper and a cup of coffee. I was a mess. I hadn't even washed up before I ran out. Then I spilled the stupid coffee all over me."

"You spilled something? Now there's a surprise!"

Celia knew exactly to what Kate was referring.

"Tell me about the cute guy you bumped into." Kate folded her arms across her chest as she leaned back to hear Celia's story.

"There isn't anything to tell. Except that he had nice eyes. But we know that doesn't mean anything, don't we?" Celia poured more water into the palms of her hands and this time splashed the water around her neck. "Think about how many guys I've met with nice eyes who turned out to be the biggest idiots." She waved her hands back and forth by Kate's face. Kate could list a dozen obnoxious men who wasted Celia's time, Geoff included. "Don't answer that!"

"It's funny how you're an eye girl. That always seems to be the first thing you notice."

"I was embarrassed that I spilled the coffee. I'm grateful I didn't spill it on him. I don't remember what he was wearing. But when I got home, I saw last night's makeup smudged around my eyes and the big brown stain on the front of my sweat shirt." Celia cupped her hands and then plopped her head into them. "Oh, forget it. Ugh!"

Celia dug through her bag for her cigarettes.

"I see you're still smoking?"

Celia glared at Kate. "Yes, I am."

"I didn't expect an answer. You do know it's passé to smoke these days, don't you? Not to mention it's disgusting and stinky. I thought you said you were going to quit."

"Why do you say that same thing every time you see me smoke? It's become a little Kate cliché. Did you think I'd quit since last night? You saw me have one then and you see me with one now. I told you I'm going to quit this week, or maybe next week." She took a long, slow drag.

"Celia, let me ask you something. Hypothetically, of course. Would you ever ask a guy for his name and number? You know, like the guy you bumped into, and I do mean bumped into, this morning?"

Very rarely did a man get a second chance from Celia. In the event someone got beyond the first date, she found something wrong with him in a relatively short period of time. The men she dated were too short, too tall, too thin, too fat, too boring, too silly, too pretentious, too poor, too rich, too smart, too dopey, or just plain too available. She had something negative to say about nearly every guy she dated. Once, after Geoff, she dated a man in whom she was remotely interested, but the relationship never amounted to more than fleeting friends. She tried to give him a chance, which was something she never thought would happen. For now, she had her work and her friends to keep her busy.

"I don't think so. Why? Because I mentioned someone with great eyes?"

"No, I was wondering, that's all. You don't usually talk about guys that you see. I thought if you met someone and found him to be a little interesting, you might think about being the one to make the first move."

"What are you? Insane?" She turned her head and blew smoke away toward the ocean. "Simply ask a stranger for their number? Are you nuts? How would I know if he was a psychopath or something? Oh, that's right, I wouldn't know, would I? Besides, I don't need a guy. I think I'm happy the way I am. And this is exactly why I never talk to you about guys. Because if I do, you make it a conversation, rather than a comment. It was a comment. That's all. Plain and simple. I thought you'd be entertained by the fact that I spilled coffee all over myself first thing Sunday morning."

"There is nothing wrong with wanting to date or having someone significant in your life. Sometimes you act as if it's a weakness to want to share your time with another person."

"I do not. I prefer being alone. At least for now. I happen to enjoy my own company, and I don't have time for a relationship."

"I'm not saying that you don't like your life now, Celia, but didn't you like being in a relationship? I know Geoff turned out to be crazy, but there were some relationship-kind of things you appreciated in your life. Weren't there?"

"Kate, I hate this conversation. You know I hate it because I tell you every time you bring it up. And I hate it even more when you mention HIS name, especially when we're about to eat. I know you mean well, but I'm not ready. I hate talking about him. I can't even say his name."

"Celia, THIS is a relationship. Our friendship is a relationship. Is this so bad?" Kate moved her hand back and forth between them.

"I know that's not what you're talking about, Kate."

"As I said, there's nothing wrong with wanting a romantic relationship. I just want to say that. I know you don't need one but need and want are two different things."

"I know. I know. It's not something I can handle right now. I'm scarred from the insanity of my past. Let's leave it at that."

"I get it. Just one more thing. If you recall, you did want to get married–that's why you got engaged to Geoff. You must have seen something good about it at one time in your life. And just because that idiot turned out to be a major league asshole doesn't mean that all guys are bad."

"Ya know, I'm not sure I would have gone through with that marriage. Even if I never found out who he really was, I don't know what might have happened. Sometimes I think being engaged was the perfect excuse to not date. I didn't have to deal with all the other jerks in the world, because I could tell them I was already committed to one. It wasn't the marriage I wanted–being committed to someone was the perfect excuse I needed to not date."

"Maybe we should order those orange margaritas now." She motioned to the waitress.

Boop

A small cluster of white clouds fragmented the vista of a solid blue sky. Celia enjoyed the ocean view from her window. *Should I call in sick? I could spend the day with my feet buried in the sand and my nose buried in a book.* She could feel the freshness of the air, a wonderful change from the muggy and oppressive previous two weeks.

She stared out the window while she pulled her sleeveless yellow dress over her head and fastened the buttons down the front. She stood silently for a moment as she gazed out toward the water. *At least it's Thursday. One more day to the weekend.*

Celia moved forward into the window. She placed both hands on the windowsill and pressed her face against the screen. She inhaled the ocean air. *How can I spend such a glorious day cooped up in my office? I should get a waitress job down at the dock. I could serve oversized veggie sandwiches dripping with melted cheese and cool fruit smoothies to tourists all day. I would be able to enjoy the golden sunshine and fresh air.* A puff of pollen wafted from the window. Celia sneezed. *And how about those cold winter blizzards? Fun at the dock then?*

Celia buckled her seat belt, placed the key in the ignition, and started the engine. She patted the dashboard. "Thank you, sweetie." Her little green car didn't always start.

She drove the scenic way, which took her by the ocean. She pulled into the parking lot at the beach, took the first space closest to the sand, opened the windows, and smelled the ocean air. From behind the steering wheel, she watched the waves roll onto the shore. She was mesmerized by the water.

The crash of a shell smashing onto the hood of her car startled her back to reality. In an instant, a filthy seagull blocked her view. The bird pecked at the shell and pulled out a tiny piece of meat. It then pooped on the car's hood. *Thanks for the gift, birdie. Guess this beach break is over.* The dashboard clock read 8:17 a.m. She left the beach and headed to the T station.

Regardless of how beautiful the day, the subway car was either too cold or too hot. Today the underground travel was sweltering and unpleasant. Celia took the last seat in the row, which limited the number of passengers surrounding her to one. A woman doused in cheap perfume took the seat next to her and took Celia's breath away. *Damn. That stinks.* Celia opened her bag and pulled out a tissue, which she then held under her nose. *How about a no perfume area? Did anyone ever think of that? Cigarette smoke isn't nearly this offensive. Said the smoker.* She saw the humor in her idea.

Her office was neat and simply decorated. She was one of the lucky ones on the seventh floor who had the luxury of a window. A window that showcased a skyline view of larger buildings in the city. Prints from local street artists covered the dreadfully painted light-blue walls. A four-foot silk ficus tree stood by the door. Her old mahogany desk was large and took up half of the wall across from the window. She enjoyed people-watching on the pedestrian mall below.

Celia's eyes focused on her monitor, and her fingers flew across the keyboard. She was engrossed in the database she was developing. Sadly, she was oblivious of the glorious day outside.

"Knock, knock. Am I interrupting anything?" Ramona moved her fist back and forth in the air, as she pretended to knock on the nonexistent door that led into Celia's office.

"Oh, you startled me. You're not interrupting anything. Come on in. I could use a break. I'm going blind from this computer screen." She nodded her head toward the monitor. "What's going on?"

Ramona stepped into her office and took a seat in the old black chair across from Celia's desk. She immediately crossed her legs and rapidly shook her foot back and forth. Her dangling shoe appeared as if it would drop to the floor at any moment. Celia knew Ramona had something up her sleeve. She appeared anxious, which was different from her usual nondescript expression. Ramona was grinning, as if she held a secret she was about to share. She dressed fashionably, and her clothes were always perfectly pressed. Her almond-shaped brown eyes were encased by long, thick, dark eyelashes. Her highlighted hair, cut short above her neck, accentuated her chin, which appeared too large for her face.

"You busy tomorrow after work? Would you want to meet me for a drink or something?"

"I guess so." Celia took a deep breath. She wished she could inhale the words back into her mouth. *STOP!* She had made a mistake when she answered too hastily. She hesitated. "Just you and me? No one else, right?" Celia waited. Ramona did not respond fast enough for Celia's liking. "Ramona?" Celia said her friend's name slowly and inquiringly. Ramona constantly pestered Celia to let her fix her up. This visit would prove no different.

"My brother Walter is coming in from New York, and I thought you might like to meet him. I think it could be fun. He'll treat us and maybe we'll even get dinner or something."

"Ramona, I don't know. I hate fix ups, and this has the definite feel of a fix up. Besides, he's your brother. How could I ever look you in the eye if I sleep with him the first time we meet and then decide I hate him?"

"Ha ha. I know you're little too uptight to even kiss a guy the first time you meet him, let alone get intimate."

Ramona's shoe dropped to the floor. "Listen. It's not a fix up. I promised to do something with him and think it will be more fun for him, and for me, if you come out with us. He lives in New York City, so it's not as if you can have a dating relationship with him anyway."

"I guess you're right." She picked up a paper clip and tossed it onto Ramona's lap.

"It's drinks, maybe dinner. No big deal. Really. What else will you do?" She threw the paper clip back onto the desk blotter. "You never go out anymore. Do something different for a change. Come on. I'm begging you." Ramona clasped her hands together in a pleading fashion and put them under her large chin as she raised her head high.

How could Celia refuse her?

Walter and Ramona were seated at a table when Celia arrived a few minutes before six o'clock. Ramona's brother was handsome. He had the same almond-shaped dark eyes and long lashes that Ramona had. They were unquestionably brother and sister. He was much taller than his sister, and his physique more athletic, but the resemblance, including the large chin, was uncanny. He wore khaki slacks and a white collared button-down shirt. His sleeves were rolled up and exposed tanned, muscular forearms covered with shiny blond hairs. His smile was fabulous and produced a twinkle in his eyes, which were surrounded by fine character lines.

"Sorry I'm a little late. My computer froze, and I had to restart to make sure everything was working before I left." Celia pulled out the empty chair conveniently left between Ramona and Walter. Walter stood and helped Celia as he slid her chair in toward the table. The appropriate introductions were made as they sat together in the crowded bar. *Ramona, I'm surprised you never mentioned your handsome brother before.* "How you guys doing?"

Neither sibling responded. Walter and Ramona blankly stared at Celia but didn't answer her question. No one spoke. Except for the noises from other patrons, there was silence at their table. Celia expected one of them would say something. But no words were exchanged. Celia was uncomfortable with the quiet. After a few more speechless moments, she glared at Ramona. *Are you going to respond? Are you going to say anything to help break the ice?* Neither sibling spoke.

"When did you get to Boston, Walter?" Celia took the burden of conversation upon herself.

"Flew in last night around nine o'clock and popped over to Ramona's place. Had a bite to eat and then hit the hay. Boop!" Walter made a fist as he punched his hand into the air.

Celia acknowledged his response with a grin. He simply answered the question and offered no further conversation. Ramona picked up her napkin, rolled it into a long tube, unrolled it and rolled it again. She presented nothing.

Did they have an argument or something on the way over? Within minutes of their get-together, Celia was sorry she had accepted Ramona's invitation. "Where in New York do you live?"

"I live outside of New York City, in Bergen County, New Jersey. Boop." He again popped his fist in the air and remained silent after his answer.

"Do you like living in New Jersey?" *Wonder if this is how a talk show host feels when they have a boring guest?*

"Yup, a lot. Boop!" He punched the air and stared at Celia, as he waited for the next question.

She watched his hand move up and down. "Do you have a long commute to get to the city?" *Why am I asking this question? Am I really the only one conversing here? Can they not hear me?* The lack of conversation, along with the absence of their server, annoyed her. She glanced around the room for someone to take their order. Her patience was wearing thin.

"Nope. I hop on the train and in less than half an hour, I'm there. Boop!" He punched his fist high into the air as he finished speaking.

She inquisitively turned to Ramona and then back to Walter. "I'm jealous. It seems so easy. I wish it took me a half an hour to get to work. Don't you Ramona?" *I guess I'm on my own here, right, Ramona?* "I hate taking the T into Boston. First, I drive to the station, sit on the subway for what seems forever, and then I walk down here. Unless it's raining or snowing; if that's the case, then I switch trains two or three times, which is slower than walking, but at least I keep dry. You're lucky you can get to your office that quickly." *That filled about forty-five seconds of conversation. Nice long sentences. Lots of information. What do you think, Boop Boy?*

"I do have to walk a little way to my office, but it isn't far. Maybe a block or two. Boop." He again punched the air above his head.

Good job. Speaking without it being a direct response to a question. He freely offered up the fact that his commute included a walk to his office. *I didn't even ask about your travel by foot.* Although Walter had become somewhat engaged in discussion with Celia, the conversation was nonetheless tedious and labored. *How long can we talk about our commutes? Ramona, chime in any time and take part in this conversation, or at least change the topic.*

Ramona glanced around the bar and paid no attention to Walter or Celia.

Celia was anxious for an iced coffee and distrusted the waitress would ever make it to their table. She was uneasy talking to Walter. If she wasn't asking him questions, no one was talking. The silence was annoying.

"Are you Ramona's older or younger brother?"

"Why don't you try to guess that one. Boop!" He again punched his fist in the air.

"Oh no!" She waved her hand back and forth and shook her head in the same direction. "That's a lose-lose topic, and quite frankly, at this exact moment I'm very sorry that I asked the question." She studied his chin and then Ramona's. *Are they the same size? Ramona's chin seems larger, but maybe it's because the rest of her face is smaller. That chin-accentuating haircut doesn't help.* Celia was bored and distracted.

"I'll let you off the hook. I'm Ramona's older brother. I'm the oldest at thirty-eight. We have another brother, Stan, who's thirty-four and then there's our little Ramona baby at twenty-nine. Boop!" He reached over to his sister and rubbed the top of her head for a few seconds and, as expected, punched his fist into the air.

The waitress arrived and took their order. Celia ordered an iced coffee while Ramona and Walter each ordered a Long Island Iced Tea. After they ordered, Walter took it upon himself to repeat the order back to the waitress.

"So. That's an iced coffee here." He nodded his head toward Celia. "And two Long Island Ice Teas here and here." He pointed to Ramona and then to himself. "Boop! Boop! Boop!" The first boop was synchronized with an air punch toward Celia, his second toward Ramona, and the last one at himself.

Celia watched his fist move in the air. *What the fuck is this booping thing?*

Celia's attention diverted from the painfully mundane conversation to the boops and air-punching fist. She counted the boops as Walter spoke to see whether he punched his fist in the air after every boop. For the most part, there was a punch for every boop. By eight o'clock, she had lost count of the boops but had concluded there were more boops than punches. The boop count became unbalanced when he emphatically finished one sentence with a "boopity, boop, boop, boop."

She fidgeted in her chair. Celia wanted a good reason to escape and was aware that finishing the mystery novel on her coffee table would not do, at least if that was the reason she verbalized to the siblings. She ordered a second drink and waited another twenty minutes. "I better get going. It's a long commute home and I need to get up early. Thank you for the invitation. It's nice to meet you, Walter." She lied.

By the time she arrived home, she was wired from the caffeine. She picked up her book from the kitchen table and walked into the living room where she plopped herself onto her couch. *Boop that.* She propped her feet on the coffee table. *I should have stayed home in the first place.* She finished her book and then flipped through ridiculous sitcoms. Strained conversation with strangers was not her idea of a good time out. *Another wasted Friday evening.*

TIMMY'S

Celia walked into her kitchen and picked up her phone and listened to her voicemail.

"Hey, we're going down to the beach for ice cream. We'll swing by at six o'clock. Be ready if you want to come with us." Kate's voice sang through the message.

Celia gladly abandoned a healthy dinner to join Kate and Tom for a visit to Timmy's Ice Cream Shoppe.

"Did you go out with Ramona last night?" Kate turned around from the front seat. She draped her arm around the headrest.

"Ramona AND her brother." Celia curled her lips and scowled.

"I'm going to guess, by the expression on your face, it didn't go well?"

"Nope. Not at all. What a weirdo."

"What happened?" Kate moved her arm down and squeezed Celia's knee.

"When I first got there, he seemed normal. He was polite and handsome. He got up when I arrived at the table. Pulled out my chair too. The whole chivalry thing. After I sat down, neither of them said a word."

"What do you mean?"

"They didn't speak. The only time the brother spoke was when I asked him questions. Then every time he said something, he punched his fist over his head and made a booping noise."

"What do you mean, booping noise?" Tom shook his head curiously at his wife. She was surprised he was paying attention and joined the conversation.

Celia punched her fist in the air and mimicked Walter's catchphrase. "Boop."

"Come on. Are you exaggerating?"

"No. I'm not exaggerating or making this up. I counted how many times he said that word, and I think he said it a million times. Well, the million is a slight exaggeration."

Kate poked Tom in the shoulder. "Do you believe this guy?"

Tom kept his eyes on the road as he turned in to Timmy's parking lot.

The trio walked to the dilapidated old shack. Timmy's had been the beach's snack bar for years. The building was situated behind a bench-lined pebbled walkway.

"What flavors are you guys getting?" Celia read the list of flavors.

"Vanilla. How about you girls?" Tom stood at the counter and waited to place their orders.

"I'll have coffee and moose tracks." Celia reached for her wallet. "In a waffle cone, please."

Kate pushed Celia's hand down. "Put that away. Our treat. I'd like caramel turtle and black raspberry. Thanks."

Celia scrunched her nose. "Caramel and black raspberry? Together?"

"Yes, together. I love both flavors. They don't have to complement each other. It's ice cream. It's fun food. Tell me more about last night."

They walked to the walkway and sat down on the benches facing the ocean.

"Another waste of time." Celia licked the coffee ice cream from the top of the cone. She wiped a large drip from her shorts. "Why can't I eat ice cream without it dripping all over me?"

"What did you do with Ramona and her brother?"

"Oh, Boop Boy? Not much. We went to the bar across from my office. I left as soon as I could." She wiped another spot of ice cream from her shorts. "Why is mine melting this fast? Yours isn't."

"Even if you didn't have a good time, I'm still glad you went out. It's good to get out occasionally." Kate used her napkin to wipe another drop from Celia's leg. "I think the bottom ice cream wasn't as cold as it should be. That's why it's melting so fast. The kid should have put that flavor on top."

"Forget about my night with Boop Boy and his big-chinned sister."

"What? What about her chin?" Kate closed her eyes for a second and shook her head.

"They both have unusually large chins. They're attractive, but, as I said, they have big chins."

A boat raced toward the harbor–its engine loud and disruptive. "He's not supposed to be going that fast right there." Tom pointed his finger to the boat, as the driver cut the engine.

"What did you guys do last night?" Celia quickly licked the ice cream as it dripped down the sides of her cone.

Tom snickered, and Kate squinted.

"Watched television. Caught a little *Jeopardy!*." Tom took the last bite of his cone.

"I didn't know there was parasailing around here." Celia pointed to the person who soared high above a speedboat in the distance. "You're still competing with each other for Final Jeopardy?"

"Yes, we are. Your little friend here is a sore loser. Aren't you, Kate." Tom touched Kate's head and ruffled her hair.

"Don't be so smug. You had a lucky streak, that's all." Kate smacked Tom's hand away from her head.

"I think I should get another dog. Boop." Celia punched her fist in the air.

Kate glared at Celia. "Don't do that. That's how bad habits start. You think you're fooling around and then before you know it, you're not conscious of doing it."

"Don't do what? Get a dog?"

"No! Don't do that boop thing. It's not funny, even as a joke. But I think you'd be crazy to get a dog now. You live in a third-floor walkup. Do you want to walk a dog at five o'clock in the morning in the middle of a blizzard? Boop. Boop. Boop." Kate bopped Celia's forehead three times.

Celia seized Kate's hand. "You make a good point. I do love being comfy in my bed when it's snowing."

They watched the sailboats off in the distance.

TRUDY

Celia felt triumphant when she beat the paper thief to her Sunday *Globe*. She flipped through the headlines and the lifestyle section, as she relaxed with a fresh cup of Kona coffee. The coffee was a gift from Kate and Tom after their recent trip to Hawaii.

She barely rinsed her coffee mug before she placed it in the wooden dish rack to the right of the sink. The dish rack also held her ice cream bowl from the previous day and four large soup spoons she had used to scoop the ice cream from its container. Daily, Celia would use one of her largest spoons to shovel out an oversized serving of ice cream, lick it dry and then toss the used utensil into the sink. After three or more samplings, she inevitably gave in and filled a cereal bowl to the top. For Celia, pint size meant single serving. A carton of ice cream lasted a very short time in her freezer.

She gathered the magazines, circulars, real estate section, and a bowl of fresh cherries and then walked down the three flights to her front steps. The sunlight streamed in between her building and the one next door. The dwellings were close together. The driveway was narrow, barely wide enough for the tenants' cars to pass through.

Like most summer Sundays, the street was quiet and somewhat deserted. Celia opened her first magazine when, in a flash, her solitude and serenity ended. He raced toward her. His tan and white ears flapped up and down, his tongue hung out to one side and his leash jingled as it dragged behind him. His tail wagged wildly as he put his front paws up where Celia sat. He pushed his shimmering wet nose into the circular. She moved the paper to her other side as he plopped himself down, just about in her lap, and nuzzled against her. "Aren't you the cutest little thing?" She stroked his floppy ears and the top of his head. "And who have you escaped from?" He was barely full-grown and extremely energetic. She continued to rub his head and neck while she checked for tags. He was well-cared for, with a shaggy light-tan coat dappled with swirls of white.

Within seconds, a young boy dressed in baggy denim shorts, a dark-green T-shirt, and a dingy white and red baseball cap, worn backward on his head, appeared at the opening of her driveway. Except for the panicked *lost my dog* expression, he was like every other kid in the neighborhood. He walked toward Celia and his liberated puppy, who sat comfortably by her side.

"Trudy! I thought I lost you! Stay there!" He relaxed his shoulders and let out a big sigh. "Stay!"

"I'm holding his leash. He won't be going anywhere, at least not right now. You have a friendly little dog! Quite the leaner." The dog continued to lean into her pale-blue sundress. "If he leans against me any harder, he'll push me off these steps."

"Oh yeah, she's wicked friendly, and she loves to run off. I'm in the middle of training her now. Sorry if she's bothering you."

"Oh, he's a she. Don't be sorry. I love dogs, and she's adorable. She can run this way any time. Here you go." Celia moved forward and handed the boy Trudy's leash. She patted the dog's head one more time.

"Thank you, ma'am." He took the leash from Celia.

No, not ma'am. Not that word. She cringed. "You're welcome. My name is Celia." She responded immediately to keep him from calling her the "M" word again.

"Hi, I'm Noah. I don't know what happened. I reached down to tie my sneaker and she took off. We had just left my uncle's house. We're staying with him for the summer." He stepped into the handle of Trudy's leash, and wrapped it around his ankle.

"You have her now, Noah. Hold on tight."

Noah bent down and picked up a large rock at the side of the driveway where he and Trudy stood. He tossed the rock up into the air as they spoke. Trudy's head moved up and down and her ears bounced along while her eyes followed the stone into the air and back down again into the palm of Noah's hand.

"My uncle lives around the corner on Washington Street. He moved in last winter and he invited Trudy and me to stay with him for the whole summer. He doesn't want me to walk Trudy by his house because it's a wicked busy road. Uncle Bill is a huge worrier.

Ya know, it's a good thing I listened to him too, because if Trudy got away from me over by his house, she could have gone into the street. I hate to think what could have happened if she did that, ya know." Noah dropped the rock, and before he could grab it, Trudy pounced on it and took it into her mouth. "Trade, Trudy, trade." He extended his arm as if he was about to give her something in return. She wagged her tail furiously and plopped the slimy wet stone into Noah's hand as she waited for her reward. "She turned one about a month ago. She's still got that puppy behavior, if you know what I'm talking about." He reached into the pocket of his shorts and pulled out a biscuit, which he then gave to Trudy as her prize for trading the rock.

"Oh, I know exactly what you mean. I used to have a dog and I remember all too well that puppy behavior. Mine would run away every chance she got. I guess they love the feeling of freedom. It drove me nuts."

"Yeah, it drives me nuts too. Thank you for catching her. I was wicked scared I wouldn't find her. My parents would be super mad if they came back and Trudy had run away."

"I'm happy I could help you. But I didn't find her. She sort of ran to me."

"Thank you, thank you, and thank you again." He rubbed Trudy's head. "My parents wanted to board her while they were away for the summer, but I promised I would take care of her by myself. Uncle Bill helps me too."

"It's nice you get to stay with your uncle for the entire summer."

Noah took his baseball cap off and tucked it into his back pocket. "Yeah, my dad's doing research in California and I didn't want to go. I begged them to let me stay here. I'm a ballplayer, ya know. I didn't want to be away because I was hoping to make the All-Star team. I'm almost sure I'll make the team. At least, my coach says I will! If I went to California, I wouldn't have been able to play, and I would have been wicked upset about that. That's for sure. Playing on the All-Stars is like a once-in-a-lifetime chance, ya know?"

Celia was entertained by his innocence and enthusiasm. He was full of conversation. "That's terrific, Noah. You must be a great ballplayer to make that team."

"I'm not terrible, but I'm not the best. My regular team usually plays down the street at the park near the church. If you ever see us, you should watch. It's wicked exciting."

"I'll watch for you. I walk by there every day."

"Uncle Bill lets me go down to Pete's to pick up stuff. We're having company for lunch today to celebrate his new job. I'm going down there now to get soda. Maybe we'll see you on the way back." He stepped out from the leash's handle and wrapped it around his hand and wrist. "See ya." He waved as they walked out to the sidewalk.

"Bye." *It would be nice to have a dog again. Would be a lot of work to train. I could get a rescue and then wouldn't have to deal with the puppy stuff and would save a dog at the same time. Hmm.*

"See, here we are again. Told ya." Noah held the leash tight as Trudy pulled toward Celia's driveway.

"Have fun at your celebration."

"Bye-bye. And thank you for catching her." They disappeared from Celia's sight.

She thought of her last dog. A salt-and-pepper schnauzer named Heidi. For a small dog, she had a ferocious appetite. Much to Celia's dismay, Heidi's favorite treat was a bar of soap. Heidi would sneak into Celia's bathroom, jump into the bathtub, and grab the soap from its dish. Without fail, after each soapy snack, she would proceed to vomit on a carpet somewhere in the house. Never would her upset stomach reject the soap on the tile floor–Heidi always got sick on something plush. When Celia cleaned the mess, the regurgitated soap would foam, lather, and stink. Celia began to keep the soap too high for Heidi to reach. In the end, a new bar of patchouli-scented soap took Heidi to the great beyond. She was fourteen years old. Her little body couldn't take the upset. Celia felt sad as she remembered her sweet Heidi. She never bought patchouli soap again.

She picked up the real estate section and read descriptions of ocean-front homes for sale in nearby communities. *I have an ocean view.* She could see a tiny square of the ocean from her bedroom window. This patch of water was Celia's definition of an ocean view.

Celia popped a cherry into her mouth. She ate the fruit and then sucked the pit. She glanced around to be sure no one was watching and then spit the pit across the narrow driveway. *Why can't I reach that strip of grass?* She ate another cherry and spit the second pit. With cherry after cherry, she attempted to get the pit across the driveway. Not one pit made it to the grass. Finally, she reached the strip of grass. “Yes! I did it!” She pulled her fist to her side.

Celia heard the church bells ring and then cleaned up the spit pits.

Emma

Celia pulled the comforter up to her neck and nestled into her bed. She opened one eye and peeked at the clock. *Shit. Four minutes to go.* She raised the comforter up to her nose and closed her eyes.

Four minutes later, the radio blasted her awake. With both hands, she pulled the pillow next to her and covered her head in a feeble attempt to muffle the noise. "No!" She squeezed the pillow tighter over her ears.

From beneath the comforter, she slid her hand out and powerfully smashed the snooze button. The clock flew off the side table. The music blared as it became wedged between the mattress and nightstand. "SHIT!" *So much for that extra ten minutes of sleep.*

Sluggishly she dragged herself from her warm bed and knelt on the carpet. She wiggled the clock back and forth as she tried to dislodge it from the tight space. Finally, she yanked it free and slammed the stop button. *Guess it's senseless to hit the snooze button again. I'm wide awake now.* She was irritated.

A pounding headache joined her morning routine. *I'll never again drink that much wine on a week night.* She removed a small bottle of aspirin from the bathroom medicine cabinet and walked into the kitchen. She poured herself a large glass of orange juice, popped two pills in her mouth, and took a big gulp.

Celia stood against the counter, drank the last sip of juice, and pushed the *brew* button to start her coffee. Instantly, the wonderful smell filled the room. She inhaled slowly.

The rescue of the alarm clock turned what should have been a ten-minute snooze into twelve minutes of frustration. Celia was now late. She turned on the shower, dropped her nightgown to the bathroom floor, and rubbed her eyes. After the two-minute wait period, the length of time it took for the water to heat up, she stuck her hand through the shower curtain and checked the temperature. *Finally*. Every day, the water took at least two minutes to heat up, and every day, Celia expected it would be faster.

She showered and then savored the warmth from the hot water that poured down her body. She turned the shower off and reached for a towel. Although the shower was off, she still heard water dripping–it came from the kitchen.

With the towel wrapped around her soaked body and her feet still drenched, she raced into the kitchen. Hot coffee coated the countertop and dripped down the cabinets to form a small puddle on the floor.

"Fuck!" She gazed at the empty space where the coffee pot should have been placed. "You idiot! How did you do this?" She looked at the coffee pot in the dish strainer.

Celia grabbed a cup and placed it under the lip of the counter. With her bare hands, she pushed the residual pool over the edge and filled the cup halfway. She gulped it down and shuddered. *Ugh!* This second mishap of the morning further delayed her. There wasn't time to brew a second pot. She clutched a fistful of paper towels and haphazardly wiped the cabinet doors and the floor.

"How was your weekend?" Emma walked into Celia's office and plopped down in the chair across from her desk. "Why's your hair curly?"

"Didn't have time to dry it." Celia raised her hand to her head and twisted a cluster of curls.

"It looks good. You should wear it that way. Look at MY curls." She shook her head back and forth. Emma's jet-black curls danced around her face.

"My weekend was stupid."

"Why was your weekend stupid? No, let me rephrase that. What constitutes stupid?"

"I don't know where to begin. I went for drinks with Ramona and her brother." *What was the booper's name? Why can't I remember? Think. It's not Booper Boy. I can't remember.* "A total disaster. Why don't you tell me about your weekend instead?"

"Nah. I'd rather hear about Ramona and her brother. Go on." Emma put her elbows on the desk and placed her hands under her chin. "Start chirping." She lowered her hands and wiggled her fingers toward her face. "I'm all ears."

Celia began to recount the evening with Ramona and her brother. Emma's cell phone rang and interrupted her a second after she began to describe the booping fix up.

"Hello?" She glanced at Celia and crossed her eyes. "Hello? Hello? Hello?" Emma was visibly annoyed.

Celia picked up a pen and doodled on a pink sticky pad. A. B. C. D. *I think it began with R. Was it R? Ralph? Richard? Roy? What WAS it?* R. R. R. *Walter. That's it! Walter! So, it ends in R. Same thing. Glad I remembered.*

Emma put the phone down on the edge of Celia's desk. "Sorry. Go on. Tell me about the brother."

Celia began to speak. Again, Emma's phone rang.

Emma glanced down at the phone and pressed the Decline button.

The phone rang a third time, and Emma once more pressed Decline. "I'm sorry. I want to hear your story."

"Who the hell is that?" Celia nodded her head toward the phone.

"Don't ask." Emma shrugged. "It's no one. Now tell me about the night out with Ramona. Why was it stupid?"

Celia put her pen down. *Something's up with you, missy.* She chose to respect Emma's privacy. "He was cute, but he was strange. He did this thing that–" The ring of Emma's phone interrupted Celia yet again. Celia stopped speaking and frowned at Emma.

Emma picked up the phone and turned it off. "The phone is off. No more interruptions. I'm very sorry."

"Emma, now it's your turn to start chirping, as you say."

"It's no one. Honestly."

She tilted her head and furrowed her brow. *What is going on with you, Em?* "Emma, I was in your office last week when this phone game happened. Why does someone keep calling you? And why don't you accept the call?"

"Trust me, Celia, it's no one."

"Come on, Emma, it's me. You can tell me."

Emma breathed in deeply. "Okay, I'll tell you." She banged her knees as she pulled her chair closer to Celia. "This has to be OUR secret. Can you keep a secret?"

"I can keep a secret. It's the people I tell who can't."

"Ha ha ha." Emma took another breath, this time more deeply than before. "It's my ex-wife."

Celia peered at Emma. "What?"

"It's my ex-wife."

"Yeah, I heard you. Your ex-wife? What does that mean?"

Emma moved in closer to Celia. "It's Fredric's ex-wife, but she annoys me as much as she annoys him, so I claim her as my ex-wife too."

"Fredric was married before?" Celia shrieked as softly as anyone could shriek–she was shocked.

"Yes. He was married before. It was years ago." She reached over and picked up the pen Celia had put down. Nervously, she flipped it back and forth from hand to hand.

"I'm totally flabbergasted. How have you not told me this?" Celia moved both hands to her face, stretched her fingers out, and covered her cheeks. "We've worked together for more than three years. We talk so much. We talk too much. How has this little surprise ex-wife not made it into our conversation?"

"Celia, it's not important. I don't talk about it anymore. It's off my topic list of things to discuss."

"So, that's it? You don't talk about it?"

"Nope, not anymore. I used to tell my cousin Jillian everything. She would call me every Monday morning, excited to hear some crazy story that happened over the weekend. We'd laugh for hours as I detailed the pathetically unbelievable actions of my ex-wife. I talked about the stories as a sanity check for me. She always agreed they were crazy. Not sure if it was out of loyalty or if she honestly thought the situation was nuts." Emma's lips turned downward, and her chin quivered slightly.

"I'm sorry." Celia reached over and touched Emma's hand. "I remember Jillian came in for lunch occasionally. She was hilarious."

"Do you realize she's been gone over a year? She was more than my cousin–she was my lifelong best friend. We shared everything." A tear formed in the corner of Emma's eye. "Oh God. How did we get on to this? I'm sorry. I'll tell you more later. I have to get back to my office." Emma stood and took a tissue on her way out.

"Lunch! Lunch is when you'll tell me. We're having lunch today." Celia was eager to know more.

"Okay, okay, okay. Come get me around noon. Let's eat outside."

Morbidly Entertaining

Shortly after noon, Celia and Emma found a small square table on the terrace outside the cafeteria. Celia placed her dish of sushi on the table and put the empty tray on the chair to her right. Emma set her tray on the table but didn't remove her lunch.

"I'm all ears." She was bursting with curiosity.

"This is for your ears only, Celia. Got it?"

"Got it. Go on." Celia slapped the bottom of her cranberry juice and twisted off the cap.

"When Fredric and I started dating, he and his ex-wife were divorced. Freddy was five years old. He wasn't even a year old when they split up. She married someone else about a year after the divorce was final."

"Oh my God! Freddy! He's your stepson!" Celia's voice escalated to a squeal. "This is amazing! How could I have never known this about you?" Celia was stunned by the new information. "How does someone get married that soon after a divorce?" She shook her head.

"I know, it's confusing. She's confused too. She seems to confuse marriage for dating."

Celia laughed. "What's she like?"

"That's a tough question. I'm sure when someone meets her, they think she's nice and maybe even attractive. She puts on a good act."

"How long was Fredric married to her?"

"About two minutes. I've had leg cramps that lasted longer than that marriage."

"Get out! Seriously! How long were they married?"

"Not long. Not even two years. I think it was less than a year and a half." Emma took a forkful from her Asian chicken and rice bowl.

"Oh my God." Celia sipped her juice. "Oh my God."

"She was three months pregnant when they got married. They dated about a year. She wanted to get married and Fredric wanted to break up because they fought all the time. She got pregnant and he married her. She won that battle."

"Whoa!" Celia put her hands up with her palms facing Emma. "How old-fashioned! Who pulls that trick these days?" She put her hands down and picked up a piece of sushi with her fingers. "Keep going. You talk, and I'll eat my lunch." Celia popped the salmon and rice into her mouth.

"It was around 1988."

"That wasn't THAT long ago. Maybe the sixties or early seventies would make sense for the marriage thing, but the eighties?" Celia nodded her head, rolled her eyes, and motioned for Emma to continue.

"I think he hoped it would work out. He was young, trusting and naïve. Plus, he loves kids and was excited about becoming a father."

"When did they get divorced?" Celia was enthralled with the story.

"She was three months pregnant when they got married. She left when the baby was ten months old. They got divorced not long after she moved out."

"She took the kid and left?" Celia was shocked.

"Not exactly. She didn't take Freddy with her. She left both of them. Fredric got custody. She moved in with a guy she met at work. They were married within a year. She spent time with Freddy, but he didn't live with her and her new husband. A year before I met Fredric, she went to court and got custody. It broke Fredric's heart–it simply devastated him. He was a single dad for close to four years."

"What? I'm in total shock about this. How does that happen? She left her son for over three years and then gets him back?" Celia shrieked in horror.

"Sympathetic female judge? Who knows. Fredric still spent a lot of time with him, even though she got custody. Freddy usually stayed with him from Friday afternoon until Monday morning. Freddy was in daycare during the day and the new husband had a night shift. It worked out. Let's not forget the supplemental income from the child support. She never paid him anything when he was the single parent, but when she got Freddy back, Fredric paid child support to her."

"Unbelievable!"

Emma snickered. "See, I told you it's not that great of a story."

"Oh yes, it is." Celia rolled her hands and motioned for Emma to go on with the no-longer secret information.

"That's it. Voila. I have a miserable ex-wife and now you know." Emma stirred the chicken, veggies, and rice and then took the fully blended mixture to her lips. "This is delicious." She scooped another forkful.

"How come you want to keep it such a secret?"

"I don't know." Emma lowered her fork onto the plate. "I don't care that Fredric's divorced. She's a total nut and it's mind-boggling that Fredric could have been with someone who behaves the way she does. I'm afraid I'll know someone who knows her, and I don't want the association. She's an embarrassment. Like I said, I needed to share the stories as a sanity check. Jillian made it fun to talk about. I miss her terribly."

"You've done a good job keeping it out of your conversation." Celia popped another piece of sushi into her mouth. "I'm dying to hear more."

"Good to know." Emma grinned. "It isn't all that interesting, I promise you."

"Why does she call you continuously? And why do you bother to answer when you hang up on her anyway?"

"I answer because I'm never sure it's her. She blocks her number and it comes up *Unknown*, but a few of my friends have private numbers too. When *Unknown* displays, I can't tell whether it's friend or foe. And I don't hang up on HER—she hangs up on ME."

"Are you sure it's her?"

"Yeah. I've heard people in the background say her name. A couple times she didn't hang up properly, and she stayed connected to my voicemail. I have recorded conversations of her talking to people where she works."

"Get out!" Celia slapped her hand on the table.

Emma's eyes sparkled. "I'm glad you're enjoying this, my dear. You might be sorry you know. I may need to vent to you the next time I have to be around her." Emma took another bite of her rice bowl and then a drink of water.

"This is incredible. You have to tell me more."

"Celia, I could keep you amused for years."

"I'm going to look forward to this. I'm still in shock. What fun it will be to hear more detail."

"Yeah, fun." Emma shook her head. "The actual living it isn't fun, but the stories are kind of comical. I must admit, if I don't get a good story out of a visit with her, I'm a little disappointed. Sick as this might sound, I find it morbidly entertaining."

"This is amazing."

"Celia, every time I see her, there's a new episode. For years, I've kept a journal. It isn't in any order right now, but I hope to write a book someday. The stories are ridiculous and quite comical."

"You want to write a book? Think you'll publish it?" Celia was intrigued.

"I'd love to, but I don't know where to stop. What if I publish it and after it's published, she does something stupendous? Then it would be too late to add the new chapter."

"That's what sequels are for."

They both laughed.

The Shark

The mouth-watering menu at Soma had been in her thoughts all day. She was delighted to be out of work and on her way to dinner.

She thought about the menu choices the entire subway ride to her car. *Should I have the scallops and pumpkin sage ravioli? Maybe salmon and homemade gnocchi, or homemade pizza covered with cheese, steak, onions, and arugula? I could try one of the pesto chicken or shrimp dishes.* She could almost taste the delightful dinner on which she was about to indulge.

Remarkably, she arrived at the T parking lot on time. Celia walked to her car, unlocked the door, tossed her bag over the headrest into the backseat, slid into the driver's seat, inserted and turned the key, and groaned. There was no sound: no whirr of the engine, no clicking. Nothing. She tried again. Nothing. Again and again she tried. Nothing. Nothing. Nothing. The car was dead. Her long, thick hair fell into her face as she dropped her head to the steering wheel. She paused for a moment and then called her dinner date to deliver the bad news.

"Hello?"

"Kate!" The panic in her voice resonated through the phone. "What are you doing?"

"Plucking! I've got some perfect plucking light coming in through the window." Kate heard the anxiety in Celia's voice and chose to ignore it. "I can see even the tiny, thin, blondish hairs on my chin. I love my new magnifying mirror! What's going on?" She held her breath and waited to hear what she already knew.

"My car won't start. Can you come get me? I'm in the parking lot at the T station."

"Where are you?"

"Ahhh. Hellllo? I'm still at the T station parking lot." She rolled her eyes.

"Don't roll your eyes, Celia. I get that you're in the parking lot. I want to know WHERE in the lot you're parked. If I come to get you, how can I find you? Or perhaps I should ask if you're in the same place as the last time?"

"Ha ha ha! Aren't you funny? And I didn't roll my eyes." She lied. "I'm all the way down on the left side. A little farther from where I normally park, but in the same area. When you come in, take a left at the booth where you pay and go down to the end of the lot. You'll see me. Do you have any jumper cables?"

"Will I have to pay to get in there?"

"Kate!" Celia's tone was emphatic.

"I want to know if I have to pay? Is that an unreasonable question? You said I'll pass the booth where I pay."

"Have you ever had to pay before?"

"Come to think of it, no. They must know me as the pick-up friend for the idiot whose car always breaks down." Kate secured her tweezers around a sprouting hair on the lower right side of her chin. She yanked out the hair. Her eyes watered from the sting of the pluck.

"I guess you want to hassle me, huh?" Celia didn't wait for an answer. "Do you have jumper cables?"

"You asked me that already. Celia, since when have you ever considered jump-starting your car?" Kate held the magnifying glass up and inspected her chin.

"Yeah, I guess you're right. You don't have any though, do you?"

"No. I don't have jumper cables. I don't even know how to use them. Would you like me to stop somewhere to get them?" Kate's sarcasm was unmistakable.

"No, we don't have time. We have reservations for dinner."

"Yeah, sure. As if we'll make THAT reservation. Why don't I pick you up and we'll leave your car there the same as we usually do? You've never considered jumping the battery, don't start now. That's why you have Brian." Kate tugged a thin hair from her upper lip. This time, in addition to watery eyes, she winced in pain.

"Yeah. I'll call him now. He can tow it to his garage. I'm sure it won't be a problem to leave it."

"Celia, it's never been a problem before. It won't be a problem today."

"Okay, I'll call him now."

"Ahhh!" Kate paused. "Do you agree it might be time to get a new car, honey? Or at least buy yourself a pair of jumper cables?" Kate's question and comment irritated Celia, but Kate could get away with it. She was the only one who could, considering Kate always came to Celia's rescue.

Celia knew Kate was right. "Come when you're ready! We can discuss my being vehicle-challenged later." Celia was not in the mood to have a conversation about her car problems. She was anxious and excited to get to their fabulous dinner. Celia no longer was surprised or upset when her car broke down. Kate was more surprised when Celia's car DIDN'T break down.

"I'll head out in a few, but I've got to finish plucking. You never know when the light's going to be this fabulous again. I'll be there as soon as I can."

After thirty minutes, Celia saw the big bright shark headed toward her. Behind the wheel was dependable Brian, looking exactly the same as always.

Brian was hot. There was no denying his splendor. He was tall, with muscular arms. His greasy T-shirts displayed the name of his towing company across his broad chest–Sharky's Garage and Towing. Long black hair, slicked to the back of his head, clearly exposed his gleaming smooth skin. At all times, a cigar hung from his mouth.

Sharky's tow truck was enormous, with a huge towing crane at the back. Except for a colorful shark's face with big white teeth painted around the grill, the truck was bright red. It was fierce.

"You know, Celia, for what you pay to get this piece of junk repaired, you could buy yourself a jazzy little new car. I'll bet you drop a pretty penny on repairs every month."

She knew he was right but couldn't bring herself to deal with monthly car payments. She owned this car outright for over eight years. The car was old, rusty, and falling apart, but she didn't want to part with it. The cloth interior on the inside roof was coming loose from the body of the car. To keep it in place, Celia had purchased a package of star-shaped thumbtacks. The little stars were pushed through the fabric into the car's ceiling. One afternoon, a thumbtack shook itself loose and found its way down the back of her shirt. She felt the sharpness on her back and almost crashed while she jumped around in the driver's seat. She thought a bee had flown down the back of her shirt. She loved that old green car and she was deathly afraid of bees.

Kate arrived as Brian finished the hook up to Celia's car. "You do realize we'll never make the reservation, don't you?"

"Yeah, I know. I'm super sorry." Celia moved her head closer to inspect Kate's chin. "Why is your chin all red?"

"I told you when you called; I was plucking."

"I'm sorry, Kate. The car has been running great and I've been adding oil every week."

"Celia, I think you have a keen sense for the obvious. Don't you think there's a problem when you have to put oil in every week?"

"Yeah, I guess that is a problem, but it's been running fine and I didn't expect that to stop."

"Maybe you should start to plan on it breaking down, Celia, because it always does. I plan on it breaking down every time you drive when we go out. You should plan on it too. I don't understand the emotional attachment you have with this car. It's not worth a dime, it's unreliable, it's rusted out, it's..."

Celia put her hand over Kate's mouth. "Stop! I know all the faults this car has. You're right. You're right and I'm sorry we missed the reservation. Do you want to try to make Soma, or do you want to grab a burger somewhere? My treat."

"No kidding it's your treat!" Kate reached over and touched Celia's shoulder. "I still love you, but you and your little car are royal pains in the ass. You know that, don't you?"

"Yeah, yeah, yeah! I know. And I appreciate you always being there to help us."

"There is no *us* here." Kate shook her index finger back and forth. "I never help the car. It's YOU I help, not the car. Got it? You need to get over this passionate bond you have with this piece of aluminum."

"I think it's steel, at least for the body, hood, doors, and trunk. The bumper might be plastic, but it's an old car. I'm not quite–"

"Whatever it is, it's some kind of metal and it's junk," Kate interrupted, cutting Celia off mid-sentence.

"Hey, I thought you go to electrolysis. Why are you plucking?" Celia changed the subject onto Kate's face.

"What do you mean?"

"Your chin is all raw and you told me you were plucking. You could get them waxed, you know. I got my brows waxed last week. Aren't they great?" She traced her fingers over her eyebrows.

"I've never had to pluck my eyebrows." Kate pointed to her chin and scrunched up her nose. "No, no. I don't have hairy eyebrows. I couldn't get that lucky. No, I have to have a full beard and a thick mustache." Still pointing at her chin, she curled her lip in disgust at the fate of her hairy face. "I've spent a fortune to get the roots shocked and now they're growing back. I don't have time for those appointments."

"You shouldn't be plucking. It makes them grow back stronger."

"Silence!" She rubbed her hairless pink chin.

They stopped for burgers but had chicken Caesar salads instead.

Kate glanced out the window as Brian drove by, towing Celia's car emulating a minnow trailing behind a ferocious shark. "Well, well, well. Will you look at that? Talk about timing." She nodded her head toward the street.

"Sorry." Celia didn't look out the window.

They shared a brownie sundae dripping in hot fudge.

The Original

Emma's phone conversation was winding down when Celia stepped into her friend's office. She carried with her a small folder. Emma motioned for Celia to come in and sit down and then put her finger up to indicate she'd be a moment.

Celia took a seat and placed the folder on her lap. After a minute, she put the folder on Emma's desk, got up and straightened a picture on the wall, walked over to the window, and took a hard candy from the candy dish on the table. She returned to her seat, unwrapped the candy, put it in her mouth, and then took the folder off Emma's desk and placed it back on her lap.

Emma hung up the phone. "Hey. How's it going?"

"You busy?"

"I was taking care of loose ends with the engineers on the Cerise Street project. How's your week going?"

"Good. I have some questions." Celia took a piece of paper from the folder. "Here you go. Take a glance." She handed the paper to Emma.

Emma burst out laughing. "I see you've been busy with the news I've shared." Emma put the paper down and pushed it toward Celia.

"Busy? Try obsessed! I need some information."

"And exactly what kind of information do you need?" Emma was amused by Celia's diligence.

"As you can see, I have a list of questions."

"Go ahead, shoot. But that looks like a long list–not sure we'll have time for that kind of session. I have a meeting in ten minutes." She reached over to the side of her desk, picked up a white box, and put it down next to her keyboard.

"That's why I wrote everything down. I figured we could check things off as we go through it. But honestly, it's a few simple questions." Celia scanned the page.

"Let me see that list again." Emma put her hand out.

Celia handed Emma the document. "This is your copy. I've got my own." Celia opened the folder and removed an identical piece of paper. "Aren't you lucky you shared this secret with a friend who has as much free time as I have?"

"You're very organized. We need to get you a hobby or a boyfriend." Emma perused the list of twenty-five questions. "I have time for one question this morning. Which question do you want me to answer?" She reviewed the list again and took a deep breath. "In five minutes or less." Emma opened the box and displayed freshly baked chocolate chip cookies. She took one out and placed it on a napkin and slid it toward Celia and then took another one for herself.

"Thank you." Celia put the napkin and cookie on her lap. "Let's see here." She lifted her paper and scanned the list of questions. "I think we should start with question one. When did you first meet her?"

"Hmmm. That's a tough question." Emma furrowed her brow and put her hand on her chin. "I first SAW her before I officially MET her. Fredric had picked me up on his way to take Freddy home. As soon as Fredric rang the bell, she ran to the window facing the driveway. She turned the light off in the room and stared out the window toward where we were parked. I guess she wanted to know if I was in the car."

"If she turned off the light, how could you see her?" Celia picked up the cookie and took a bite.

"Is that legal to add a question if it isn't on the list?"

"Yes, it's my prerogative, since it's my list. Let me ask the question again. How could you see her if she turned the light off? This is delicious–it's still warm." She licked a sliver of chocolate from the corner of her mouth.

"There was a window behind where she stood. I could see her silhouette. She did that every time Fredric dropped Freddy off. One time I gave a little wave and I saw her duck down. I felt she was tormented by the fact that I was in the car, so I stopped going with him."

"Do you see her a lot?"

"Now that Freddy's an adult and has his own place, he often has parties and barbeques, which puts me in the position to be around her more than I care to be. I could let Fredric go alone, but I don't want to do that. I go, and I tolerate her. Freddy tries to schedule things separately between us, but she inevitably shows up. It's quite pathetic."

"Does she bring her husband? Do you like him?"

"Two questions at once? This is more than one question, but I'll answer for a few more minutes." The banter was obviously entertaining Emma. "Yeah, she brings him. He's gross. He's a racist and doesn't censor anything he says. I stay clear of him." Emma chuckled at Celia's ability to fire questions as fast as she could answer them.

"You said there are stories you used to tell Jillian. What kind of stories? Do they bother you?" Celia was enthralled by Emma's information.

"Wow. You're good. Have you ever thought of a career in journalism?" Emma broke off a tiny piece of her cookie and put it in her mouth. "Honestly, I don't care WHAT she says. I care WHY. It's more about the intention of her actions. Her intent is mean-spirited. I didn't know Fredric when they got divorced–it wasn't my fault. I've had relationships longer than their marriage. I truly don't care he has an ex-wife–obviously it would be better if he didn't. Celia, she constantly tries to disrespect or diminish my existence in Fredric's life and make her two-minute marriage a focus of every encounter we have together. It's hard to explain." Emma shook her head. "She started being conniving when I first met her in 1995. This was my initial introduction to her."

Fredric, Emma, and Jillian walked across the football field and found the shadiest seats they could locate. Freddy had asked them to come to his Step-Up ceremony into first grade. Although Emma knew Freddy, she had yet to meet his "extended" family. She asked Jillian to join them and hoped her cousin's support would help calm the knots in her stomach. Fredric had warned her about his ex-wife.

"If we find seats before she gets here, we might be able to avert an invasion." Fredric rubbed Emma's back.

The trio settled in their seats in the eighth row, feeling somewhat sheltered by the sea of strangers surrounding them.

"Oh brother." Fredric motioned his head toward a woman headed in their direction. He opened his can of cola and took a sip. "She has radar. That's her coming this way. The one in the red pants and the white high heels. Just want you to be prepared. I'm sure Freddy told her you would be here." He put his arm around Emma's shoulder and pulled her close.

Emma bit her lower lip as she anxiously made eye contact with her cousin.

His ex-wife rushed over and sat down in the empty seat next to Jillian. She leaned forward in front of Jillian and made direct eye contact with Emma. "Good afternoon. I'm the original Mrs. Fredric Cerezo. You know? Fredric's first wife and first choice." She emphasized the word "first" as she glared at Emma.

"Is 'The Original' a hyphenated first name? You know, like John-Paul?" Jillian antagonistically asked the question.

Emma pushed her elbow into Jillian's side.

"You must be Emily." Her eyes still fixed on Emma, she ignored Jillian's harassing comment. She turned toward Jillian. "And you are?" She curved her lips to a snarl.

Fredric stopped her in her tracks. "This is Emma! Not Emily, which I know you know. And this is cousin Jillian."

The ex-wife stood from her chair just enough to lean over Emma and Jillian. She reached for Fredric's cola. "I'm so thirsty. I'll just take a sip." She seized the soda and sat back down before Fredric realized what happened. She held the can up to her lips and took several sips. Again, she leaned in front of the other women and attempted to return the cola to Fredric.

"Keep it." He moved his hands away from her and motioned he no longer wanted the soda.

Before anyone could say another word, she got up from her seat. "Good to meet you girls." She turned and walked away.

Jillian's eyes opened wide and she slapped her hand over her mouth. She couldn't control herself and she laughed out loud. "What the fuck was that?"

"She's a piece of work. You weren't kidding." Emma snickered at the ridiculous show she had just witnessed.

"She called us girls. Was that supposed to be an insult? If you didn't push your elbow into my side, Emma, I would have kicked her down a notch. Did she actually introduce herself as the original Mrs. Cerezo?"

"No. She said, 'the original Mrs. FREDRIC Cerezo.' Don't forget to include the first name. Isn't she married to someone else now?" Emma giggled.

"Yes, she changed her name to his last name. It would have been more appropriate to say 'Hi. I'm Mrs. Shit for Brains.' She was hoping to create a problem."

Emma touched Fredric's leg. "I don't think it went that badly. I expected much worse."

"Give her time, my dear. Give her time." Fredric leaned over and kissed her forehead.

They watched as the parade of boys and girls marched onto the field. The sun crept over their seats. The day became very hot.

"She sounds psycho. She's been nasty since the first time you met her?" Celia shot out the question before Emma had fully exhaled from her last sentence.

"She is psycho. And yes, since the first time I met her, she has been harassing me in one way or another. It's a good thing I believe in karma." Emma flipped her phone over and looked at the time. "Damn. I forgot about my meeting. Too late now." Emma moved her index finger in a slashing motion across her neck. "Off with my head. It was only with Ramona, anyway. I'll tell her I got tied up with something important."

"That's the truth."

Safety First

Celia couldn't believe it. Truth be told, not only could she believe it, she anticipated it would be worse. She turned on her computer and launched Google. *What did he call it?* She tried to remember what Zach had called the problem with her car. *Fuck it!* She dialed Brian's number.

"Brian. It's me, Celia."

"Hey, Celia, did you talk to Zach?"

Celia heard loud noises in the background and wasn't quite sure what Brian had said. "Sorry, Bri, it's noisy there. Do you know what's wrong with my car? I don't understand what Zach told me." She paced from the kitchen to the living room and back again.

"Listen, kiddo, you got a big problem with that little buggy. He can rig it for a while, but it's not going to last long."

"How long does he think I can drive it?" Her panic boomed through the phone.

"Bottom line, you need a new car. I have a few out front, if you want to see them. Honestly, if you buy one of these used cars, you'll buy someone else's headaches."

Celia was silent on the other end of the phone.

"Kiddo, if I were you, I'd get a new car. Something with a few bells and whistles. You could have air conditioning that works in the summer and heat that works in the winter. It won't cost you more than what you pay to keep this junk going."

Celia cringed when he called her car junk. *Maybe Brian and Kate conspired to make this happen? Coincidental they both used the word junk.*

"You there, Celia?"

"Yes. I'm here." She paced back and forth. "You've been telling me this for a while. I shouldn't be surprised."

"Listen, it's a car. Once you get behind the wheel of something jazzy, you'll forget about this clunker. I promise."

"I can't handle this." She finally stopped pacing. She lifted a spoon from the drawer and removed a carton of cookie dough ice cream from the freezer. "Should I get it fixed this one last time?" She exhaled and then dug the spoon deep into the carton.

"You'll be throwing $1,500 out the window. You could use that money for a new car. If you're too freaked, you could lease, but I recommend you buy. You keep cars for a while. Right?"

Celia made a decision. She would begin to think about buying a new car. She wasn't going to actively shop for one; she was going to think about car shopping.

Abruptly, Celia's plan was kicked into action when Kate stopped by unannounced.

"I got gas this morning and saw Brian. He told me about your car, and I'm here to help. Aren't you lucky you have me as your friend?"

"Not in the mood."

"Celia, sweetie, I've lost track of how many times we've changed our plans or missed out on something because you got stranded somewhere with that stupid piece of junk. I want you to look. You don't have to buy anything right this minute. Come with me and we'll browse around. We'll make it fun. A little adventure! Sound good? Your car is not safe."

Celia covered her ears. "I can't listen to this."

Kate glared directly into Celia's eyes. She didn't need to say a word. Celia knew Kate was right. She was about to be held captive in Kate's car-searching mission. "I swear, I heard you sing 'nyah nyah nyah' when you covered your ears. Did you sing that?"

"No, I didn't sing that." Celia's annoyance rang clear as the church bells on Sunday morning.

"Oh, I guess it seemed that way, because it's so mature to cover your ears. Come on. We'll have fun. I promise."

"I can't deal with car payments and decisions, and all that crap." Celia knew Brian was right when he said the expense would be a huge waste of money. She wouldn't admit that little tidbit of information to Kate.

Kate went into the kitchen for Celia's bag. She walked to the sofa, grabbed Celia's hand, and pulled her up. "Come on. Let's go for a ride."

The first showroom had two customers–AFTER Celia and Kate entered the room. Three different sales people, two men and a woman, pounced upon them.

"Just checking things out." Celia made it clear she was not going to buy at this time. The men walked away, but the black-haired woman, wearing a pale-yellow suit that was too tight for her little round body, followed them throughout the showroom. They left after seven minutes.

"I don't want that kind of pressure." Celia pushed through the doors out toward the parking lot.

"I'll admit being followed around is annoying, but there was hardly any pressure."

"Did you check out that yellow suit?" Celia giggled.

"I know. Hideous color."

"Do you think she got up this morning and saw herself in the mirror and thought that suit was a good choice?"

"Celia, you need to get serious about this. You have no transportation for work on Monday."

"I can walk to the commuter rail. I don't have to take the subway."

"You know–you're truly difficult. Your car is seriously dangerous, and you need a new one. I'm trying to help you. You know I'm right. You can't keep that old junk of yours." Kate shook her head and dramatically rubbed her forehead. "You know it's not safe, right? Safety first! Let's find another dealer. We can make fun of the yellow suit later. Or maybe not at all."

The second dealership was less than a mile away from their first stop. The huge building was surrounded by colorful flags, which were attached to ropes strung between several light poles. The new cars were lined up diagonally along the side wall of the structure.

Celia and Kate walked down the row of cars and then back up to the first one. They were silent. Celia pulled the handle of the front car. The car was locked. Her nail broke and the skin at the top of her finger was pinched. "Shit!" She shook her hand up and down to shake away the pain. "Every car is locked. It's not even possible to look inside without someone's help."

A group of salesmen stood smoking by the front of the dealership. They continued to smoke as they watched the two women walk among the parked cars. They offered no assistance.

"Can you believe they let their salespeople smoke by the entrance? Who smokes at work these days?" Kate whispered to Celia.

Celia scowled at Kate, her jaw pushed forward. "Yeah, who smokes these days? Oh, that's right. I do." Celia's attitude had gone from resistance to bad to worse. Kate's comment antagonized her and downgraded her frame of mind.

They roamed the row of cars and peeked through the windows of two or three.

"I'm out of here. I don't appreciate being ignored. If we were guys, or maybe young hotties, they'd be all over us." Celia turned away from the cars.

"First and foremost, we ARE hotties! And second, we don't have to waste any more time on this new car nonsense." Celia picked up on the exasperation in Kate's tone. "I can take you home and maybe your cute little car will miraculously go for another couple of years without needing to be fixed once or twice a month."

"I'm willing to look, but I won't tolerate being ignored. How are we supposed to see them if they're all locked?" Celia was frazzled. Her eyes became glassy. "I'm totally intimidated by this entire process. I don't want to have to beg someone to help me. I don't know what questions to ask." Celia was more upset than Kate had seen her in a very long time.

"Celia, do you want Tom to help us? He knows a lot about cars. I'm trying to be supportive. I'm sorry, but I don't know any more than you do." Kate stepped closer to Celia and took her hand. "Honestly, if you don't want to do this, I don't want to push you. I understand it's stressful and scary and a huge commitment, but I think you'll thank me for this."

"No, I'd rather do it without Tom. I could research more online. I'm mad that I haven't done that already. It is a daunting decision for me. I don't do well with change. Let's go to one more place and

I'll take it more seriously. There's another dealer down the street. Let's go there and see what they have. I'll try to relax."

"Don't worry about buying something this second. Let's see what they have and find something fun about this."

At the next dealership, they parked at the front door and walked into the well-lit showroom, filled with gleaming new cars. Immediately they found themselves in front of a sparkling black Navigator.

"This is beautiful. The black has a little glitter." Celia opened the door and peeked inside. "This is gorgeous. Is this real leather?" She rubbed her hand across the seat. "What am I saying? Of course, it's leather. And I'm sure it's way too expensive for me."

Kate pointed to the sticker on the window and scowled.

Celia read the sticker and gasped. "This is what freaks me out. The cars I like are too expensive. This price is exactly why I'm nervous about getting a new car. Who can afford this?" Celia was anxious. Kate tried to remain calm and supportive.

"How about these?" Kate stood between two SUVs on display and swayed her arms between the vehicles. "Let's get some information. These are as nice as that one. Right?"

Celia walked away from the Navigator and over to Kate. They ambled around the SUVs and peeked through the window. Kate reached for the door of the dark-blue one. Celia suddenly clutched Kate's arm. She squeezed it hard and pulled her back.

"What's wrong?"

"Shh! That's him. Don't look!" Celia stared at the entrance at the front of the large room.

"That's who?" She immediately turned her head to look.

"Kate! I told you not to look and the first thing you do is look! Why did you look? What part of 'Don't look' didn't you understand?"

"Sorry. Who are we not looking at?"

"That guy by the door. That's the guy I saw at Pete's Market." Celia was still squeezing Kate's arm.

"When?" She pulled her arm free.

"I don't know. Maybe a month ago. I told you about him. Spilled coffee on myself. Remember?"

"Yeah. Yeah. I remember. Are you sure it's him?"

"Yes! That's definitely him! I couldn't forget that face or those eyes. Should we find out if he works here? Maybe I could buy a car from him. Come on, let's walk over there."

Kate groaned and shook her head. She let her bag fall from her shoulder. Slowly they proceeded in his direction. Before they reached the handsome stranger, a salesperson greeted him. The two men walked past Celia and Kate.

"Are we invisible? He didn't even notice us. I looked directly at him. We should have stayed by the Navigator. I don't want to leave right now."

"I think you seem to be forgetting the reason we're here. Besides, you're not interested in guys these days. Remember?"

"Very funny. I don't think he's a booper." Celia took a deep breath. "Do you think he's a booper?" She wrinkled her nose and tilted her head. She was serious with her question, though she knew she wouldn't get a serious answer.

"You never know, Celia. Don't forget, you told me that you thought the booper was cute at first sight too. Hey, maybe we can use the word booper as the code word for when you meet a guy who's a jerk. You know, he's a real *booper*. Good idea?"

They laughed at the same time. At every vehicle, Kate jumped into the front seat and pointed out all the visible features on the dashboard. Celia read the sticker and groaned. She held her heart as she recited the price aloud.

"This is a beauty. I might buy it if you don't want to." Kate sat up straight and looked through the front window.

"You know, Kate, that's not a bad idea. You buy this one, and I'll buy your car. I'll be broke if I buy one of these."

"Broke or broken down, take your pick. I could get used to driving up this high. It's as if you're a notch above everyone else." She stepped down and out of the SUV. "I want you to sit in the driver's seat. I'm not kidding. I think you'll love it."

Celia stepped onto the side panel and settled into the driver's seat. A salesman in olive trousers and a light-blue button-down shirt approached.

Celia adjusted the seat and kept her eyes forward as if she were driving. She continued to peek in the rearview and side mirrors for the man with the nice eyes. Her concentration on the car was distracted, to say the least.

"How do you like it?" The salesman watched Celia and Kate inspect the car.

"I don't know. I think it's too big for me." She turned her eyes away from the mirrors and toward the back window. "I'll be afraid to back up."

"You look fabulous in it." Kate leaned into the window next to Celia.

"I need to think about this. I'm just shopping around today." Celia glanced in the direction of the potential non-booper as they left the dealership. He never glanced in her direction.

Kate talked Celia into one more stop as she spotted a Jeep dealer up ahead. After she took the Jeep for a test drive, Celia knew her car search was over. She was in love with a steel-gray Wrangler. A decision was made, and Kate couldn't have been happier.

Noah was walking Trudy past her building when Kate dropped Celia off.

"Hey, Noah. How are things with you and Trudy?" Trudy jumped up on her. Celia bent down to Trudy's level and rubbed her head.

"I'm doing great! We're on our way home from the store. Got some ice cream this time. Uncle Bill is waiting at the corner for us. He watches me walk to the corner when it's late and then waits up there for us." He pointed to the top of the hill. "He can see us all the way to Pete's Market. I guess he still thinks I'm a little kid."

Celia saw the shadow of Noah's uncle under the streetlight.

"I'm right here, Uncle Bill." Noah waved his hand high.

"I see you, Noah." Celia heard him reply.

Celia motioned a wave to his uncle, and the uncle returned the wave.

Celia locked the door behind her and walked through the kitchen into her bedroom. She stood by the window and gazed into the distance at the minuscule patch of the ocean. The moon created streaks of light on the water. Celia moved her face closer to the window and bumped her head on a puppet's foot. She took a long, deep breath. She breathed in the ocean smell and instantly felt calm.

Cigarette? Calories? Cigarette? Calories? Maybe both? No! *Don't do it. Think of the wrinkles it will cause with every puff you take. Think about your lungs. Don't do it.* A lollipop and a carton of ice cream replaced her urge for a smoke. With the rounded candy of the lollipop, she dug out small bits of ice cream.

Celia sat at the kitchen table under the window and stared out as she sugared up. On the street below, she saw a couple walk together through the glow of a streetlight. *Look how cute they look holding hands. Would I ever be open to another relationship?* Geoff's face popped into her head. Her blood ran cold as the hairs on the back of her neck stood straight. It had been a very long time since she thought about him. She walked to her night table and picked up a book of matches on the way.

Keep the Fizzy

The text came through Celia's phone minutes after she arrived in her office. C. *can u meet me 2day 4 lunch.* E.

Celia responded immediately: *c u at 12. did u remember a good story 4 me?*

Emma responded: *Yup.*

At their usual table in the courtyard outside of the cafeteria, Celia waited for Emma to arrive with their lunch.

"Great idea to share a pizza." Celia opened the box and took out a slice covered with cheese and pepperoni. "It smells amazing." She put the slice on a paper plate and handed it to Emma. She took another for herself. "Yum!" The cheese was stringy and stretchy, exactly the way she liked it. "This sauce is spicy and sweet. It's perfect! What's the lunchtime entertainment today?"

"It's stupid. After Jillian was diagnosed, I visited with her more than usual and entertained her with these stories. I told her about a dopey drink episode. After this incident, she made me make a promise to her. I promised that whenever I'm put in an uncomfortable situation, I'll take a deep breath, pause, and respond with a question. Ya know, something like 'What do you mean?' or 'Why do you say that?' Throws the attention right back at the attacker. It took me awhile, but I practiced a lot and finally got better at controlling my actions. I still try to be prepared, but I don't always do the right thing for me."

"What was the drink story?"

"It happened a couple years ago." Emma took a bite of the pizza. "I told this incident to Jillian right before she passed. Here's what happened."

Fredric and Emma arranged to meet Freddy and his friend Mitch for lunch in Essex. Freddy arrived, without Mitch.

"I thought he was bringing Mitch." Emma moved close to Fredric and whispered in his ear. *This doesn't surprise me one bit.*

"So did I. Not sure what happened."

"Hey. I was going to bring Mitch, but he had to work late." He looked powerlessly at his father and then at Emma.

"Hope you don't mind that I tagged along." She flashed a huge smile. "I didn't want Freddy to take the drive by himself."

"Really, Mom? It's a twenty-minute drive," an irritated Freddy snapped.

"No problem at all." Emma was outwardly polite. *Let's walk over to that dock and I can push you off. Don't stoop to her level. Stay calm.*

Emma resented lunch being hijacked by Freddy's mom—she did a terrible job hiding her discomfort. *How inappropriate are you? This is Fredric's time with his son, and you have to encroach on their visit, don't you?* Fredric rubbed her back, but she remained anxious and trapped with this sudden guest list modification. She anticipated a pleasant and peaceful lunch where they would talk about his job and life in general. That plan vanished into thin air as soon as her stepson arrived with his mother.

"What's this fizzy on the menu?" Freddy's mom jumped in to ask the waiter before anyone ordered.

"It's a new fun drink this summer. It's a concoction of fruit and citrus juices and a splash of seltzer to make it fizzy."

"Is it any good?"

"Mom, you think the waiter's going to tell you it isn't good? Order one and try it." Freddy's tone remained annoyed at his mother.

"Okay, give me a fizzy."

Emma ordered shrimp cocktail. The rest of the group ordered lobster rolls with French fries.

The server brought Emma's shrimp and the ex-wife's fizzy to the table. He assured the group the other lunches would be delivered momentarily. He forgot to fill their water glasses.

Freddy's mother immediately reached across the table and helped herself to a shrimp from Emma's plate. She dipped it into the small cup of cocktail sauce at the edge of the dish. "You don't mind if I try one, do you?" She took the entire shrimp into her mouth at once.

Emma was horrified. She sat speechless and frozen. *How can you be this rude? At least you ate it so fast you didn't have time to double dip.* Her stomach felt tight and jumpy. *Relax. Don't let this person make you uncomfortable. Ignore her. Breathe. Pity the fizzy drinker.*

The other lunches were served, but the server had yet to bring water to the table. Emma glanced around the room to locate the waiter.

"Do you need something, hon?" Fredric asked.

"I'd love a drink. He never brought water. I should have ordered a seltzer."

"Let me share my fizzy with you. I haven't even touched it." The ex-wife pushed her chair out, got up, and walked to the booth across from their table. She picked up a glass that sat on a tray of dirty dishes. The glass contained a tissue at the bottom—a ketchup-covered fork stood upright in the glass. She used the fork to pull out the dirty tissue that was stuffed inside. She removed her straw from the fizzy and poured half of her bubbly beverage into the germ-filled glass. She grinned and handed the disgustingly used glass to Emma. "Here you go, Em." She winked at Emma as she moved her hand away from the glass.

Emma was fuming, her anger plainly visible. The harder she tried to hide her irritation, the more noticeable it became. She felt her rage race up and down inside her. She was aware of her neck as it became hot and turned red.

Fredric instantly reached over and pushed the glass to the edge of the table. The original fizzy sat on the table in front of his ex-wife. She had yet to take a sip. Emma stared at the untouched glass and took a deep breath. She stretched her arm across the table, grasped the ex-wife's glass, and took a big gulp. "Thank you for sharing." *You are truly a fucking bitch. I never gave you permission to use my name, let alone turn it into a nickname.*

Freddy witnessed the entire episode and turned his head away. His mother sat speechless with her lips tightly squeezed together.

"This is wonderfully refreshing. You should try it." She motioned to the revolting glass she had placed down by her husband's ex-wife.

"You ARE kidding me. Who DOES that? That is absolutely disgusting. She's hostile, aggressive, hateful, gross, disgusting. Absolutely disgusting. Did I mention disgusting?"

"I know."

"I am so excited to hear you took the drink from her. You didn't have to say a thing. I'm sure she got the message. She's disgusting!"

"I wanted to vomit when she brought the dirty glass to the table. I was in shock and couldn't believe someone could be that big of a bitch. I'd rather eat dog poop off the street than something that witch offered me. Later, when I told Jillian, I'll never forget, she shook her head and she was livid. She was lying in her bed, IVs in her skinny, frail arms. She said, 'Emmella, you should have thrown the fucking fizzy thing in her face. You should have said, "Keep the fizzy, fuck face!" That's what you do if something like that happens again.' She held a crumpled tissue in her hand. As she said those words, she took the tissue, flicked her wrist, and tossed it over the blanket onto her thighs."

Emma took a long sip of water and then continued. "Jillian died the next day and that entire next day I kept saying over and over in my head, 'Keep the fizzy, fuck face.' I must have recited it in my brain a thousand times. Every time I said the phrase, I could picture Jillian's little hand flip the tissue into the air and onto the blanket. She asked me to promise her I would take a deep breath and then calmly ask a question. If all else fails, toss it back and say, 'Keep the fizzy, fuck face.' Now I ask a question to throw back the focus. She is undeniably a bitch, and so is karma. I can sit back and watch her be an idiot, because the bitch that is karma will get her."

"I'm glad you're taking Jillian's advice. That's her legacy to you."

"You know, Celia, I have never done anything unkind to her. I'm cold to her and stay away from her, but that's to avoid her vicious conduct toward me."

"You're an innocent victim who happened to fall for a guy with baggage."

"I know, right?" Emma flipped her hands in the air.

"Does this ex-wife have a name?" Celia took another slice of pizza.

"I despise her to the point that I can't bring myself to say her name, and I hate when she says mine. She's too vulgar and detestable for me to say her name." Emma took a bite of her now cold pizza; the cheese was no longer stringy.

"Oh. I see. You have no problem saying fuck face a million times, yet you can't say her name." Celia's voice was lowered to a whisper. "You do realize how funny that is, don't you?"

"I call her Edie. Let's leave it at that."

Comfy Cozy Sheets

The changes that came along with her new car were now part of Celia's weekday routine. The biggest change was setting her alarm clock twenty minutes earlier than usual. She hoped the extra time would provide a better chance to obtain prime parking at the T station.

She parked against the fence in the last parking space of the lot, which significantly reduced her chances of someone banging her car by fifty percent.

Celia despised people who parked their cars at an angle. She parked her Wrangler, pressed lock, and looked back at her parking job. There was no denying it: her car was ever so slightly parked at an angle. She never concerned herself with dents to her old car–its metal bruises were camouflaged by the rot and rust.

"Hello, this is Celia. How can I help you?" She didn't bother to read the caller ID.

"Hey, it's me. What's new?" Ramona's voice was particularly upbeat, which caused Celia concern.

"Not much. What's going on?" She punched her fist in the air as she remembered their last evening together.

"My brother is coming back to Boston. He asked me to ask if you want to get together again."

Oh, the booper. "Wow, he's coming back again? So soon?" She reached for an advertising circular from the newspaper on the chair next to her desk. She started to leaf through the pages as they spoke.

"So soon? Celia, he was here over a month ago! I want you to know he specifically asked for you. He liked you a lot, Celia. You should consider yourself honored. He doesn't take to people too easily."

Wonder if anyone has ever confronted him on that booping thing? "I'm kind of busy. I don't know." Celia hedged. She didn't want to decline too rapidly. She picked up a green highlighter and flipped through the pages of the Linen Closet circular. She began to highlight pictures of sheets, towels, and kitchen gadgets. She was half-listening to Ramona.

"He'll be here over the weekend. He said he truly enjoyed meeting you the last time he visited. He thought you were very nice and wants to get together with you. That is, if you're available."

Celia pushed the circular to the side of her desk and focused on their conversation. "I think he's nice, too, and very handsome." She told the truth about his appearance. "Unfortunately, I have plans for the weekend. If they fall through, I'll let you know." She felt guilty for lying, but knew she had to lie to avoid another night out with Ramona and Booper Boy.

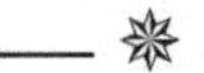

The Linen Closet was a luxury-only shopping spree. She needed nothing, except a new, fresh feel for her home. The thought of refreshing, crisp, cotton sheets against her cool, smooth skin when she got into bed at night made her happy. Soft, unspoiled bath towels hugging her body after a hot steamy shower would be delightful. Her old and soiled dish towels could be replaced with clean, new 100% cotton ones. She removed a shopping cart from the corral at the front of the store and enthusiastically began her shopping adventure.

Aghast at how incredibly gigantic the superstore was, she stood motionless at the entrance. With her hands clasped around the handles of the shopping cart, she took in her surroundings. Kitchen gadgets, bedding, artificial plants and flowers, dishtowels, picture frames, and bathroom and kitchen supplies filled the shelves. She pushed the cart and began her search for new possessions. Before long, she crammed the cart with bedding, linens, kitchen items, towels, and lotions.

Purchasing pillows was not even a distant thought when she set out on her excursion. At aisle four, the oversized fluffy pillows screamed out to her. *Touch Me* tags dangled from their packaging. She couldn't resist the fluffy queen-size pillow. She squeezed it and held it to her chest, closing her eyes for a moment. She loaded three of the pillows on top of the dish strainer, the kitchen towels, and the comforter, which had all been tossed into the cart somewhere between the entrance and the beginning of the fourth aisle. She stuffed three more onto the bottom shelf of the cart, above the wheels. She selected new pillows to sleep on, new pillows for the pillow shams that came with the new comforter, and new pillows for the extra pillow shams that would match the comforter.

This cart was full. She should have taken a second one, but she was certain she could handle the awkwardly overloaded cart.

At the back of the store, a magnificent display of brightly colored plastic wastebaskets was set up in four tiers, each perfectly uniform. As Celia navigated around the display, one of the pillows popped up and slid down the side of the cart. She seized the pillow and pulled the corner up. The large *Touch Me* tag caught the rim of the second tier on the display. The plastic baskets crashed down; the fourth tier fell on the third, plummeted down to the second, the first and then the floor. She tried to stop the imploding event, which made matters worse when she pushed her overloaded cart deeper into the collapsing display. She watched in horror as the red, orange, green, and yellow baskets collided into a colorful pile. The implosion stopped, and a shallow sea of brightly colored plastic baskets surrounded her. She reached down and picked up two of the fallen items. She awkwardly searched the area to see whether anyone had witnessed the incident.

A man nearby observed the collision between the shopping cart and the fallen display. He looked at the debris at her feet. She was uncomfortable, and nervously began to laugh. Not a full belly laugh—simply a quiet shaking laugh of self-consciousness. She was caught. How could she not be? He was right there. It would have been impossible for him not to notice. And equally impossible for her not to notice his eyes. In a split second, she realized he was the same man from Pete's Market and the car dealership. The brilliant and colorful display encircling her paled in comparison to the bright red her cheeks had become with the hot flush of embarrassment.

"How about this being our little secret?" She smiled at him, scrunched her face, and tilted her head with a begging shrug.

He grinned. "Sure, no problem."

She bent down and picked up a few more baskets. "I guess I should organize them, huh?" She spoke without raising her head from the mess.

"Nah, I'm sure that's somebody's job. I would, however, suggest you leave before someone arrives with police tape to block off the area."

"Yeah, I think you're right." She stood, took hold of her cart, and walked toward the cash registers. An announcement for cleanup assistance in the back of the store came over the loudspeakers. She paid for her purchases and was happy—very happy—to leave.

Celia loaded her purchases into the back of her car. She got into the driver's seat, fastened her seat belt and dialed Kate.

"Kate!" She all but screamed into the phone.

"You're calling from your cell phone? Please tell me there isn't anything wrong with your new car. Tell me you're not having a problem. Please."

"I'm fine. The car is fine. This is much worse."

"Celia, what's wrong?" Kate prepared herself for terrible news.

"I just saw him!" she shrieked. "I'm at the Linen Closet and I saw that guy with the nice eyes! The one from Pete's Market and the car place! The non-booper! Oh my God! He was in the store when I was there." Celia started the car, but didn't drive away; instead, she sat, idling the engine.

"You scared me, Celia. I expected something terrible."

"This felt terrible. I'm so embarrassed." Kate heard the panic in Celia's voice.

"Why are you embarrassed? Celia, you were shopping in the same store. It's not a thing to be embarrassed about. I'm sure there were other people shopping too. Right?"

"The store was almost empty, and he was right near where I was. I knocked over a few trash barrels. He watched the whole thing. He was right there! I felt like an idiot! I asked him to keep the little accident our secret. I'm an idiot, an absolute idiot. Now I hope I never see him again. I'm totally embarrassed."

Kate laughed, and Celia knew why. "Don't say that. This is what they call a *cute meet*. You see this in movies all the time. It's a fate thing or something like that. Maybe your clumsiness will help him remember you better. What was he doing in a store like that?"

"What do you mean, a store like that? What's wrong with that kind of store? I was in there."

"I usually don't see a lot of guys in linen stores. You know what I mean?"

Celia was silent for a minute. "I guess you're right."

"What kind of stuff was he buying?"

"I have no idea. I had just taken out an entire end-cap display of trash thingies. I was thinking about how stupid I looked. I never thought to check out his purchases."

"What do you mean, an entire display? You said you knocked over a few trash barrels." Kate laughed. "You took out an entire end-cap. I knew it! I knew it wasn't as simple as you tried to make it sound. You're too funny."

"Stop." Celia was used to feeling this sort of embarrassment.

"You're so klutzy, it's comical. Are you still in the parking lot? See if there's a Navigator in the lot. Maybe he bought that car he was looking at." Kate found Celia's mishaps, of which there were many, very amusing.

"You're a genius. Why didn't I think of that?" Celia turned to her right and then craned her neck to look behind her car. "I don't see anything." She continued to peruse the parking lot for his car.

"You could wait until he leaves the store, then you could see what car he goes into. Would this be considered stalking?" Kate didn't expect a serious answer to the question.

"I don't know. I think it is stalking. I'm going to Google stalking to see if I fit into the stalker category."

"He probably lives somewhere around there."

"I wonder if he does. I feel like a real jerk."

"Don't worry. I'm sure it wasn't that bad. Right?"

"Yeah, right." Celia didn't believe her own words.

Before going up the three flights to her apartment, she ran down to the basement, unlocked the padlock to her storage bin, pulled out her laundry detergent, ripped open the package of sheets and pillowcases, and threw them into the coin-operated washing machine. She fumbled into her pockets and found the correct change, fed the money into the coin slot, and tossed in the bath towels as well. She wanted the sheets as soft as possible when she climbed into bed and the towels fresh and fragrant for her morning shower.

The comforter made its way onto the bed, the pillows into their pillow shams, and the dish strainer and knickknacks were placed appropriately around the small apartment. She was excited and looked forward to getting into bed with her brand-new comfy cozy sheets, a book, and a lollipop—or cigarette if she couldn't shake the image of the trash barrel incident at the Linen Closet. Decision made: her treat would be a lollipop. She didn't want to lose the fresh scent of the cleaned linens.

We Have a Winner

"Lunch. Noon. I've got a funny story for you." Emma barely stuck her head into Celia's office to make her lunchtime announcement.

Celia was about to respond when she realized Emma was no longer at the doorway. She anticipated an entertaining lunch.

"I'm excited to tell you this story." Emma sat down across from Celia. "It's one for the books–literally."

"Start chirping." Celia took her sandwich from her lunch pouch and then poured out a bag of mixed nuts from a small plastic container.

"It's probably not as good as I think, but it's classic of how she lies to antagonize me. She fabricates stories that go on and on."

"Since yesterday was Father's Day, I'm going to guess you spent some time with Freddy and Edie?" Celia pushed the nuts to the center of the table.

Emma laughed. "Yes, I did."

"Why'd you laugh?"

"It's funny to hear you say 'Edie,' that's all." Emma placed the bowl of salad on a paper towel. "As you know, I've cut my visits down tremendously. I was foolish to think we would get a quality visit without her. When she's going to be there, I need to prepare myself with a suit of armor."

"Don't you prepare yourself every visit?"

"Of course I do. A month ago, Freddy told us she was busy on Father's Day and would not be there. When we turned onto Freddy's street, she drove past us in the opposite direction. Fredric and I were happy that she was leaving. Five minutes later, she came back to spend the entire day with us. Not sure how her plans changed so quickly. Fredric once told me she doesn't stay if I'm not there. Obvious or what?" Emma took a Jillian-inspired deep breath.

"Yeah, I'd say it's obvious."

"She parked right next to Fredric's car and went into Freddy's apartment as soon as she arrived." Emma shook her head as she recalled the event. "The plan for the day was a cookout with some of Freddy's friends in the afternoon and then the three of us were going out to dinner."

"By three of you, you mean you, Fredric, and Freddy?" Celia picked up a few nuts and popped them in her mouth.

"Exactly. She wasn't in the plan. She wasn't supposed to be there. Instead of going into the house, we hung out with Freddy in the garage–while he fixed his bicycle. Within two minutes, she was standing right next to me. My jaw tensed up, but I tried to remain relaxed. Her other kid was with the husband."

Celia had taken a bite from her sandwich and appeared as if she were about to choke. "What other kid?"

"Her little girl."

"Emma?" Celia said in a singsong tone. "What are you talking about?"

"Geez! Did I forget to tell you about her daughter? I think she's in third or fourth grade. She spent the weekend in Maine with her dad and the grandparents."

"Aren't you full of surprises?" Celia's eyes were opened wide. "That's a big age gap between Freddy and the daughter."

"I guess she had a hard time getting pregnant this time."

"Go on." Celia listened intently.

"She walked up to me and stood so close we nearly touched elbows. I can't even tell you how uncomfortable I was to have her breathe down my neck. Then the guys needed a chain or something and were going to go to the bike shop."

"What did you do? Were you stuck alone with her?"

"I whispered to Fredric that I planned to take a walk. She listens intently to every word I say. I don't know how she heard me, but in a second, she invited herself on my walk. I told her I was taking the walk to avoid spending time alone with her."

"Get out! Did you really say that?"

"No, but I desperately wanted to. I didn't need to go for a walk if she was going to join me. The entire purpose of the walk was to get away from her. She didn't ask–she told me she would come with me. As if we're friends. I stayed civil. She wasn't nasty or insulting. Not THIS time." Emma took a bite of her lunch and a sip of her drink.

"Emma, I don't know why you try to be civil. She doesn't." Celia put a few more nuts in the palm of her hand. "I'm dying to hear what happened this time."

"I honestly can't remember how everything transpired, but here's what happened."

Her plan to escape mundane conversation with Fredric's ex was commandeered when Edie invited herself to join in on *Emma's avoid the ex-wife* walk.

"Are you still working in Boston?" Edie asked Emma.

"I am. I love the job, but I'm not a big fan of the commute."

"That drive must suck."

If I had stayed back at Freddy's, I could be on my phone texting or playing solitaire. Now I'm stuck. Emma was annoyed with herself. She never made the right decision with situations that involved the ex. She could feel her stomach tense up and churn while she waited for an inevitable insult to spew from Edie's mouth.

The two women turned the corner and came upon a garage sale. Three tables of knickknacks, utensils, and bottles were lined up in the driveway. Fireplace irons and grates were off to the side. The little gray-haired woman selling the items sat in a shaded chair close to the walkway.

"Good afternoon." Emma smiled at the woman.

"Welcome to my yard sale. Look around. Take your time and let me know if you're interested in anything." The woman remained seated.

"Why are we here? This is just that lady's junk." Edie picked up a wine glass with a red stem. She put it down and touched a few more glasses.

"Ah, one person's junk is another person's treasure. I once found an antique desktop in someone's trash. It turned out to be worth thousands. It's one of my favorite pieces."

"Gross!" Edie seemed disgusted. Emma ignored her.

Emma examined crystal wine glasses and silver serving spoons. She walked around to the back of the table. On the ground below, she found a large cardboard box filled with crystal and glass items. She lifted out two uniquely shaped vases. "If these are for sale, I'd love to buy them. They're beautiful." Emma carried them closer to the woman. *This isn't so bad. I'll get these new vases and we'll walk back and everything will be fine.* She felt the tension lessen in her stomach. "Are you selling these vases? They were in a box under the table." She held out the larger vase to show the woman.

"Oh yes, dear. I love those. In my younger years, I owned a flower shop. I searched everywhere for beautiful vases."

"Are you buying those?" Edie interrupted.

"I think so. Do you see how the glass sparkles?"

"I wanted to get them, and you got to them before me." Edie stared at Emma as she whined.

"Oh?" Emma squinted, tilted her head, and lowered her eyebrows in confusion. She felt the all too familiar knot in her stomach reappear. *You little liar. You couldn't have seen them without coming around the table. They were underneath and out of sight.* Emma's stomach was once again tight with anxiety. *That was a quick reprieve of stress. It's not possible to have a normal minute with you. Is it?* "There are others in the box. Did you see any of them?"

"No. Why would I? I was going to get those." She whined once more.

I wonder if I could smash you to little tiny pieces with those fireplace irons. "All right." Emma took a deep breath. "Why don't you take one and I'll take the other one. Which one do you want?" She held out both vases for Edie's inspection.

"Which one do YOU want?"

Oh God! Just fucking pick one. "Honestly, I don't care. Take the one you want, and I'll take the other." *How can I make this any easier for you, you idiot? Take the fucking vase you want from the two you never saw in the first place.* She knew Edie would never have looked at the vases if Emma hadn't picked them up. Edie took the vase that wasn't Emma's favorite. Emma selected a few pieces of silver serving utensils to add to her collection.

They paid for their items and walked away. Emma stopped at the end of the driveway and walked back to the box below the table.

She found another magnificent vase. "I want to add this too." She handed the vase to the woman. "It's beautiful. How much is it?"

"That's my favorite, dear." The woman double-wrapped the vase in paper. "I want you to enjoy this vase as your gift from me." The woman winked at Emma. Emma hugged and thanked her.

"I should have taken that one." Edie snarled when they returned to the sidewalk.

"Yeah, I love it!" Emma's smile had victory written all over it. She requested they cut the walk short. She didn't want to carry the fragile vases any longer than necessary.

Friends of Freddy's had arrived and were drinking beers in the backyard when the girls returned. Emma placed her purchases securely in the backseat of her car.

She walked over to Fredric, who sat around the fire pit with a small group of friends and neighbors. She sat down next to him.

"Hey, babe, I think Freddy could use my help with the burgers. You need anything?" He kissed her cheek as he got up.

"All set. Go cook."

Fredric hadn't been away from his chair for more than a minute when, in a flash, Edie took the now empty seat to the right of Emma.

"We went to the little garage sale down the street today. I got a beautiful glass vase and Emma did too," Edie announced to the group.

Emma tightened her jaw. *Whatever!*

"The woman was selling figure skates and ski equipment." Edie scooped potato chips from a bowl next to Emma.

"I didn't see any sports equipment." Emma was baffled. "Where was it?"

"Right up front by the first table. How could you miss it?"

"She had only glass, silver, and fireplace tools. She told us that." Emma was curious as to why this conversation was taking place. She knew Edie didn't bring this up without a reason. *What are you up to this time?* Emma remained silent and waited for what was about to happen to actually happen.

"I saw the skates and ski boots and all I could think of was the 1988 Winter Olympics in Calgary."

Here we go. For a millisecond, Emma's eyeballs disappeared into her top eyelids. *We're enjoying a beautiful sunny day in June. Let's talk about the Winter Olympics from twenty-six years ago.*

Edie smiled as she began her story. "Fredric and some buddies from college went to Calgary to watch the Olympics. I was supposed to go, but I was pregnant and not feeling great. I was afraid to fly, being preggers and all." She took a sip of her wine cooler and smirked at Emma—it was a mocking smirk. "Fredric kept calling me and sending me pictures of the figure skating, so I could feel like I was there with him. That's how he shared the experience with me."

Emma sat back in her chair and crossed her legs. *Wait a second. How can that be*? Emma thought of Jillian and took a very deep breath. *Remember, breathe and ask a question. Breathe and a question.* "You must have watched them on television. Right?" Emma stared at Edie.

Edie ignored the question. "The cell phone was the only way we could be together. He was upset I couldn't go to Calgary with him and he missed me so much. He sent me pictures all day long."

Go slow. Breathe. Take your time. "Have you ever seen that sort of sporting event before? What did you think of the pictures?" Emma stared straight into Edie's eyes.

"They were amazing. I couldn't believe how close he got to the athletes. Fredric must have texted me more than twenty-five pictures from his phone. And that was just in the morning."

And there it is! "That's great he was able to text you all those pictures. That way you didn't need to feel left out." Emma grinned. She restrained her desire to burst out laughing. *You truly are a fool!*

"I know. Right? I felt like I was there with him." Edie shoved a handful of chips in her mouth. "We spent hours on the phone going over the pictures. Amazing, don't you think?"

"Yes. Very amazing. Especially since the camera phone wasn't invented for another nine years, not until June of 1997. Nobody texted back in 1988."

"I didn't mean text," Edie snapped loudly as she tightened her lips. "I meant to say he emailed the pictures to me." Edie desperately attempted to reclaim and validate her fictional story.

"Save it! Fredric's never been that technologically astute, let alone ahead of his time. Even today he struggles with taking pictures from his cell phone." Emma picked up her plate and walked away chuckling. "Another harebrained story." She mumbled under her breath and left the cookout for about twenty minutes.

Celia's sandwich was long gone by the time Emma finished her story. The plastic bowl of nuts was empty, and her chocolate caramel cookie was merely a crumb on her plate. "No more phone calls–we have a winner!" She slapped her hand loudly on the table. "That is truly a crazy story. What a witch!" Celia shook her head in disgust. "That woman is absolutely, positively insane." She picked up her spring water, twisted off the cap, took a drink and then put the bottle down. The bottle tipped over and spilled half the water on the table. She put the cap back on immediately and wiped up the water with a couple of napkins.

"How on earth did you know off the top of your head the camera phone was invented in June of 1997?" Celia spun the bottle around inside her paper plate.

"Coincidentally, I heard an electronics guy on the radio talking about cell phones. He mentioned it was the birthday of the camera phone, which was June 1997. The fact that I heard that story on the radio at that time was total luck. And I mean absolute total luck. If I hadn't heard that segment, I wouldn't have known. I never would have put together the inaccuracy of the timeframe. It would have hit me days later how chronologically inaccurate her stupid story was. Then I'd be pissed at myself that I didn't catch the lie immediately, when she made up the story during the cookout."

"How did she act after you exposed her?"

"I don't know. I left for about twenty minutes, but she was quiet when I returned."

"I want to know, but I think I already know the answer. Where did you go when you left?"

"Guess." Emma laughed.

"I think I know, but I want you to tell me." Celia laughed and pushed the tip of her tongue to her upper lip.

"I went back to the garage sale. The lady was still outside. I asked what happened to the skates and ski equipment she had for sale."

Celia slapped the table. "I knew it! Let me guess. There weren't any skis or skates?"

"You got that right! She said her kids took all their winter stuff out of her garage years ago. She couldn't stand the clutter."

"Did you tell Edie?"

Emma laughed.

"Emma, why do you always laugh when I say her name?"

"It's funny to hear you say Edie. I guess it's because I don't talk about her to anyone else. That's all. And no, I didn't tell her; it would have served no purpose."

Strike Three

"Celia! Celia!" Noah screamed from his bicycle as she stepped out of her Wrangler. He wore his white and green striped game uniform. "I hoped I would see you! You won't believe this! We're winning!" He jumped off his bike and lowered it to the ground. He ran toward her. "We won this morning and now we've won every game so far! We're undefeated. We have a big game next Saturday. It's against our biggest rival. You should come. I've invited the whole neighborhood. The game is at the field by the church!"

"Congratulations!" They walked together to her front door and stopped before the steps. "The other day I saw a sign about it in Pete's. Let me know the time. I'll try to stop by to cheer you on."

"It's 11:30 in the morning, right next to the church. Can you believe it? Home team advantage! My Uncle Bill and Aunt Sophie are coming to watch. My dad finished his work a month early, and my parents will be back from California by then. They're coming home Friday morning. I'm wicked excited. It's a really important game." Noah shrieked with excitement. "The only bad part is that Trudy can't come. Last week she chased one of the balls and the coach yelled at me."

"That stinks. Wasn't anyone holding onto her?"

"My Uncle Bill had her leash, but she still got away from him. You might remember that she's wicked good at escaping. Coach might not have been mad if it was the first time, but she's gotten loose before."

"Your uncle took her to the game after she had already escaped once before?"

"I sort of never told him about the first time, so don't say anything."

"I won't say a word."

"I gotta get home. I just wanted to tell you about the big game. Please try to come if you can. Tell everyone you know to come! We have to win this game!" He lifted his bicycle, jumped over the bar, and pedaled out of sight.

Celia often walked past the ball field and occasionally stopped and leaned against the fence to watch an inning or two. Noah's games were far from the most exciting sports events Celia had ever watched. They were amusing nonetheless. The errors and young boys' tantrums were comical, although she wouldn't say that to Noah. She had never officially attended an entire game, but he asked her personally, so she expected she would attend Noah's game–at least a few innings. She was certain she could coerce Kate into tagging along. She also knew she would have to bribe her with lunch or some sort of treat.

Saturday's weather prediction was overcast. Not rain, just overcast. Nothing to ruin the big game, just enough cloud cover to make the conditions tolerable for the fans. Celia's plan to lure Kate with the "catch a few rays at the game" idea instantly washed down the drain.

Kate reluctantly agreed to go. Her wakeup call to Celia was full of commentary. "Why are we going to spend Saturday morning at a kid's ball game? We're supposed to shop for makeup or something ridiculous. The sun's not even out."

"It will be over by 1:00. Besides, didn't I agree to buy you dinner tonight? Park behind me and we'll walk to the game. We can head out from the ball field when we're ready to leave. They have a great concession stand with incredible slush. I'll buy you a slush too. We'll stay a few innings."

"Is the slush in addition to, or instead of, dinner?"

"It's in addition to dinner. Why do I have to buy your friendship? Just come over." Celia twirled an unlit cigarette between her fingers–she didn't light it.

"I was kidding. You don't have to buy my friendship or dinner. I'll be there in a little while. You think they'll be done that early?"

"I think so. I've seen portions of other games and the innings didn't take long. They're kind of funny to watch. I have to hang up now. My hair is at critical." Critical was when Celia's hair was damp, but dry enough to go any which way it desired. If she waited much longer to use the hair dryer, she would have no control on the direction her curls would take. "Ring the buzzer, and I'll come right down."

The ball field was less than packed. Parents and fans sat by the sidelines in nylon folding chairs. Coolers filled with soft drinks and snacks had been placed on the ground nearby. The bleachers were nearly empty. A group of small children and young teens played on a swing set far behind third base.

Celia, dressed in white shorts, a pink gauze shirt, and sneakers, along with Kate in jeans and a T-shirt, climbed to the middle section of the bleachers. They both wore sunglasses on top of their head and hoped for sunshine. Noah stood by the home team bench and talked with three adults, presumably his parents and his aunt.

At 11:30 sharp, the game began.

"Do you think we're the only two people here who aren't parents or relatives of a kid on one of these teams?" Kate's sunglasses had fallen forward–she pushed them back to the top of her head.

"Probably." Celia reached in her bag for a lollipop.

"Which one is Noah?"

"He's the one who just walked up to practice his swing. I think he's up next. He's number 27. You want a lollipop?" She held out a handful of the sugary treats.

"I can't see his face. Damn!" Kate took an orange pop, removed the wrapper, and put it in her mouth.

An elderly man climbed up and sat in the row in front of them. He turned to the women. "Which team does your son play on?"

Kate turned toward Celia and raised her eyebrows. Her lips curved upward.

"We came to watch a boy from my neighborhood." They looked at each other. Kate winked at Celia.

"Do they have root beer slush?" Kate bit her lollipop and crunched on the hard candy.

"I doubt they have anything other than lemon and pineapple. You want me to get you one?"

"Nah. We'll get an ice cream or something after. Can I exchange my slush credit for an ice cream?"

"You bet! Ice cream sounds better anyway. I think that's Noah's family over there, on those navy beach chairs. He was hanging out with them when we got here." Celia inconspicuously pointed in their direction.

"I love those chairs. I wonder where they got them. If that's his dad, he's kind of cute, don't you think?"

"Kind of. The tall one must be Noah's aunt."

"Why do you assume the little one is his mother?" Kate leaned forward and examined Noah's family.

"Because I heard him call her Mom as we walked by."

"Celia, you've always had such a keen sense for the obvious." The sun poked through the clouds and the sky became a beautiful shade of blue. "That sun feels great. Don't you think?" Kate lowered her sunglasses to cover her eyes.

"Yeah. See, I can make good on a promise."

Noah was at bat. "Strike one!" The umpire clenched his fist and pounded out as he lowered his elbow. "Strike two!" the ump bellowed loudly. "Strike three!" His voice echoed through the ball field. Noah threw his bat to the ground and walked to the bench with his head down.

"Oops!" Kate nudged Celia. "Hey! Who's that guy over there in the suit? He looks familiar."

"Where?" Celia leaned into Kate. She tried to get a clear view of the man in the suit walking toward Noah's family.

A tall, handsome man, wearing dark sunglasses, walked in the direction of Noah's parents and aunt. He took off his tie, folded it, and neatly placed it into the pocket of his jacket. He unbuttoned the top button of his shirt, removed his jacket, and threw it over his shoulder.

"Right there." Kate pointed. "He's heading toward Noah's family. Doesn't he look familiar?" She sucked on the empty stick from the lollipop.

"Yeah, he's got a familiar face, but I don't think I know him. Do you?" Celia pulled a tube of suntan lotion from her bag. She poured a small amount into the palm of her hand, rubbed her hands together and then smoothed the lotion over her nose and cheeks.

"I can't tell. I wonder if he's someone who works with Tom or something."

As the man approached Noah's family, he removed his sunglasses.

Celia took hold of Kate's wrist. "No way! That's the guy!"

"What guy?"

"Remember? You saw him at the car dealer the day you took me car shopping." Celia continued to hold Kate's wrist.

"The one from the Navigator?" Kate squinted in his direction to focus better. "I think you're right! I think that's him. Maybe that's why he looks familiar. He does kind of look like the guy from the car place, but I'm not sure. Are you sure?"

Celia gasped as she remembered the trash barrels tumbling down in the linen store.

He leaned over and kissed the woman who wasn't Noah's mother on the cheek. He knelt by her side for a few seconds and then stood behind her with his hands on her shoulders.

"I can't believe this. I can't believe this." Celia's heart beat rapidly. "He must be Noah's uncle. I've even said hi to him from a distance." She released her grip from Kate. "And AUNT! That's the aunt and uncle who Noah talks about–the ones he's been staying with. Now I have to see him more clearly."

"You want my binoculars?"

"You have binoculars with you?" Celia sounded surprised.

"No. But I might have some in the car. I can go back and look if you want. Are you okay? I wish I had something more helpful to say." She rubbed Celia's arm.

"I'm sure he's the same person." She took an anxious breath. "I think I might puke. I can't believe Noah's uncle and my mystery man are one and the same. That's why he was at Pete's. He lives in my neighborhood. And to boot, he's married." She took another long, hard breath. "Have I got luck or what? What are the chances of this happening? I wish I had these odds when I bought my lottery tickets. I cannot believe this. In a split second, my little fantasy washed down the drain!"

"Aha! So, you were interested! I knew it was more than you made it out to be! You should be happy you didn't waste too much time or energy thinking about him. That would have sucked more. Geez! The guy's married. Who would have guessed he'd be the same guy as the kid's uncle?" She shook her head back and forth a couple of times for sympathetic emphasis and then wrapped her arm around Celia's shoulder. "Celia, I'm sorry he's married."

"I can't breathe. I want to leave now. How can we sneak out of here without Noah seeing us?"

"Don't worry, Celia, I'm with you. We can leave now if you want, or we could hide in the crowd when everyone leaves."

"The huge crowd of fifteen people here in the bleachers? Would that be the crowd we could hide in?" Celia's sarcasm rang loud and clear.

"Sorry, I wasn't thinking. If you want to leave right this minute while everyone watches the game, I'm with you." Kate squeezed her arm tighter around Celia's shoulder. "Chances are he doesn't remember you from the little incidents when you saw him the other times."

"Let's wait and watch the game a little longer. I need a moment to think." Celia tried to concentrate on the game but continued to stare in the direction of Noah's uncle. She hoped he would leave before the game was over. The uncle was apparently staying to until the final score.

"One o'clock, huh?" Kate checked her cell for the time. At 2:00, Noah's team won the game. Celia and Kate stepped down one row and then descended from the bleachers.

"How was I supposed to know the game would go extra innings? I'm glad his team won. Now let's get the hell out of here. Fast!" Celia stepped up her pace.

Celia and Kate held hands and tried to sneak off the ball field. Noah called out from home plate. "Celia! Celia! Over here." His arms flailed frantically.

Celia turned around and waved to Noah, who raced toward her.

"Can you believe it? We won! We won! We beat our biggest rival!" Noah's family strolled in the direction of the trio.

"Hey, these are my parents." The family approached them. "This is my dad Glen and my mother, Melanie. And this is my Uncle Bill and Aunt Sophie."

"Nice to meet you." Celia's throat tightened. Her heart pounded. She wondered whether they could hear the thumping. "This is my friend, Kate." She turned back to Noah.

"Congratulations on a great game. It's nice to meet you." Kate reached down to shake Noah's hand.

Noah's Uncle Bill put his hand out to greet Celia. "Hi, I'm William Charles. Noah has told me a lot about you. I'm glad to finally meet you."

"I hope Noah said nice things." *You didn't just make that lame and unoriginal comment. Did you?*

"He's had only nice things to say." William Charles had a remarkable twinkling smile.

"My pleasure to meet you all." Celia made eye contact with Noah's four relatives. She held Kate's elbow as they walked away from the ball field.

"Did you see him wink at me, when Noah introduced us?"

"I'm not sure if he winked, Celia. He has twinkly eyes. You've said that since the first time you saw him, and you're right about that. The guy's eyes are amazing. Do you truly believe he winked? What would that mean?"

"Kate, I think he winked."

"Then if he DID wink, Celia, he's a real asshole, because his wife was right there next to him. Don't you agree?"

"I still think it was a wink."

"What kind of guy winks at another woman with his wife right there? Geoff who? Hellllllo?" Kate shook her head.

The pit in Celia's stomach was piercing. There was silence for a few moments. Celia looked at the pavement as they walked down her driveway. "It sucks because I don't trust these jerks anyway. Deep inside, I've never lost hope I'd find someone who doesn't totally suck."

"I hope you aspire to more than 'doesn't totally suck,' Celia. They don't all suck. Some guys are nice. Ice cream? I'll buy," Kate sympathetically suggested.

"Nope! Drinks! Alcoholic beverages are the way to go." Celia dug into her bag for a cigarette. "Please don't say a word." She played with the package she held in her hands. "I was going to quit this week, but I think I'll wait until next month."

"Whatever. This is an extenuating circumstance." Kate fished her keys out of her back pocket.

They drove to Tequila Maria's to enjoy an afternoon margarita.

MEMORY LANE

The one negative about autumn was the impending doom and gloom of winter. Celia loved everything about the fall, from the fresh air to her non-frizzing hair. Unquestionably, fall was her favorite season.

What better time to do spring cleaning than the beginning of autumn? Her staycation plans would include time to clean, shop, and relax. Daily trips to Pete's were on the agenda. She would try a different flavor of ice cream each day and test her luck with the lottery.

Today, the first Saturday of her week off, encompassed a carton of chocolate mousse with macadamia nuts and caramel swirl. A can of whipped cream and a package of pecans could not be passed up. Two bags of lollipops, three two-dollar lottery tickets, and one pack of fresh cigarettes–just in case–rolled down the conveyer to the register.

"Good morning." Celia handed the girl at the checkout thirty dollars from her wallet.

"Celia?" He walked up and stood in line behind her. "I thought that was you." He smiled. His eyes sparkled. His teeth glistened.

She instinctively turned toward him when he mentioned her name. "Hello, William." *Is there any part of you that isn't shiny and perfect?* She felt her heart skip a beat. "How are you?" Noah's game was over a month ago. She was surprised he recognized her or remembered her name.

"I'm great, thank you. How about you? Getting groceries for dinner?" He was friendly and sweet, which annoyed her.

"Stopped in to pick up a few things and cash in my big lottery winnings. I won a free ticket yesterday." She fumbled with the orange scarf draped around her neck. She held out her hand as she waited for her change.

"I should play the lottery one of these days, but I'm not lucky with scratch tickets."

"You'll never win if you don't try." She put the change into her wallet.

"I guess you're right. Maybe I'll try my luck one of these days. Hey, I'm heading across the street for a cup of coffee." William pointed to the small sandwich shop across from Pete's. "Would you care to join me?"

"No thank you." Celia's response was as quick as it was cold.

"Are you sure I can't entice you into coffee, or maybe something sweet– perhaps a pastry or slice of cake?" He was surprised she turned him down so rapidly. He sounded sincere and authentic.

Just like Geoff. You're all the same, aren't you? "Please don't take this personally, but I prefer to stay away from certain situations. Thank you anyway."

"I'd like to get to know you better. Would you ever be interested in dinner?"

You're relentless. "Thank you anyway!" She turned and faced the door. "Have a nice day, William. Say hello to Noah and Sophie for me." She pushed the glass door–her scarf caught on the handle. She instantly dislodged the fabric and checked to see whether William witnessed her clumsy move. The incident at the Linen Closet flashed through her brain. She was reasonably certain he didn't recognize her from the barrel-tumbling scene.

She walked home and focused on the beautiful day. Better said, she TRIED to focus on the beautiful day. Her main goal was to clear her head and forget about William. Married William. William Charles who had invited her for coffee or something sweet. *He invited me to coffee and probably thought nothing of it. Geoff seemed to have no problem having his little adventures. I don't get it. I just don't get it.*

Celia stopped walking and put her bag on the front steps of a neighbor's entryway. She reached in and took out her cigarettes. She tapped the bottom of the package into the palm of her hand. She threw them back into the shopping bag and stood silent as she stared into space. She took out the lollipops and selected a red one. She sucked the pop for a few seconds, removed it from her mouth, and slid it back in the wrapper. Within minutes, she exhaled a puff of smoke.

Wearing black jeans, a baggy blue shirt, and his baseball cap, Noah approached her. Trudy walked by his side.

"Hey, what are you doing around here? I haven't seen you for a while." She moved her hand down, in an attempt to hide her lit cigarette.

"Visiting Uncle Bill for the day. Aunt Sophie said he's down at Pete's. I want to surprise him and meet him at the corner."

"Would you like a lollipop?" She lifted the bag of pops and handed them to Noah.

"Sure!" Trudy lay down on the sidewalk and plopped her head on her front paws.

"Take a couple. I always have plenty."

He peered into the bag. "Cool!" He took three pops and opened the grape one.

Celia took a handful of the candies and gave them to Noah. "Please. Take these. I have more than I need."

"Thank you. Did you see Uncle Bill at the store?"

"Yes, he was in the same checkout line as I was."

"He thinks you're pretty and..." Noah stopped without completing the sentence.

"That's always nice to hear. Does your Aunt Sophie mind that he told you that?" She knew she had said the wrong thing, but that didn't stop her from speaking. Celia imagined her social status had been a topic of conversation among Noah's relatives.

"Oh no. He thinks Aunt Sophie is beautiful too, but I guess he has to think that. Right?"

"That's good." Celia was at a loss for words. *Why is he telling me about Uncle Bill and Aunt Sophie?* "I have to get home. It's always nice to see you, Noah." She ended the conversation as quickly as possible. Before she left, she patted Trudy on the head.

Celia walked into her living room and fell backward into the couch. She pushed her sneakers off and rested her legs on the coffee table. She was surprised and bothered by William's invitation for coffee and pastry. *How can guys so easily lie and cheat without any regard to their wives or partners?*

She was disappointed–mostly at herself. She had fantasized of a man she knew nothing about. A married man who made subtle advances toward her. He was a handsome stranger. She needed to not think about him.

She clicked on the television but didn't hear a word. Her thoughts brought her back to the day, a little over three years ago, when she left Geoff and moved into this three-room apartment. She wanted to return to the place where she had grown up. The logical and comfortable choice was to move back to Massachusetts.

Geoff had been the love of her life. At least, that's what she thought. He was handsome and full of charm and charisma. He was broad shouldered, with a wide face and strong jaw. His thick, wavy hair was the color of chocolate. And similar to William Charles, he had nice eyes.

From the moment they met, there were sparks between them. Their chemistry was incredible. She remembered the time they were together. It seemed a lifetime ago. She felt as if she were recalling someone else's life, not her own.

Geoff told her immediately that he had been married when he was twenty-one, a "huge mistake," he claimed. He and his ex-wife were the same age when they married while still in college. In his words, "a silly thing to do" and after nine months of marital experimentation, the short-lived union was annulled.

He was romantic in a way that Celia had never known and could never have dreamed about. He would send her gifts for no reason. Several times a month, she would find flowers at their doorstep or in the mailbox when she arrived home. Every now and then, a wonderfully scented bouquet was delivered to her office. He thought nothing of picking her up at work on Friday afternoon. They would take a limousine into New York City for dinner or a show. Sometimes they would stay overnight in the city, and other times they would have a long, intimate ride home. She tingled at his touch. Twitterpations–like butterflies dancing within her, even when he just touched her hand. She became lost in her thoughts.

It was Celia's twenty-ninth birthday and Geoff surprised her with tickets for a long weekend in Bermuda. They left for their island adventure the following week.

A pale-green bungalow enclosed with a salmon-hued roof became their home for the next few days. The bungalow was a delightful private little hideaway with steps that led to a white sandy beach, where waves brushed along the seashore.

Winding walkways, each lined with fragrant blossoms and shrubs, surrounded the tropical resort. As they walked hand-in-hand from dinner on their first evening, geckos raced across the footpaths. Instead of going directly to their cabana, they strolled along the beach. Eventually they arrived at a secluded area, where they stopped. They sat in the cool sand. With their arms wrapped around each other, they talked about life, family, and a future together.

On Sunday morning, they strolled to the ocean-side dining room for a tropical island brunch. They devoured several servings of pineapple pancakes drenched in coconut syrup, banana fritters, fried potatoes and onions, strawberries lightly dusted with colorful sugars causing their juices to spill onto the platter, pecan and apple muffins covered with sweet butter, tropical drinks, and fresh brewed coffee.

They walked back toward their bungalow along the beach. Geoff rested his arm on Celia's shoulder. Sporadically, he twirled her ponytail between his fingers. He then pulled her arm tightly and she stopped walking. He took her hands in his and gazed down into her eyes. Her stomach flipped once and then again, the same twitterpations she had felt since the first time they kissed.

"Celia." He smiled at her. "I love you. I can't remember my life without you, and I can't imagine my future the same way. I want you to promise to spend the rest of your life with me. Can you do that?"

"I love you too, Geoff. Of course I want to spend the rest of my life with you."

"So? What do you say? Will you marry me? Say 'yes'–it's that easy."

"Are you asking me to marry you, Geoff?" Her heart skipped several beats. "Oh my God! Really?"

He knelt on one knee. She tried to pull him up, but she was giggling too hard. She then plopped down on her knees to be at his level. He grabbed her hand and slid an exquisite solitaire diamond ring onto her finger. She fell back onto the sand and pulled him down with her.

"Well? What do you say?" His eyes were pleading for her to say she would marry him.

"I think I should have gotten a manicure." She teased him as she stared at the dazzling diamond glistening on her finger. "It's beautiful! Can I keep it even if I say no?" She tilted her head and smiled lovingly.

He grabbed her by the waist and leaned in to kiss her lips. "You won't say no."

"No kidding, I won't. I'm officially saying YES. Y-E-S." She spelled out the second yes.

"I love you, Celia." He squeezed her tightly and hugged her again.

Suddenly a neighbor's door slammed shut and snapped Celia out from her depressing and miserable recollections of the past. She unconsciously lit a cigarette as she remembered their relationship and how she found out about Geoff's secret. *Shit! I'm never going to quit.* Frustrated and angry at herself, she squashed the cigarette in the ashtray and selected a red lollipop. She picked up the television remote and flipped through the stations to make herself stop thinking of Geoff. *Stop thinking of Geoff! Stop thinking of William or Uncle Bill or whatever you want to call him. Don't be a loser. You're fixating on a total stranger! Get over it!* The thoughts screamed in her head. *Stop thinking—period!* She watched sitcoms, ate ice cream, and sucked on lollipops.

Now, three years after Geoff, Celia was happy and living alone in her drama-free, one-bedroom, third-floor hideaway. She convinced herself she didn't want to clutter her simple life with another relationship. She concentrated on the television and her channel surfing.

The Clap

"You interested in dinner tonight?" Kate asked the question before Celia finished saying hello.

"Dinner again? I think you're trying to fatten me up." Celia reached for a lollipop.

"Yes, I'm trying to fatten you up. If I can't be thin, then I want my friends to be fat."

"I think we weigh about the same. Too bad you're eight inches shorter than I am." Celia tasted the pop. The disgusting flavor of sour apple seized her tongue. *Gross! I thought this was lime.* She pulled it from her mouth, threw it in the trash, and rinsed her mouth with water.

"Ha ha. You know I'm taller than you, don't you?"

"Barely an inch. You really want to go to dinner again?" Celia searched for a new flavor in the bag. She found another green pop, removed the wrapper, and smelled it. *Smells like lime.* She took a quick lick to confirm the flavor and then sucked on the candy.

"My in-laws are driving home from Maine. They'll be driving by here around dinner time and want us to meet them. They invited you to be my date. Tom could never be home early enough to meet them. He's seeing patients until 6:00."

"Aren't you sick of me yet? You took me to dinner less than a week ago."

"Come on. They love you–I think even more than they like me. Please come. Don't forget I went to that baseball game for Nolan. I don't want to get into a thing about why we haven't given them grandchildren. I don't think they'll talk about that if you're with us."

"I already put on my sweats and clicked up the heat. I'm too comfortable to go out. And by the way, his name is Noah, not Nolan."

"I was close. Noah. Nolan. It's almost the same name. Come to dinner. I'm begging you. You'll be doing me the biggest favor. It's always more fun when you're there." Celia could hear Kate's desperation radiate through the phone. "You can wear your sweats."

"Where are you going?" Celia chewed the last bit of her lime pop. She walked to the sink, took a spoon from the dish strainer, and removed a carton of caramel pecan turtle ice cream from the freezer.

"I don't know yet, but I'm sure they'll pick someplace quick. They don't want to be on the road too late. I think they have a place in mind. I'll call them now. Pick you up at 4:00."

"Four? Is this lunch or dinner?"

"I know. I know. They always eat early. You'll come, right?"

"All right. I haven't seen Bernie and Doris in a while. It might be nice to catch up with them." She licked the spoon dry before she dug in for a refill.

"Do you want me to call when I find out where they want to meet? If they haven't decided yet, I'll try to suggest someplace casual."

"Don't worry about it. I'll meet you in the driveway." Celia proceeded to finish the pint of ice cream and left the empty container on the table. She changed from her grungy clothes to jeans and a sweater.

The waiting area was nearly empty, 4:30 being on the early side for the dinner crowd. Bernie sat quietly and glanced through the local real estate circulars. He crossed one leg over the other and exposed his dark-brown socks, which contrasted greatly against his out-of-season white slacks and shiny white shoes. He held the paper high to avoid getting the black print on his clean trousers. His thick gray hair was combed back. Although his reading glasses rested low on the bridge of his nose, he tipped his head back slightly as he peered down through the frames.

Doris's emerald-green jogging suit revealed satin squares across the front and swirls of gold glitter down both sleeves. She stood out from the small group of casually clad early-birders who also waited to be seated. Her bangle bracelets clinked as she raised her arms to hug Kate and Celia.

"This is some line." Doris sat down next to Bernie. "We could be here for hours and I'm starving."

"We won't be here for hours. There's less than a dozen other people waiting," Kate reassured Doris. "Even when it's crowded, you can usually get a table fast." Kate scanned the crowd and assessed the number of people. "There are only eleven people, and that includes us." She spoke quietly to her mother-in-law.

"You look thin, Celia. Doesn't she look thin, Bernie? Do you eat enough? I hope you don't have that anorexia disease. I think you girls don't take care of yourselves properly." Doris looked at Celia and then Kate. "You both look too thin."

"Doris, I feel great." Celia was caught off guard by the weight conversation. *I thought you were supposed to focus on your childless daughter-in-law.*

"You better be sure you don't catch that disease."

"Trust me, Celia would never be anorexic. It isn't a disease you catch. Besides, if anything she'd be bulimic, where she could get the best of both worlds. Eat to her heart's content and then stick her finger down her throat."

Celia turned toward Kate in horror. Her jaw dropped, and her mouth opened wide. Kate's comment made her uncomfortable, but not as uncomfortable as Doris's topic choice. She shook her head and turned away from the women. *Why did I accept? I was comfy and warm in my cute little apartment with my fuzzy sweats. I must remember to never again accept a dinner invitation with this crazy crowd.*

"Kate, that's disgusting. That's a terrible thing to say. There is nothing funny about that illness. My neighbor's granddaughter is too thin. They always take her to doctors to make her better. I would hate for that to happen to you girls."

"Doris, Celia's healthy as a bull. Try not to worry about her, or me, or anything. I'm sure we can find something better to talk about in a restaurant." Kate rested her face in the palms of her hands and rubbed her forehead so hard she left a huge red line above her brow. She tilted her head toward Celia and mouthed the word *sorry*.

The two starving patrons, along with Kate and Celia, were seated at a rectangular wooden table pushed up against a half wall.

On top of the short wall sat oversized bunches of artificial green plants that obstructed the view of the adjoining section of the dining room. The paper placemats displayed a city map with the menu printed in the center. Flimsy silverware and empty water glasses were positioned at each place setting. Bernie picked up his knife and anxiously twirled it between his fingers. Doris reached over without saying a word and took the knife from Bernie. She put it on the placemat in front of her. A minute later, Bernie unconsciously stretched his arm toward Doris and again picked up the knife. She didn't bother to take it away.

Doris held her placemat and began to examine the menu. "Did these prices go up, Bernie? I don't remember this place being this expensive the last time we were here." She never took her eyes off the menu as she spoke.

Bernie continued to fiddle with his knife as he took a moment to read the menu selections. "I think you might be right. Did these prices go up, Kate?" He lowered his menu and peered over his glasses toward Kate. "Let's ask the waitress. She'll know if the prices went up."

"I have a better idea. Don't worry about the prices or anything else. It's my treat. Enjoy the dinner and worry about nothing," Kate pleaded with her in-laws.

"You know, why don't we share something, Bernie? We can share an appetizer. That could be dinner."

"They don't have appetizers here. They have soup and salads. You each get what you want and enjoy yourselves. Please, don't worry if you don't finish. Remember, it's my treat."

"If we don't finish, we'll take a doggie bag. We hate to throw Tom's money away." She stared at Kate as she spoke.

"Maybe there won't be any leftovers to worry about." Celia slid her hand across the bench and supportively touched Kate's leg.

"Do they take coupons here? Maybe we have coupons." Doris lifted her purse onto the table and began her search for coupons.

"Yeah, that's a good idea, Doris. See if you have coupons." Bernie pushed into his wife's side and visually searched the contents of the purse as he continued to spin the knife between his fingers.

"Listen. Even if they take coupons, which I have no idea if they do or not, they won't take coupons from Connecticut. Please, I want you to relax and order whatever you want. And don't forget,

I'm treating." Kate picked up her empty glass and glanced around the room for the waitress.

Celia silently read the menu printed in the map.

A young woman in a blue and white sailor outfit arrived at their table. She took their orders, filled the water glasses, and left warm rolls and butter at the table. Fisherman's platters were ordered all around, with two pitchers of lemonade.

"Celia, how are things going with you? Anything new?" Doris sang the word new.

Kate and Celia instantly knew where this was heading. They knew the musical tone in the mother-in-law's voice meant Celia was about to be pounced upon by Tom's mother.

How clever. Bring me along and they won't annoy you about not having kids. They'll interrogate me about my lonely, loveless existence instead. I hope you can read my mind, Kate.

"Everything is terrific. I love my work and my apartment. And this weather is magnificent. Fall is my favorite season. Don't you love the fall?" Celia stupidly expected the question to turn the conversation to another direction.

"Yes, the fall is lovely, a bit cooler here than in Connecticut, but quite nice. So, let me get to the point." She directed her conversation toward Celia. "How's your love life?" She tapped her long red fingernails on the table. The sun was low and the slivers of light through the window triggered Doris's diamonds to sparkle like the stars of a clear night's sky. Bernie continued to play with his knife. As usual, he was predictably quiet.

"It's fine. Thank you. Where in Maine were you? Did you get to Kennebunkport?" Celia was stubborn and desperately tried to avoid a discussion about romance in her life, or lack thereof.

The waitress stopped to deliver their first pitcher of lemonade. She disappeared quietly and quickly.

"Maine, schmain. Who wants to talk about Maine? Tell me about your situation."

"Celia is fine with the guys. In fact, she's been seeing the brother of someone she works with and she's very happy. Right, Celia?"

"Oh? Is this serious?" Doris interrupted before Celia could confirm Kate's statement.

"It's still new, but I hope so." Celia wasn't sure which way to go with her answer to the question. If she said the relationship was serious, an engagement or wedding discussion would follow. If she told her it wasn't serious, the conversation about to take place would begin.

"Good. I hoped you weren't seriously involved with anyone. I have a friend who I play bridge with and she has a son who got a new apartment in Boston about six months ago. He's dying for a girlfriend. I'll give Brock your number." Her bangle bracelets collided melodiously as she clasped her hands together in pure delight.

"Please don't give Celia's number to anybody. It would be very awkward. Besides, no one wants a guy who's dying for a girlfriend. There must be something wrong with him if he's that desperate. How's that card group of yours doing?"

"Celia doesn't mind or think it's awkward. Do you, Celia?"

Celia smiled unnervingly at Doris. She picked up the pitcher of lemonade and filled the four empty glasses. She wished she could say something to stop the conversation but became speechless and said nothing. She knew she would curse herself later for not taking a stand.

"When Brock gets your number, he can call you and take you out. If you don't like him, you don't have to see him again. In the meantime, maybe you'll get yourself a nice meal. You look as though you could use a nice meal." Doris took a roll from the basket, ripped it in half, spread butter on it, and topped it off with a sprinkle of salt.

"Brock? What kind of name is Brock? Did he make that name up?" Kate's irritation with the conversation was clear. "I think we should change the subject. I'm uneasy with this, and I'm sure Celia is too."

Doris ignored Kate's suggestion to change the subject. She addressed the inquiry regarding Brock's name. "No. To answer your question, he didn't make up his name. His name is Brock." She defended the man they were discussing–the man whom they did not know.

"I think his name was Bruce." Unexpectedly, Bernie chimed into the conversation. "I think he changed it when he was younger because he didn't like Bruce. If he likes Brock better, he should call himself Brock. There's nothing wrong with the name Brock."

"I think it's a nice name. What do you think of that name, Celia?" Doris asked.

"It's a lovely name." *Dear God, please make this dinner be over soon.* Noah's game or not, Kate would owe her for this one.

The waitress delivered their platters filled with crispy clams, shrimp, scallops, and golden-brown French fries piled high. The young waitress brought a side of pickles and a large bowl of coleslaw, along with another pitcher of lemonade. Silence enveloped their table as they began to eat dinner.

A few moments into their dinner, a swinging door collided with a waiter on the other side of the room. His tray, weighted down by dirty dishes, smashed to the floor. After the burst of noise from the crash, the room became silent. Bernie pushed his chair from the table and stood up. He lifted his head and gazed over the artificial foliage to catch sight of the commotion. Bernie sat down and broke the silence as he evenly and methodically clapped his hands together. Kate kicked Celia under the table. No other patron in the restaurant clapped or attempted to applaud the misfortunate accident. His clap was loud. Doris grasped his clapping hands and forcefully pushed them onto the table.

"Why do you have to be the only one to clap? What's wrong with you, Bernie? The poor boy drops his tray and you make applause!" she snapped at Bernie. "I figured some dope would clap! I didn't think that dope would be sitting next to me at my table."

"Everybody claps when someone drops a tray. You're supposed to clap." He held his fork in the air as he defended himself.

"Everyone claps? Look around, Bernie. You were the only one to clap. Why? Can you tell me why?"

"Listen, Doris." Kate attempted to halt the argument from escalating. "Let's not make a big deal about the clap. Let's eat our dinner and forget about the clapping, trays smashing to the floor, and fix ups with Brock. And remember, I'm buying!" Kate kept an unnatural smile on her face. Her attempt to hide her frustration was rapidly deteriorating.

"Yes, dear, that's a good idea. This smells absolutely delicious. Please be sure to thank Tom for us."

Kate bit her lips together and shook her head up and down.

Hannah and Blake

Emma knocked on the wall to Celia's office. Celia was on the phone but motioned for Emma to come in and take a seat. Emma stepped into the office and sat down in the chair opposite Celia's desk.

Celia crossed her eyes and stuck out her tongue as she looked at Emma. "Ryan, I understand your frustration, but I'm sure you saved your data as you went along. Right? I know I told you to do that during the training." Celia paused and let Ryan speak, his voice inaudible to Emma.

"Yes, Ryan, as a matter of fact, I can tell you how to make sure this doesn't happen again." Celia again allowed Ryan to complain.

"Ryan, if you don't want this to happen, close the program and don't ever launch it again." Celia smiled at Emma and made the motion of sticking her fingers down her throat. "No, I'm not trying to antagonize you, but there is nothing you can do. It's an old application and we have the newer version up and running. I told you last month during training, the old version is no longer supported. It's not stable." *Just like you.* "It's your choice to use something we can no longer help you with." Celia paused again. "Ryan? Ryan?"

Celia put the phone down. "Guess he hung up. Oh well."

"Let me guess. Ryan Krumpett?"

"You got that right. He's been sent to anger management classes. I don't have to take his crap anymore. If he can't speak to me in a professional manner, I won't help him. He's using an old program that I told him not to use, but he insists. If he's not going to listen to me, then he shouldn't come to my training sessions. And he definitely shouldn't call me for help."

"He's nasty to everyone."

"You're here early. Can't wait until noon, huh?" Celia slid her keyboard tray under the desk.

"I know this disrupts our lunchtime tradition, but I didn't want to wait until noon. Do you have time to chat?"

"Before you begin, let me show you a present I bought myself. Check it out." Celia motioned for Emma to come around her desk to see the cubby on the side of her desk. "It's a beautiful thing. May I interest you in a French vanilla?"

Celia's newly purchased coffee machine, along with a gallon-size jug of water, paper cups, and napkins, was stored neatly into the area.

"That would be delightful."

Celia prepared two coffees and removed a container of biscotti from her bottom drawer.

"Aren't we the hostess with the mostest?" Emma took the coffee and biscotti from Celia.

"This little coffee maker is a time-saver in the morning. I make my second cup here and have a sweet breakfast too."

"Always thinking. That's you." Emma took a sip from her cup. "I want to tell you this story, because it's a perfect example of what a witch she is." Emma no longer had to say her name. It was understood the stories were about Edie, the ex-wife.

"Go ahead. I'm ready to hear. Should I be nervous?" Celia dunked her biscotti into her coffee-filled paper cup.

"No, not at all. Sit back, relax, and enjoy your beverage. She's such a jerk. She must stay up at night thinking of hateful and nasty acts to perform."

"What happened?"

"We were at Freddy's this past weekend. His cousins were visiting, which is why he had a late afternoon get-together."

"And I take it bio-mom was there?"

"She was there. She wouldn't miss an opportunity to impose on our time. She had no business being there since it was for Fredric's side of the family."

"Did you guys talk to each other?"

"I did this time, but normally I don't. It's usually a quick hello—I try to be polite. If we happen to be in the same conversation, I won't leave; but as you know, I try to stay clear of her."

"I would have a hard time being nice to someone like that."

"I do have a hard time with it. She has mistaken my kindness for weakness. This time she crossed a line and was nasty to my niece—that's worse than being nasty to me.

"Continue." Celia was all ears.
"Here's what happened."

Emma and Fredric's nineteen-year-old niece Hannah and twenty-two-year-old nephew Blake stood at the table, making sandwiches from a deli platter. Hannah's sandwich of roast beef, Boursin cheese, Russian dressing, and coleslaw on rye bread was complete. Blake finished his ham and cheese sandwich as he spread Honeycup mustard on pieces of bread.

Blake took his first bite when Fredric's ex-wife walked up to say hello. "You must be Blake and Hannah." She put her hand out to shake hands. "You're so lovely. From what your aunt said, I thought you would be scrawny, mousey, and homely. I'm surprised that you're actually quite striking." She took Hannah's hand into her own.

Emma walked into the room the very second Edie insulted Hannah.

The two women glared at each other. Edie acted smug and Emma was enraged.

Emma stepped closer to Edie and stood straight. She was easily four inches taller. Abandoning Jillian's advice, she didn't take a breath. She instinctively spewed her comment, followed by her question. "Even if that were true, which it isn't, why would you say that to my niece? Why would you say that to any young woman, for that matter?" She took a breath after she confronted Edie.

"Said what?" Edie acted innocent.

"Why would you tell a young woman that her aunt said she was scrawny, mousey, and homely?"

"Hey, that's not what I said." She tensed up and became stiff.

"I know what I heard. Let me ask you again. Why would you say that to my niece?" Emma kept her eyes on Edie as the little ex stood speechless. "I'll ask you now, for the third time, why did you say that to my niece? I'm sure my niece and nephew want to hear your explanation as much as I do." Emma was relentless and enraged. She had no intention of letting this go. Her heart pounded as she tried to keep it together, but her rage was more evident than it had ever been.

Blake swallowed the bite he had taken from his sandwich and looked back and forth between his aunt and the ex-wife. Hannah stood motionless, with an expression of horror on her face as she, too, looked at her aunt and then at Edie.

"Well." Edie fidgeted. "That's not what I meant. I guess I said it as a back-handed compliment. You know, it's my way to say your niece is beautiful."

"That's not a back-handed compliment. That's not a compliment at all. I'm still waiting to hear your explanation of why you would say such an unkind thing to anyone." Emma was not giving up.

"It's not what I said." Edie's voice was louder than usual as she shrieked her denial.

"It's exactly what you said. Not only did you insult my niece, but you lied. You told her I said she was scrawny, mousey, and homely. That is simply not true. While you insulted Hannah, you also tried to implicate me." Emma regretted her words. She was talking too much. *Questions, questions, questions. Don't tolerate this behavior. Ask another question.* She couldn't think of anything else to say. She was frazzled.

Emma stood straight and tall as she silently stared down at Edie.

Edie stepped back and leaned against the counter. She bumped into and spilled a jar of pickles as she fidgeted in awkwardness. She picked up a paper towel and wiped the liquid, shoved the pickles back into the jar, and then twisted the wet towel between her fingers.

"I guess you're not going to answer my question." Hannah and Blake had never seen their aunt this angry.

Fredric's ex remained silent; her hatred toward Emma appeared intense. *Mission accomplished. Anything now is a bonus.* Emma stepped to her niece's side and draped her arm around Hannah's shoulder.

The ex-wife scowled at Emma. Emma walked to the corner and grabbed a cold water from a tub of ice. "Why don't you guys come downstairs? Uncle Fredric's excited to see both of you."

Edie turned around and stormed out of the room.

Emma apologized to her niece that Freddy's mother was rude to her. "Please ignore her. She stirs the pot because she wants to start trouble. I'm sorry if this made you uncomfortable. I can handle her insults to me, but she crosses a line when she extends her nastiness to you."

Hannah seemed slightly amused. "She's totally nuts!" She bit into her delicious sandwich. They walked downstairs together.

Edie snuck away from the party.

Celia laughed as she took out two more biscotti. She handed one to Emma. "I'm delighted that you didn't let her off the hook and you questioned her."

"It's bad enough she constantly insults me, but I can't let her offend my niece. Hannah knows I don't chat with that psycho." Emma refused the second biscotti.

Celia shook her head. "That's just mean, crazy, and vicious. Is there no limit she'll go to try to make you seem like the bad guy? Did you say anything else to her?"

"No. I had said too much already. If I didn't badger her a little, I would have been pissed off all day that I let her get in some nasty dig toward my niece. Did she think I would allow that?" Emma snickered. "Of course she did–I've never confronted her before. Why would I start now? She must have been shocked. Fredric divorced her over twenty-five years ago. This was the first time she's met Hannah and Blake. At least they saw firsthand a true depiction of who she really is."

"How come she's never met your niece and nephew before?"

"They live in Chicago, and they don't come out here much. When they do visit, we do things with OUR family. It would never include her. Fredric's sister and brother-in-law don't care for her and choose not to see her."

"I can see how asking a question works. Takes the focus right off you and puts it on the villain. I would have frozen and then thought of something to say at 3:00 a.m. the next day."

"You know, Celia, I used to be that way. I could never think of the right thing to say in the moment. When she insulted Hannah, my adrenaline started to pump. I know I talked more than I wanted to, but she wouldn't answer the question and I was frustrated."

"It's good you can laugh about it. Don't know if I could."

"I have to laugh, because if I don't, I'll get too mad. I made her uncomfortable and it's about time I did that back to her. I think the fact that she went after Hannah gave me more motivation than if she insulted me."

"Clearly the woman is miserable. I'd be fuming mad, if I had to deal with someone like her." Celia made a sad face and pushed out her bottom lip. "Does this mean we aren't having lunch together?"

"No, I'm still planning on lunch." Emma reached for the second biscotti. "I'm loving this little espresso and biscotti break."

The Call

Celia didn't recognize the name on the caller ID. *Who the hell is Goodwin B*? She knew the first three digits were a Boston number and assumed someone from work was calling. "Hello?"

"Is this Celia?"

"May I ask who's asking?" She couldn't identify the voice.

"You don't know me, but we have a mutual friend." The caller was briefly silent.

Celia was not interested in playing guessing games with a stranger on the telephone. She was about to hang up when the caller continued. "My mom's friend Doris recommended I contact you. My name is Brock Goodwin. I hope you don't mind that I called you."

The fisherman's platters of two days earlier flashed into her brain. She clenched her fists tightly and leaned against the refrigerator. Several souvenir magnets fell to the floor. "Oh yes, Doris." Celia went silent. She looked down at the magnets strewn across the tile floor. She wasn't going to carry the burden of this conversation. It was a conversation she didn't want in the first place.

"I hoped you would be interested in getting together. I think we might have a lot in common, and I would really enjoy meeting you."

She resented the position she was put in; Doris shouldn't have shared her personal information. She sighed. "Brock, I'm sorry, but I'm very uncomfortable right now. Plus, I'm involved with someone." She lied and was annoyed with herself that she used the word sorry.

"Oh. Gee! I'm disappointed to hear that. Doris said that your relationship wasn't terribly serious."

Celia clenched her teeth tight—her jaw protruded. *I'm going to kill Kate's blabber-mouth mother-in-law first chance I get. The nerve of her to classify my relationship as not terribly serious.* She snickered quietly at the fact that she was defending a relationship that didn't exist. "I'm sor–" She stopped short and didn't finish the word. "I do hate to be rude, but I'm not comfortable with this at all. If I change my mind, and you're still willing, I'll get your number from Doris and give you a call. At this point in time, I don't think it's a good idea. I hope you understand."

"Let me give you my cell. That way you'll have the number and won't have to call Doris."

"Fine." The number was on her caller ID, but she recited it as if she had written it down. She moved her right hand over the palm of her left hand and pretended to write down the number. "There, I have it. Thank you for calling. Bye!" For Celia, the conversation was over. She heard Brock say bye as she clicked off the phone.

She moved away from the refrigerator, picked up the magnets, and plugged her phone into the charger. She was proud of herself for not being backed into an unpleasant situation. She was honest–except for the part when she told Brock she was involved with someone. And the part when she pretended to write down his telephone number. And especially the part when she said she would consider calling if she changed her mind. She didn't say she would like to meet him if the situation were different. She didn't say she was busy and suggest they meet at another time. She was direct and as straightforward as possible.

She opened the freezer and hung her arm over the door as she gazed into the icy space. Nothing appealed to her. She walked to her pantry and pulled out a Snickers. She savored her chocolate victory snack. She smiled and was pleased that she did what she wanted to do. A triumphant rush ran through her body. She was proud for not being coerced into this date with the stranger.

Celia's phone began to buzz. She unplugged the charger, read the caller ID, and rolled her eyes. "Hello?" She pushed the speaker button and placed the phone on the counter.

"Hello, Celia? What happened?"

"Nothing. Why?" She knew the voice all too well.

"Brock's mother told me that you turned down Brock's offer to take you out. Couldn't you go out to dinner with him? You might think he's nice. He's good to his mother–he calls her every day. You can tell a lot about a man by how he treats his mother. He would be as nice to a girlfriend or wife. You should have told him you could go."

Celia cringed at the word *should*. "Doris, first of all, he didn't ask me to dinner. He said we should meet. And secondly, I don't have the time or the desire to meet this guy. It's nothing personal. Honest!" She made a fist and banged the wall behind where she stood.

"Couldn't you go out with him for me, dear? Just one date? You can go out to have a nice dinner. Wear something pretty. You'll get a delicious meal. How terrible can it be?" Doris was persistent.

Celia breathed a loud and frustrated sigh, which Doris ignored.

"His parents are a very handsome couple, Celia. I'm sure he's a fine-looking boy himself. It took a lot of courage for him to call you. I wish you would reconsider."

It couldn't have taken that much courage considering you most likely spoke to his mother within the last day or two. He didn't waste any time in calling me. So much for mustering up all that courage—Mr. Dying for a Girlfriend. She shook her head in disapproval. "Listen, Doris, I would try to reconsider at some other time, but you must realize this is a very awkward situation you have put me in. I'm involved with someone else and not interested." There was that little fib again, nudging itself into her conversation. She was beginning to believe her own lie. She rejoiced at her strength in dealing with Tom's mother and sticking to her guns.

She hadn't given in, and for that reason she still felt victorious. She did not say she would go out with Brock. She had no intention of partaking in this blind date. She was sorry she mentioned she would reconsider. She had no intention of reconsidering anything. She went to the freezer, grabbed a pint of chunky peanut butter brownie sundae ice cream, walked over to the drawer, and selected a spoon—a big spoon. Within the next ten minutes, slouched on her couch with her feet propped up on the coffee table, she managed to finish the entire pint.

Satisfied from the sugar fix, she was eager to contact Kate to relay her conversations. She picked up her phone and punched in Kate's number. The call didn't connect. *Did I not disconnect from Doris*? She held the phone to her ear. She dialed the number again—the call didn't go through.

"Hello?" She couldn't get a tone. "Hello?"

"Hello," a voice said back to her.

"Who is this?" Celia's tone was rude and angry.

"It's Brock Goodwin."

"Brock? The phone didn't even ring. I was trying to make a call. Why are you calling again?" She didn't attempt to hide her annoyance.

"Well, my mom told me that Doris called her to say you had second thoughts about meeting. So, I'm happy to say I'm calling to schedule the date."

"What?" Celia's voice escalated to a shout. *Schedule the date*?

"My mom told me Doris said you were home now, and I should call you immediately to set up the date."

Again, with the date? "Do you do everything your mother tells you to do?" WTF? *Are they all sitting in the same room together? How can they communicate back and forth this fast? This is not normal. Not normal at all.*

"Doris, my mother's friend, told my mother to tell me to call you now."

"Semantics!" She got up threw the empty carton into the trash.

"Well?"

"Well what?" She felt trapped. She hated this feeling. She was provoked into being unkind. She believed she was appropriately and acceptably standoffish during the first conversation. She was sorry for one thing. She regretted that she tried to be polite the first go-around with Brock.

"When do you want to get together?" Brock asked anxiously. He sounded sadly pathetic.

She was softening and felt bad for Brock. *This is pathetic. He's pitiful.* She pressed the Speaker button and plopped down on the kitchen chair. She had an icky feeling. She was about to cave. What she felt was all too familiar and unwanted. She accepted his ridiculous invitation. The date was made. Her victorious moment was short-lived and long gone. She stood from her chair, and with her open hand, she smacked the bottom of a hanging basket above her head. A cloud of dust billowed into the air.

"You need to have a baby!" Celia shouted into the phone when Kate answered her call.

"What do you mean?"

"I think you need to have a kid. Your mother-in-law has way too much time on her hands. She needs to focus on a new grandchild."

"She already has three grandchildren–she can focus on them. Why are you saying this?"

"Because she needs to bother you, not me. I'm not even related to her. I'm simply a poor, pathetic project to her. The lonely old spinster friend of her daughter-in-law."

"Oh shit! What did she do?" Kate prepared for the worst. "I'm sorry."

"Let's just say that tomorrow night I'm having dinner with Mr. Dying for a Girlfriend, the momma's boy. I think since he doesn't know either of us, you should go as me. You can respond to Celia, can't you?"

"Knowing Doris, I assure you he's already seen a picture of you."

"That's great!" Celia's sarcasm was apparent.

"How did this happen? Why did you agree to go with him? Is he picking you up? Where is he taking you?"

"I can't believe you're asking where we're going! That isn't the point here, Kate. The point is that I'm going at all."

"Sorry. Why are you going?"

"He called. I turned him down. Then your mother-in-law called. I told her I didn't want to go. I felt trapped and idiotically told her maybe at another time I would have considered it–"

"Whoa! Big mistake there." Kate interrupted Celia from finishing.

"Yeah, no kidding, and don't make me feel worse." Celia took a deep breath. "Doris hung up from me and she called the guy's mother. The mother called the guy back and then..." Celia took another breath. "I tried to call you–to scream at you, by the way–but he called me back before I could get to you. I'm about to vomit right now." Her hands flailed around her face.

"Where are you going?"

"Once more, with the same question? I don't know. Some place called The Cod. I'm supposed to meet him at the Town Center and I guess we'll walk to the restaurant. I don't want him to know where I live. I was going to tell him to pick me up at your house, but I considered he could be a nutcase and didn't want to put you in danger too. Bad enough I'm putting myself in harm's way. Besides, you owe me BIG TIME and I want to make sure you're around to pay up."

Celia told Kate the entire story, including the parts when she lied. She tried to sound stronger and more self-assured than she was.

"Celia, he could be nice. Try to have an open mind and play it by ear. I've told you before and I'll tell you again: not all guys are jerks."

"Whatever." *There are no nice guys left.* She thought about the fool she had become when she was with Geoff. She believed in him until she found out what he had done.

The Cod

Celia's anger about the evening was directed more at herself than anyone else. She was furious that she felt a twinge of optimism about the date. She knew any positive thought would lead to disappointment but couldn't help herself. *Maybe he won't be a jerk. Maybe his name really* IS Brock.

She would never admit this out loud. *It would be funny if he turned out to be a nice guy.* She became more and more irritated as the absurdities took up space in her brain. The second call from Brock, the call that proved she was a pushover, had turned her off completely. She would never have called someone back if they blew her off so quickly.

She decided she wouldn't like him. He could be an Adonis, and nothing would change her opinion. She didn't wash her hair, although in a last-minute decision, she rubbed a little blush on her cheeks. *He'll be a jerk, like the rest of them. Even if he starts out nice, you know he'll morph into a jerk. It's the curse of his gender. It's not his fault.*

As she approached Brock, she felt her anxiety rise and a knot rocket into her stomach. She was more uncomfortable than she anticipated.

Brock waited under the street sign at the designated meeting place. He was tall and slender with dark-brown hair, and not nearly as unattractive as she had expected this desperate momma's boy to be. Dressed in black slacks and a dark-blue shirt, his appearance was neat but unfashionable. Except for a sheen around his left eye, he had a very pleasant appearance. *Maybe he won't be an idiot.* She shook her head quickly to shake out the thought.

"I'm glad you made it." He extended his right arm to shake her hand. "I was certain that you would stand me up."

Good evening, Son of Sam. "I would never do that. It's not my style. Is the restaurant close enough to walk?" She felt a gentleness for his insecurity and his sincerity.

"Not that close. It's about three miles away. I'll drive." They walked together toward his car.

Celia was not fond of getting into a car with a stranger. *He's good to his mother. He calls her every day.* The words from Doris rang in her ears. *I wonder what kind of relationship Ted Bundy had with his mother? How about little Jeffrey Dahmer? Were he and his mother close? Did they call every day? I think they found a victim of the Boston Strangler near here.* Her paranoid thoughts continued as she buckled the seat belt on the passenger side of his Ford Explorer. Two minutes into the ride, she heard a rustling sound in the backseat.

"What's that noise?" She turned to check out the backseat. Shiny black eyes stared up at her.

"That's Gracie, my dog."

"What's she doing in the backseat?"

"Eating grapes."

The dog's presence surprised Celia and cleared some of her paranoid thoughts of having dinner with a mass murderer. "Do you leave her in the car?" She reached into the back and patted Gracie's head. "Hello, Gracie girl. Aren't you a little cutie?" She spoke in a high-pitched, dog-friendly voice. *He loves his dog. Maybe he's a decent guy.* She rubbed Gracie's head again and smiled at Brock. She relaxed.

"I don't usually take her with me, but since it's a cool night, I figured she'd be happier in the car. I hope you don't mind, but I knew she would prefer to wait for me in the car rather than in the house. She loves to take a ride."

Celia shifted the conversation to the evening's event. "So, I've never been to The Cod. In fact, I've never even heard of it. What's their specialty?" She watched the speedometer on his dashboard.

"The Cod?" He glanced at her curiously. "We're going to the Fieldstone. What's The Cod?"

"Isn't that the name of the restaurant? The Cod?"

"No, I said we're going out on the cod."

"Out on the cod? What does that mean?"

"You know. The cod! It's a great deal."

"I've never heard of the place." Celia tried to keep an open mind and remain calm.

"I can't believe you don't know about it. I thought everyone knew about the cod?"

"I don't." The icky feeling was back. *Well, that was a short-lived nice guy reprieve. I've never heard of the place, so shoot me. Oh God, could he have a gun?*

"It's the entertainment cod. Where you get half off or the less expensive meal free. I can't believe you don't know about it."

"The CARD?" She shouted her words. "The entertainment CARD?" She clearly enunciated the word card. "Is that what you've been saying? The card that provides discounts at restaurants?"

"Yeah, the cod."

"Wow, that's quite an accent you have." *I don't remember this accent from the phone call. I wonder if maybe he had a friend make the call. This accent is too strong to forget.*

"Yeah, I took a girl there a couple weeks ago and I loved it. Made sense to come back since it was delish."

"You can go to a place twice on the card?"

"No. You can use it once at each restaurant, but I borrowed my mom's cod for this date."

Celia didn't respond.

Brock walked into the restaurant ahead of Celia. He let the glass door swing back into her. She threw her arm up and stopped the door from hitting her. *I wonder if he lets the door swing into Mommy.* The hostess seated them right away. The restaurant was dimly lit and nearly empty. His dark-blue shirt was now purple. When he moved, the shirt shimmered while the hue changed back to blue and then to purple and then back to blue again.

He sat down at the first seat. Celia walked to the other side of the table and sat down. *What the fuck?* His eyes didn't sparkle, but the left one glistened. She couldn't control her curiosity as she stared at his eyes. The light overhead reflected on a glossy gunk around his upper and lower lids. *Did he put glitter on his eye? Maybe he wanted the sparkle around his eyes to match his shirt.* She continued to stare.

"Hey, honey." He was loud as he called the waitress to their table.

"May I help you, sir?" She looked at Brock, then Celia, and then back at him.

"Yeah, could ya get me a toothpick?" His tone was pompous and rude.

Celia slouched down in her seat. *Save me!* She now dreaded the evening ahead of her. *Case closed. Dog lover or not, he's a loser!*

"Certainly." The waitress looked away from Brock and inquiringly at Celia.

"I'm all set, thank you." Celia's tone was apologetic. She smiled an embarrassed smile at the waitress. The waitress walked away. *How weird.* Celia tried to hide her bewilderment toward his strange request and arrogant attitude.

"I see you staring at my eye. It's an ointment I have to put on it. I had surgery awhile back, and I need to use the salve for a few more weeks. Slimy, huh?"

"Sorry, didn't mean to stare, but I did notice." The waitress brought over menus and water-filled glasses. She placed a small round dish next to Brock's water glass—it contained his toothpick. He immediately tore open the cellophane, removed the toothpick, picked at his front teeth, and then sucked on the tiny wooden stick.

"Let me tell you about our specials." The waitress recited the day's specials. She concluded with, "And I must inform you, coupons or the entertainment card cannot be applied to any lobster dinner choices."

"I guess you ain't getting lobstah!" Brock waved his menu under Celia's chin as he shouted his comment. "If I can't use the cod, it ain't gonna be your meal."

Celia was speechless. She was horrified and embarrassed. *Please dear God, don't let anyone I know come into this restaurant.* She looked away from Brock and sheepishly at the waitress. "Thank you. I'll need a few minutes to read the menu."

Let's see here. She read the left side of the menu. *Filet mignon?* She glanced to the right. *Nope. Hmm. No rib eye on this menu? What should I get? There's that lobster. It's only $29.95—not that expensive for lobster. Too bad it's prohibited from the dinner choices.* She continued to read the left and then the right. *There it is. Sounds delicious. I love paella.* She read the column to the right again. $34.95. *Perfect!* She found exactly what she wanted. When the waitress returned, Celia ordered the most expensive item on the menu.

See Brock, *the paella is greater than the price of lobster, and I never would have ordered lobstah, as you say, in the first place. Good thing you didn't take me to a nice restaurant—you'd be spending a fortune, you moron.* She smiled at the waitress. *Jury is in. This date is officially a disastah. Idiot!* She wasn't sure whether she referred to Brock or herself as the real idiot. *Decent guy, my ass.* He interrupted her thoughts by speaking.

"Let me tell you about my eye." He told her the long and boring story of his eye surgery. "They had to remove the eyeball and everything to fix the problem." He didn't tell her what was wrong with his eye, but he described each gory and disgusting detail of the surgery and subsequent care.

Their dinners arrived. Without missing a beat, he continued to discuss the surgery. "And to make matters worse." He paused and started to laugh. "I had to have a hemorrhoid operation a week and a half after this surgery." He pointed his fork to his eye. "Talk about having a problem at both ends." He continued to laugh at his own joke. Again, he pointed his fork to his eye. He swung his hand down and pointed the same fork to his butt and then again to his eye. He concluded the minutiae of his surgeries and segued into chatter about his food allergies, skin rashes, and intestinal problems.

Your little decoy dog in the backseat doesn't fool me. You are so obnoxious. It's probably not even your dog. The evening nosedived into the catacombs of terrible dates.

Celia ate a grain or two of rice from her plate. She reached her goal when she ordered the most expensive item on the menu. To drive her plan home, she was not eating more than a morsel from her dinner. She envisioned him scratching his skin rashes or tending to his hemorrhoids, which made it easier to avoid ingesting her half-price meal.

"Are you finished with that?" He pointed to her dinner and pushed his plate away.

"I'm done, thank you." She smiled.

"That ain't going to waste." He leaned over and began to eat her leftovers. She was unnerved. She picked up the food-covered plate and plopped it down on his side of the table. "You can pack it up and take it home or give it to Gracie." *Before you take her back to her rightful owner.*

The waitress arrived to clear the table. "Would you care for dessert menus?" She handed a small menu to Celia and another to Brock.

"Would love them." Celia opened the menu and smacked her lips. Once again, the most expensive item became her choice.

"I'll try the Kitchen Sink." She handed the menu back to the waitress.

The enormous dessert was placed down on the table between Celia and Brock. The Kitchen Sink consisted of a double chocolate brownie covered by oversized scoops of vanilla, chocolate, and peanut butter ice cream dripping with fudge and caramel sauce, covered with pecans and almonds, topped with a chocolate chip cookie, spiced whipped cream, sprinkles, and a cherry.

"In case you want to share." The waitress put down two spoons before she walked away. It was obviously a share-with-a-group-of-people kind of dessert.

"Do you want a separate bowl? I'd be happy to share with you." Celia smiled as she offered her dessert to Brock. *You'd have been better off to not tell me about that little nut allergy you have.* "Oh, I forgot. You said you're allergic to nuts. I guess if you only get a rash, you could try some, but if you'll go into a full-blown anaphylactic shock, you should perhaps pass on the sharing. Do you have an EpiPen with you?" She moved the dessert away from Brock and closer to herself.

He scowled and shook his head right and left.

She ate half of the scoop of vanilla ice cream and left the rest of the multi-layered treat on the plate. *Finish THIS, you jerk!* She was delighted that she ordered the most expensive dessert—the bonus of his nut allergy made it that much more enjoyable. Allowing the door to slam in her face was his first mistake. Embarrassing her with the lobstah routine was his second. The trivial toothpick was barely a blip compared to his other disgusting and rude actions.

"I think you should have ordered a plain dish of ice cream, if that's all you wanted." Brock's tone was angry, to say the least.

"That wasn't on the menu." She shyly tilted her head toward him and smiled.

"I'm certain you could have ordered it, even if it wasn't on the menu."

"Oh, it's not the same. I love it with all the sauce and nuts and stuff."

"But you didn't even eat that stuff."

"It trickles into the flavor, and it's not the same without it." Celia dipped her spoon into the bowl. She pulled it out and licked a smidge of the peanut butter ice cream. "So good." She smacked her lips.

"I should make you pay for the dessert," Brock said under his breath.

"Excuse me?" Her tone was loud and clear.

"Never mind. I'm just talking to myself." Brock pulled the coupon from the booklet. "So, what do you want to do now? Walk down by the shops, get a drink?"

Celia felt repulsed from her head to her toes. *Are you out of your fucking mind?* Celia was shocked. *Why would you want to continue this painful excuse of a date any further?*

"You're still recuperating from all those surgeries. I think you should get home early to rest. Besides, I have a big day planned tomorrow and quite frankly, I'm exhausted." Celia was elated that her date with Brock was about to terminate.

Celia couldn't get into her apartment fast enough. She texted Kate. *Meet me at T Ms immediately.*

Kate responded. *On my way.*

Celia arrived at Tequila Maria's first and took a seat at the bar.

"How was the date?" Kate sat down on the seat next to Celia.

"Let's just say he's not the kind of guy I want my kids to spend every other weekend with."

"You need therapy."

They sipped cocktails as Celia recapped the entire story for Kate. Starting with the glass door slamming in her face, the toothpick, and the lobster, Celia covered every disgusting aspect, including the look on the face of the waitress.

"He was feeding her grapes? Dogs can get sick, even die, from grapes."

"That's what you're commenting on? The grapes? How about the gooey eye, the hemorrhoids, the forbidden lobster? You have nothing to say about that stuff?" Celia's snap was loaded with attitude.

"Well, I might add the dessert sounds delish." Celia glared at Kate. "Okay. Okay. Sorry, the date sounds like a disaster. I'm sorry. It's sounds absolutely horrid."

As Celia continued to share the story, two women and a man walked behind them. Celia and Kate both turned at the same time as the man passed them. "Hi, Celia. Nice to see you again." He touched the back of Kate's chair.

"He was kind of cute. Who was that?" Kate smiled.

"That was Mr. No-lobstah Brock." Celia covered her mouth and laughed softly with her eyes wide open in surprise.

"Get outta here! I could see the shine around his eye. I guess he's recovered from your failed date."

Geoff

Another wasted night. When are you going to learn? Give it up. Celia walked slowly up the three flights to her apartment. She was still annoyed that she followed through on the Brock date. *Nice to his mother. Right! Obnoxious.*

She shook her head, took a bottle of water from the pantry, and sat on top of the comforter on her bed. She picked up her iPad and read her email. She was unable to concentrate. Her stomach felt queasy from eating only morsels of rice and ice cream for dinner. *Probably would have been better to have at least eaten some of the fish. Never should have had that drink with Kate.*

She thought about the wedding she and Geoff never had. It was planned as a small intimate event, with a few relatives and their closest friends. The plans vanished when she discovered his secret. She never understood how he could hide it so effortlessly. She blamed herself for stupid and blind trust of love. He lied when she confronted him. Each lie led to another and before long he was in too deep. She would never have forgiven him anyway.

Geoff's stealthy hobby was discovered quite by accident. Three months before their scheduled wedding, Celia took a personal day to organize the storage area in the basement of their rented townhouse.

Dressed in ratty old clothes, with her hair carelessly clipped on top of her head, Celia began to organize the basement. She took a box of extra-large trash bags from under the kitchen sink and headed downstairs. The cement room was dark and dusty. A single bright light bulb at the foot of the stairs lit the area. At the back wall, an insignificant amount of sun filtered in from a tiny rectangular window. Lawn chairs and garden tools cluttered a small space in the corner below the window.

Old furniture left by the previous tenants added to the stale and musty smell in the basement. Celia pushed a stack of boxes to one side of the dank room and swept the newly cleared area. Dust floated around her legs.

Celia noticed a collection of shoeboxes under the stairs. She peeked inside the small containers and saw pictures—she paid no attention to the images. To protect the photographs from the cold, damp floor, she picked up a few boxes and carried them toward the storage shelves against the wall. She stumbled over the top of a rake—the boxes toppled to the floor. The photographs were strewn about the area.

She knelt and carelessly gathered the pictures into a stack. She lined the three empty boxes in a row and picked up a handful of the snapshots, which she tossed into the first box. As she grabbed a second fistful of photos, she glanced down at the pictures. Shock and revulsion overcame her. Nausea and dizziness followed. She sat down on the cold floor and focused on all that was scattered around her. Distributed on the floor and over the rake were pictures of Geoff and women in graphically sexual poses.

Celia couldn't breathe. She couldn't fully grasp what she was viewing. She clutched another bunch of photos, picked herself up, and moved to the bottom of the stairs where the light was brighter—where the repulsive photographs could more easily be seen.

She examined the first picture. Geoff sat on a lounge chair with a woman. She had her hands across his chest and her big, full, red lips pressed against his cheek. In the second photograph, two women wearing bright-red wigs snuggled close to Geoff. They wore only thongs, while Geoff wore leopard bikini briefs. His hands were draped over their shoulders, barely reaching their breast. Their hands pulled at his leopard bikini. She viewed picture after picture after picture. The women were striking. Celia counted nine, maybe ten, different females. Each face covered in bizarre makeup, with peculiar hairstyles. She felt another wave of queasiness. Bile bubbled up to her esophagus. She was sure she would vomit.

The back of her neck moistened with a rush of perspiration. Droplets of sweat trickled down between her breasts as she felt her heart pound into her throat. This flash of disgust was far from the twitterpations she had associated with Geoff's touch.

She got up and hastily collected the pile of pictures, along with the other boxes, and threw everything into one of the trash bags. She dragged the over-filled bag to the foot of the stairs. She exhaled slowly in an aborted attempt to calm herself. She repeatedly dug into the bag and removed handfuls of pictures each time. The pictures formed a mound high on her lap and onto the floor, surrounding her feet. She pulled a pack of cigarettes from her pocket, took one out, and nervously lit it. She inhaled fast and exhaled faster. Her anxiety intensified with each picture she viewed.

With clammy and trembling hands, she examined the photos of the man who was to be her husband, posed with a pageant of different women. *When were these taken? Were they new? Were they old? If they were old, why did he still have them?* Knowing these answers wouldn't have calmed her down. She scrutinized the pictures. Geoff appeared comfortable, as if it were commonplace for him to be photographed this way.

She took another picture and examined it closely. Celia froze. Her blood raced to her head. Geoff was wearing the watch she had given to him last Christmas. Her grandfather's gold watch. *You asshole. You fucking, fucking asshole! You couldn't take off the watch? My grandfather's watch? You pig!* The watch was visible in every picture that showed his wrist. *How did I almost miss this?*

She was immobilized by her angst and sat anxiously as she studied the pictures.

For forty-five minutes, she sat on the basement stairs and shuffled through the photographs. After an hour, her heart resumed to a normal beat. She could breathe. Her horror was devoured by anger. She was no longer soaked in perspiration. She was infuriated and sickened by the thought that she would see him when he returned home from work in less than an hour. *How should I confront him?*

She pulled the bag up the stairs and into the kitchen. She continued to sift through the pornography that was Geoff. The man who was no longer her future husband.

Celia silently sat smoking at the kitchen table when she heard his keys rattle at the front door. He entered the kitchen with his usual, "Hey sweets, how ya doing?" He walked over to her and leaned down to kiss her forehead. "I thought you were giving those up." He pointed to the cigarette she was now inhaling. She didn't respond. He walked to the refrigerator to get a beer and stopped in his tracks. The door was covered with a collage of the photographs. For a few seconds, he stood frozen by the gallery she had created. She didn't turn toward his direction.

"What's this?" He laughed.

Celia spun her head around in a rage. *Are you fucking laughing, you asshole?* "I hoped you could tell me."

Geoff laughed again and shook his head. "They're composites put together as a joke from one of the guys. They were made for a bachelor's party. He used pictures of all the ushers' heads on a body from the internet. Ridiculous bachelor party nonsense."

"Wow. That's a lot of work for someone to do for a party. There are over a hundred pictures there." Celia didn't believe his story. "Whose party were they made for?" She expected to not believe another word he spoke.

"I don't even remember. It was a long time ago." Geoff opened the refrigerator door, took out a beer, and swiped his hand across the front of the door, causing a dozen pictures to float to the floor. "I didn't even know you then."

"Oh, really?" She got angrier by the second. She knew he was lying and didn't want to let him off the hook or screw up her plan of attack. "You don't remember how long ago? Why do you still have the pictures? Did you actually bring them here when we moved in? You're such a liar. They were taken while we lived here together."

Celia could see Geoff becoming irritated. He was clever, and she knew she would lose this argument and be the one apologizing to him if she wasn't careful about her strategy.

"Celia, knock it off. I'm not talking about this. Throw them out. I never even looked in half of that stuff when we moved here. They're old and absurd." He walked over and grabbed the rest of the pictures off the door and then threw them, along with a few magnets, into the trash. He glared at her in anger and started to leave the room.

Celia jumped up and stood between Geoff and the trash can. She reached into her pocket and pulled out the picture of him wearing the watch she had given to him. "Is this picture from before you met me also?"

"Of course it is." He grabbed it from her hand and threw it down.

Celia bent down, picked it up, and clutched it in her fist. "That's amazing, Geoff!" Her voice escalated from the calmness she tried to display. "How the fuck did my grandfather's watch get into a picture from before you knew me? Can you tell me that? You're a sick fucking liar, Geoff! I would have thought you could come up with something better than that childish fucking story." She turned away from him and stormed out of the room. "That watch better be on my bureau within the next five minutes."

Deep down in her gut, Celia wanted to believe him, but her brain knew he was lying. *Don't try to intellectualize your emotions. He's a lying fuckhead.* The twitterpations of her past turned to stomach-churning nausea.

Although the pictures were gross and upsetting, she was more troubled by how easily Geoff had lied to her and how effortlessly he came up with the excuse of the composites for the party. *Was he expecting me to find the pictures? Is that why he had them in the house? In OUR house? Was he prepared with his response? Or was he that clever and creative at lying?* She would never know.

"Where are you going?" he asked as she walked down the stairs with her suitcase.

"It doesn't matter, Geoff. It doesn't fucking matter. You lied to me and you lied too easily. If you had told the truth, maybe we could have gotten you help, because you SERIOUSLY NEED help. You desperately need help. I don't think even a team of psychiatrists could help you, quite frankly."

She threw her suitcase in the backseat of her car. For the next hour and a half, she loaded her car with whatever she had brought to the relationship and a few choice items they had purchased together. She nearly fell down the stairs as she pushed the iron headboard down along the railing.

"I'll get counseling. Please don't leave, Celia. I'm sorry. I got caught up in the game." Geoff stood at the front door and sobbed. He dropped down to his knees and covered his face with his hands. His broad shoulders hunched over as he trembled. He looked up at her, his brown hair disheveled. His chin quivered as tears rolled down his cheeks. For the first time since she had fallen in love with him, she saw him as a pathetic, empty loser.

His behavior horrified her. He had been someone she respected and loved, someone she thought the world of, and someone she held dear to her heart. With her iron bed hanging out the back of the hatch, she drove away, and she didn't look back.

Celia was heartbroken but more than that, she felt foolish for not having known such a thing about someone she trusted and deeply loved. She drove back to Massachusetts with a lump in her throat, a pit in her stomach, and tears in her eyes. She crossed the border from Connecticut to Massachusetts and glanced at the sparkly stone on her finger. How swiftly she had come to hate that ring and hate that man.

She never regretted leaving the sick and deceitful man she had just revealed. The door to that chapter in her life was slammed shut–along with the belief she would ever trust again.

TWINS

"Thank you for lunch, Kate." Celia sat in the passenger seat and buckled her seat belt.

"Listen, this has been bothering me for a while. I wish I had said something sooner, but I'm truly sorry about Tom's mother telling Bruce or Brock or whatever his name is to call you. She has no boundaries and believes that everyone should think the way she thinks. I wish I could say she meant well, but I'm not sure what her motives are. I feel terrible you got sucked into that date. Although, you must agree, it makes a good story."

"You should have seen the gunk oozing from his eye. I would have been kind about it had he been decent, but the eye thing raised his gross level tenfold." Celia motioned her index finger to her mouth, as if she wanted to vomit. "The name is Brock." Celia laughed. "Don't apologize. I could have said no. Maybe deep down I had a one percent hope that he wouldn't be a jerk. I'm a jerk magnet. If I walked into a room with a hundred guys and ninety-nine were great, the one jerk in the room would corner me and I wouldn't know how to get away. I guess, as tough as I think I am, I'm quite weak. I can't even say it's because I'm nice and don't want to hurt someone's feelings. Being nice or not nice has nothing to do with it. It's because I'm weak and I can't think of the right way to handle these situations until it's too late."

"Don't be so hard on yourself. It's not easy when someone you know fixes you up with someone they know. I spoke to Doris and firmly requested she stay out of your love life. At first, she was offended, but then I pushed the fact that you're involved with someone and didn't want to ruin your chances with your imaginary lover."

"Did you honestly say imaginary lover? You're such a bitch."

"No, I didn't say imaginary, but I thought it. I hope you forgive me for bringing you into her craziness."

"Stop apologizing." As they neared Celia's driveway, they saw Noah walking Trudy, who pulled her leash taut as she struggled to break free.

"Geez, is that kid stalking me?" Celia was annoyed to see Noah and Trudy.

"Try not to take it out on the kid that his married uncle's another jerk on earth. After all, you're a self-proclaimed jerk magnet." Kate pulled into the driveway and glanced into her rearview mirror. Noah and Trudy followed behind her car.

"Hey, Celia!" He raced over as the two women stepped out.

"Hi, Noah. This is Kate. Do you remember her from your game?"

"Yeah, I do. Wasn't that the best game?" He was still excited about the win. "Uncle Bill told me he saw you AGAIN!"

"Yep. I guess we have the same shopping schedule." Celia glanced at Kate, who shook her head sideways.

"He was down at Pete's buying aspirin for Auntie Sophie when he saw you."

"Oh, is she sick?" Kate asked and then smugly smiled at Celia.

Probably pregnant. Celia remained silent.

"I think she had a headache. No big deal. I'm here with my parents, visiting for the day."

"How long have they been married?" The question jumped from Kate's lips without a second of hesitation. Celia's mouth dropped as she shot Kate a look to cease and desist.

"About thirteen years." Trudy inched over to Celia and sat down on Celia's booties as she leaned her furry body into Celia's pant leg.

Kate mouthed the word *sorry* to Celia and turned the right side of her lip up with a snarl for only Celia to witness.

Celia walked to the cold steps and sat down. Noah let go of the leash and Trudy jumped into Celia's lap and licked her face. Celia pulled her heavy jacket to wrap around Trudy, who was comfortably nestled against Celia's warm body. Celia was uncomfortable with, and yet in awe of, Kate's nerve.

"Do they have kids?" Kate ignored the *I'm going to kill you and you better stop asking questions* look Celia gave her.

"Just me." He took his baseball cap off, scratched the top of his head, and then put the cap back on his head.

"What do you mean, just you? I thought he was your uncle?" Kate's curiosity intensified.

"Oh, you mean Uncle Bill? I thought you were asking about my parents." He walked closer to Celia and Trudy. "My mom and dad have been married for thirteen years."

Kate glanced over at Celia. Celia's piercing eyes were focused entirely on her friend. Kate continued to interrogate Noah. "No, I was asking about your Aunt Sophie and Uncle Bill. How long have they been together?"

"Ah. Like forever." Noah took off his baseball cap again, but this time stuffed it in the pocket of his jacket. "They're fertinol."

"What's that?" Kate turned away from Noah and toward Celia.

Celia attempted to play with Trudy but was more focused on the question-and-answer session between Noah and Kate.

"You know, fertinol. They're fertinol twins."

"You mean fraternal? Fraternal twins? Your Aunt Sophie and Uncle Bill are fraternal twins?" Kate's eyes popped wide open. Celia saw the shock on Kate's face, but the fraternal reference hadn't registered, and she didn't fully comprehend the conversation at hand.

"They aren't married?"

"Who's not married?" Celia jumped into their discussion. She knew she had missed something important.

"Auntie Sophie's married. My Uncle Matt is in the service and coming home soon. But my Uncle Bill isn't married."

"Noah's Uncle Bill and Aunt Sophie are fraternal twins." Kate spoke loudly as she tried to clarify the situation to Celia.

"What? Your Aunt Sophie is your aunt because she's your uncle's twin? Is that what you said?" Celia's voice had an unfamiliar tone, a sound Kate had never heard before

Noah reached over and picked up a small stick from the ground. He waved it up and down for Trudy. She jumped from Celia's lap and grabbed it into her mouth. "Yeah. It's no big deal. She's been my aunt as long as I've been alive. She's wicked cool."

Celia stood. Her face changed its shade. She immediately thought about her conversation with William at the store. *I was unbelievably rude.* "Tell me you're kidding." She wasn't thinking about her words or the fact that she was conversing with a young boy.

Kate laughed an out-of-control laugh. Celia sat down on the steps again and Trudy jumped back up onto her lap.

"I have to get back to Uncle Bill's house. My parents are probably wondering what's taking me so long. C'mon, Trudy." He reached to get the leash.

Celia was no longer flush; she was rather pale. Kate's shoulders shook as she tried to hold in her laughter.

Celia slumped over, rested her elbows on her knees, and buried her face into her hands. "If he ever thought I WAS nice, he doesn't now."

"Let's go. I'll buy you a glass of wine or maybe something stronger. How's a nice hot Irish coffee sound?" Kate leaned over and reached for Celia's hand and pulled her up from the stairs.

"I should have told Noah to say hello from me or something."

"Celia, it's better you didn't. You'll see him again. I'm sure he'll understand."

"I was unbelievably cold to him." Before they left for drinks, Celia ran upstairs to grab a pack of cigarettes.

When We Were Newlyweds

Celia sat on the edge of her mattress and pulled the coated band out of her ponytail; her hair fell scruffily below her shoulders. She sluggishly walked into her bathroom and thought about Noah's unmarried Uncle Bill. *Was I a little unfriendly or was I super rude?* She stood over the small bathroom sink and stared at the water as it flowed down the drain.

She dressed with extra care. She wore a freshly laundered red camisole and a black wool suit. An additional brush of blush and a dab of lipstick made its way to her face and lips, as did a touch of mascara, which emphasized the sparkle of her bright-green eyes.

At Pete's, she ordered a large French vanilla coffee. She hoped to bump into the very single William. The William to whom she had been very cold. *I'll explain everything, and we'll laugh about it and make plans to meet for drinks or coffee, perhaps even that dinner he mentioned.* She lingered around Pete's longer than usual. William was nowhere in sight. *Sure, now that I want to see him, I don't. Doesn't that figure?* She called herself an idiot, not for the first time.

You ARE a stalker. You're stalking a total stranger. Well, not a totally total stranger. You're pathetic. You're not even a good stalker. What are you, twelve? Her ridiculous thoughts annoyed her. She knew dating meant disappointment. Geoff, Booper, and Brock were a few names that came to her mind.

Celia pushed the up button for the elevator as Emma and Ramona walked toward her. She took off her gloves and turned to greet the two women as they approached her. "Hey, great timing.

This doesn't usually happen." The women stepped into the elevator. "It's sooo cold outside."

"Okay, I'll bite," Emma said. "How cold is it?"

"It's so cold I saw a chicken cross the street with a cape on."

Emma and Celia laughed. Ramona smiled, but seemed confused. "I don't get it. The chicken was wearing a cape?"

"No. It's a silly chicken joke. I said *cape on*, but it's supposed to be capon. You know. Those little chickens called capons. C-A-P-O-N." Celia spelled out the word capon. "The two different types of chicken crossed the street together. It's a cold weather joke. Never mind, it's nothing. That's why I don't tell jokes in the first place. I'm not funny."

"Oh, I get it now." Ramona smiled again but continued to appear confused.

Ramona got off on the fourth floor. Celia and Emma rode together to the seventh. "Do you have time for some coffee and sit for a few minutes?" They walked together to the kitchen area to get coffee, and then they walked to Emma's office to catch up after the weekend.

Emma's corner office was sparsely decorated, with a few knickknacks strategically placed on a bookcase by the back wall. On her desk was the only photograph in the room. It displayed Jasper, a chubby Golden Retriever, running with a stick in his mouth. Although Jasper had passed the previous year, Emma was not emotionally able to take his picture down.

"How was your weekend?" Emma asked as the two women sat down.

"Sucky. I've told you about that guy I met. Very attractive guy who turned out to be the married uncle of a kid who spent the summer in my neighborhood. I told you about him, right?"

"Yeah, the flirty jerk?"

Celia refreshed Emma on the incidents with William–from bumping into him with her coffee, to the ball game, to the invitations for coffee or dinner. "I was basically very cold to him."

"I would be cold too." Emma tried to be supportive.

"I'm not even sure I would say I was cold to him. I think I was just plain rude. Either way, friendlyis not the word I would use to describe how I treated him. I didn't know–I THOUGHT he was married."

"What do you mean, thought? He's not married?"

"No, he's not."

"How come you thought he was married?" Emma's tone was one of confusion.

"When I met him, he was with a woman. All signs pointed to her being his wife. Turns out the wife is his fraternal twin sister."

"What?" Emma uncrossed her legs and leaned forward, her eyebrows raised high.

"Exactly. I'm totally out of my mind about it." Celia took a big gulp of her coffee. "When he was married, I bumped into him a few times, but now that he isn't married, I haven't seen him at all." She air-quoted the word married each time she said it.

"Hey. You said he seemed nice. If he's truly a nice guy, which he probably is, next time you see him, explain the situation. I'll bet he understands." Emma's words were reassuring.

"Yeah, maybe. I hope I get the chance to tell him soon. It's driving me nuts."

"You'll get a chance, Celia. I'm willing to bet on it."

Emma's phone rang and interrupted their conversation. "Hello?" She mouthed the word *Ramona* to Celia.

"Ramona, I think I've made it clear, I won't commute in a snowstorm. If we have the storm as predicted, I won't be in."

Celia watched her speak to Ramona. Emma leaned back and punched the speaker button and put her finger up to her mouth to indicate for Celia not to say anything. She then flipped her hand in the air above the phone.

"Emma, I'm not changing the meeting. We have to meet tomorrow. Maybe you can conference in." Ramona sounded snippy and annoyed.

"As I said, I won't make it in if it's snowing. And guess what, neither will a lot of other people." Emma was biting her bottom lip as she glared at the phone.

"Well then, you can conference in." Ramona's tone was condescending.

"Nah, I don't think so. I'll be outside making snow angels." She snarled at the phone. "Let's wait a little longer and listen to the forecast. I'll talk to you later." Emma hung up the phone. "Pain in the ass—she drives me crazy. Whenever I call her, she answers the phone in a snippy voice and it makes me uncomfortable. I always feel like it's a huge bother to speak to me. She confuses being better off with being better."

"What do you mean?"

"Celia, she might be better off than I am, but she isn't better than me or you or anyone."

"What did she want? A meeting tomorrow?"

"Yes. She refuses to change a meeting for tomorrow and it's supposed to snow. We're saving lives here. It's human resource paperwork she wants to discuss. I refuse to commute in here if the weather is bad. My martyr days are over. If she wants to be one, good luck to her. It's not mission critical. Now, Celia, tell me about single Uncle Bill."

"I want to get my mind off it. It's making me very anxious. I need to think of something else. Why don't you tell me one of your stories? You must have a story to tell me to get my mind off my own craziness."

"I could tell you what happened this weekend. It's nutso."

Celia loved hearing about the crazy stories and antics of Fredric's ex-wife. She hoped she was a comfort to Emma in a way her cousin Jillian had been.

"The woman is relentless! Celia, I am not kidding, something happens every single time I'm there. I can't believe how creative she is. How can she continually come up with new stuff? She must spend hours conjuring up these stories. Funny thing is, she never tells me the stories when Fredric's in the room. The second he leaves, when we're forced to be alone together, she starts. Here's what happened."

Emma and Freddy sat on separate couches in his living room, each of them on their iPad. Fredric had gone back to his office to get his computer.

The peaceful visit was instantly interrupted when the front door slammed shut.

"Anybody home?" Freddy's mother barged into the house and disturbed their quiet moment.

"We're in here." He turned toward Emma. "Sorry, I had no idea she was coming over."

Emma rolled her eyes. "Don't worry about it."

"Yeah, I know—we should assume she'll stop by." He was aware of the friction but felt bad for his mother.

Edie walked into the living room and sat down next to her son. "What are you guys doing?"

"Not much." Emma kept her eyes on her iPad. "Checking out shampoo on Amazon."

Edie looked over his shoulder to see what Freddy was viewing on the screen. "I have a work party on Friday and I think I'll make Gramma Millie's lemon poppy seed cake. Think that's a good idea?"

He nodded in agreement that it sounded good.

Emma kept her eyes on her iPad.

Two seconds later, Edie reiterated her party plan. "So, you think it's a good idea to make Gramma Millie's lemon poppy seed cake for that party?"

This time he nodded and made a verbal acknowledgment. "Sounds good, Mom."

Emma silently perused shopping sites, while she wondered why Edie deliberately mentioned the cake twice. *Does she want me to ask about her party? She's up to something. I can't imagine any recipe from my mother-in-law being good enough to cook, let alone bring to a party.*

"Let's see now, I'll make Gramma Millie's lemon poppy seed cake on Thursday night and then bring it in to work on Friday."

So that's the third time in two minutes that you've brought up the stupid lemon cake. Emma feigned interest in her iPad shopping. She did not want to make eye contact and be sucked into the conversation.

Edie was talking about the cake for some reason, but Emma couldn't imagine why. *Is this to remind me that you have recipes from my mother-in-law? I refuse to acknowledge this cake conversation and your thirty-year-old recipe swap activities with my mother-in-law.* Emma continued to scroll through her iPad and pretended she was unaware of the discussion.

Finally, after a few minutes more, Emma believed the cake chat had concluded. She put down the iPad and was about to make tea. Before she got up from the couch, Edie stopped her.

"Emma!" Fredric's mother shouted and had now captured Emma's attention.

Shit! Aren't you clever to use my name. I can't avoid you now. Emma regretted that she put down her dodging device. Without the iPad, she became a prisoner in her ex-wife's cake dialog.

"Emma!" Edie said her name louder than before. "When we were newlyweds, Fredric and me, I made Millie's lemon poppy seed cake. We always shared recipes. I turned the oven to 450 instead of 350 to make it cook faster. Isn't that funny?" Edie didn't wait for a response. "As you can imagine, the cake was horrible. I cried and called Millie and she consoled me and laughed about it. Later it became our joke on how I started our marriage as such a bad cook. Millie taught me how to cook after that."

Emma remained silent. She resented being commandeered into the cake conversation. *Why did I put that iPad down?* She smiled and held back a laugh. *Millie's a horrible cook–how could she teach you anything?*

"Then when Fredric came home from work, he was so loving about the cake mistake. He comforted me and made me feel much better. I cried in his arms."

There it is. All that work to depict the happy loving newlyweds. Who cries over a cake anyway–spilled milk...maybe. Emma laughed, but not at the story. She was entertained by her thoughts. She took a deep breath. She couldn't think of a question and she could feel a knot forming in her gut. *Question. Question. What can you ask? Keep the fizzy, fuck face? Nah, that won't work. Think! Let it go. Let the newlywed and the loving comments go. She's a loser and you're not.*

Emma was willing to let it go, but Edie wasn't. She kept the story active. "It was weird, cooking as a newlywed. I wanted to make beautiful, romantic dinners every night. This was a silly mistake that Fredric and I ended up laughing about as we snuggled in our bed that night."

Maybe if you cooked better, you could have saved your marriage, fuck face. Say something to her. You're smart. Think of the promise to Jillian. This witch is going to keep taunting you if you don't stop her. Ask her how she can remember that kind of detail from thirty years ago. Ask her something. "Well, you were married such a very short time, I guess you were always newlyweds." Emma's smile toward Edie was insincere. "Seriously, who could perfect their cooking skills in just a few months?" She picked up the iPad and smiled.

Edie left.

Celia finished her coffee and shook her head at Emma's rendition of the story.

"Celia, she was pissed. I hate to admit this, but I enjoyed it! She always tells totally made up cutesy stories about the past. She does it deliberately to taunt me. I need to have some fun with it. If I don't, it will bother me for days, maybe even weeks. I never flaunt my successful marriage in her face. I never talk about things I know will upset her or make her jealous. I never talk about our vacations or activities. I don't talk about OUR pillow talk to her. I won't even wear good jewelry if I know I'll see her, except for my wedding band. I feel bad for her, yet she continues to go out of her way to bug me. Plus, I promised Jillian I wouldn't allow her to continue to pull this crap. I have to keep that promise."

Celia played with her empty coffee cup. "What's her problem?"

"That story, if it even happened, was over twenty-eight years ago. Does she think I forget that they were married? Does she have to remind me each time I see her. Get over it, chickee poo."

"What adult uses the word snuggled in that context? I could never do it. I couldn't tolerate that constant bullshit. I don't think it's normal. Most divorced people don't have to see each other that much once the kids are grown. I know I couldn't do it."

"Fredric told me from day one that she's *F'd in the H*."

"What's F'd in the H mean?"

"Fredric always says she's fucked in the head. F'd in the H. One of the first things he told me about her was how horrible and nasty she is. I told him not to tell me anything because I wanted to make up my own mind. He told me he would enjoy saying ITYS."

"ITYS?"

"Yeah. I Told You So. Whatever."

Ping and a Symbol

"Hello?"

"Hi, Celia. Have you seen him again?"

"Kate, you're so funny. I knew you would ask that immediately. I almost answered the phone and told you I hadn't seen him again. Doesn't it figure, I see him all the time when he was married, and now that he's single, I haven't seen him once." Celia shuffled papers on her desk and then picked up a scented marker.

"Celia, I hate to tell you this, but I think you're forgetting he's been single all along."

"I know. I know. It's hard to change my thought process on him." She took the cover off the marker and sniffed the cherry scent. "Did you know they make scented markers for dry-erase boards?" She smelled it again, and inadvertently touched the marker to her face; a bright-red spot was now centered on the tip of her nose. "Watch. I'll never see him again, or at least not until he's found someone new. Someone who's not rude to him the way I was."

"You probably weren't as rude as you think. Be patient. It hasn't been that long. People don't go out as much when the weather gets colder." Kate's tone was compassionate and supportive. "Can you still meet me for dinner?"

"You bet. I've been fantasizing about their coconut shrimp all day. A little snow isn't going to stop me from getting there. I'll park in the lot off Cabot Street. Should I wait for you or go in?"

"It's cold out–let's meet inside. Celia, isn't it great to make a plan and have the confidence to know it will come to fruition? I love your new car. See you then."

It felt like snow. *Snow has a distinct feeling.* Celia inhaled the wintery smell and watched her breath as she exhaled. She crossed her arms tightly against her body and shivered. She opened the door, hopped into the seat, and started the engine. *Right on time.* She drove down the narrow streets on her way to meet Kate.

When she approached the stop sign before she entered the main road, Celia heard a ping and saw an amber symbol display on the dashboard. Like Pavlov's dog, the sound and symbol caused a knee-jerk reaction of panic. This wasn't the first time she heard a strange car noise while driving to meet Kate. She had hoped delays from car trouble were a thing in her past. "Shit!" She was panicked. "This can't be happening!"

She feared the worst. *Great! I'll freeze to death waiting for Brian, if I need a tow. I spent a small fortune on a new car and I'm no better off. Now I have another car problem* AND *I'm poor from payments.* The tension in her stomach was all too familiar. She drove into a nearby parking lot. To keep the car warm, Celia left the engine running as she reached into the glove box and pulled out the manual.

Celia rested the operator's manual on the steering wheel and searched for information to help identify what would cause a ping and a symbol. *Holy cow! I have heated seats? I totally forgot!* She flipped from the index to the pages with instructions for the heated seats and then fiddled with the levels to control the driver's side seat heater. *I can't believe I forgot about the heated steering wheel too? I've wasted all those cold mornings.* She pressed the button to set the steering wheel heater and then wrapped her hands around the wheel until she felt the warmth. *Focus!*

She was distracted from her mission of locating the issue at hand. She searched for details related to the ping and the symbol. She found nothing. She examined the manual, she read the index, and once more skimmed through the pages. Finally, she located the answer. She leaned back and laughed. *When the outside temp is 32F or lower, layers of black ice can begin to form on the roadways.* She studied the symbol on the dashboard. *It's a snowflake, you idiot!* Aside from the heated seats and steering wheel, she had a lot to learn about the features of her Jeep.

Celia arrived at Soma first and requested a table by the fireplace. She welcomed the warmth and the comforting glow. She was reading the specials when Kate approached the table.

Kate bent down to kiss Celia hello. "Happy New Year! What's that red thing?" She leaned in closer to better see Celia's nose.

"What red thing?"

"You have a red dot at the tip of your nose." Kate pointed to Celia's face.

Celia reached into her bag and pulled out her cell. She launched the camera and set it to selfie to view the red spot. "What is that?" She rubbed it softly. "Oh, it's from the scented marker. I sniffed it when I was talking to you. It must have touched my nose." She dipped her napkin into the glass of water and rubbed the spot. "Better?"

"Better. Now it's a pink smudge. Don't worry about it. People will think you had too much to drink."

Kate removed her coat and hung it on a nearby hook. She sat down across the table from Celia and slowly and deliberately unwound her thick winter scarf. With the scarf now draped over her shoulders, her neck was exposed. She leaned toward the fireplace. "I love this table. It's warm and cozy. I feel spoiled from the mild weather we've had, but this freeze smacks of January." She shrugged and rubbed her hands together. "Have you missed me?" This was the first time the two had gotten together since the holidays.

Celia ignored Kate's question. She was more intrigued by Kate's new adornment. "What's that around your neck?" Celia held the menu in her hands.

"Christmas present from my mother-in-law. What do you think?"

"What the hell is it?" Celia wrinkled her nose and squinted, her eyes fixated on Kate's neckline. She put the menu down and moved her head across the table to further inspect the artwork around her friend's neck. "What is it?" She reached out and touched the chain. "A gift from your mother-in-law? Is it a necklace? What's it mean?" She released the chain from her hand and leaned back.

"It's the Christmas present Tom's mother gave me." Kate touched the chain and rolled it between her fingers and thumb. "What part of Christmas present don't you understand?"

"The part where it looks like an unscratched two-dollar lottery ticket on an ugly chain. I have that same chain for the light in my storage bin. Is that a joke? It's crazy."

"No, it's not a joke. But I commend you for seeing the ridiculousness of it. You are correct. This is a two-dollar lottery ticket." Kate continued to twirl the chain from which the lottery ticket hung.

"What's the story?"

"Before I tell you the story, I want you to see this picture." Kate handed her cell phone to Celia.

The waitress arrived with pita bread triangles, a bowl of hummus, and a small dish with oil, olives, and spices. "You ready to order?"

"Can you make the coconut shrimp with lemongrass/curry an entrée portion?" Celia handed the menu to the waitress after she ordered.

"Certainly, the chef would be happy to do that. And for you?" The waitress turned toward Kate.

"That sounds delicious. I'll get something else and we can share. I'll start with grilled octopus." She looked at Celia. "You'll have some?"

"Absolutely."

"And for my main course, I'd like the chicken under a brick. Does that sound good to you, Celia?"

"It sounds wonderful!"

"Would you care for an arugula salad?" The waitress picked up Kate's menu.

"No thank you. I think we have enough food for now. We need to leave room for dessert."

Celia inspected the picture displayed on the cell phone screen. She was not sure what she was looking at, or better said, what she was looking for. "It's a Christmas tree. It's a nice tree. Is it real?"

"Not the point." Kate's tone was huffy. "Keep looking."

"Am I supposed to find something in particular?" Celia kept her eyes focused on the picture.

"Sort of." Kate offered no further explanation. "Please, just humor me." She leaned over and swiped her hand across the screen to display the next image. "Look carefully at the gifts. Check for details. Let's make it a fun little challenge."

"Okay." Celia's response was harmonic. "I'm looking at the gifts, and what do I see? I spy with my little eye." She continued to sing her words.

"Please, it won't be any fun if I have to explain it. Zoom in if you need to but read the name tags taped to the gifts. That's the most of a hint that I'll give you."

"Okeydokey." Celia read aloud. "Tom, Russ, Sara, Alex, Dawn, Kate, Heather, Caleb, Krystal. What kind of phone is this? It takes great pictures. Incredible detail."

Kate snarled. "Celia! The phone is not the topic here. Focus on the names. Will you?"

"Okay, okay, okay. Don't yell at me."

"Sorry, I'm not yelling, I want you to concentrate. It's an LG."

"What?"

"The phone is an LG. Please, read the names again–you left one out."

"Sorry. I love how detailed the graphics are." Celia read the names again and stopped at the last name. "Magpie. Who's Magpie?"

"It's Dawn's dog. Now slide to the next picture."

Celia swiped her hand on the screen to move to the next picture. "What's this?" She turned the phone to show Kate the picture.

Kate took the phone. "You went too far." She swiped back to the correct picture and then returned the phone to Celia.

"What was that?" Celia referenced the last picture she had seen.

"That was an accidental picture of the floor and my shoe. Please, look at this one." Kate sounded frustrated. "Celia, get serious. I want you to see the opened gifts."

"Sorry if I didn't take this seriously enough for you. I think the chained lottery ticket draped around your neck threw me off and caused me to think this is some sort of silly joke. Think about it! You're wearing an unscratched lottery ticket as a necklace. Think about it."

Kate got up, grabbed an empty chair, and pulled it next to Celia. Together they looked at the screen. The gifts depicted on the screen were organized in a straight line. "I staged them. I wanted you to be able to tell which gift went to which relative." She took a sip of Celia's water.

Celia inspected the picture. "I see a sweater with Tom's name on it and a stack of books for Dawn." She continued to recite the details of the photo. "Oh, I see Magpie got a brand-new bed." Celia opened her mouth, put her hand up to her cheek, and then looked at Kate. "Oh no." She lowered the phone. "I see what's happening here. Please don't tell me."

"Yup. You got it." Kate took a bite of pita covered with hummus. "The dog gets a $50 bed for Christmas, and I get this two-dollar lottery ticket." Kate grabbed the ticket and flicked it into the air. The chain flipped up and then dropped back to its original position around her neck.

"And? What else did Doris give you?"

"Nothing. This was my Christmas gift. Nice. Right?"

Celia was speechless. She tried not to laugh. She couldn't tell for sure whether Kate was angry or whether she saw the humor in the situation.

"That's not nice, right?" Kate took another piece of pita and dipped it into the hummus. "I bought his mother a gift card to her favorite store. When she opened it, she asked if she had to pay an activation fee to use the card. I told her I took care of it and the card was ready to use. She thanked Tom for his generosity. Tom didn't even know what the gift was." Kate drank the rest of Celia's water and reached across the table for her own water glass.

Kate took the phone from Celia and placed it down on the table. "I don't care about a gift. Honestly, I don't. But the fact that she took the time to get everyone, including fucking Magpie, a gift and then threw a two-dollar lottery ticket in an envelope for me is antagonizing. It wasn't even an envelope to a holiday card or a nice envelope. It had a window in it and looked like it came from a bill or something. I continue to be nice to her and help her and I can't win. No one is good enough for Tommy." Kate popped another piece of pita into her mouth. "Whatever!" She raised her hands up and placed them on top of her head. "Nuts! Right?" She curled her upper lip.

"Do you plan to scratch it?"

"No, my dear, I saved it for you." Kate pulled the homemade necklace over her head, and in a ceremonious gesture, placed it over Celia's head and watched the ticket dangle from Celia's neck. "I don't even play the lottery, and I know how much you love it."

"If it's a winner, do I have to share it with you?" Celia took the necklace off and placed it on the table. She searched for a coin at the bottom of her bag. She scratched small circles to expose each of the numbers at the top of the ticket. "Will you tell your mother-in-law if I win big? Boy, that would truly piss her off."

Kate watched as Celia scratched the numbers in a most organized and systematic fashion. "You always scratch them that neatly?"

"Yeah. I make a game out of it. It's more fun that way."

All the numbers were now exposed, and Celia read and compared the bottom numbers to the winning numbers above. "Nothing." She tossed the chained ticket onto the table.

"Figures." She put her hand out, palm up. "I want the necklace back."

"You're kidding, right?" Celia slid the necklace closer to Kate, who was now back in her original chair.

"Nope. Not kidding." Kate lifted the necklace, slightly bent her head, and adorned herself with her hand-crafted jewelry.

Celia turned on all the heated options she could find when she got into her car: the seat, the steering wheel, the backseats, and the dashboard. She blasted the warm air as high as it would go.

Her phone rang as she started to leave the parking lot. Without checking the incoming number, she answered. "Hi, Kate. I can see you in your car. What'd you forget to tell me?"

"Celia?"

Her stomach knotted up and a rush of heat ran down her back. Her neck got clammy. "Why are you calling me?" She turned on the air conditioning as she felt beads of sweat around her neck.

"I wanted to check in and see how you are."

"Don't call me again." Her voice was strong and fierce. "Goodbye." She pressed End as hard as she could and threw the phone onto the passenger seat.

Celia leaned on the horn.

Kate drove over and pulled up beside her. Both driver sides were next to each other. "Car trouble, miss?"

Celia's face was white as a ghost.

"Celia, what's wrong?"

"Geoff just called me. Talk about ruining a good evening."

Kate turned off her engine, got out of her car, and jumped into the passenger side of Celia's Wrangler.

"What did he want?"

"Not sure. I didn't give him a chance. I told him to never call me again and I hung up. Got a smoke?"

"Of course I do. You want regular or menthol?"

Celia didn't laugh. "I haven't had a smoke in weeks. This is the first time I've felt the urge to have one."

"Why don't we sit here for a while and let this gross feeling pass?" She handed her the mint she had taken when she left the restaurant.

PRINCIPLES

On her way home from dinner with Kate, Celia stopped at Pete's to collect her winnings from a lottery ticket she had purchased earlier in the week.

As she received her prize money, she saw William at the next register. He didn't see her. She smacked her lips together. She anxiously tapped her foot. Her heart thumped inside her chest and her stomach flipped about. She tried to time her exit to bump into him at the door where she would explain everything. The cashier counted her change too slowly; the delay would hinder Celia's meet-at-the door plan.

"Do you mind a few ones?" She held the ones out to show Celia. "I don't have a lot of big bills."

"Whatever you have is good." She moved her hand back and forth as she waited for the girl to count out fifteen ones.

William glanced down at the front page of the newspaper he had just purchased. He paid no attention to his surroundings as he walked past the checkout where Celia stood.

"William!" Without thinking, Celia blurted out his name as she stuffed the winnings into her bag.

He smiled. "Hi, Celia. How are you?"

"I won fifteen dollars. Imagine that?" She felt foolish as she walked toward him.

"You seem to always win on those tickets, don't you!" He continued to smile.

He sounds normal. What's normal for him anyway? Will he stop for a minute or walk away? Will he ask me for coffee again? Before he had a chance to move, she spoke. "You know, this is going to sound funny. At least I think it might sound funny." She smacked her lips again. They were still dry from her nervousness. "But the last time I saw you, I might have spoken—" Celia paused for a minute as she tried to grasp the right words. "I might have spoken—what I'm trying to say is that I thought you were married and I think I was rude to you because of it." *There. She said it.* She breathed out a deep breath and waited for his response.

He said nothing.

She began to speak again. "I hope you don't think I was rude. I'm not usually that way. I thought you were married and I couldn't fathom why a married man would ask me to join him for coffee. Sorry, maybe I'm not making any sense." Her stomach did a little dance inside her and she stopped talking. She knew she would say something ridiculous if she continued to speak while she was on edge.

He narrowed his sparkling eyes. "Is that what you meant about my *situation*?" His smile was still present.

"Yes. I'm sorry." She tilted her head and smiled a weak half-smile at him. "I feel terrible, but I assumed you and Sophie were married."

"Sophie?" He laughed out loud. "Sophie's my twin sister. Why did you think we were married?" He laughed again.

Celia's face was slowly heating up. The more she thought about it and the more she wanted it to stay normal, the redder it got—especially the pink smudge she had forgotten was at the tip of her nose.

"I assumed you were a couple. I never considered siblings."

"How did you get the idea we were married, though?"

"At the ball game." She played with the strap on her shoulder bag. "I'm so embarrassed about this." She moved her arm toward her face and pressed her knuckles against her lips. She was visibly nervous.

"I guess it's good that you have your principles."

"Yeah, I guess so." *Is he going to walk away*? The ruckus in her stomach turbulently continued.

William lightly touched her arm and she felt a tingle. "Would you ever consider that coffee again? That is, if I muster up the courage to ask you?"

"I'm shocked you would even think to ask me again. I feel like such an idiot. I'm very sorry, you have no idea."

"I believe you already apologized. So? Can I take you for coffee?"

"How about this? I won fifteen dollars. Let me buy YOU a cup of coffee." Her face was still scarlet, her palms somewhat sweaty.

"You're not married, are you? Because I don't do coffee with married women." He touched her back as they crossed the street. "You know, Celia." He glanced into her eyes. "I have another sister in New York. I'm not married to her either."

With her face still flushed, she looked back at him and smiled.

They shared a pastry. William paid the bill.

Part 3

One Year Later

I Promise

White fluffy snowflakes floated into the streaks of sunshine as the sun peeked through the clouds. Like tiny diamonds, the delicate dusting of snow sparkled on the windowsill. An enormous window framed the almost bare harbor, while abandoned fishing boats rocked back and forth at their moorings. Celia loved this view of the harbor. It was a marvelous setting for a magnificent day.

The guests stood as Celia entered the room. She slowly walked through the arched doorway and halfway down the aisle to where her father stood. He greeted her with a kiss on each cheek. They walked together past the thirty-six witnesses to this special occasion.

Her off-white calf-length dress swayed as she walked. A cluster of purple, yellow, and white freesia shook as her trembling hands grasped the stems of her bouquet. Celia was excited with anticipation and wondered whether her nervousness was visible to her guests. *Are twitterpations visible*? Twitterpations she thought she would never feel again.

Celia paused for a moment and looked at William. He smiled as he eagerly waited for her to approach him. She felt a calm overtake her. William reached for her hand as she walked up to him. She turned and hugged her father before he sat down next to her mother. William and Celia held hands and faced each other.

Celia and William turned their heads toward the justice of the peace as he spoke. "We welcome you here today to join in the marriage celebration of Celia Beech and William Charles." William's brother Glen, as well as Noah, stood by his side. An extremely emotional Kate was Celia's attendant.

"Do you, William, find within yourself the love and commitment to be a husband to Celia?" The justice of the peace waited for William's response.

"I do."

"And do you, Celia, find within yourself the love and commitment to be a wife to William?"

"I do." Celia's voice was softer than usual.

"Do you both find within yourselves the love and commitment to share life together, regardless of the obstacles that may confront you?"

"We do." They responded together as Celia tightened her grip on William's hand.

"Good! Then we shall continue." The JP smiled at the couple and Celia giggled. "William, please proceed with your vows to Celia."

"Celia, you have renewed and enriched my life. When I met you, I realized how much we could share together. I choose you, Celia, to be my wife and my best friend. In doing so, I commit my love and my life to you. I want to share with you all that is to come. As we begin our new life together, I know we have developed a trust and commitment that is strong enough to support both good times and bad. I promise to encourage and support you in all that you undertake."

William took a deep breath and then continued his vows. "I will believe in you even when you doubt yourself. I promise always to listen to you and to encourage you, and to protect you from people taking advantage of your kind nature." Celia and the group of witnesses laughed. "I promise to share with you my wit, my strength, and my heart. I promise to respect your wishes and let you select most of the movies we watch." The crowd laughed again. "Let me be the rock on which you rest, the companion of your life, and the one to keep your car shiny and clean."

The guests enjoyed the lighthearted touches added into his serious and loving vows. "I pledge myself now to be ever faithful to you and most importantly, I promise to love you forever. I join with you, Celia, to seek the meaning and fulfillment of our lives together. May our love deepen and grow with the years, and may we always share in the changes of life with flexibility and respect for each other. I truly love you, Celia."

Kate sniffled as she stood by Celia's side.

Celia, much to her own surprise, was calm and composed as she began her own vows to William. "William, I used to be afraid of falling in love and trusting someone to love me in return. I had begun to believe there was no such thing as true love. And after I had given up all hope, you appeared in my life like a miracle."

Celia became distracted by Kate's whimper and loud sniffle. Her concentration was broken, and she became anxious. Her bottom lip quivered, and her eyes filled up. *No, Kate! Get a hold of yourself. What was I saying? Would it ruin the party if I killed Kate right now?* Her focus had waned. William lifted her hand to his lips. She closed her eyes, took a breath and regained her composure.

"William, when I met you." Her lower lip trembled as she spoke. "I realized how much we could share together..." *Oh no! These are William's vows. Why did I memorize both sets of vows?* She was again anxious. *Will someone pick up my heart if it beats out of my chest?* She took a deep breath and paused.

Her vows bounced back into her brain. With her voice even softer and slower than before, she continued her vows. "With you, William, I will work toward our common goals and share our leisure joyfully. I will share with you the small daily pleasures and chores, as well as exciting new ideas. I pledge myself now to be ever faithful to you, William, with my body, my mind, and my heart. I promise to stand by you and to care for you. I promise to respect your wishes and your feelings, and to share in your laughter and to laugh at your jokes, even when they aren't funny." The small group laughed again.

"And most of all, I promise to like you and love you with all my heart." A single tear trickled down her cheek as she momentarily paused. "I join with you, William, to seek the meaning and fulfillment of our lives together. Thank you for coming into my life, for loving me, and for seeing the best in me. I am deeply in love with you, William."

William winked at his bride. The justice of the peace spoke of love, marriage, and commitment. Celia and William exchanged rings and were pronounced husband and wife. Mr. and Mrs. Charles kissed, embraced, and listened to the full-fledged sob that Kate broke into.

"Well, well, well!" Celia snickered at Kate as the guests walked up to congratulate the newlyweds. "I never would have figured that you'd be the one to lose it during the ceremony."

"I was fine until you started with the giving up on love, and never finding it, and whatever it was that you said. I'm super happy for you. For both of you!"

"Thank you." Celia hugged Kate and didn't let go.

"Was it obvious that I was crying?"

"Kate, it's a wedding–you're supposed to cry."

"I think people were focused on you and Billy Boy anyway."

"You're right." Celia let go of Kate and wiped her eyes dry. "Are you ready for the most delicious curried shrimp and rack of lamb you've ever tasted?"

Puppies

Celia was settled into her new home, previously known as William's apartment. It was THEIR place now, and Celia enjoyed adding her personal touches. Her puppets were hung in a corner window, her iron bed was set up in the second bedroom, and a host of decorations and knickknacks were dispersed throughout the two bedrooms, kitchen, den, and living room. It was perfect.

A glimpse of the ocean could be seen from the small window in the bathroom. Much to Celia's surprise, she could still hear the church bells ring on Sunday morning, although not as clearly as she used to hear them. Their lives combined nicely together. She loved waking up next to her husband.

Noah and a very pregnant Trudy would arrive soon to spend the weekend. With William's excellent culinary skills, Celia continued to pick up new cooking techniques and recipes. Celia, the non-baker, was trying her hand at chocolate chip cookies in an unfamiliar oven. *This will be interesting, little homemaker that I am.* She measured the ingredients and started to mix them into a large bowl. Before adding the chocolate chips, she poured a handful into the palm of her hand and popped them all at once into her mouth. *Don't want too many in the cookies–they'll be all chocolatey.*

"Hello?" She held the phone between her chin and her shoulder as she wiped batter from her hands with a paper towel.

"Hey, Celia! I mean Aunt Celia. Right?"

Celia laughed. "Hi, Noah. You still coming? How's Miss Trudy doing? Anything new?"

"Yup. I have five new things! When can you come over to see them? They're wicked cute."

"WHAT! I can't believe Trudy had her puppies. That seems so fast. What did she have?" She put the phone down and pressed Speaker.

"Puppies, Aunt Celia. Puppies. Five cute little puppies! I want to keep them all. I doubt my mom will let me."

"How many girls and how many boys?"

"I think it's two girls and three boys, but Mom says she isn't totally sure right now. Trudy had them last night. When can you and Uncle Bill come to see them?"

"How about later? I'm baking some cookies for your visit. I'll finish them and bring them over. That is, if they come out decent."

"WOW! That's wicked awesome!" Noah's excitement flew right through the phone. "I'll tell Mom you guys are coming over."

"Great! I can hardly wait to see them."

"Is Uncle Bill there? I want to tell him about the puppies."

"He's out right now. Try his cell. I'm sure he'll be excited to hear the news." Celia blew Noah a kiss through the phone.

The smell of puppies greeted Celia and William the moment they walked into the house. Noah raced to the door with his mother's cell phone. "Come see the pictures. Here they are right after they were born. I didn't see them get born, because Mom wanted to give Trudy some room and didn't want us to crowd her. Mom went in a lot to make sure Trudy was doing okay."

Celia placed a plastic container of cookies on the table in the front hall. "Wow!" She scrolled through the pictures. "When can we see the pups?"

Trudy rested in a large homemade bed filled with fresh towels as the puppies slept by her side. All five puppies were visible–Trudy lifted her head and fixated her eyes on the visitors.

"Does Trudy look sad?" Noah asked.

"I don't think so." Celia rested her hand on Noah's shoulder. "She's probably very tired and doesn't want to leave her little babies alone right now." Celia took her cell phone out of her pocket and snapped a few pictures of Trudy and the puppies.

"Can you send those pictures to Mom? I want all the pictures I can get." Noah sat down next to Trudy and rubbed her head.

"I'll send them right now."

Celia and Uncle Bill left the puppy room and walked into the hallway, where Melanie met the visitors. Celia greeted her with a hug. “How’re you doing?”

“It’s been twenty-four hours straight and I’m exhausted.” She leaned in closer to Celia. “I might scream if Noah asks me one more time if we can keep them all.”

Deals for Dinner

Celia felt the building sway as the fierce winds gusted outside. She watched the liquid swish back and forth in the bottle at the water cooler.

On the seventh floor, Celia walked to the kitchen to get a cup of steaming hot coffee and wrapped her hands around the warm cup as she walked down the hall back to her office. She stopped at her coatrack and removed the scarf from the sleeve of her coat before she returned to her desk. She shivered as she sat down and draped the scarf on her shoulders.

The snow had stopped, but the temperature outside remained freezing, and it wasn't much warmer in her office. *I'm getting a space heater tomorrow. If they don't want us to have space heaters, then they better turn up the heat.*

Celia was mesmerized by the frozen crystals on the ledge outside. The ring of her cell phone broke her frosty trance.

"Hi, Kate."

"Sadie Sadie, married lady." Kate sang into the phone.

"Hey, it's snowing again. Is it snowing there?"

"No, not yet. It's not coastal snow. It is dark and gray, though."

"Do you still want to get together for dinner?" Celia sipped her coffee.

"Absolutely. I've been looking forward to it."

"What time do you want to meet? I can leave early."

"Well, about that." Kate drew a long, slow breath. "I have good news and I have bad news. Which do you want to hear first?" She spoke slowly.

"Neither. I don't want to hear any news. But go ahead, spit it out."

"Kate? Where are you?" A high-pitched Doris was heard over the phone. Her voice sailed through the speaker of Celia's cell phone.

"What was that? I mean, who was that?" Celia closed her eyes tight as she pressed her hand against her cheek. "That's Doris, isn't it?"

"I'm sorry. I'm so, so sorry. They surprised me with a visit. SURPRISE! I had no idea they were in the area. I told them we had plans, and they sort of invited themselves, and I didn't know what to say. I'm sorry."

"Kate, I'm sorry too. Because after the Brock fiasco, I promised Celia—that's me, in case you've forgotten—that I wouldn't go out to dinner with that triangle of characters ever again."

"Oh, come on. You're married now. You're no longer a pathetic project for my mother-in-law to fix. You're all fixed. We can go and enjoy. I'll pay." Kate sounded animated and cheerful.

"You were taking me out to dinner to celebrate my marriage. Remember? You were planning to pay for dinner anyway."

"I'll make it up to you. I'll take you to The Cod and you can even order the lobstah."

"Oh brother. I'll go just to get the lobstah at The Cod."

"Celia! Really? You'll come with us?"

"Nope. Not a chance. I was kidding about wanting the lobstah. Not going to dinner with you."

"I want my wedding gift back," Kate kidded.

"Fine. I'll go. Relax. But it has nothing to do with your gift. You sound desperate. What kind of friend would I be to not go? Think of it as me doing a good deed for you."

"Great!" Kate exuded excitement. "Just one more thing."

"And what would that one thing be?"

"They called and made a reservation someplace and it's a little earlier than usual."

"How much earlier?"

"4:30 earlier."

"Still waiting for the good news."

"I'll text you the name and address of the restaurant." Kate hung up before Celia could renege.

At 4:37, Celia walked through the door of the restaurant. Kate and her in-laws sat on a bench in the waiting area. She glanced at Kate, shook her head, and rolled her eyes.

Kate jumped off the bench and ran to Celia. She put her arms around her and hugged her tight. "I honestly thought you weren't coming." Her voice was soft and low.

"I wouldn't stand you up. The subway was slow. Are they leaving tonight? It's already dark out, and they don't like to drive in the dark."

"They're staying over. SURPRISE! Again." Kate released Celia from her grip.

Celia walked over to Doris and Bernie. "Hi. It's nice to see you again. How are you?"

"We're good. But, how are YOU? That's what we want to know. Let me see those rings." Doris grabbed Celia's left hand and pulled it toward her chest. "Beautiful. Your husband has good taste."

"Yes, he does. He chose Celia." Kate put her arm around Celia's shoulder and squeezed her.

Celia leaned into Kate's ear. She whispered in the softest voice possible. "Don't try to butter me up."

As usual, Bernie remained quiet; he appeared frustrated as he focused on his cell phone.

"So, Celia." Doris's voice sang in an all too familiar sound. "I guess it's time to get that baby factory started. Right?"

No! This can't be happening. Kate doesn't have kids. Hop on her factory. Mine's not even in the planning stage.

In a nanosecond, Kate jumped in. "Sorry. This conversation isn't going to happen. Celia hasn't been married long enough for THIS to be a topic. Let's leave her to enjoy the honeymoon phase."

"Well then, Kate. When is your baby factory going to get into motion? You're not getting any younger." Doris snapped as she finished her sentence.

Celia was horrified as she turned to Kate. *She's relentless. How can she say such a thing?* "Where are you coming from this time? Last time I saw you, you were driving home from Maine." *Remember? Maine, schmain.*

Kate didn't allow Doris time to answer. "This time, we're having a nice, pleasant dinner and we're not questioning anyone's lifestyle or life decisions."

Bernie put his phone down. "I can't get these damn coupons off the phone. Do you know how to do this, Kate? I wanted to buy you girls dinner, but I have to get the coupons and I can't get them on the phone." He held the phone out for Kate. "Can you take a look?"

"Celia teaches computer stuff. I'm sure she can do it." Kate passed the phone to Celia. "Do you mind? I can't see without my reading glasses."

Celia took a long, deep, exasperated breath. *This is proof that no good deed goes unpunished. And you felt sorry for Kate.* "Let me see what I can do." She clicked their website and displayed the coupon on the screen. "There you go." *This must be why they loved Brock. A man after their own coupon.* "What did you all do today?"

"We drove around to find deals for dinner. I wanted to search the web for restaurants, but Doris and Bernie wanted to see the places firsthand. They wanted to make sure we'd pick a clean restaurant and that it took the coupon they got in an email. Right?"

"Absolutely. I want to see the place in person. You can't tell if it's clean by looking at the Google."

"I agree." Bernie held the phone tight in his hand and kept tapping the screen, to be certain the coupon didn't disappear.

"Yup. We drove around ALL day. Doris and Bernie surprised me around 1:30 and we commenced our coupon-taking-restaurant search around 2:00. Luckily, we found this place, and the early bird coupon goes to 5:00. It's all good." Kate smiled.

Doris glanced at her watch. "It's 4:49. They better seat us soon."

"We're here. I'm sure we'll be fine." Kate touched her mother-in-law's hand reassuringly.

At 4:58, the hostess led the group to their table.

At 5:00:03, the waitress delivered the regular menu and walked away.

At 5:00:25, Doris had a conniption fit.

"Excuse me. Miss?" Doris's voice was elevated. "Miss? You brought the wrong menus."

The waitress turned around and returned to their table. "Is there a problem?"

"Yes, you brought the wrong menus. We're here for the early bird, and you brought the regular menus." Doris collected the menus and attempted to hand them to the waitress.

The waitress ignored the menus and looked at Doris. "That offer stops at 5:00. It's after that now."

Doris looked at her watch. She was flabbergasted, with her mouth opened. Her hand remained in the air as she held the menus.

Celia became outraged. “Excuse me.” She leaned in to read the name tag on the waitress’s shirt. “Excuse me, Stacy.” She dragged out and emphasized the word Stacy. “We were here before 4:30, and we were ushered to our table before 5:00. Your delay in coming to our table pushed the time ahead. We were here in time for the early bird. Now please get the proper menus and bring them to our table.”

The waitress walked away.

“Don’t worry, I think she got my point. Don’t you, Kate?” *Oh no. Coupon craziness must be contagious. What am I doing? That little bitch better bring us the right menus.*

“We drove around all day. I almost got carsick from being in the car stopping and starting and stopping and starting.” Kate failed to distract the group from the early bird debacle.

“Ah-uh. That’s great, Kate.” Celia didn’t hear a word Kate said. She got up from her seat and walked to the hostess station. “We were here in time for your early bird special. We waited over twenty minutes to be seated at a table that was empty the entire time we sat in the waiting area. The waitress came over less than a minute after 5:00 and has refused to give us the special menus. Please provide us with those menus.” She put her hand out to receive the menus. Celia’s voice could be heard back to the table where Kate, Doris, and Bernie sat.

“Sorry. Our policy stops the early bird menu promptly at 5:00 when the chef changes for the evening. The chef working now doesn’t prepare the items on the early bird menu.”

“Great, then we’ll order from the regular menu and get the early bird prices.” *Terrific idea! You got her now. She can’t back out of that option.*

“Sorry. We can’t do that. It’s not fair to the other patrons.”

“You mean the other patrons who will arrive after 5:00 for the non-early bird menu?” *What the fuck is a non-early bird menu? You’re making stuff up. Forget about this and return to your seat.*

“If you visit with us another time, before 5:00, we can provide you with the earlier menu.”

“This is such a scam. You know that, don’t you? We were here long before 5:00 and we sat in your waiting area for no reason at all. So, what should we do? Should we get here at 3:00 just in case you take your damn sweet time seating us?" Celia glanced back at her table. Doris and Bernie seemed content as they ate breadsticks from a basket. Kate stared at Celia.

Kate motioned for Celia to come back to the table.

"You have to do something about this situation. These people came a long way and were very excited about your special."

"Here's what I'll do. We'll provide you with free soup and dessert. Will that help the situation?"

"I guess that helps to compensate for your early bird scam." Celia quieted down.

Kate approached Celia. "Please come back and sit down."

Celia turned and walked away with Kate. "Hey, I negotiated free soup and dessert."

"You're not fooling me. I know you're doing this to avoid sitting and talking about babies."

Celia burst out laughing. "Brock would be proud."

"Thank you. That was delicious." Doris rubbed her full stomach as they walked out through the waiting area.

"Celia and I will get the car. You guys stay here where it's warm."

Celia walked beside Kate. "No offense, but that dinner sucked. The lemon gelatin with the oranges was disgusting. I hope I vomit so I'll get a better taste in my mouth."

"I know. It was horrible. But they enjoyed it. Funny how a revolting meal becomes wonderful when you get free stuff."

"Still waiting to hear that good news, Kate."

"How's this? Dinner is over."

"That works."

EXTRACTION

Celia had barely settled at her desk when Emma appeared at the door.

"I'll be by at 12:30." Emma didn't step into Celia's office; she simply made the announcement confirming their lunch together.

"What happened?"

"I'll tell you about it at lunch."

Celia raised her head and turned toward the doorway. Emma was gone.

At 12:30 sharp, Emma arrived at Celia's office, ready to share her weekend tales.

"Emma, I'm been looking forward to your story all morning." Celia pushed Emma's shoulder and laughed.

"Glad I can amuse you by having a bizarre ex-wife. My pain is your pleasure," Emma teased back.

They walked into the cafeteria. "I hate this cafeteria in the winter. It's too crowded. Want to sit in the quiet room? It's too busy and noisy in here."

"Where's the quiet room?" Celia was surprised to learn of a special dining area. "How do I not know about this quiet room?"

"It's around the corner. There are usually a few free tables in there. It will be quiet, and we can talk softly."

"Oh, I get it. This is a special room for the bigwigs that little peons like me don't have access to. Right?"

"Try not to view it that way. It will make you feel you're not worthy." Emma turned toward Celia. "Honestly, it's just a room. Anyone can use it."

"Ha, ha, ha." Celia followed Emma into the quiet room.

"This is the quiet room?" Celia mocked Emma. "I'm in this room all the time. I never thought to eat lunch in here or label it the quiet room—the way you did."

Celia opened her lunch bag and started to assemble her salad of spring greens, veggies, nuts, and avocado.

Emma eyed Celia's lunch. "That looks great." She placed two pieces of cold cheese pizza on a paper plate. "Wanna swap?"

"No but thank you anyway. Why don't you nuke that? There's a microwave around the corner."

"Nah, it's fine cold."

"You want half my salad? I brought a lot."

"Nope. But thanks. Cold pizza's a treat for me." Emma picked up a slice of pizza and then plopped it down on the paper plate.

"Tell me what happened." Celia licked the avocado off her knife and then cut the salad into bite-size pieces.

"It's a ludicrous story, but I have to share it. Jillian would absolutely kill me if I told her this one. On Friday, Freddy had his wisdom teeth out. I told him he should stay with us after the procedure in case he didn't feel well. He couldn't stay at his mother's because she was changing his old bedroom into a study. She has a guest room, but I guess it was too much work for her to set it up for him."

"Wow! She sounds like Mother of the Year."

"Doesn't she? I picked him up from the dentist. He was fine, but I took him back to my house anyway. He was still numb, and I didn't want him to be alone later in case he started to feel bad. Fredric was home when we got there. He brought dinner and snacks that Freddy would be able to eat. Here's what happened."

Still woozy from the medicine he had received during his tooth extraction, Freddy settled comfortably in an oversized couch in the family room. It didn't take long for him to fall asleep.

Upstairs, Emma changed sheets in the guest room. She had purchased flowers and placed them on the night table next to the bed. She knew Freddy couldn't care less about the flowers, but she wanted the room to feel fresh and happy.

Fredric had gone into the garage to get the last few bags of groceries from the car. He brought the bags into the kitchen and stopped in his tracks.

His ex-wife stood next to the kitchen table as she greeted him. "Hello, Fred. Nice to see you."

"What are you doing here?" His voice was raised higher than usual.

"MY son is here, and he is sick. That's what I'm doing here."

"How did you get in? You can't just walk into our house."

"I can walk into any place where MY SON is, especially after he's had surgery!" Edie put her hands on her hips as she shouted at Fredric.

Emma heard the voices and the unfriendly tones. She tiptoed to the top of the stairs and listened closely to the conversation coming from the kitchen. *Whose voice is that? That's a woman's voice. She sounds vaguely familiar.* A chill ran down her spine the second she recognized the voice. *I don't believe this! She's in my house? What the–?*

She pulled the cell phone out of her pocket and touched the contacts button. She felt a sting in her stomach and her heart sank. *Jillian, I could kill you for dying.* This was the first time in months she impulsively attempted to call her cousin. The sad reality of Jillian no longer being there hit Emma hard. She took a deep breath and leaned against the wall at the top of the stairs. *Should I go down there? What would Jillian tell me to do? What should I do, Jilly?* She stood frozen in the upstairs hallway.

"I'm asking you nicely to leave. I'm not comfortable with you here, and you have not been invited in." Fredric was calm but firm.

Edie ignored Fredric's plea as she walked past him, over to the refrigerator. She opened the door, gazed into the cold space, grabbed a soda, and sat down at the kitchen table.

The noise woke Freddy and he hesitantly walked into the kitchen. With a concerned and confused expression, he looked at his father. He pulled out a chair at the table and sat down across from his mother.

Emma remained in the hallway upstairs as she listened intently.

The ex-wife tapped the top of the can and then opened the soda. She swirled the can around the table surface for a moment and then took a big gulp.

This is where Jillian would bop me on the head for standing frozen. I know, Jillian—I should stop hiding up here in the hallway. I know. I know. Emma's one-sided conversation with the memory of her silenced cousin brought a lump to her throat. She realized this was the coward's way out. Nonetheless, she was pleased she wasn't in the middle of the drama.

Fredric was fuming. Freddy could read the expression on his father's face.

Freddy asked his mother to walk with him to the foyer. By the front door, he spoke in a soft voice.

Freddy walked back into the kitchen and took his seat at the table. His mother stomped behind him, grabbed her soda, and stormed out the front door.

"Sorry, Dad. I don't know why she does this stuff."

"It's not your fault, Freddy. No one blames you. I'm sure your mother planned this entire little act with the hope to annoy Emma. She most likely planned it the day you told her about your wisdom teeth coming out."

From the stairs, Emma breathed a huge sigh of relief. She ran downstairs to change the conversation.

"Freddy, why don't you lie down in the other room? I'll bring you something to drink. What's your pleasure?"

"Some water would be good. Thank you." He looked at Emma and then turned away. "My mom doesn't understand why you don't like her."

"She knows why I don't like her and it's an odd situation she has brought on by herself."

"It sucks." He put his hands up to his face and rubbed his jaw.

"It sucks for all of us, honey."

"You don't like her, do you?"

"Why would I like someone who is so blatantly rude and nasty to me? I've never done or said anything rude or nasty to her; it's not who I am. If I'm cold to her, it's to protect myself and keep my distance."

"I don't get it."

"Freddy, this isn't a good conversation for us to have. I have never said anything negative to you about your mother, and I'm not going to start now. But can I bring up one thing, if you don't mind?"

"Sure. What is it?"

"You saw how she behaved when we met for lunch by the river. She tried to make herself seem generous by sharing her drink. Did you see her give me that disgusting germy glass from a tray of dirty dishes?"

Freddy lowered his eyes and stared at the floor. "I did see that, and I thought it was gross. How come no one said anything?"

"We aren't going to start a problem with her, and we don't want to make it more uncomfortable for you than it already is. Both your father and I see it. We can't figure out if she wants a reaction or if she thinks we're stupid and we don't know it's intentional. I guess all we can do is make fun of it when we leave. Right?"

"I guess that is the best way to handle it."

"Let's find something else to talk about. She's not going to change and there's nothing anyone can do about it. It's trivial."

"I'm sorry about her."

"Honey, it's not your fault. Like your dad said. I wouldn't have even told you had you not asked. Again."

"I'm glad you answered. And I know I've asked you a million times about this. Thank you for answering this time."

"Well, buddy, I won't talk about it again, but I guess this time she crossed a line, and you've caught me at a weak moment. Oddly, it brings your father and me closer. We share the same thoughts about the situation and talk about it together."

Freddy looked up at Emma. "Well, I guess every cloud has a silver lining. Right?"

"Let me get you that drink. I'll bring in some Tylenol too."

Emma picked up the larger slice and took a bite of the pizza, shook her head, and then tossed the pizza back onto the plate. She sighed.

"I'm glad you said that to Freddy. She's out of her mind." Celia scooped up a large chunk of avocado.

"Yes, she certainly is out of her mind."

Celia opened a package of brownies. "I don't think I could separate my bad feelings toward the mother from the kid."

"It hasn't always been easy. But he's basically a good kid—he's not nasty. I agree with Fredric that she choreographed the entire performance before Freddy had the extraction. It was more important for her to barge into our house than to help her son. Now we have to move."

"What do you mean? You're moving?" Celia broke off a piece of the brownie and placed it in her mouth.

"I can't stay in a contaminated house."

Celia laughed out loud. "She's never been there before?"

"Nope!" Emma played with her second slice of pizza.

Celia's Shadow

"Wow! They're getting big." Celia reached down to pat the puppy Noah held.

"Here, take this one." He raised the adorable light-tan and white ball of fuzz up to Celia.

She took the little pup and held him close to her face. "I love this smell. There is something special about stinky puppy breath. Don't you think?"

"I like it too! But Mom hates it." He raced back for another puppy. "Here, Uncle Bill. You hold this one." Noah ran back and forth to show off a different puppy every few minutes. "I can't decide which one to keep. I want them all! Are you going to take one? You can have first choice if you want one. I love them all."

"They are cute, and they are smelly. Aren't they?" William lifted the puppy from Noah's arms.

Noah led them from the front hall into the laundry room where the puppies were spending their first few weeks on earth. Newspapers were scattered on the floor by the back door, and a low cardboard box, filled with old blankets and T-shirts, rested under the dryer. The puppies, those who were escaping Noah's hold, cuddled together into one large ball of fluff.

Celia kissed the puppy's head. "Don't you love them? They're amazingly cute. We should think about taking one."

"They kind of stink." William let the puppy lick his hand.

"William, they're puppies. It's the paper that stinks, anyway. Think about how much fun it would be to have a dog."

"You want to worry about a dog? You'll have to walk it in the rain, feed it, pay veterinarian bills and all of the other stuff that comes along with owning a dog."

"Yeah, I do. Plus, if the weather is terrible, YOU can take the dog out." She walked over to William and put the puppy up to his face. "How can you say no to this cute little face?" She turned the pup around, cuddled him like a baby, and then put him back in the blanketed box. He immediately escaped from his group of siblings resting in the box.

"You were here last week, Uncle Bill. Do the puppies look any bigger? They're over four weeks old now. I don't think they are getting bigger yet."

"You're with them all the time, Noah, so you don't see the difference. But I see it. They are definitely getting bigger." William put the puppy back in the box. He patted the head of the tan and white puppy Celia had been holding.

"Do you think they're really big too, Aunt Celia?"

"They're not big, Noah, but they're bigger every time I see them." Celia walked into the kitchen; the little tan and white dog followed her. When she left the room, he followed her again. When she came back, he followed her back in.

"Is that the puppy you were just holding and put back in the box?" William looked down at the little puppy by Celia's side.

"Which one?"

"The one that follows you around." He pointed down to the floor.

"Yeah, that's the one I gave Aunt Celia. I think he knows her." Noah was excited his uncle had paid attention. "He follows Aunt Celia around whenever she's here. See? Aunt Celia walked over to the table and he did too."

"He does?" William pointed to the little guy standing at Celia's heels.

"Yes, he always follows her." Noah picked up the puppy at her feet and handed him to Celia again. "It's like he's Aunt Celia's shadow."

"Noah's right. He's been following you around like he's your shadow since we got here."

"I guess he loves me." She hugged him and nuzzled her face into the puppy's furry face. She kissed the dog's head and then cuddled him some more.

"Someone's coming tomorrow to check them out," Noah announced to his uncle and aunt as he sat down on the floor and let the puppies jump all over him and lick his face as he laughed. "They're thinking of taking one or two of them for their grandkids. I'm trying not to think about it."

As he spoke, Celia's heart sank. She held the little puppy closer to her chest. "Try to make sure they don't take this one. Please." From the expression on her face, her fear was evident.

"Uh oh. I think your Aunt Celia has become a little too attached to this little one. I wish our lease didn't exclude pets."

"Trudy's there all the time." Noah challenged his uncle.

"Thank you, Noah. I think your uncle should be reminded of that. Trudy spent the entire summer at the apartment last year and there wasn't a problem." She tilted her head toward William.

"Let me talk to the landlord. But I signed a lease and it is a legal document."

A House

Celia kicked the covers off—she was drenched in sweat. She watched William, who slept comfortably with the pillow over his head. She moved his pillow and nudged him awake. "How can you sleep in this heat?"

"What?" He sounded drowsy.

"It's too hot. I can't believe you're able to sleep."

William, with barely opened eyes, turned toward Celia. "I was able to sleep until someone woke me up to ask me how I can sleep."

"Did you know it was going to be this hot today? There's still a little snow on the ground. How can it be this hot?"

"Celia, open a window or turn on the fan or something. I need to sleep a little longer." His voice was groggy. He rolled to his side and pulled the pillow back over his head.

Celia got out of bed, walked into the kitchen, and opened the door to the small screened porch. She stepped out and fanned herself with her hands. *Could the cold weather be over? It was freezing yesterday and now it feel like summer. What a difference.*

She started her coffee and threw on a pair of shorts and a tee shirt. She dragged a kitchen chair out to the porch and drank her coffee in the fresh air.

"Don't get too excited about this. It can change to cold as fast as it changed to warm." William leaned out the kitchen door. "I know it's officially spring, but it's supposed to cool down again tomorrow. You know what they say in New England: *If you don't like the weather, wait a minute.*"

"Oh, you're awake. I thought you wanted to sleep longer."

"I wanted to, but someone woke me up to ask me how I could sleep."

Celia apologetically grinned at William. "Sorry. I don't care if it's cold tomorrow. I plan to enjoy every second of this weather today." She propped her feet up on the railing and sipped her coffee.

William walked over to her, played with her messy ponytail, and then walked away. He drank his coffee at the kitchen counter as he read the Sunday *Globe* on his iPad. "You want to go out for brunch?"

Celia basked in the warm sunshine on the back porch. "That's a great idea! Can we bring Noah? Melanie told me he won't leave the puppies, and she needs some space and time to clean their room."

"Sure. I'll text her to see if he can come with us."

"That will make her very happy. Yesterday she told me Noah's driving her nuts with the daily barrage of questions. He pleads with her every two minutes to keep the three puppies that haven't been taken yet."

Celia's yogurt parfait was filled with homemade granola and topped with coconut and toasted almonds. It was tasty but paled in comparison to the boys' breakfast. Their pancakes covered in caramelized bananas, brown sugar, and praline pecans, topped with maple syrup was irresistible to Celia–she finished William's leftovers. *Maybe I'll try to be healthy again tomorrow. That was worth the sugar rush.*

"What should we do after brunch?" Celia wanted to spend more time with Noah. *Let's give your mom a longer break than this hour and a half.*

"Can we take a drive by the beach? We can get Trudy." Noah smacked his hand to his forehead. "Oh wait, Trudy can't leave the puppies. What was I thinking?"

"We can still take a ride if you want. Maybe we can stop for a treat someplace." Celia turned to Noah.

"Breakfast wasn't sweet enough. Right, Noah?" William picked up the check from the corner of the table.

"Meet me outside." William took out his wallet as they walked to the cash register. "I'll be right there." He handed the car keys to Celia.

Celia started the car and opened the sunroof.

William got into the car, sat in the driver's seat, buckled his seat belt, and handed Celia and Noah the same house hunter guide he held in his own hand.

"What's this?" Celia inspected the house on the cover of the guide.

"I picked them up at the cash register."

"Was this a plan?" She flipped through the first few pages.

"No, I swear. I saw the booklets and spontaneously decided to pick them up." William grinned. "I thought this would be fun. Let's each look at the pictures and circle twenty houses we want to see." He handed pens to both Celia and Noah. "Should we limit the selections to five cities?"

"I thought we didn't want to do this right now?" She formed a question from her statement.

"I know. But I thought this would be fun. Don't you think it will be?"

"I do! I think it will be a lot of fun!" Noah's response was filled with excitement. "I've already picked out some houses."

"Should we limit our choices to five cities?" William waited for her response.

"Good idea!" Celia studied the guide.

"Noah, you pick a city and Celia will pick another one. Then I'll pick one. How's that sound?"

They each selected a nearby city and discussed the last two choices together.

"Let's take a few minutes and each of us will go through our booklets. Circle your favorite twenty houses. If we find houses that match, we'll visit those. Oh, and they have to be open houses." William clicked his pen and opened his booklet.

"Hey, I have a match game that works like this. If you turn over two cards at the same time and they match, you get to keep them. The one with the most cards wins." Noah's excitement intensified.

Celia laughed at William and then bit off the cap from her pen. Other than the sound of the pages turning, the car was silent as they reviewed homes for sale and made their selections.

"We all set?" William turned to Noah, who sat in the backseat. "Let's compare our choices and see if we matched any of the houses. We'll go through them all and then pick the top seven choices. How's that sound?"

"It sounds crazy." She recapped the pen.

"This is wicked fun!" Noah leaned forward and pushed his head toward the front seat between Celia and Uncle Bill.

With each match found, Celia tore the page from the guide and held it on her lap. They agreed upon six houses.

"Let's find new construction first and then we'll head out to the other houses if there's still time. Agree?"

"Whatever you say, Mr. Full-Of-Surprises." Celia organized the new construction by location. "We can begin with the one closest to this starting point."

William plugged the address into the GPS. Within ten minutes, they drove up to the first house on the list.

"Here we are." William turned off the car.

"It's beautiful. What do you think, Noah?" Celia looked at the big gray house.

"Is there a pool in the back?"

William laughed. "Let's hope not."

"A pool would be wicked awesome!"

"Maybe we'll get friendly with neighbors who have a pool." Celia was also not interested in a pool.

"My parents don't want a pool either. I guess a kid can hope, right?" Noah's excitement dropped down a level.

Celia turned around and observed him as if he were a stranger. *Funny kid.* "Remember, Noah, the beach is less than a half hour from here."

"Well, Celia, should we check it out? It's nice from the outside, and I like this neighborhood. How about you, Noah—other than the pool thing?"

Celia unbuckled her seat belt and was out of the car in a matter of seconds. Noah ran out back to see if there was a pool, even though he was told there wasn't. William and Celia walked through the front door into an amazing foyer.

The real estate agent walked into the room with a piece of paper and a pen. "Would you mind filling out a little information? The school system is wonderful in this town." She handed the sheet to Celia.

She must think Noah's our son. Until that moment, Celia had never given much thought to school systems or bus routes. She now envisioned their children as they boarded the school bus with their lunches and backpacks. *Maybe two children, perhaps more. We'll get a big fluffy dog who sleeps in their bedroom.* She shook her head back to reality and continued to walk around the house.

The house was large, certainly large enough for a family. An oversized family room was open to the kitchen. The kitchen could hold an army of friends and relatives.

"Hey, I thought you were trying to surprise me, but there really isn't a pool." Noah walked through the kitchen's sliding door, his disappointment obvious by his slouched shoulders. His aunt and uncle were engrossed in the details of the kitchen.

Celia and William walked to the beginning of the hall and looked down toward the bedrooms. "I hate this." She pointed to the seams where the bedroom carpets met the hallway carpet. "The different colors come together like patchwork. It's all broken up."

Noah remained downstairs, where he ate cookies and drank lemonade. Celia heard him tell the agent about his cute puppies. She also heard him ask whether it would be hard to put a pool in the backyard. Noah then suggested the agent show them only houses with pools.

"Sounds like he's trying to sell his puppies. Can you hear him? He asked her to show us a house with a pool." Celia was amused by her new nephew. "I couldn't buy this house, based on the carpet colors. It would be expensive to replace all the carpeting. This could have been a great house, if the decorator had any taste."

William gave her a slight push and put his finger to his mouth.

Their conversation was cut short as the agent approached. "Any questions?"

"It's not exactly our style," Celia glanced down at the flooring.

"What are you searching for? I have many other listings."

"We're not sure."

"This is the first house we've seen. We just started to look at houses." William glanced into the adjoining bathroom as he spoke.

"If you're interested, let me know. Another couple came in for their second visit and they might make an offer."

"Too much color for our taste." Celia refrained from making a face.

"It is colorful, isn't it? Let me give you my card. There are a lot of new homes in this area. Why don't you stop by a few of our other open houses? You might find something more suited to your style. Cherry Tree Lane has a lot of new homes." She handed Celia a paper with information on the development. "They're designed similar to this one, but more neutral, if you know what I mean. Some are still in the construction phase, which gives you an opportunity to select your own colors, cabinets, paint, floors, and even appliances." She winked at Celia as she finished her sentence, and then gave directions to the other home sites.

"I think my head is spinning. I'm starting to confuse one house with the other." Celia walked next to Noah as they headed toward the car.

"Me too." Noah joined in. "Sure wish at least one of the houses had a pool."

"Yeah, the pool thing isn't going to happen. Sorry, honey."

"Yeah, I know. Sprinklers are fun too. And Trudy loves to bite at the water."

"Anyone ready to call it a day?" She put her arm around Noah's shoulder and gave him a hug. "Let's get you home to the puppies. How's that sound?"

"That sounds great." Noah's excitement for getting home sounded greater than his excitement for visiting pool-free houses.

"Thank you. I got a chance to clean up the puppy room, take Trudy for a quick walk, and chill for a while. Glen's still at a ball game and I had a happy day of me time." Melanie showed Celia her freshly painted fingernails. "How was your day?"

"We had fun, but I think we bored him to pieces this last hour. We got involved with taking a ride to see open houses."

"He'll be fine. He's already in there with the puppies. Are you guys buying a house?"

"We spontaneously decided to visit open houses. We found a new development on Cherry Tree Lane in Georgetown. It was fun. I'll keep you posted."

"Was Noah bummed we didn't see the houses we circled?" Celia asked William.

"No. He was too busy being bummed because we didn't see houses with swimming pools."

"Is this the right time to buy a house?"

"If you think about it, Celia, this is as good a time as any."

"Yeah, you're right. I'm a little confused about all the options they talked about. Aren't you?"

"A little bit. Which one was your favorite? The one on Cherry Tree with the big white kitchen, right?"

"Yup. If you couldn't figure that out, then you don't know me very well. I have the spec sheet right here." She lightly hit his cheek as she waved the sheet in the air by his face.

"You want to drive by it again?" He was already driving in the direction of the house with the big white kitchen.

"Definitely. I want to see it again and pay more attention. Right now, I feel confused and overwhelmed by everything. I need to focus on it." She picked up the spec sheet and read the details again.

"It might be too late to go inside. The open house is probably over, but we could call and make an appointment to see it tomorrow or later this week."

"You do realize this is totally insane, right?" Her voice elevated with excitement.

"I don't know about that. Why do you say it's insane?"

"Because no one in their right mind goes out for brunch and buys a house. Maybe they buy house supplies, towels, sheets, and ice cream, whatever. I've never heard of spontaneously buying a house. Have you?"

"No, but–" He didn't finish his sentence–there was no rebuttal. It was insane. He knew it.

The open house was closed.

The Flower

"Hey, Celia, I missed you yesterday. How was your weekend?" Emma walked into Celia's office.

"Interesting." Celia giggled with enthusiasm.

"How was it interesting?" Emma sat down and excitedly waited to hear Celia's news.

"I think we bought a house."

"WHAT?" Emma jumped up and threw her arms around Celia. "This is so exciting. Tell me everything!"

"There isn't much to tell. We saw a house Sunday and then again yesterday. We put an offer in this morning. Now we're waiting to hear. I've been anxious since Sunday and I need a distraction. You better have a good story."

"Forget about that crazy one. Those stories aren't important but hearing about the house is. Tell me about the house. I want details from YOU this time."

"I can't talk about it, because I don't want to jinx anything. I haven't told anyone else. Well, except you and Kate, but that's it. I need a distraction before I get the call that they've rejected our offer." Celia leaned to her right and started her espresso machine. "Our coffee will be ready in a minute." She took a container of biscotti and placed it on her desk.

"Come on. Don't say that. If they reject it, you'll counter. Then they'll counter and then you'll all negotiate and then you'll move in. Do you love the house? Tell me about it."

"I wasn't even going to tell this much, but I'm too excited to hold it in. I'll tell you more this afternoon when we get an answer. I mean, IF we get an answer. I need you to entertain me, or I'll burst."

"I get it. I'm that way too. You'll have to tell me every detail once your offer is accepted. I want to know the whole shebang. Where?

How many rooms? Bedrooms. Bathrooms. Kitchen. Especially the kitchen. Everything."

"Absolutely. But you have to have something to distract me with today." Celia put her hands together as she pleaded for a story from Emma.

"You have to beg? I told you, I have years of stories. I didn't see Freddy over the weekend, so nothing new here. But you know I have an encyclopedia of tales from the past."

"Start chirping."

"Celia, it's cathartic to write about it. Jillian always told me it would be therapeutic, and she was right. When the event I'm telling you about happened, I barely knew Edie. It's a quickie, but it's clear what a schemer she is. Freddy was on the basketball team in high school. Edie went to every game, which she should be, since she's the mother. She always arrived later than us, and she always sat a row or two behind us. Fredric said she wanted us in front, so she could watch us. I told him he was nuts. One time we got there later than she did, and we were the ones who sat behind HER. When everyone stood for the national anthem, she got up and moved right behind Fredric."

"Emma, you have got to be kidding."

"Crazy, right? It was the first time ever that she hasn't sat behind us."

It was chilly inside the basketball court. Emma nuzzled close to Fredric for warmth. She felt a nervous pit in her stomach each time she saw Fredric's ex-wife walk into the gymnasium. She was uncomfortable being scrutinized and taunted.

Minutes before the game, right on schedule, Edie walked across the wooden floor. She stopped, glanced around, and located Emma and Fredric. She walked up the steps to their general area. And then, in the row in front of them, four people to the right, she sat down. Emma kept her head faced forward but moved her eyes to watch Edie. *That's odd. She's never sat in front of us before, at least not intentionally.*

At each pass or shot that involved Freddy, Edie stood up, cheered, and turned toward Emma. Edie didn't look at Emma; she simply turned her body toward her. Emma tried to ignore the ex-wife but found herself sneaking peeks throughout the first half of the game. *Shit! I've become her. I'm the one gawking now. I have to stop.*

Edie stood up at least a dozen times and turned toward Emma every time. Emma tried to act calm and disinterested. Finally, she leaned in toward Fredric. "Have you noticed she's not behind us?"

"Uh huh." Fredric kept his head straight as he faced the court.

"What is she up to? She keeps turning toward us."

"Not sure. But I wondered the same thing. I can guarantee you it's not innocent that she sat there. My guess is it has something to do with the flower."

"What flower?" Emma furrowed her brow and turned toward Edie. "I don't see a flower."

"She has a flower on the front of her sweater. I noticed a few women around her also have flowers."

After the second quarter, fans got up and moved around. Edie worked her way toward Emma and Fredric. Unlike most people who faced the court as they left the stands, Edie's back was to the court. She stopped walking when she arrived face-to-face with Emma.

"Didn't you get a flower? We all got them." Edie smirked at Emma. "Oh, I guess the flowers are only for the mothers of the players. Fathers' girlfriends don't count." Edie snickered and continued her way out of the stands.

"Wow, she's more small-minded than I could have imagined. It's amusing." Emma couldn't help but laugh.

Fredric squeezed her thigh. He whispered into her ear. "I thought they were for the mother fuc–"

Emma cut off his words as she put her hand over his mouth. "Shhh! I hate that phrase. Someone could hear you."

"I've said it before and I'll say it again. I don't know how you do it."

"I view it this way, Celia. It's a chronic condition that no one else can truly understand unless they have experienced it firsthand."

"I don't think anyone could experience this same craziness. Don't you ever want to say something to her?"

"There's nothing to say. She's a nut. Freddy got several baskets during that game. When the game was over, we all walked out of the gym together. The father of one of Freddy's friends came over and wanted to take Freddy's picture. Freddy was out of his mind excited. Edie told the man he should take HER picture since she's the mother and without her, Freddy wouldn't be here to score the points."

"Wow! What kind of mother tries to steal their kid's thunder? You think it was for your benefit?"

"I guess so. The entire team should have thanked her for birthing Freddy, so he could score those points."

"You're funny."

"Let me know the second you hear anything on the house. Then you can tell me all about it."

A Strange Noise

As Celia walked up the front steps to their apartment, she saw a light coming through the front door. *Why isn't the door closed?* She pushed the door fully open and then closed it securely behind her, bolting the lock and hooking the chain.

"William?" She waited a few seconds for an answer. "William, I'm home. Where are you?" She curiously checked the front room and searched for William. She heard a strange noise coming from the kitchen. It sounded like clicking or scraping, certainly a noise she had not heard before. "William?" She anxiously called out to him again. *Something's wrong! I just know it.*

Suddenly the sound of clicking stopped as the little paws reached the rug and the puppy ran to her. "Oh my God! What are you doing here, you little muffin?" She reached down and grabbed the pup. A grinning William and an excited Noah appeared by the kitchen door.

"Surprise!" Noah jumped into the hallway.

"What's this?" She closely held the puppy she knew so well. Her little furry friend was now securely in her arms. He licked her nose, cheeks, and chin.

"Celia, this is Shadow. He's been anxious for his new mom to get home."

"This is the best surprise ever. Why didn't you tell me?"

"Then it wouldn't be a surprise, would it?" William walked over and patted the puppy's head.

"No, I guess not. When did you pick him up?"

"This afternoon. Noah and I were dying as we tried to keep this a secret."

"How long have you been trying to keep it a secret?"

"Since about the first time you saw him. Last week when I watched him follow you around, I knew he belonged to you. I hope you don't mind, but when I heard Noah call him Aunt Celia's shadow, I decided his name had to be Shadow."

"I agreed!" Noah shrieked with enthusiasm. "Will you keep his name? You can change it, but we thought it kind of fit."

"Fit? It's perfect. I love the name! I love him! I love you guys!" She squeezed Shadow and held him with his belly up. She rubbed his stomach and kissed his little wet nose. "This is the sweetest surprise ever." She continued to cuddle and kiss Shadow. "What about the no-pet clause in the lease?"

"There isn't a pet clause in the lease. We didn't want you to know about the surprise we were planning. Right, Noah?"

"He's adorable. I love him." She nuzzled her face in his belly.

"Good. I'm glad you're happy. I think he needs to go out for a quick walk." William handed her the leash.

"Oh no! It's cold out." Celia shrugged and shivered as she put Shadow down on the floor.

"It's not cold, my dear. It's a little chilly, but not cold."

"I'll take him. We can go together." Noah took the leash and hooked it to Shadow's blue collar.

Together, Noah, Celia, and Shadow headed out to the street. It was Shadow's first walk to Pete's.

THE CLOSING

"Ready to do this?" Celia sounded anxious. She and William sat on the front steps of their almost-new-home.

"Yup. No turning back now." He reached over and gently rubbed her back.

"I guess we're close now." She watched a little white car pull into the driveway. Keith's truck arrived seconds later. "Why is Keith here? Does the developer need to be at the closing?"

"I don't think so. I'm more curious why the attorney isn't here than I am why Keith is."

"Who's the guy in the white car? I thought that was going to be the attorney, but it's not. Why isn't she here?" Celia sounded anxious. "Not getting a good feeling right about now." She squeezed her lips together and glanced at her watch. "No lawyer and we're supposed to close in ten minutes. What's going on? Who's the guy in the car? This is falling apart. I can feel it."

"No idea who that guy is. Let's wait to see what Keith says. Don't worry." William paused and watched the stranger in the car. "Don't worry. YET!"

"Hi guys." Keith walked up to the nervous couple. They watched the man in the white car gather papers and slowly get out of his car. Keith looked reassuringly at William and Celia. "Stay calm and follow my lead. Everything will be fine. This guy is from the town and I'll explain as we go along. I spoke to your lawyer and she knows there's a delay."

"What's going on, Keith?" Celia's stomach dropped at the fact that Keith called their lawyer. *Nope, folks, it wasn't an earthquake. It was my stomach plummeting. Stay calm, like Keith said. Stay calm. Calm is the key word. Did I put on deodorant? Doesn't feel like I did. I know I did. Shit! This isn't a good thing. I can feel it.*

The pudgy bald man slammed the car door shut and marched toward them. The long thinning hair from the left side of his head was combed over to the right side and bounced up and down as he clomped in their direction. He pulled off his light-brown wrinkled jacket and threw it over his left shoulder. His sweat-stained short-sleeved shirt was too tight for his protruding stomach; his shirt buttons appeared as if they would pop off if he took one big breath. He didn't look happy.

"This is definitely deodorant failure." She leaned in and whispered to William as the man approached them.

"Got a little problem here, ladies and gentlemen." He stopped in front of Celia, William, and Keith, who now stood at the front steps of the house they might not buy.

He handed a stack of papers to William, who read a few lines and then passed them over to Celia. She glanced at the papers and gave them back to the little man.

"What's this all about?" Celia's voice quivered as she spoke. She tried to take Keith's advice.

"You can't move into this house without a CO."

"A CO?" *Too bad I don't buy houses every day. Maybe if I did, I could understand your stupid lingo, you ass.*

"A Certificate of Occupancy. You can't move in without one, and I'm the guy to give it to you, and I'm not giving you one."

"Oh, sorry. I guess I should have known what a CO is. And why won't you be providing us with that CO?" Celia's sarcasm was obvious. William tugged at her elbow.

William stood straighter than normal. He was much taller than the little, bald, pudgy town worker, but a great deal less powerful in this situation.

"Hi, I'm Keith Warren, the developer of this community. What seems to be the problem, sir?" He stretched his arm out to shake the other man's hand.

Ignoring the intended handshake, the short balding man with the tight shirt began to speak. "Mr. Warren, I won't issue a CO unless those trees get moved closer to the sidewalk." He pointed to the two young sugar maples that had recently been planted by the edge of the property. "Without a CO, the bank won't release the funds for the closing." His tone was confrontational and disagreeable. "That's what the problem is."

Why would they want to move trees closer to the sidewalk? They're smack in the middle of the strip of land now. Celia was annoyed. She was about to question the man when William inconspicuously shook his head to signal her not to say anything else.

Celia walked with William to get his cell phone from the car. "You don't have to be an MIT engineer to know that if they move the trees closer to the sidewalk, the roots are going to lift and crack the pavement as they grow. This guy's an asshole." Her frustration was apparent.

"Shhh! This guy has the power right now. Let's hang tight."

"Where's Keith?" She was beginning to panic.

"I don't know. I didn't see him leave. Did you?"

"I just asked where he is. I think that would indicate that I didn't see him leave! Oh God."

"Calm down. It's going to be fine."

"Sorry."

Keith walked onto the property. Several tall, well-built men followed him into the driveway. Each of them carried large shovels.

"What's going on?" Celia raced up to Keith.

"These guys work with me, and they'll move the trees to wherever this dickhead wants them to go. We can move them back next week once you get into the house. Don't worry, I've had to work with morons from his office before. Usually he won't issue the CO if the driveway isn't paved. They throw their power around and hope we'll pay them off to allow us to keep the trees as they are. We'll move them now and then again. It's no problem. Trust me."

Famous last words. "What about the closing?" She had fear in her voice.

"Your lawyer called me. She'll be here in an hour. I figure this jerk will be gone by then. My lawyer is on his way too," Keith assured her.

"Why didn't she call us?"

"She said she tried, but there was no answer."

Shit! We left the phone in William's car when we got here.

"Sorry about this." The lawyer referred to her four-year-old son who trailed along by her side. "With the delay, I was afraid I'd miss his pick-up time from day care, so you have me and my sidekick for the closing."

"It's all good." With tears in her eyes, Celia laughed. "I'm happy to see you."

"Let's go into the model home and get the paperwork done in the office there." Keith motioned for them to follow him across the street.

"Is this normal?" Celia walked next to Keith.

"It's not common, but we've had to deal with situations like this in the past. The town has strange guidelines for these new developments." Keith handed Celia and William a bottle of champagne and a gift box, which held the keys to their new home. "You're all set for now. We'll move the trees back next week. Don't worry about anything."

"We're homeowners now." William gave Celia a huge hug and kissed her forehead. She squeezed him back. They walked across the street to their new home.

Celia stood in the foyer and looked up the staircase, into the living room, and then into the dining room. "Can you believe this? It feels like yesterday this was a construction zone and now it's our home? I love it! I simply love it."

Moving Day

Celia sat on the front porch as she waited for William to return with iced coffee. When he pulled into the driveway, she breathed a huge sigh of relief.

"I'm afraid to be in the house without you here. It's foreign to me. And with Shadow at Noah's, I freaked about being alone."

"Why are you worried, Celia? You've moved before. And it went relatively smoothly–once the trees were repositioned."

"I think the crazy closing zapped me a little. Plus, the way things started out, I'm surprised we're not having a torrential storm right now."

"Don't let the tree thing take away from the excitement of being homeowners. We'll get a lot done today and it will be fine." William reassuringly kissed her forehead before he walked away.

"Yeah, you're right."

Celia walked through the house and wiped down windowsills and countertops. "The truck's here!" She ran into the hallway to get William and greet the movers.

"You check off the boxes on this sheet." She handed him a printed sheet that contained box numbers. To the right of the number, the contents were listed. "I want to keep track of everything to make sure nothing is missing."

The five movers paraded into the house and filled the first floor with furniture and cartons. The kitchen was bursting with cardboard containers. *I don't remember this many boxes. I'll never get them emptied.* She spun around the kitchen as she counted the boxes.

She moved to the sink and pulled the tape from the carton closest to the sink. *Don't look at any other box. Focus on this one. Pretend they aren't there. One at a time–one at a time.* She lifted the wrapped glasses from the top of the box, unwrapped the paper, and placed them into the sink. She pushed the sink stopper, poured in liquid soap, and ran the water. As the glasses were unwrapped, one by one, she placed them into the warm soapy water. When the oversized white farmhouse sink was filled, she let the glassware soak.

Half of Celia's ponytail had fallen out of the coated band. The hairs on the back of her neck were drenched and clammy. Her tee shirt clung to her body and was splattered with water.

Of course, it's the hottest day on the face of the earth. She filled a Styrofoam bucket with ice and dropped in a dozen bottles of water, which she brought outside to the movers. "Sorry I don't have anything else to offer you, but we're just moving in." *You're such an idiot. Of course you're just moving in. Why do you think they're here in the first place?*

She brought a water over to William, who obediently attempted to check off the boxes on the list.

"Celia, we have to give up on your little checklist. There are five guys and they're hustling. I can't keep stopping them to check the box number. You good with that?"

"Sure. Whatever. I guess I'll have to trust that a box marked *dining room* will be delivered to the dining room."

"Yeah, I think that's a good idea. I'm willing to bet these guys have moved people into houses before."

She laughed and walked back into the house.

As Celia wiped down the sinks in the master bedroom, a large, attractive man entered the bedroom. He carried a nightstand as easily as Celia carried a bag of groceries. His skin was flawless.

"Where do you want this?" His voice was deep and musical.

"The bed is going on this wall." She pointed to the large empty wall between two windows. "If you can put it anywhere over there, that will be good. Make sure there'll be room for the bed." Two other men, one short and one tall, walked into the room as they carried a large bureau.

"How about this?" The taller man held most of the bureau. The shorter man was obviously his helper.

"I don't know where to put it. How about there?" She pointed to the wall between the closet and the bathroom door.

The men all looked at one another and stood momentarily still. They placed the large piece of furniture across from the bed and not at the location to which she pointed.

Hmm? What's this about?

"Here's the deal, ma'am," the first man said. "We're going to put the dresser over here and if you want to move it once the other furniture is in, we'll rearrange it. We promise."

Oh, there's that stupid M-word again. Celia looked confused but agreed to their deal.

They left the room to return with the box spring, mattress, and bed frame. "Put it against this wall." The tallest man pointed to the wall as he instructed his helpers where to place and set up the bed structure.

"I guess you know your business, don't you? I don't think I would have picked that wall for the bureau, but it looks great and I'm leaving it there. Thank you." She walked over to the bureau and wiped off the dust on top of it.

"I've been moving furniture for a long time. You get an eye for these things. If we had put it on the other wall, you would have wanted it over here." He pointed to the perfectly placed bureau.

"Looks great!" She followed the big man with the melodious voice out of the room.

Celia opened another box in the kitchen. *This must be the millionth box I've unpacked.* She opened the cooler and took out a bottle of water. She twisted off the cap and gulped down half of the contents.

Her forearms were raw and red. Each time she pulled an item from a box, her arms rubbed against the hard cardboard. Her hands were chafed from washing dishes and glassware.

Celia reached in for another glass. *Shit.* She instantly pulled her hand out of the box–her index and middle fingers dripped with blood. With her bloody hand wrapped in her tee shirt, she carefully searched until she found the broken glass and the shards around it.

"Hey, hon, do you know where the box with the suntan lotion is?"

"You're kidding, right?" She looked up at him with her eyes opened wide. Between the water that had splashed from the gooseneck faucet and her own sweat, her shirt was soaked and bloodstained. "I think you'll have to live with your sunburn, darling, because I haven't a clue as to where the suntan lotion is." Her sarcasm was evident. She continued to rinse her stemware.

William walked up to her. He stood behind her and put his arms around to the front of her waist. He leaned in and kissed her clammy neck. "Delicious!" He placed his strong hands on her shoulders and began to massage her upper back. "Do you want me to stay in here with you and do this stuff?"

She moved her head back and rested it against his shoulders. "No. We need to make sure that truck is empty as soon as possible. If you could run down to Pete's and get sandwiches for the guys, that would be great."

"Ah! Remember? Pete's is no longer a run-down-to kind of place."

She laughed out loud. "I forgot where we are. Well, run down to that little shopping strip mall over by North Street. Make sure you get some ice and something cold for the guys to drink. Then get back to work. I mean get to work. No more standing in the sunshine."

"You got it." He saluted her and then kissed her sweaty cheeks before he walked away.

The home of Celia and William Charles was slowly coming together. Every bone in her body ached.

Cherry Tree Lane

"Welcome back. That was a long two weeks without you. How'd the move go?" Emma sat down at their corner table.

"Check these out." Celia handed Emma her cell phone set to a selected photo gallery. With her index finger, Emma slid the screen from right to left.

Celia removed her chicken and pesto sandwich from her lunch bag and placed it on the paper towel she had included with her lunch.

"How did you get everything organized in such a short time?" Emma advanced through the pictures. "Wow! It's beautiful!" Celia leaned in toward Emma to more clearly see the pictures as they displayed on the screen of her phone. "It looks as if you've lived there forever."

"I worked nonstop that entire time off. Threw out the last box yesterday. There's still a lot to do, but I'm done with the worst part. Now I need to put things away and organize. I can take that slow and do a little every night. I'm getting used to it, but it's weird when I wake up in the middle of the night. It takes me a minute to realize where I am."

"I know what you mean. Isn't that such a strange feeling?" Emma continued to swipe her fingers on the screen to see the pictures.

"There you have it! 18 Cherry Tree Lane." Celia beamed.

Emma dropped the phone onto the table. Her color faded. "What's the address again?" She seemed anxious as she took a deep, slow breath and picked up the phone.

"It's 18 Cherry Tree Lane." Celia loved to say the address of her new home.

"I can't believe we never discussed the location." Emma still held the phone in her hand.

"It all happened fast. We went for brunch and now we have a house. I didn't realize I never told you where the house is. Do you know the street?" Celia looked at Emma, whose face had gone white.

"Um." Emma took another deep breath and hesitated. "No, I don't think so. I thought you said something else."

"What's wrong?"

"I don't know. I got a little dizzy or something. I'm sure it's nothing. I'm a little freaked out today because it's the anniversary of Jillian's death. Something must have prompted me to think about her." She continued to flip through the pictures.

Celia was concerned. She put her hand on Emma's arm. The color in Emma's face returned to normal. She was obviously distraught about something, and Celia didn't believe the anniversary of Jillian's death was the problem.

"Are you sure you're all right, Emma? Take a sip of water." Celia opened her bottle of water and handed it to Emma.

Emma took the bottle and sipped slowly. "Tell me about each room in the house." Emma's breathing returned to normal. She turned the phone inward, to help Celia more easily see the screen. "I want to hear every detail about each picture."

Celia looked at her friend with a curious eye. "Should I be worried about you?"

"No, you shouldn't be. Please, I'm fine. And in case you are wondering, no, I'm not pregnant. It was a moment. It happens sometimes. I'm good to go. I want to see these pics. What's this?"

Celia leaned in. "This is my favorite room," Celia explained with pride. "It overlooks a small pond in the back. There's a great blue heron who has been there every day since we moved in. The builder said it's lived there as long as he's worked in the development. Can you see him through the window?" Celia extended her fingers over the screen and enlarged the picture and then moved her hand away.

"That's amazing! He's beautiful!" Emma took another sip from the bottled water and examined the pictures. "I love it." She scrolled to another photo of a small room surrounded by windows. "And what's this?"

"That's a little sunporch right off the kitchen. The family room is on the left of the kitchen and this room is off to the right. It's a three-season room. It has heat, but it isn't insulated that well."

"I love it, Celia. It's beautiful. Show me the kitchen."

Celia took the phone and found the first of a stream of kitchen pictures. "You'll have to come to visit." Celia watched Emma's color drain again. "Emma, you look pale."

"I'm fine. It's a tough day for me. I was exhausted over the weekend. I think I need a vacation."

"I'm sorry. Here I am going through this and you're upset about Jillian."

"I'm good. I want to see these pictures." Emma scrutinized every picture. "I love the white cabinets. Is the countertop marble?"

"No, it's quartz. Doesn't it look like marble? It's the appearance of marble without the headache and scratches."

"It's beautiful. The white cabinets are fantastic. The beading around the shaker border is fabulous. It's subtle, but you can still see it." Emma stopped at a picture of the range. "Is that a commercial stove?"

"Yes, it's incredible–I love it." Celia reached over and swiped to the next picture. "Can you see the hood? It's custom made and the nail heads make it look like a piece of art."

"It's magnificent. I'm super happy for you and William. It's amazing! Find me a picture of the master bathroom." Emma handed the phone back to Celia. Celia scrolled through a group of pictures and then returned the phone back to Emma.

"Nice whirlpool tub. What's this?" Emma pointed to a unique fixture on the ceiling over the tub.

"Get this. This rain showerhead fills the jetted tub from the ceiling. It makes the most wonderful sound as it rains into the tub. I've never seen that before. Have you?"

"Ah, no. Never. I've never seen anything like this. It's beautiful." Emma leaned toward Celia and hugged her. "I'm so excited for your new home and puppy. The husband? He's already old hat." She laughed. "How's Shadow enjoying the new house?"

"He's good. He runs around in the backyard all morning chasing the birds. I'm glad it's fenced in."

Lemon-Scented

Celia backed into a parking space across the street from the restaurant where she was to meet Kate. As she turned off the car, Kate pulled into the space directly ahead of her. She flashed her lights twice and waved out the window. Kate lightly tapped the horn.

"Thank you for meeting me for dinner. William and Shadow are fending for themselves. I badly need a break from house stuff." Celia made a dramatic gesture of exhaustion.

"How're you doing and how's the house coming along?" Kate greeted Celia with a kiss on her cheek.

"Doing great. Love the new house." She pulled her sweater together and buttoned the bottom four buttons. There was a chill in the air.

"And how is Shadow doing? I know you were concerned." Kate walked with her arm snuggled into Celia's elbow.

"He's doing good. He tells me every morning how much he loves the new house." Celia laughed.

"I'm sure you actually believe he tells you that."

Celia rolled her eyes at Kate. "Do you mind if we stop in here first? I'm afraid they might be closed by the time we finish dinner." Celia pointed to the Soap Chest, which was across the street from the restaurant. "I want to get something special for Emma. She's been in a funk. She lost her cousin a few years ago, and the anniversary was the other day."

"What an adorable little shop." Kate held the door for Celia. Brass chimes rang as they entered the shop.

A woman wearing a flowery print dress came out from the back room. "Can I help you? Are you looking for anything special?"

"We're just browsing. Hoping to find a lemon-scented body cream or scrub, but I'm open to other options too."

"Take your time and let me know if you need my help. The moisturizers and bath gels are all grouped together in the back. The soaps, loofas, oils, and bath toys are on both sides up here in the front. Most everything comes in a variety of scents. The brand on the front table comes in a soft lemon scent you might like. There are testers all over the shop. Feel free to sample anything."

A display up front consisted of beautifully packaged massage oils, body washes, and bath powders. "These are gorgeous." Kate opened one of the oil samplers and inhaled the fragrance. "I love lavender. Did you see how pretty this foaming soap is wrapped?"

"I can't decide what I want to get. Should I get a perfume she can wear or something for her house or office, maybe a room diffuser?"

"I think I'll start my Christmas shopping." Kate's excitement for Christmas shopping was apparent. "Great idea! Right?"

"A little early for that, isn't it? Can't you at least wait until the fall?"

"Yeah, but this kind of stuff doesn't take up much space."

Celia walked toward the back of the store and Kate ambled to the right where a display of body mitts hung on the wall. The table by Kate held a variety of lovely gifts all packaged like antique treasures. Kate picked up each one and sniffed the wrapping. Celia sprayed her way through the colorful dispensers on a back shelf.

Celia pumped the handle of a ginger cream. The ginger lotion squirted out and splattered onto the front of her sweater. She checked to see whether Kate saw the lotion spit on her and then quickly wiped it off. After testing eight or nine *Try Me* samples, she walked over to a display against the back wall of the store.

With the absence of a dispensing pump, Celia twisted the cap open and poured a little into her palm. *Wow, this is a full-bodied lemon smell. This might fit the bill for Emma.* The consistency was watery, and more than she anticipated poured out from the bottle. She rubbed her hands together and tried to absorb the liquid and then rubbed it on her wrist. The fragrance was overpowering in such a large dose. She rapidly waved her arms in the air to dry the moisture and calm down the scent. She walked over to Kate and put her wrist right below Kate's nose. "What about this scent?"

Kate pulled her head away. "Phew! That's strong." She then leaned in closer and smelled it again. "You hit the jackpot with the lemon. Maybe when it wears down it will be nicer."

"I kind of like it." Celia put her wrist up to her nose and inhaled deeply. "It's too watery, though. I'm not sure it's a good choice, because so much poured out when I took the cap off."

"Let me try that again." Kate sniffed Celia's wrist. "Something about that smell is strange. Where did you get it?"

"Over in the back corner. I'll show you." As they walked to the back of the shop, they tested various hair products and bath gels along the way.

Celia sniffed her wrist again. "I like this. I think I'll get Emma this lemon stuff. It's fading a little bit now, don't you think?" She once more put her wrist under Kate's nose.

"It's a little better now." Kate rubbed her nose.

When they arrived at the back corner, Celia picked up the lemony lotion she had sampled. She removed the cap and poured a small amount into her palms. "See how watery it is? Is it a shower gel or a lotion? It's not an oil." Celia put the cap back on and smelled it again. "The front of the container is cute with the flowers on it. Can you read it? The print's too small for me." She gave Emma's potential gift to Kate. "Is it a regular body moisturizer?"

Kate pulled her glasses down from the top of her head and turned the bottle around to read the small print on the back. "Celia, you're too cute." She burst out laughing.

"What? Kate, what's so funny? Is it a bath gel?"

Kate's infectious laughter caused Celia to laugh as well, although she had no idea why Kate was laughing.

Kate put the bottle down. "I don't think you want to get this for Emma." She teased Celia as she held back from revealing the intended purpose for the watery solution. "Celia, I want you to try to guess what this is."

"Oh no! Is it some sort of sex lube? Was I about to buy her porno potion?"

Kate laughed again. "No, it's not sexual, you dope!"

"Tell me what it is!" Celia demanded.

"I'll tell you, but I wanted to make you guess first. It's poop stuff."

"What do you mean? What's poop stuff?" Celia seized it back from Kate and held it out as far as her arm could go. "I still can't read what it is. Tell me what you're talking about."

"It's that stuff you spray in the toilet bowl. You spray it in the water and the poop doesn't stink. Haven't you ever heard of this?" Kate didn't wait for Celia to answer. "It's the refill for the toilet spray. You almost got Emma a really shitty gift." She air-quoted the word shitty. "You're quite entertaining, Celia. You have no idea."

Celia was now laughing. As she winced with disgust, she rubbed her hands together vigorously to get the lotion off. She saw the humor in the incident but was also embarrassed and horrified that she almost bought this as a gift for her work friend.

"Celia, don't freak out. It's only a smell. It's not as if you rubbed poop all over your hands." Kate put her arm around Celia's shoulder.

The saleswoman came over to ask whether they had any questions.

"Can this be used as cologne or body wash?" Kate held up the refill container.

Celia grabbed it out of Kate's hand and put the item back on the shelf. "Sorry. She doesn't get out much."

Celia purchased the lavender gift they saw when they entered the store. As soon as they arrived at the restaurant, she ran to the ladies' room and washed her hands three times.

Holy Crap

"Hey, what are you doing around here?" Kate opened the front door. She was disheveled.

"I have to pick up Shadow in a while and figured I could extend my break from organizing the house to come surprise you." Celia held a small plant in her hand and walked into the house as Kate opened the door wider.

"Where's Shadow?"

"Shad's with Noah and Trudy. Probably having a lot more fun than when he's with me these days. I spend most of the time doing house stuff and pushing him out of the way. I went to the nursery and bought some cool perennials. Here, I bought you a gift for the week." Celia followed Kate into the kitchen and placed the plant on the counter.

"What do you mean for the week?" Kate picked it up from the counter and placed it on the sill of the bay window above her kitchen table.

"Well, you know. You aren't that great with flowers and garden stuff."

"What are you talking about? I have a great garden out back."

"They're wild flowers. You're lucky they grow wild. Hence, they're called WILD flowers."

"Yeah, yeah, yeah. Well, thank you for the plant. I'll try to keep it alive for a while. Does it need water?"

"A little when the leaves start to droop or fall off. Or if you want it to live, you could water it on a regular basis. It's a big responsibility, but I think you can handle it."

"I meant right now. Does it need water right now?" Kate touched the soil of the small plant with her fingers. "I hope you don't mind if I clean while we talk." Kate motioned for Celia to follow her into the small hallway bathroom.

Splatters of toothpaste stretched halfway up the mirror. "Isn't it strange how toothpaste gets up high on the mirror?" Kate took her index finger and rubbed the hardened paste. She leaned down and opened the cabinet door beneath the sink. Reaching into the back of the small storage cubby, she pulled out spray cleaner and a jumbo-sized roll of paper towels. "This will never be enough!" She looked at the paper towels and then sprayed the mirror and attempted to wipe off the sticky substance.

"It's not that bad." Although the room was a mess, Celia tried to comfort Kate.

"Two people for two days! Not sure how this bathroom turned into such a mess in just two days. It looks as if a bunch of teenagers were here." She scrubbed the mirror. "Bernie didn't like the color of the toilet paper. What's wrong with blue toilet paper? I had blue, and I used blue. Remind me to never buy that again! I didn't mean to buy blue, but the package was white, and it didn't say blue anywhere on the wrapper." She sprayed and wiped the mirror. Her entire body shook as she moved. Her elbow pushed a metal soap dish off the counter–it clinked on the floor as it landed.

Celia held paper towels out and handed them to Kate, bunch by bunch. She bent down and picked the soap dish off the floor and pushed it to the corner of the counter.

Kate rubbed the clumps of toothpaste, which finally began to soften and slowly dissolve into cloudy smudges.

She looked down at the sink. The same pasty substance lined the sink. Remnants of powder and dark-orange blush covered the faucet and countertops. As Kate wiped the cosmetics, the colorful powder encrusted into the counter. The more she wiped, the more it smeared.

"Look what this is doing to my countertops! I need heavy-duty chemicals." She reached again into the cabinet, pulled out a few more cleaning products, and placed them on the counter. She rested against the wall.

"Tom!" Kate's voice echoed in the small room. "Why didn't he answer? Do you think he heard me? He never hears me. He has selective hearing, that guy."

"Did he go out?" Celia stuck her head into the hallway.

Kate waited a moment longer before she called for her husband again. "Tom, can you come here for a minute." She suppressed a scream.

Tom walked into the tiny room.

Kate shook her head and looked at him. "Can you put the wash in the dryer? I'd like to get something accomplished today."

"Already done. I folded the towels that were in the dryer and got the sheets started. Hi, Celia. How's the new house coming?" Tom kissed her cheek as he greeted her.

"The house is coming along. I've unpacked everything." Celia looked down at the mess. "Kate, I can help you clean. I don't mind. I'm in my grubby clothes anyway."

"Don't be ridiculous. You're on a break from house stuff. Remember? Besides, it's a small room, and we're close to being finished." She swung her hand into the air. As she turned her head, she noticed masses of toothpaste on the wall. Her shoulders drooped, and she closed her eyes for moment. "Maybe I'm not as close to being done as I thought. I keep finding little dirty surprises."

"I'll clean the toilet." Tom stepped behind her. He knelt and reached into the well-used cabinet below the sink. He pulled out toilet cleaner and a disposable brush.

He flushed the toilet. The water slowly swirled and then stood still. He reached to flush again.

"NO!" Kate grabbed his hand away from the lever. "Don't flush it again. It will overflow! Wait a minute!" In the crowded small space, they all stood over the toilet bowl and stared down at the motionless water.

Kate ran out of the bathroom.

Celia unconsciously wiped the countertop with a square from the paper towels.

The water level in the toilet was stagnant.

Kate raced from the garage back into the bathroom. "Let's try this." She was out of breath. She filled the old rusty pot with hot water. She poured the water from the container into the porcelain bowl. The water level lowered slightly. There was no rapid swish or flush of disappearing water. She repeated the procedure two more times. Each time the water drained from the bowl more and more sluggishly, until it stopped moving at all.

Kate again raced out of the room. Tom and Celia attempted to hide the fact that they found the situation amusing.

Kate returned from the garage holding a large black and yellow plunger. "Here." She handed the plunger to Tom. "You do it! Try not to splash." She leaned back against the wall next to Celia. Celia reached over and held Kate's arm. Kate rested her head on Celia's shoulder.

Tom plunged for a few minutes. The water in the bowl went nowhere. Aside from the water becoming dark and murky, nothing happened. The suction pulled the water within the bowl, but the water level remained unchanged. Each plunge was more vigorous than the one before it. His actions were futile.

Celia was nervous to chime in. "Have you tried a snake?"

"I don't think the snake will work! I'll never finish this work today. I just want it done!" Kate's tone was anxious as she snapped out her words.

"Hey! Don't yell at Celia," Tom barked back at Kate. "It's not her fault the toilet's clogged."

"No, it isn't, is it now? And whose fault is it?" Kate looked at Celia, put her fingers to her chin, and slightly tilted her head sideways. "Hmmm. Let me think. Doris complained all weekend about being constipated. Information I didn't need to know, by the way. I guess $85 worth of Chinese food solved her personal plumbing problem."

Celia burst into laughter. Kate couldn't help herself from laughing along.

Tom left the room and returned with the snake. "I doubt this will work." He cranked, wiggled, and jiggled it for twenty-five minutes. Nothing. "I give up. I'm calling the plumber. I'm not wasting another minute on this. We'll clean the rest of the bathroom and let the plumber deal with this."

"You sure got frustrated fast." Kate's comment was unmistakably antagonistic. She turned to Celia. "Are you going to have to leave soon? What can I do to make you stay?"

"I have a couple of hours. I told Noah I'd get Shadow around dinnertime."

"Oh, thank you, thank you, and thank you. It's nice to have someone normal to keep me company." She glared at Tom.

Tom left the tiny bathroom.

A half an hour later, a handsome young plumber in navy-blue overalls arrived. He carried with him a snake comparable the one Tom had already tried. Celia and Kate looked at each other but never mentioned that an identical snake had already failed to open the current in the toilet. They followed him into the bathroom.

"Let's hope he can get things GOING." Kate emphasized the word going.

"Yes." Celia laughed. "Let's hope he can get some MOVEMENT." She emphasized the word movement. The plumber laughed as well.

Tom was within earshot of the two friends in the bathroom. "Glad you're all enjoying the party. Wonder what this will cost?"

"Come on, I'll make some tea." Kate motioned for Celia to leave the bathroom with her. She turned to the plumber. "Can I get you something to drink? Coffee? Tea? Water?"

"No thanks." He didn't lift his head from his tool box as he answered. He stood and put the snake into the bowl and started his work.

"Boy, he's a cutie," Kate whispered to Celia as they entered the kitchen.

The cutie was having no luck loosening the blockage or lowering the water level.

"Did someone stuff a soda can down here or something?" The plumber stuck his head out of the bathroom. "I'm not having any luck."

Kate walked from the hallway and into the bathroom. "No, I'm sure no one did that."

Celia snickered under her breath and joined Kate and the plumber in the bathroom.

"Do you have kids that had a party or something? I've seen kids put cans and all kinds of stuff down toilets. Maybe a sneaker or some socks?"

"No, nothing like that." Kate looked at Celia.

"How about a dog? Have you got a toilet-trained Great Dane or something?"

Celia couldn't contain herself. She stepped into the hallway and burst into laughter.

"We don't have teenagers or potty-trained pooches. Just a previously constipated mother-in-law."

Celia's laughter escalated as tears rolled down her cheeks.

The plumber laughed too. Kate covered her face with her hands.

The plumber maneuvered the snake to no avail. "Something's gotta be stuck back there and it ain't budging." He shook his head back and forth. He unsuccessfully struggled another twenty minutes.

Tom checked his watch. "He bills by the hour," he whispered to Kate as he walked by the bathroom.

Kate kept an eye on the floor and surrounding area, wiping splashes while trying to stay out of the plumber's way. Celia watched the cute plumber struggle with the clogged bowl.

"Sorry, guys, but I can't do anything here. I have to call in my partner. This could take some time."

Forty minutes later, an older man in gray overalls arrived. They dismantled the toilet.

"What are you doing?" Kate was ineffective in hiding her angst.

"Sorry, we have to remove the toilet. We'll take it outside."

"Drag it through the house?" Kate put her hands up and covered her mouth.

"Afraid so."

"Wait!" She disappeared briefly and returned with rolls of plastic. "Please wait until I line the area with this plastic. I don't want toilet juices dripped through my house." She unrolled yards of plastic and laid it out on the floor from the bathroom up to the front door. The two men followed closely as they exited the house, holding the heavy commode between them. They placed it down in the middle of the front lawn. Celia joined the toilet parade to the front door.

"Aren't you so proud to have your toilet displayed as a lawn ornament out front, Tom?" Kate moved to the door and looked out to watch the men work on their clogged fixture. "I'm not going outside to have neighbors see me and my toilet on the front lawn."

Kate stood within earshot of the men working. "I'm horrified by this."

"It's not that bad." Celia was still laughing.

"You got a soda can or something in here?" the newest plumber asked the man in blue overalls.

Kate and Celia looked at each other and at the same time opened their mouths wide.

"We already got that one covered. No kids, no party, no cans, no potty-trained Great Dane or Saint Bernard," the young plumber informed his helper.

"Just a constipated mother-in-law!" Kate cupped her hands around her mouth as she yelled out her response.

Everyone, except Tom, laughed.

The first plumber took a hose and connected it to the water-spout at the front of the house. The second plumber held the other end of the hose tightly to the bowl. They blasted water as high as the pressure allowed. The water sprayed full force into the opening of the toilet bowl. Within a few seconds, flying feces exited the back of the bowl. It rocketed through the air onto the other side of the lawn. The clog culprit landed just short of the driveway.

"Holy crap!" The second plumber could be heard clearly as his voice echoed through the yard.

A hysterical Celia could be heard at the doorway. She grabbed her sides as she bent over in laughter.

"This wouldn't have been a Great Dane–it would have been a HORSE! Someone ripped themselves a new asshole, if you ask me." The cute plumber had been relatively quiet until this comment.

Celia's laugh escalated.

"I guess your mother-in-law isn't constipated anymore," the man in blue yelled back to Kate.

The older plumber waved to a neighbor, who slowed his car down to look.

"Glad you enjoyed the show." Tom huffed as he walked into the kitchen and poured himself a glass of wine.

"I would never have appreciated this story if you had simply told it to me." Celia continued to laugh as she spoke. Mascara streaks stained her cheeks.

"Hey, how about some Chinese food for dinner?" Tom surprised the girls with his comment. Celia fell back into a chair. She was out of control and held her stomach and laughed. Kate, also hysterical, leaned against the wall.

"I'm glad you see the humor in this, Tom. It's not believable."

"I think I better get my dog." Celia took her keys from the kitchen counter and walked toward the door. "Thank you for the entertainment." She was still laughing as she drove away.

TAMMIE

Shadow sat in the passenger seat and bit at the wind as it blew in through the half-opened window.

In the rearview mirror, Celia could see her new colorful garden shrubs and flowers bounce up and down. "We'll plant these flowers as soon as we get home, Shadow." He turned around when he heard his name and moved close to lick her cheek. She rubbed his head and kissed him above his eyes. They were inseparable.

"Come on, Shad." She opened the back of the Jeep and walked to get the garden supplies in back. Shadow sprung onto the driveway and ran up to the porch. He plopped down in the shade by the front door.

From the garage, Celia pulled her green wagon over to the walkway. She pushed her fingers into her red and white polka dot garden gloves and was ready to plant.

Shadow sprang from the porch the instant Celia squeezed the nozzle on the hose. He growled at the water and backed away each time she sprayed. "Ah, something new, Shad. You like the water?" She couldn't tell whether her canine companion liked the water or hated it. "Let's get you used to this." She aimed the hose into the yard, away from Shadow, and showered the lawn. She released the handle and stopped the flow of water. He barked and sat down in the grass. His tail wagged, and his ears spiked up. He wiggled his butt in the air and then again sat down. Celia turned the handle to lower the pressure and sprayed the water into the air. She released the nozzle and sprayed once more. She squirted the water onto her feet–he lunged at her toes. He rolled around in the grass near where Celia stood. She sprayed the water again. This time, Shadow sprung up and again attempted to bite the water.

"What are you doing, you silly mutt?" Her voice was high-pitched as she spoke.

Celia directed the spray at her now drenched dog. He rolled on his back in the grass, with his paws in the air. *You're going to stink.* "How's a little shampoo and bath sound?" Again, she raised her voice to a high pitch as she spoke to Shadow. *Oh God, I'm that person I hate.* She loved Shadow's reaction to her high tone and she continued to talk to him in that way.

They played with the water on the front lawn while the garden supplies sat abandoned at the edge of the driveway. He was soaked and had had enough. He walked to Celia and vigorously shook his wet coat. Celia became drenched from his spray. Shadow passed by the bowl of water Celia had brought out for him and then sipped from a small puddle on the walkway. *Glad I brought out a nice fresh bowl of water for you.* He walked to the front porch and found a small pool of sunshine.

Celia's hands were saturated through her garden gloves. She pulled them off and grabbed a small shovel. *Shouldn't have bought fabric garden gloves.*

She moved the plants to the small dirt-filled area below the porch and started to dig. "Let's try to get this finished before Daddy comes home." She paused for a second and shook her head in disgust. *Did I really say Daddy? Ugh, you idiot.*

Her bare hands dug into the worm-filled rich soil. "You guys are gonna love it here." She spoke as if the plants could hear her. She focused on digging holes and planting flowers. *Damn, I wish I had bought better garden gloves.* She looked down at her filthy nails and then over at her soaking wet gloves that lay on the sidewalk.

Crouching down, excavating intently, she was oblivious of all that surrounded her. Shadow never lifted his head from the cool shaded porch where he dozed. Suddenly, a short chubby woman in jeans and a glittery tee shirt walked up next to her.

Celia jumped. She was startled by the unexpected appearance of the woman. "Oh, my goodness, you surprised me. I didn't hear you walk up the sidewalk."

"I'm so sorry. I didn't mean to scare you. I wanted to come over and introduce myself. I'm Tammie Lagarfils. Tammie with an I E."

Her short brown hair was outdated with its frosted streaks. Her features were sharp, with a pointy chin and equally pointy nose.

"Hi, I'm Celia. Nice to meet you." Celia stood up and wiped her hands on her shorts. She put her hand out to shake Tammie's hand, but immediately pulled it back. "Sorry, I'm way too filthy." She rubbed her hands together.

"I know." Tammie pointed to the taupe house with brown shutters across the street. "I live right there. We watched you guys move in."

"I thought they'd never empty that truck." Celia brushed a bead of sweat from her brow which left a streak of dirt across her forehead.

"We were the first ones in the neighborhood. We've watched all the other houses go up. I had extra help when we moved in. We have two kids who we could order around." She laughed at her own comment. "Where'd you move from?"

"We rented in Salem but spontaneously decided to buy a house. We went out for brunch on a Sunday morning and found this house while we took a drive. It's exactly what we wanted, although we do miss being right by the ocean."

Tammie nervously moved her head up and down while she waited for Celia to stop talking. "We moved here from Springfield, which is in Western Massachusetts. The school system here is supposed to be great. At least that's what we've heard. So far, we love it. We wanted the schools to be our top priority in finding a neighborhood. We moved during the second half of the school year. We looked all over, but when we found this, we fell in love with it. We're so glad we found a neighborhood with all new construction. Don't you love it?" She didn't wait for Celia's response. "Well, we love it. My daughter loves it too. There are already a ton of kids in the neighborhood."

Tammie spoke without taking breaths between her words. "I love to shop and there are oodles of shopping places nearby. We're near New Hampshire, not far from Boston and along the highways there are several malls. Do you like to shop?" Celia was about to respond when Tammie continued her monologue. "I love to shop. If you ever want to go shopping, I'd be happy to take you around. I promise, you won't have to ask twice." She laughed again at her own words. "I know all the best bargain places. Most of my friends are still out in Springfield so I'm usually available."

"Thank you. I'll keep that in mind." Celia responded quickly to get her words into the conversation.

"Got any kids?"

Celia hated that question and didn't want to answer. The question was premature, abrupt, and intrusive–and asked too often by too many people. She valued her privacy more than Tammie's curiosity, but she answered anyway. "No, not yet."

As Tammie spoke, white foam formed deep in the corners of her mouth. Celia looked at the foam and hoped Tammie would wipe it away. She didn't. She continued with her endless chatter. Celia barely heard the woman's words. She was distracted by the white froth, which had hardened to a crust.

"We have two kids. Oh, I already told you that, didn't I? My daughter goes to camp for the summer. I work mornings in the school office and have a lot of time off in the summer. Summer my time to enjoy peace and quiet–if you know what I mean."

"Does she go every day?"

Tammie laughed. "Every day? What are you–joking, honey?" She threw her hands in the air. "She gets out of school and a week later, she's off to camp and away for the summer." Tammie dramatically swiped her hand across her forehead. "Phew! I get her out of my way as soon as possible. She won't come back until the week before the fall season starts. I'd send her off sooner if I could. I don't want to ruin my entire summer carting a kid around the world. One day she would want to go swimming, and the other day to the arcade. It gets way too hectic. If you know what I mean! If she doesn't have something to do, she sits around and whines all day that she's bored. I can't take that nonsense. If you know what I mean!"

"No, I don't know." Celia attempted to sound interested.

"Kylee's my youngest. Her brother Rickie's in college and he works during the summer and on his school vacations. He's never around."

Celia fixated on the crust that had hardened on both sides of Tammie's mouth. Unconsciously she pushed her tongue to the left corner of her mouth, as if she were the one with the crust gathering.

Celia bent down and picked up a small shovel. She flipped the shovel from one hand to another. *Gotta get this garden done.* She was anxious that it would be too late to finish planting if she spent more time with Tammie. Celia dropped the shovel to the ground, which caused a loud noise. Shadow sat up and barked at Tammie. Celia left the shovel on the ground.

"Oh, I didn't even see the dog there. Isn't he cute?" Tammie looked at Shadow. She leaned forward and rested her hands on her knees. "Hi there, fella."

"That's Shadow. Took him long enough to notice you. Not much of a watchdog, I guess."

"Yeah, right. Good thing I didn't come to rob you. Hey, he must be giving me a signal to leave. I guess I should get going. Alan said he would come home early today so we could go out for Chinese."

Celia recalled the bathroom event at Kate and Tom's house.

Tammie continued to speak. "Maybe some time you and your husband—what did you say his name is? Did you say William? I see him leaving for work in the morning, but I've never spoken to him. I've waved to him a few times, but he must not have noticed me. He sure is a looker, if you know what I mean! What was I saying?" She paused briefly and dramatically put her hand to her chin. "Oh yeah, maybe you and William could join us for dinner some time. Get to know the neighbors. Ya know?" Tammie scraped the crust at the corners of her mouth and then sucked her finger.

Celia cringed. *I'm certain I didn't mention my husband's name to you.* "That would be nice some time."

"Don't forget my offer to go shopping. I love to shop. Ring my bell and I'll have my credit cards ready."

Celia walked up the steps and put her lips to Shadow's forehead. "You could have barked a little sooner, love." She rubbed his ears, and he tilted his head into her hand. "She's checked us out already. At least, she knew William's name."

Celia picked up a six-pack of pansies and walked toward her cart. With the flowers in her hand, she didn't see the shovel. She stepped on it with the heel of her sneaker and slipped. Smack on her butt, she landed hard. The pansies sat colorfully in her lap as the dark-brown dirt surrounded her. She looked up to see whether Tammie had witnessed the spill. *Shit!*

"Are you okay?" Tammie ran back up the driveway to Celia. She put her hand out to help her up.

Celia's hip was sore, and she wanted to scream. "I'm fine. Honestly. I'm a bit of a klutz." She stabilized herself and brushed the dirt off her legs.

"You sure you're okay? Do you need anything?"

"I'm good. Thank you. I think I'll take Shadow in and forget the garden for today." Tammie walked away, and Celia turned toward the porch as she rolled her eyes at her own clumsiness.

"C'mon, Shadow." She pushed away the rest of the dirt and threw the pansies into the cart. Shadow followed her into the house.

"Celia, why are you limping?" William watched Celia walk into the kitchen.

"I fell when I was working out front."

"How'd you do that?"

"I tripped on a shovel." Her voice snapped. She wasn't in the mood to be teased about being clumsy.

William looked at her and raised his eyebrows. He didn't pursue it.

"One of the neighbors came by to introduce herself. She knew your name and said you were a looker."

"What else did she say about me?" William stood at the counter and sifted through the mail.

"William!" Celia rolled her eyes. "I find it a little odd that she knew your name."

"Think about it, Celia. She probably Googled the house or recent sales on the street and found out who we are. People do that these days. Was she nice?"

"She was all right. I give her a lot of credit for coming over to say hi. She talked a lot; maybe she was nervous." Celia didn't mention the disgusting white crust at the corners of Tammie's mouth.

Introduce Me

With dark circles under her eyes, Celia looked as tired as she felt. No concealer on earth would mask the exhaustion on her face. She smashed the snooze button six times to gain an extra hour of interrupted sleep. Finally, she dragged herself out of bed.

She walked downstairs and looked into the living room, the dining room, and the kitchen. She smiled.

"Hey, Shadow, I guess it was worth it to run myself ragged and get this done. Even the pictures are hung." She sent a text to work to say she was running late. "Let's go out for a quick walk, buddy. Does that sound good?" She again used the high-pitch, annoying voice that Shadow loved. Shadow ran and sat by the front door. "You're a good listener, aren't you?" She bent down and hugged him. Except for her time at work, she was always with Shadow.

She put out some treats, a fresh bowl of water, and threw his toys around the room before she headed out for work.

"Oh, you're here?" Emma seemed concerned when she bumped into Celia. "I was worried you weren't coming in."

"No, I'm here. Better late than never."

"Ah yes, but never late is better." Emma walked down the hall with Celia.

"Hey, I found a golf magazine on the seat next to me this morning. Would you want to take golf lessons with me? Think it would be fun?" Celia showed the magazine to Emma.

"Nah, I used to golf. I started to play in college. The last time I played was with Fredric and a guy he works with. I got stuck with the wife. Snooty little one, she was. I played horribly. I let them both intimidate me. It was soggy as hell on the course. I hit the ball and when it landed, it sunk into the ground and I couldn't find it. The wife snapped at me and told me I'm supposed to keep my eye on my own ball."

"I thought when you golf with someone they're supposed to help with that?"

"Yeah, I thought that too. The funny thing is that on the very next hole the same thing happened to her and she couldn't find her ball. You have no idea how much I wanted to tell her she was supposed to keep her eye on her own ball."

"Did you?"

"No. Like an idiot, I helped her try to find her ball, but we never found it. I let her get in my head. I did everything wrong from that point on. I even lost control of my pull cart and my clubs took off down the hill without me. When people take it too seriously, I get derailed. If you want to try it, I'll golf with you, but it has to be fun and not competitive." Emma scanned Celia's face. "You look tired."

"Tired? I'm beat." Celia rubbed her eyes and smudged her mascara. She yawned. "I got to bed at 3:30 on Saturday night and woke up at 7:00 Sunday morning. I guess it was 3:30 on Sunday morning, huh?"

"How's it all going?" Emma motioned for Celia to join her in the kitchen area.

Celia immediately walked over to the coffee maker. She selected a French vanilla coffee for herself and pushed the button. "You want one?"

"No, I'm all set. Tell me about the house. I'm dying to hear how it's going. And I want to see more pictures."

"I finally have the curtains and shades hung. Now it has that finished look. This is the fun stuff, especially compared to how exhausting the unpacking was." Celia removed the cup from the dispenser and poured in a single creamer and two packets of sugar. She stirred the coffee and then took a huge gulp. "I still have a few closets to organize to make it perfect. I've shoved some of the extra items under the bed in the guest room. I hope I don't forget about them later."

She guzzled her coffee and walked back to the machine to make a second cup. *You're going to have heartburn.* "How was your weekend?"

"Huh!" Emma laughed. She turned her lips up and then scowled.

"You have a story, don't you?"

"Here's how my weekend was." She handed a piece of paper to Celia. "Take a gander at this, my friend. Read it out loud. I want to hear it read back to me. I love to be entertained."

Celia picked up the letter and leaned against the counter. "Let's see what we have here. *Dear Emma, It was nice to see you this weekend. I hope you had fun at Freddy's party. I thought it was fun. That said, I did not appreciate you're introducing me as Freddys' mother, since that does not identify who I am in the big scheme of things. It's very insulting to me. Next time me and you are together at some thing, and we can agree that their WILL be a next time, I must insist that you introduce me as Fredric Cerezos' first wife. That will make the relationship much more clearer. By saying I am Freddys' mother, does not tell my status, as it could misleed some one and they might think that maybe I had Freddy with some one else or before I was married to Fredric. It was very disrespectful to me. I can not tolerate it if you introduce me any other way than Fredric Cerezos' first wife. Do you understand? If we could get passed your problems things would be so much more better.*" Celia dropped her hand to her side."What the fuck?" She almost laughed. "What on earth is this all about?"

"It's a love letter I got from Edie this weekend. I printed it out for your reading pleasure."

"Emma, where do I start? Should I start with the fact that she doesn't know how to use an apostrophe? Does she honestly think anyone would care about her past marriage?" Celia perused the letter again and for a moment was silent as she read a few of the lines a second time. "I would not be able to contain myself. I would want to redline this, edit her grammatical errors, and then send the marked-up letter back to her. She sounds illiterate. What did you do?"

"What did I do?" Emma snickered. "What CAN I do? She's a moron. I can't even acknowledge it."

"I'd be most pissed about the fact that she said they were YOUR problems." Celia waved the letter up and down in the air.

"WHAT?" Emma shrieked. "Give that back to me." She grabbed the letter out of Celia's hands.

Celia couldn't help but laugh at Emma's surprised outburst.

"Where does it say YOUR problems? I must have read the letter too fast and missed that." Emma scanned the letter for the sentence Celia mentioned.

"In the last paragraph." Celia pointed to the line in the letter.

"That little bitch. I thought it said 'OUR' problems. I didn't even realize she was blaming the bad situation on MY problems." Emma clenched her teeth together and growled as she squinted with anger. "I should have introduced her as Freddy's egg donor."

"Ha ha. Edie the egg donor." Celia let out a laugh.

Emma smiled. "That's funnier than you think."

"What do you mean?"

"Nothing."

"Yeah, the last time you said nothing, I found out about your secret ex-wife. What upset her? Why did she write this to you in the first place?" Celia sipped her coffee.

"I don't know if you remember the story I told you when I first met her, and Jillian was with me. She introduced herself as the original. I guess she wants everyone to know she was the first wife. We were at a party at Freddy's on Saturday. Freddy has become friends with a few people in our neighborhood, and he invited them to his house. I was talking to my neighbor when Edie came up and stood next to me. She was almost touching me. She was standing right there and didn't walk away. I felt I had to introduce her. I had no idea how cold-hearted and terrible it was to say she was Freddy's mother. Isn't that the most terrible thing you've ever heard? That I said she is his mother? I told you she is F'd in the H."

"Hey, I remember that one–fucked in the head. You're right about that. Every time you tell me a story about her, I think you can't beat it with something better." Celia was laughing. "I don't think you could even make this stuff up. This is totally, absolutely, undeniably insane."

"Ya think?" Emma crossed her eyes and looked at Celia. "What am I supposed to do with this? I didn't even show Fredric."

"Why not?"

"I don't know. I guess I have to process it by myself, or with you. It's beyond my realm of comprehension how crazy she is."

"Are you going to respond?"

"Nope. No response. If I respond, then she knows I read it. If I don't respond, it will drive her totally nuts. And what would I say?

Any response to this insanity would bring me down to the same level. There is nothing to say. I suppose I could send it back with a few recommendations for therapists in her area."

"She would need more than a few therapists to help her." Celia laughed. "Hey, here's another idea. You could send it back with a book on spelling and grammar. That would always come in handy for her."

"Right?"

"Can I keep this copy?" Celia fanned her face with the letter.

"Please, be my guest. Enjoy it. Share it. Show your family and friends."

"You don't mind? I have to show Kate."

Emma suddenly went motionless and seemed deep in thought. "No, wait! I think I'm too paranoid for anyone else to see it. But you can tell Kate about it."

"I get that. Emma, I can go back to my desk and write a rebuttal if you want me to help you out. It would be a lot of fun."

"Ha ha ha. That WOULD be fun. Problem is I would be too tempted to send it, and I have to rise above this."

"You do know that silence is the same as acceptance. Right?"

"I do. I know that if I am silent, she could think I'm afraid of her. But knowing her, I think it will be more fun to not respond. Let her wonder if I received it or if I read it. That kind of torment is better than anything I could write."

"You're right about that." Celia finished her second cup of coffee. "I'll see you for lunch?"

"Absolutely."

The Drop-In

Shadow lifted his head and pointed his nose in the air. He held the position for a second or two and then put his head back down. He raised up again and let out a loud bark. The noise disrupted Celia's catnap on the couch. He barked again at the exact moment the doorbell rang. She wasn't expecting a visitor or a package. *Do people still sell door to door? What if it's a kid trying to sell cookies? I should get up.* "What do you think, Shad? Should I get the door? Do you want wrapping paper, cookies, or a tin of popcorn?" She decided to ignore the unexpected visitor.

The doorbell rang once more. Celia contemplated not budging from her restful position. The bell rang yet again. Begrudgingly, she got up to investigate who was ringing the bell. Shadow picked his head up and watched her leave the room. By the time she had reached the door, his head rested on his paws.

"Hi, hope you don't mind that I dropped by." Tammie held a coffee cake in one hand and a bouquet of fresh cut flowers in the other. Dressed in orange shorts, a faded-yellow tank top, and gold sandals with braided straps that wrapped around her skinny little ankles, she waltzed into the house the moment Celia opened the door.

"No. Come on in."

"I knew you were home. I wanted to give you time to answer the bell." She handed the flowers to Celia and walked to the back of the house into the kitchen, but not before she poked her head into the living room. "A lot of people don't care for the drop-in thing, if you know what I mean. I figured you might want some company."

Maybe on a day I'm not exhausted. "It's fine that you stopped by." There was no need to invite her in, since Tammie was already headed toward the kitchen.

Tammie ambled around the center island and over to the sink, where she could clearly see out to the small pond and woods beyond the backyard. She rested her hands on either side of the sink, stared out the window, and then turned back to Celia. "I hope you like coffee cake." She continued to move about the kitchen; she touched everything.

With each new piece she focused upon or touched, Tammie commented with a single word. "Lovely." She glided her hand across the countertop. "Nice." She touched the top of the stainless-steel range. Celia noticed the fingerprints Tammie left on the stovetop.

Tammie stroked a stained-glass lamp on the half wall separating the kitchen from the family room. "Lovely." She rubbed her hand against a panel on the hutch. "Lovely." She wrapped her hand around a water pitcher containing an arrangement of lilacs and uttered, "Nice."

"Tammie, these fresh flowers are spectacular! Thank you." Celia attempted to direct the conversation away from her house and toward the gift brought in by her new neighbor. She walked over to the counter, opened a bottom drawer, and pulled out two glass vases. "Which one?" She held the taller of the two in her hand and showed it to Tammie. "I think the flowers will look nice in this, don't you?" She filled the vase with tap water. "Do you have time to stay for an iced tea?" She arranged the flowers and then placed them on the counter next to the sink.

"That would be lovely." Tammie skimmed her hands back and forth over the shiny countertop.

Celia removed the tea from the refrigerator and added a few ice cubes. She placed the cake onto a glass plate and removed two square white dessert dishes from the shelf by the window.

Tammie walked to the side of the island, pulled out one of the round stools below the overhang, and sat down. She swiveled back and forth. Her eyes darted throughout the room as she took in the décor in Celia's house.

Tammie stopped spinning and focused on the adjoining family room. She squinted as she stared at the paintings on the farthest wall.

"Do you want to see the house?"

"I'd love to. I've been dying to see the inside of this house." Tammie didn't attempt to soften her enthusiasm.

Celia was surprised at Tammie's bluntness about her desire to see the house. Celia gracefully swung her hand back to the direction of the foyer. "Come on, I'll show you around."

Tammie was off the stool and on her feet in a split second. She followed Celia as they left the kitchen. Shadow trailed along. He wedged himself between the two women. Tammie almost tripped over him as they walked into the foyer.

"As you already know, this is the entryway to the house." Celia moved her hand around to display the room.

"Wow! Great giraffe! Where'd you get that?" Tammie touched the wooden giraffe placed by the wall at the bottom of the stairs.

"William's sister found it on a trip and had it shipped back to our old apartment. We named her Stretch. She fills out that spot perfectly, don't you think? She's seven feet tall."

"I would love something like that. I wonder where I could get something similar for my foyer. This is so welcoming. The entry to my house is bare and not at all inviting. I like the tree there too. It's like Stretch is nested in." She pointed to the tall ficus. "This is lovely. Maybe I'll do something like this too. They sell silk trees a lot of places now. They fill up empty space, don't they? I noticed you had a lot of tree things in your family room too. Are they real?"

"No, most of my indoor plants are artificial." Celia sounded apologetic. "I'm good with the outside garden, but the inside stuff is too much work. The silks look real, so I figure, why bother? Right?"

From the foyer, Tammie sauntered into the dining room. She ran her hand along the furniture as she walked by. She stopped and took in each minuscule detail of the room.

Celia watched as Tammie picked up an antique candlestick, removed the candle, and then turned the crystal over to inspect the bottom. Celia's stomach sank. OMG. *I'll kill you if you drop that. They were my grandmother's handmade antiques.*

Tammie placed the candle back into the antique and returned it to its original position. "Good thing you haven't dusted in here. I can get this back in its exact spot. See, right around the dust circle on the table." She continued to snoop about the room.

Celia felt a twinge of embarrassment for the dust on her table.

Tammie walked over to a velvet amaryllis on the floor. The flower stood about three feet high. Shadow moved next to it, his nose almost as high as the fake flower. Tammie didn't have to bend to touch the top of the display. "This is lovely. I've never seen anything quite like it. Lovely." The women and Shadow walked back out to the hall and across to the living room.

Tammie's eyes darted around each room they entered. She didn't miss a thing. She touched each silk flower, straightened a picture or two, and examined every trinket and knickknack.

Shadow had found a new sunny spot in the family room, where he lay down and stretched out his hind legs. He didn't lift his head when Celia and Tammie entered.

"This room is quite different from the family room in my house. The way you've decorated makes it look wider than it actually is. It's lovely. What a waste that you don't have kids to run around in it. My kids would kill for this room!"

Whatever. "Would you care for extra lemon or sugar? It's a sweet tea to begin with." Celia removed a couple tall glasses from the cabinet.

Tammie followed her back into the kitchen.

"How about upstairs?"

"It's a little disorganized. If you don't mind, I can show you next time." Before Celia could finish her sentence, Tammie had turned and headed toward the stairs.

The upstairs tour was brief, but enough to satisfy Tammie's curiosity. At the conclusion of the fleeting upstairs visit, the women returned to the kitchen. Tammie again sat on the stool at the island in the center of the kitchen.

"I would love to have that." Tammie pointed to the miniature shopping cart filled with papier-mâché fruit.

Celia cut the coffee cake. "I forget, did you tell me if you wanted anything in your tea?"

"If you have it, an extra splash of lemon would be lovely." Tammie reached over and fingered the grapes draping over the cart's basket. "I can't believe how completely finished and decorated you have this house. I don't mean over-decorated. I mean that it looks like you've been living here for a long time. I mean it looks like you've really worked at finishing it. Everything fits perfectly." She continued to trip over her own words. "You've really done a beautiful job. It's lovely." Little white droplets formed at the corners of her mouth as she stumbled over her words.

Tammie's Garden

Celia was determined to create a rock border by the garden of daylilies out back. At 8:00 a.m., she began to gather rocks and bring them to the edge of the flowers. By 10:00, she was drenched in sweat. With the intense heat, this project would have to wait until it cooled down later in the day, after the forecasted thunder showers.

"Come on, Shadow. We're done for now. Don't want you to get overheated." They walked side by side to the front porch. The cool whirl of the ceiling fan felt refreshing against her hot and sweaty skin. Shadow slurped from a bowl of water and then rested by Celia's feet. She closed her eyes and anticipated hours of serenity.

Shadow let out a loud bark. Celia's eyes popped open to find an unprompted visit by Tammie steal away her tranquility.

"Don't you two look comfortable, sitting around, being lazy on a hot summer morning?" A droplet of sweat ran down the side of her nose.

"It's so hot! I can't stand it." Celia fanned her face with her hands. "I should have moved my staycation further out. It's too hot to do anything."

"Well, I've been very busy. I'm on a mission, but I haven't been successful." Tammie took her hands out of the pockets of her shorts and walked up the front steps. She sat down on the rocker next to Celia. "I've looked all over for flowers and garden stuff this weekend. I love what you've done to your front garden and thought that maybe I could do something nice with mine. I basically wasted my time, since I don't really know anything about flowers or gardening." She made a sad face. "I wondered if I could ask you to help me. I wish that I had your green thumb. Would you ever come to the flower place with me?"

"I'm happy to help. I was going to go back later this week. I could get my other flowers today instead. William's out of town for a couple days, and I have a few hours today. The rest of the week is taken up with other plans. I could take you to the garden center where I bought my flowers. If you want, I can drive since I have the space in the back. I haven't cleaned out the leaves from my last visit to the garden center."

Celia opened the back door for Shadow to jump in. He jumped in and hopped into the front passenger seat before Tammie could open the front side door.

"Shadow! No!" Celia leaned into the back and patted the seat for Shadow. "Come on." She patted the seat again. He didn't budge. "Shadow. Come!" She raised her voice.

Shadow looked at her but didn't budge. He wagged his tail and barked twice. "Shadow, come on. You want to go for the ride or go into the house?" *I'm asking the dog a question in front of someone else. He's not going to answer, you idiot.*

Celia got out of the back and walked around to the side of her Jeep. She pushed Shadow into the back. He turned around and jumped into the front again. Finally, with another attempt, and a few tugs on his collar, she got him settled behind the driver's seat. Tammie sat in the front.

"Why don't you just leave the dog home?" Tammie turned and looked at Shadow.

Celia felt a defensive twinge in her gut. *Why don't you go flower shopping yourself? Since you're sitting in HIS seat, maybe I should shove YOU in the back.* "I want Shadow to be with me, and I think he needs to get comfortable with traveling and being around people and other animals. He's such a great companion. He's my baby."

"Well, he's not a kid, he's a dog."

Wow! What nerve. "If Shadow's bothering you, I'd be happy to write down some notes for you regarding what to look for in garden foliage. I'm sure the people who work there would also help you." Celia was sorry she agreed to help her neighbor who was almost a total stranger.

"Oh no. I didn't mean that the way it must have sounded. I'm so sorry." She turned around and touched Shadow's head. Shadow growled.

Dogs and kids—they instinctively know how to judge people. Gotta trust your gut. "No problem. Some people aren't dog lovers."

Celia lowered the window next to Shadow. He kept his head inside and wedged his face between the two women. Tammie inconspicuously moved away from him, but he moved closer to her. Celia took her hand and pulled Shadow's face close to her. She rubbed his neck and behind his ears. He lapped at the breeze coming from the air conditioning vents and leaned his head on Tammie's shoulder. He drooled on her shirt—she used a tissue and wiped away the slimy saliva.

Shadow walked between the two women as they browsed through the rows of flowers. He stayed close by Celia's side. Celia leaned over and picked up a box of geraniums. The bottom broke open and the flowers fell out against her clothes. She was covered in dirt.

"Celia, are you okay? You're covered. I'm so sorry."

Celia looked down at her khaki shorts. They were almost completely black with the rich soil. A few rocks mixed with the dirt had wedged between her belt and the shorts. She brushed the moist soil, which made the smudge worse. "I'm fine. These are the clothes I garden in. They're already dirty from working out back this morning."

Tammie reached out and touched Celia's arm. "I appreciate your help." Shadow watched Tammie's arm touch Celia and he jumped up on Tammie. The black soil from the bottom of his paws left dirt all over her shirt.

You're killing me here, Shadow. "I'm sorry, Tammie. He's acting a little silly today." She helped Tammie brush the dirt off her shirt.

Shadow pulled his territorial front seat stunt again on the way home–he didn't get any further with it this time either.

"He's usually much better behaved." Celia tried to convince Tammie. "I think he's afraid I'll leave him or something. Since we moved to Cherry Tree Lane, he stays much closer to me, until William comes home. Then he follows William around like HIS shadow."

Shadow settled down in the backseat, where he closed his eyes and napped.

"Are you comfortable with planting these on your own?" Celia dropped the last flat of flowers by Tammie's front garden.

"Oh, thank you, but I think I'll be fine. I'm looking forward to digging in, no pun intended."

"Great. I don't think it's going to shower, and I have some rocks to move around in my backyard."

"Have fun with your garden. I hope I get mine done before Alan gets home later. I wonder if he'll notice when it's all done. Does Wills notice that kind of stuff?"

Wills? "Yes, William notices what I do around here. He doesn't always like it, but he does notice."

"He's super handsome. He's perfect guy, isn't he?"

"Perfect? I don't think so. Nobody's perfect. But he's a great guy and I lucked out." Celia paused for a second. "And he did too." Her tone was lighthearted as she joked. "I'm sure Alan will notice your hard work."

Celia loaded large rocks into her plastic wheelbarrow. The weight of the rocks cracked the bottom of the plastic container. The heavy stones tumbled out onto the ground and onto her toes. She hopped around the yard as she breathed in and out, holding back a scream of pain.

Finally, she sat down on the ground by the garden and rubbed her toes. She swayed back and forth until the stabbing pain left her foot. "I should have known better than to think this was going to be easy." She remained by the garden, with Shadow pushing into her side. Slowly she shuffled the rocks along the edges. She gave up and hobbled inside. Her foot was throbbing.

Jeopardy

"Hey guys! Right smack on time." Kate sauntered over to Celia in her usual casual style. "How was the traffic?"

"Great! Took us less than twenty-five minutes." She took a dramatic deep breath. "The ocean air smells wonderful."

"See. It's not that far away. How's the garden coming? When we spoke the other day, you were planting."

"Yeah, I planted a bunch of stuff. It looks good, not great. Hopefully it will come together when things start to grow. I put perennials in toward the back of the garden and some annuals in front. A woman from the neighborhood stopped by to say hello when I was out there. I didn't get as much done as I wanted to."

"Go on. Who was it? What was she like?"

"Her name is Tammie something or other. I forget her last name. Not much to tell. She must have snooped on us, because she said William's name before I told her what his name is. But I know it was nice of her to stop by. I'm not sure if I would have done that. I slipped on a shovel as she was leaving and landed smack on my ass."

Celia wanted to be annoyed with Kate's laughter, but couldn't help but laugh along. "Oh Celia. Did you fall in the middle of your conversation with her?"

"Worse. She was leaving and then came back to see if I was hurt." Celia laughed as she covered her face with the palms of her hands.

"What are you two talking about?" Tom interrupted their conversation as he came around to the front yard.

"He's quite nosey, isn't he?" Kate whispered to Celia.

"Hi, Tom! I think William is looking for you out back." Celia hugged him hello.

Celia glanced into the beautiful set dining room. "Kate, you went all out."

"Oh, it's nothing. I wanted to have a nice dinner with you guys to relax and hang out. And play a game or two."

"Good luck with that, Kate. You know he doesn't enjoy games." Celia touched the flower arrangement in the center of the table. "Is this sunflower centerpiece from your garden?" she called out to Kate, who put the finishing touches on their dinner. "They're fabulous!" The sunflowers were in a huge vase of crackled green glass. Mixed among them were bunches of Queen Ann's lace and ferns. "It looks wonderful."

"I picked them this morning. There are tons out back if you want to take some home with you."

"It's incredible to me that someone as flower-challenged as you can get lucky enough to have that wild flower garden growing out back. If you told me you got them from a florist, I'd believe you. Did you honestly put this arrangement together by yourself?"

"Yes, Celia, I did." Celia caught the tenacious tone in Kate's voice. "It was easy. There's a magazine on the coffee table in the other room with all sorts of great floral arrangements and ideas. Take a look. I got the idea from that. Take the magazine too, if you want. I'm done with it."

Celia walked into the adjoining room and looked through the magazine. "I think I'll borrow it, if you don't mind."

"Will you call the guys? Dinner is ready."

Kate brought out a platter roasted chicken and an herbed crusted rack of lamb cut into lollipops. All beautifully displayed on a bed of radicchio and edible flowers, which she had purchased at the grocer's. String beans and fingerling potatoes coated in spices were served on a separate platter.

For dessert, Kate served fresh juicy blueberries and strawberries sprinkled with colored sugar, wedges of watermelon, cantaloupe, and honeydew. Pineapple spears surrounded the border of the large melon-colored plate. And of course, for Celia, a carton of vanilla ice cream was placed on the table alongside the platter of fruit.

"Delicious, Kate. You do know how to put a great meal together." William began to clear away a few of the dishes. "We'll help you clean up."

"No! My guests don't clean." Kate pushed William's hand to the table. "We can clean up when *Jeopardy!*'s over."

William looked at Celia. She turned away and picked up her water glass. Except for sporting events, William was not a fan of games. Not board games, not card games, not television games. "*Jeopardy!*?" He raised his eyebrows.

"It's *Jeopardy!*, William. You watch that show, right?" Kate was excited to have the additional competition for the game show.

"Shouldn't we be sitting on the deck, or the front porch? It's nice out. Why waste the great weather to watch television?" William attempted to sidetrack the plan to watch *Jeopardy!*.

You aren't going to win this one, dear. Celia glanced at William and rolled her eyes. She mouthed *don't even try*.

"It's too buggy out there. We'll watch the show and make it interesting or something," Kate pleaded.

"So, this betting thing between you guys is STILL going on?" Celia disobeyed Kate's demand to not clean as she gathered the silverware and brought it into the kitchen.

"We're addicted. Every night at 7:30. We can't stop. He gets so upset when he loses that it makes it too much fun to play. And win."

"Of course." Celia snickered. "So, who's winning this week?"

"Don't ask!" Kate's tone was snappish and annoyed.

"Are you winning a lot?" Celia shouted out to Tom.

"More than she wants to discuss. She takes it too seriously. She shouldn't make such high wagers, because when she loses, she's mad that she's lost all her money."

Celia's eyes opened wide as she made a realization about *Jeopardy!* and Georgetown. "Hey, Kate, can you come with me out back to pick some of those sunflowers?"

"The show's about to start. I don't want to miss it."

"Kate, it will take less than a minute. Come with me." Celia looked stern as she spoke. Kate followed her outside. "You say I don't live that far away, but I live far enough away that *Jeopardy!* is on at 7:00 at MY house. I watch it on a New Hampshire station that you don't get."

"What?" Kate instantly knew what Celia was planning.

"That's right. I'll make sure I text the answer to Final Jeopardy every chance I get."

"I love you!" Kate clapped her hands together.

Within thirty minutes, Tom was boasting about his *Jeopardy*! win. Kate looked at Celia and winked. With Kate's sneaky little secret, Tom wouldn't be winning much longer.

THE BUG

Celia was preparing dinner as William entered the kitchen through the garage. "You're home early." She walked over to greet him with a kiss. "I got home about a half hour ago. No traffic, and the subway was on time. A miracle."

William loosened his tie and walked toward the stairs in the front hallway.

"I'll get it." *Who's calling on this phone*? "Hello?"

"Hi, Celia, it's Tammie from across the street. I have a huge bug problem!" She was obviously panicked.

"Tammie! What do you mean?"

"I had a gigantic flying creature in my kitchen, and I'm afraid of it."

"Where is it? Don't you have any bug spray? Can you swat it with something?"

"Well, I have it trapped under a glass, but I'm afraid of it and I don't want to kill it. I have to get rid of it."

"It's a bug! Just kill it."

"I'm afraid that if I let up on the glass, it will come after me. It's probably enraged that I captured it."

"Slide a piece of heavy paper or something under the glass. Try a square of cardboard. That will trap it. Then take it outside and throw it on the lawn."

"I don't think I can do that." Her panic appeared to increase. "I'm way too scared of it. Can William come over to get rid of it? I just saw him pull in the driveway."

"Hang on. I'll come over and take care of it."

"You can do that? Aren't you afraid of it? Shouldn't you send William?"

"No! I'll be right over. William's more afraid of bugs than any girl I know."

Tammie greeted Celia at the front door. Tammie's one-piece skimpy bathing suit was a bikini with the top and bottom connected by mesh in the middle. Her makeup was perfect, and her lightened hair was perfectly blown out.

"Were you at the town pool?" Celia had not seen Tammie with lipstick before.

"Yes, we just arrived home when I saw the bug. I trapped it and then called for William to help."

"You go to the pool like that?"

"What do you mean?"

"You look as if you just came from a fashion salon. When I go to the pool or the town pond, someone would think I crawled out of bed a minute before. You don't have a hair out of place." Celia pointed her index finger and moved her hand in a circular motion around her face.

"I didn't do anything special."

Like hell you didn't. I wouldn't have recognized you if I fell over you. "You lightened your hair. Looks good blonde."

"Yes, I did that the other day."

"How'd you trap the bug in the first place? It's the ugliest bug I've ever seen. Weren't you scared to get so close you could trap it?"

Before Tammie could answer, Kylee walked into the room. "Mom, the beach towels are done. I took them from the dryer and folded them."

"I thought you just got home?" Celia turned away from Kylee and looked at Tammie.

"We got home an hour ago. Mom thought your husband might be able to get rid of the bug. She's surprised you aren't afraid of bugs. I'm not afraid either. I wanted to throw it outside, but Mom thought your husband should do it."

Tammie glared at Kylee. "Where are my manners?" She put her hand to her mouth. "Celia, this is Kylee. She came home from camp a few days early to have her braces tightened."

"Hi, Kylee. It's nice to meet you." Celia put her hand out to shake Kylee's hand.

She shook Celia's hand and then put her arms around Celia's waist. "I'm happy to meet you. Can I play with your dog some time?"

"Sure, come on over whenever you want. He loves to play catch in the backyard."

"Thank you. I love dogs and Mom won't let me have one."

Tammie interrupted their conversation. "Go get a snack or something in the kitchen, Kylee. Celia has to help me here." Tammie turned to Celia. "I never imagined you wouldn't be afraid of a giant bug."

"I grew up in the country. I'm not afraid of bugs, but I must admit, I freak out with snakes. Hate them. I guess if you get a snake trapped under a glass, you'll have to call someone else." Celia leaned in and looked closely at the bug. "Yuk. That is the grossest bug I've ever seen. What is it?"

"I think it's called a stink bug, but I'm not sure." With her tongue, Tammie wiped the crust from the corners of her mouth.

Celia cautiously slid a thick piece of paper under the glass and secured her hand beneath it. She carried it outside, walked to the grass, dropped it, and ran to the house. "I have no idea what kind of bug that was, but it's disgusting." She shivered with revulsion.

"Hey, Kylee! Are you home tomorrow?" Celia walked into the kitchen to say good-bye.

"Yes. I am."

"Come over around ten and you can take Shadow for a walk with me, and then play in the yard."

"Can I, Mom?" Kylee looked up at Tammie.

"I guess so, but you have an orthodontist appointment at 2:00."

"Great. See you then, Kylee."

William, I'm home. Dinner should be ready in a few minutes."

"How was the bug incident?"

"Fine. I got it outside. I think she was hoping you would come to get it."

"Oh yes, Celia, everyone wants me. But don't worry, you're the lucky winner of this fabulous prize." He moved his hands up and down the front of his body.

"No, I'm serious. She asked for you not once, but twice. A tad strange."

"That's very funny. Does she know I'm the one who will stand on the chair while you kill the creature?"

"Yes, Mr. City Boy. I told her Mrs. Country Girl is the one to handle these life-threatening insect incidents in our house. I met her little girl, Kylee. She's adorable. She told me they had been home an hour, when Tammie said they just got home. I believe the daughter."

"You did a good deed. Whatever you're cooking smells amazing. I'm starving."

Difficult People

"Kate and I start our course tonight." Celia sat down at the kitchen island and had her coffee with William. "I haven't been to school in almost ten years."

"You excited?"

"Not sure if I'm excited or nervous. Hopefully we're not the oldest ones in the class."

"Won't matter if you're the oldest or the youngest. You'll have fun with Kate. What course is it again?" William buttered a crescent roll and poured a second cup of coffee.

"Dealing with Difficult People."

"Whose idea was that course?"

"It was Emma's idea, but now she can't even make it because she has another commitment on each night it's taught. I was excited for her to meet Kate."

"Hope you didn't take it to learn how to handle me."

"I've already figured out how to handle you."

"Is that so?"

"Yup. It was easy."

"Care to elaborate?"

"Nope. I need to stop by the registration office before class, which means I'll have to leave work a little early. You'll be okay for dinner? And you'll feed Shadow and take him out?"

"Yes. Shad and I will be fine. Right, Shad?" Shadow picked his head up when he heard his name. "It's supposed to rain. Don't forget your umbrella and raincoat." William kissed the top of Celia's head as he left the kitchen.

"Even if it's raining, Shadow needs to go for a walk when you get home." She heard William walk up the stairs.

"It's under control, Celia. Nothing to worry about."

"How long do we have to wait in this stupid line?" Celia counted the number of students ahead of them.

"Hmmm? Not sure. Maybe you should have mailed in the paperwork when I reminded you five times to take care of it."

"I know. Sorry. Sometimes I'm lazy about this stuff. We're moving. It won't take long."

"That's Chris from the coffee shop." Kate motioned toward the woman who sat at the registration table. "Hi, Chris. I didn't know you worked here."

"I started a couple months ago. I'm here two nights a week. What class are you taking?"

"Dealing with Difficult People withDr. Sanford. I was told to come here to get my registration card, since I signed up late." Celia showed her driver's license to Chris and then put it back in her bag.

"Here you go. Would you mind taking the roster to the class? Dr. Sanford was supposed to pick it up, but he didn't. He never does. He thinks he's too good to do what every other faculty member does. Ironic he teaches a course on dealing with difficult people." She handed Celia her registration card and the roster.

"Oh God! Did we sign up for a bad course?" Kate's tone was filled with trepidation.

"The curriculum is good, but he's an ass. Don't take any crap from him."

"Crap? You still want to go to this class, Celia?"

"Definitely." Celia gripped the paperwork in her hand.

"You better hurry. The class starts in less than ten minutes. It's in the building directly across the parking lot. It'll be faster if you cut through the back." Chris pointed to the door behind her.

"Damn! Figures the guy's a jerk. We can make it if we hurry." Kate's attitude screamed negativity.

"I'll go as fast as I can but keep in mind I'm wearing heels." Celia followed Kate as they exited through the back door.

Kate and Celia rushed down the stairs and through the parking lot. It was pouring. Celia pulled her raincoat over her head and ran with her book, registration card, and roster in hand.

As she was about to step up on the sidewalk, she caught her foot in a puddle that concealed a large hole in the asphalt. Her foot twisted. She fell face first onto the cold, wet ground.

"Celia!" Kate shrieked. "Are you okay?" Kate started to laugh.

"I'm not okay. It isn't funny!" Celia put her hands on the curb and tried to get up.

"I know. I know it's not funny. This is a nervous laugh. I'm sorry. I'm sorry." Kate bent down and helped Celia up. Kate shrieked when she looked at Celia's leg. "You're bleeding. You ripped your pants and your knee is bleeding." She looked at Celia's face. "Shit! Your cheek is bleeding too. Do you think you broke anything? Do you need to go to the hospital? Maybe we should skip the class and take care of your injuries."

"Absolutely not! I don't want to start out by missing the first class."

"Oh God, you're so stubborn. You're hurt, and we should take care of this first." Kate pleaded with Celia, to no avail.

"Let's go." Celia was mad, and her ego was bruised. "I need this class, to better handle people like you."

They arrived at the building and Kate rushed to the ladies' room to get a fistful of both wet and dry paper towels. They entered the classroom from the door in the back of the room.

With blood dripping down her face and her clothes soaking wet, Celia found a seat and sat down. Kate sat in the seat next to her. Celia wiggled out of her coat and draped it over the back of her chair. She then noticed the drenched registration card on top of her also drenched book. *Shit! I guess I should bring this up there.*

Kate handed Celia the paper towels. She searched inside her bag and pulled out a small tube of antibacterial ointment. "Put this on the damp one and wipe your face and knee with it." She leaned across the aisle and handed the ointment to her bruised friend.

Celia bit her lip and shook her head. "I have to take this paperwork up to the front."

"Give it to me. I'll take it up to him." Kate put her hand out for the papers.

"No!" Celia's voice snapped. She limped to the front of the room with her registration. Kate tried to grab her to tell her she had forgotten to take the roster. She watched Celia at the front of the room. "Sorry we're late. I had an accident." Celia placed the card on his desk.

He looked at her and then the card. He didn't say a word.

"You're welcome." She turned and walked back to her desk. The moment she sat down she realized she had forgotten the roster. *Tough shit, Proffy. You can get this after class when I leave it on my desk. You're welcome.* She was angry, mostly at herself for being sore, sopping wet, and splattered with blood. Her adrenaline raced full force.

"Continue reading," the professor said to a student who read from her seat in the second row.

Kate leaned over to Celia. "Are you kidding me? He has someone reading from his own book? This is lame."

He looks about eighteen years old. Celia mouthed her words to Kate.

"You can stop reading now. Are there any comments on this excerpt?" He gripped the podium on both sides.

No one spoke.

"Well then, since no one has anything to add, let me ask a question." He focused his eyes on Celia's registration card. "Ms. Charles, what are your thoughts on that reading?"

Celia and Kate had missed most of the excerpt. Celia was not prepared to answer intelligently. She held paper towels against her face and her knee. *Why is he calling on me? I think they said something about passive/aggressive personalities.* "In my opinion, passive/aggressive personalities are the toughest to deal with."

The professor cut her off. "Interesting. But I'm asking you specifically about the exact excerpt your fellow scholar read aloud." From the podium, he leaned in toward the classroom.

Celia was embarrassed. Her anxiety was sky-high. She became enraged. "Why do you ask ME specifically?" She glared at the professor.

"I'm not targeting you specifically. I glanced at the roster and randomly picked the first name I focused on."

"Is this the roster you used to find my name?" She held up the class roster that Dr. Sanford had not yet seen. She waved it over her head.

Kate stared at Celia in shock.

"Excuse me?" He slammed his hand on the top of the lectern.

Blood rushed from Celia's neck to her cheeks to her head. *You want to screw with me, Professor Dickhead? I'm not in the mood to deal with bullshit from anyone.* She was in pain. She was not going to allow this man to mock her in front of an entire room of fellow students.

"It's interesting that you got my name from the roster, since you haven't even seen it." She waved the roster again, this time in a circle around her bloody face. Celia stood from her seat and hobbled to the front of the room. "I forgot to give you this."

She slapped the roster on the top of the podium and stood at the front of the room, facing her professor. Her stomach flipped and flopped, but she stood firm. *I'm not going to sit back and let you humiliate me. I'll show YOU how to deal with difficult people, Professor Asshole!* If she didn't speak up now, she would regret it for the rest of the course.

"You didn't get my name from any roster. As I've proved, you didn't even have the roster. You tried to put me on the spot. You knew I missed the reading."

The professor froze for an instant. "Don't flatter yourself. I don't even know you. Why would I want to put you on the spot?"

She could feel the moisture under her arms; then, out of nowhere, she began to speak. "I don't know why."

Celia heard murmurs throughout the room and a few chuckles from the other students.

"You." He stared at Celia as he paused and then looked again at the registration card. "You, Ms. Charles, are disrupting my class."

"I believe you are disrupting your own class. We all see that now." Celia reached out toward the professor's podium, picked up the roster, and waved it in the air. She could feel the heat intensify in her body–her rage strengthened.

Kate sat with her jaw dropped.

"You knew the registration card was mine. You also knew I came in late and wouldn't be able to answer your question. Talk about passive/aggressive! You wanted the class to focus on the lame student who couldn't answer, rather than the fact that you're not prepared for your own class. Do you think we are morons?"

The other students talked softly and rustled their papers.

"You have no idea what you're talking about!" Dr. Sanford's voice was loud and strong.

"I know exactly what I'm talking about. We read from your book and then you ask questions about what we've read. Great way to fill up two hours. I'm out of here. Feel free to give me an A, because you, sir, are a very difficult person." Celia hobbled back to her seat, gathered her belongings and stormed out of the classroom.

Kate followed her out to the hallway. "Give you an A? What was that all about?"

"I have no idea why I said that." Celia tilted her head with an embarrassed snicker. "I don't even remember half of what I said in there. Let's try to get our money back." Her adrenaline was returning to normal and she regretted her exhibition.

"Let me carry your stuff." Kate reached for Celia's bag and books. "Are you okay?"

"I'll be fine. My face hurts, my knee hurts, and I think I'm going to throw up. Can we see if there's any ginger ale in the soda machine?"

"I'm texting William to let him know you're on your way home and to get the first-aid kit ready for you. I'll get the car and pick you up at this door."

"I need that ginger ale first." She rubbed her stomach and then her face.

Quick Change

Celia sat on the front porch with Shadow at her feet and a book in her hand. The rocker moved forward and backward, but she was unaware of the motion. She was engrossed in her novel.

Tammie, wearing a faded taupe T-shirt, brown shorts, and a pair of old jogging sneakers, ran across the street into Celia's driveway. She shouted to Celia as she approached. "Hey, Celia! Are you still interested in pulling those weeds from the swamp in your backyard?"

Yes, I want weeds in my garden. "Do you mean the perennials by the pond? I was only commenting that I love how they looked around the water and would love something like that in my yard. I didn't plan to dig them up."

"Well, today's your lucky day. I have some time and thought I could offer my assistance. You want to do this?"

Oh God! Do I want to spend that much time with her? Although, the flowers would look nice in the garden and the help will make it easier and faster. "Did you want to do that right now?" Celia rubbed the top of Shadow's head as he sat next to her and leaned into her thighs.

"Yes. I have nothing else to do, so I can help you."

"I have work to do inside, but I have a little time now. Let me change into my grubby garden clothes." *That's not a total lie, right, Shadow? I always have work to do, one way or another.*

"I'll run home and change too, and I'll be back in a few minutes. Do you need any tools for digging?"

"I have everything I'll need."

Ten minutes later, Tammie returned to Celia's front lawn, as Celia mindlessly deadheaded the flowers from a hanging planter. Tammie now wore neatly pressed black shorts and a peach tank top. Shiny gold sandals with a slight pump heel had replaced the old sneakers she had worn ten minutes earlier. Fresh lip-gloss and pink cheeks brightened her face. Her hair was blown perfectly straight. In her right hand, she held the faded taupe T-shirt she previously wore; in her left hand, she carried the old sneakers.

"Tammie, there is no rush in doing this. If you're going out, we can do it another time." Celia noticed the quick transformation of Tammie's attire.

"Nah, like I said, I don't have anything else to do. I would love to help you now." Tammie clapped her hands together. "Let's go!"

"Why did you change into good clothes? There's a good chance you'll get dirty doing this."

"That's okay. I wore those clothes all day. I wanted something fresher for right now. Let's go." She clapped her hands together again as she started to walk toward the back of Celia's house.

"You shouldn't have taken off your socks. There are tons of bugs out there. You might get bitten." Celia pulled her own tennis socks up higher. "I hate the bugs around my ankles."

"I won't worry about that. Bugs don't bother me at all."

How about that bug under the jar that I had to release for you? "All right then, let's go." Celia walked by the side of the house. She stopped to pick up a shovel and a pitchfork.

As they approached the soon-to-be-transplanted flowers, Tammie stopped briefly. She pulled the T-shirt on over her tank top and slipped out of her sandals to slide into her sneakers. Neither woman mentioned the wardrobe change.

Celia dug the shovel into the ground around the root of the flower. She skillfully pushed the flower up out of the earth. Under Celia's instruction, Tammie grabbed the flowers by the root ball and gathered them into her hands. Together they dug up another five bunches of flowers.

"I can help you plant them now too, if you want." Tammie appeared eager to help as they headed back toward the house.

"This should be easy. I've already dug the holes for flowers by the back wall."

Before long, the two garden partners had transplanted the perennials into Celia's back garden.

As they walked around the front of the house, Tammie pulled off her T-shirt and exposed her tank top. She slipped off her sneakers and stepped back into the sandals. She bent over and flipped her hair back, giving it a look of freshly wind-blown hair—it was feathery and full around her face. Celia curiously watched as Tammie fluffed her hair.

"Thank you for your help with that, Tammie. I would never have done this without your assistance."

"No problem. I might even start to enjoy this garden stuff."

"It's fun. Hang on, I'll get us something cold to drink. I think I have some lemonade. It's store-bought." Celia scrunched up her nose.

"Sounds perfect. I'll meet you out front on your porch steps. We can hang out for a while. I have no place to be."

Celia came out the front door with two enormous glasses of lemonade. They sat quietly for a moment on the steps. Shadow, in the corner, never moved—he had become used to visits from Tammie.

"So, doesn't William get home around now?" Tammie fluffed her hair once more.

"Sometimes. He tries to get home before 6:30, but that isn't always possible. Why do you ask?"

"I was just wondering. I don't want to keep you from starting your dinner. What are you making?"

"I was planning on leftovers from yesterday, but now I think I'll make myself some popcorn. William's going to be home very late. He'll grab something with the guys at work."

"Oh! Well, I hoped I helped you out with the weeds. I'm going to head home." Tammie gulped down half of the lemonade and abruptly left to go home.

"Thank you again for helping. I hope I can return the favor to you."

"Oh Celia, you already have. I could never have done my flowers without your help. This little transplanting event was hardly enough to thank you."

Celia watched Tammie as she walked down the driveway and across the street. She continued to sit on the front steps until her craving for popcorn became too intense to ignore.

Shrimp Tale

"How are you doing? Celia, you look tired."

"Isn't that synonymous to saying I look bad? I'm exhausted. I couldn't sleep all night; I was up scratching mosquito bites until three in the morning. How's your day going?"

"Decent. Only five hang-ups this morning. Maybe she's working today."

"I can't believe Edie has nothing better to do. What a sicko. You haven't talked a lot about her. I take it you haven't spent much time together."

"I've seen her, but it's a waste of time to talk about her. She's been too much of a hobby of mine, and I want to find a more useful way to entertain myself."

"Well, I guess she's become my hobby too, because I very much look forward to hearing the stories. I miss them."

"I'm still keeping notes. I had a dream about her last night where she confronted me on the book. You know, the book I'm never going to write."

"Don't say that!" Celia put her hand on Emma's. "This is great therapy for you and a wonderful source of entertainment for me. You must carry on with the writing. Don't you have even one story for me today?"

"Oh brother. I swore I wouldn't get into it, but I do have one little odd event. We were at Freddy's on Saturday last week. There was a ton of food. His neighbors all got together and had a party at his place."

"Any special occasion?" Celia took out her thermos filled with vegetable soup and poured a cupful into a Styrofoam bowl.

"No special occasion. Someone had brought shrimp that looked incredible. It had some sort of garlic sauce seasoning on it. Fredric and I walked over to the table where it had been, but there wasn't any left."

"I hate when that happens. Didn't you bring lunch today?"

"I'm not hungry. They had a huge breakfast at the monthly meeting."

"That's nice. Do they always serve breakfast there?"

"No, they never have before. There was probably a reason, but I got there too late to know why. They had everything you can think of: eggs, bacon, pancakes, waffles, fruit, juices, potatoes. Everything."

"Sounds good. Now, get back to the shrimp story."

"Oh, right. Fredric and I saw the empty serving plate and I made a comment about how good it had looked. I had seen it on some of the plates people were carrying. And then, like the little phantom she is, she appeared right next to me. She had three pieces of the shrimp on her plate. She must have heard Fredric and me talking about it."

"You should have reached over and taken her shrimp the way she did to you that day in Essex."

"I know. I should have. I didn't remember that."

"Did something happen?"

Emma laughed. "You have to ask? Of course something happened. She popped two of the three pieces of shrimp into her mouth. Then she picked up the last one and offered it to me. I knew I shouldn't have responded, but fool that I am, I did."

"You need to tell this story faster. I'm dying to hear what she did."

"She held the shrimp out to hand it to me. I was about to take it and she pulled it back, bit off most of it, and left a tiny piece and the shell of a tail. Then she handed it to me."

"That's disgusting."

"I was totally dumbfounded. I felt that icky feeling in my stomach. I didn't think fast enough, and I didn't think of Jillian."

"What did you do?"

"I ate it."

"WHAT? Did you eat the shell too?"

"No, I didn't eat the shell—I bit the tiny little piece of shrimp meat. I honestly thought I was going to throw up. Why did I do that, Celia? Please, tell me what is wrong with me? I totally froze and didn't know how to react to her hateful and obnoxious behavior. I was taken off guard, which is exactly why I can't be around her. I can't have the suit of armor on every second."

"Did Fredric see her do this? What does he say about her behavior?"

"He sees it. But I've ask him to never say anything to her about it. He can't stand it. And I still haven't thought of a good question to ask her. I'm mad at myself. I thought of a few things to say, but unfortunately it was at three in the morning, a day later." Emma rolled her bottom lip and stuck her tongue out.

"Don't be so hard on yourself. Who would expect a grown woman, a mother—or anyone—to act that way?"

"I could have said anything. I could have refused it once she bit into it and told her she ate the best part. Or like a normal person would have done, I could have said no thank you when she handed it to me. I could have questioned her about her bad behavior. But no. I acted like a shrimp-deprived pathetic loser and ate it after she had it in her mouth. Her gross, little, disgusting, revolting, sickening mouth. I'm still mad at myself."

"Hey, if you write about the shrimp tail, you could call it *The Shrimp Tale*, and spell tail T-A-L-E."

"Ha ha, that's funny. I wish I had come up with a response to shoot her down, but she took me by surprise."

"Emma, it's easy to come up with retorts and better ways to respond afterward, but I get the being shocked by her behavior. I don't know what I would have done, if it were me. She's a repulsive little pig."

"I hate when you insult pigs that way."

LOST

"What are your plans today?" William sat at the kitchen island as he drank his coffee and read the *Globe* on his iPad.

"Going for a spa day with Kate. Manicure and pedicure."

"Hope you don't mind that I'm going to the football game with Glen and Noah."

"No, you'll have fun. I'm glad to spend the entire day with Kate. We haven't had a day together in a long time."

"I'm heading out. Call if you need anything." He kissed her on the top of her head and walked to the garage.

"Have fun at the game. I'm looking forward to being pampered."

Celia went into the master bath to apply her makeup. She turned on the straight iron and removed her mascara from the drawer. *Where's Shadow? I haven't seen him in a while.* "Shadow." Her voice had a singsong tone. "Shadow? Where are you?" She stopped and listened. He didn't come to her. She put down the iron and turned it off.

She tightened her robe and walked into the hallway. "Shadow!" With her voice raised to a shout, she called for him. "Shadow! Where are you?" She looked in the upstairs den. She opened the closet doors and looked inside. In the guest rooms, she opened the closets as well.

In each bedroom, she knelt on the floor, lifted the bedspread, and looked under the bed. "Shadow!" This time her voice was firm and not friendly. *Where the hell is he*? Shadow was not upstairs.

"Shadow!" Her voice echoed through the foyer as she walked downstairs. Shadow was not in the hall coat closet, nor was he under the couch in the family room. Celia scoured every inch of the first floor, the same as she did on the second floor.

She took his cookie jar from the kitchen pantry and shook it vigorously as she searched throughout the house. *Come on, Shadow. You love these cookies. Come out from where you're hiding. I know you're playing. Come on.* "Shadow!" This time she yelled his name louder.

Celia put on her boots and went down to the basement, where she checked every nook and cranny in the dark and cold area. In the garage, she looked under the carpenter's bench. The garage door opened when she pressed the button. In her robe and boots, she walked into the cool air. "Shadow! Shadow, come!" She returned to the house and opened the sliders to the backyard.

Her heart raced as fear began to set in. The palms of her hands were clammy and shaky. In a panic, she ran upstairs, picked up her cell phone, and dialed William.

"William!" Her voice shrieked as she yelled his name.

"Celia. What's wrong?"

"We've lost Shadow."

"What do you mean?" His tone smacked of worry.

"I can't find Shadow. I've looked everywhere. In every room, in the basement, outside. He's nowhere to be found. Did he follow you out to the garage?" Her voice began to quiver.

"He didn't follow me out to the garage. Did you check the den? He was in there with me earlier this morning."

"Yes, I checked the den. He wasn't in there."

"Are you sure? That's where he was earlier. I know it."

"William, I checked the den. Did you not hear me? I checked the den. What part of I checked the den don't you understand?" She hung up and threw the phone across the room.

Thank you for making me doubt myself. See. He isn't in here. In the den, she double-checked the closets, looked beneath the desk, and inspected under the couches. As she walked to the door to leave, she heard a soft thump. She turned around and stood silent in the room. "Shadow?" The noise came from the other side of the room. She looked under the couch by the window and then under the couch against the wall—still no Shadow.

The armless ends of each couch met at the corner and were hidden below the table's top. She crawled onto the couch and lay down on her stomach. Celia pushed her head between the table top and the couch. It was too dark to see anything. The thump happened again. She wiggled her way off the couch, ran into the other room and picked up her cell phone from the floor. With the flashlight shining, she crept back to the corner table and shined the light under the top of the table. Two shiny eyes stared back at her.

"Shadow!" She screamed with excitement. He had become wedged in the space at the corner and was caught between the ends of the couches.

Celia rolled off the couch and pulled it away from the table. Once there was enough room, Shadow leapt out of the small dark space, wagged his tail, and jumped on her. She grabbed him and held on tight. Her tears trickled into his fur. She didn't let him go for over five minutes. "I thought I lost you, sweetie. How did you get in there?" He gobbled the treat she gave him.

"Hello?" Her voice was nasally when she answered the phone.

"Did you find him?"

"Yes, I found him a few minutes ago." She wiped the tears from her eyes.

"Where was he?" William sounded relieved.

"In the garage." She would tell him the truth later.

Play Ball

William stepped out of the bathroom with a towel wrapped around his waist. "Hope I didn't wake you earlier. I went downstairs and made those frosted cinnamon cakes from the package in the refrigerator."

"That sounds great, William. I'll have one with my coffee."

Celia got out of bed, put on an old pair of sweatpants, and stepped into her slippers.

Shadow didn't budge when the doorbell rang. He sat by Celia and waited for her to drop a piece of her breakfast treat. She nearly tripped over him as she got up to answer the door.

"Hi, I'm Kylee. Do you remember me? I live with Tammie. She's my mom. Can Shadow play ball with me? I brought toys for him."

Celia laughed and opened the door wider for Kylee to enter. "Of course I remember you, Kylee. Come on in. You can take him out back through the sliders. Come on, Shad." Celia opened the door to the deck, and Shadow ran out, followed by Kylee.

Kylee threw her ball into the backyard–Shadow was on it in a second. He brought it back to her and dropped it at her feet. She picked it up and threw it again. He retrieved it and returned to drop it again at her feet.

"Is that your friend Tammie's daughter out there with Shadow?" William glanced out the window as he walked in with his empty coffee cup.

"Yes. Her name is Kylee. And by the way, Tammie's not really my friend. She's our neighbor. Nobody automatically gets friend status."

Celia heard the grandfather clock in the living room strike ten. “Shoot. Kate will be here at 10:30 and I'm not even close to being ready. I'm going to take a shower and I'll be down in a few. Can you keep your eye on Shadow and Kylee out back? Make sure they stay in the yard.”

“You got it. I want to clean up the garden by the side of the house. I'll be out there anyway.”

Kate arrived and walked in through the open garage. She noticed Shadow playing with a little blonde girl in the backyard. “Celia?” she called out as she walked to the sliding glass doors and watched Shadow chase and return the ball to the little girl.

“Be right down. Make yourself comfortable. There's coffee in the pot and cinnamon cakes on the counter.” Celia added blush to her cheeks and left the bathroom.

“Who's that?” Kate motioned her head toward the backyard.

“That's Kylee. Remember I told you about her mother Tammie?” Celia took out a couple of big coffee cups. “Coffee?”

“Definitely.” Kate watched out back for another minute. “She's a cute kid. She looks happy out there, throwing the ball for Shadow. Ah, to be young and innocent again.”

“Were you ever innocent?”

“Don't think so.” Kate opened the book of wallpaper samples. “I tagged the swatches I want you to see. I'm thinking of putting paper up in the first-floor bathroom. Do you think any of these are nice?” She handed the book to Celia.

“I think paper is going to be much more difficult to clean when your in-laws come to visit.”

“Why didn't I think of that? I'm such a jerk. I'd be nuts to put paper in that room.”

“I thought you were nuts when you put a shower in there. Now it's a regular bathroom and that's why they use it.”

“You're right. I never even considered that before I added the shower.” Kate heard Kylee's laughter in the backyard. She reflexively looked through the sliders and smiled. “Isn't it funny how kids don't get bored throwing a ball over and over? Who's that?”

"Who?" Celia peeked out back and saw her close the gate. "That's Tammie, the mother."

Tammie walked up to William, whom she had yet to meet. Celia and Kate watched them introduce themselves. William put his hand out to shake Tammie's. She ignored it and gave him a big bear hug instead.

"Isn't she friendly?" Kate teased.

Tammie walked through the yard toward Kylee–she noticed Celia standing by the window but didn't acknowledge her. She approached Kylee and appeared as if she were going to reprimand her. Celia opened the door and stepped into the brisk fall air.

"Tam, hope it's all right with you that Kylee is over here."

"You mean Tammie?" Tammie raised her eyebrows. "I don't care for abbreviated names. I wasn't sure she was here."

"Mommy!" Kylee put her hands on her hips. She grimaced at her mother and then reached down for Shadow's ball. "Don't you remember? I asked if I could come over, and you said I could." Kylee held the ball in her hand as she waited for her mother to recall their conversation. Shadow sat at her feet and wagged his tail wildly as he waited for Kylee to toss it farther out back.

"Oh, that's right, honey. I forgot." She looked sheepishly at Celia. "I'm forgetful sometimes."

"Do you want to come in for a cup of coffee? William made some wonderful cinnamon cakes this morning."

"He bakes?" Tammie seemed surprised.

"Well, he followed the recipe on the package, which involved opening the package, putting them on a cookie sheet, and throwing them in the oven. I still had to clean up."

"Sure. I would love to try them. I just met Wills when I walked into the yard. He's even cuter close up."

Okay, Tams. Don't like abbreviations, do you? "How do you take your coffee?"

Tammie stepped up to Kate. "Hi, I'm Tammie, from across the street. That's my little girl Kylee playing with Shadow."

"Nice to meet you, Tammie. I'm Kate."

Celia placed the coffee and cinnamon cakes on the kitchen table. "Kate was about to show me wallpaper she's considering for one of her bathrooms. I might have talked her out of it."

"Is that a trend? Are people putting up paper on their walls again?"

"I don't know." Kate opened the book. "I make my own trends." She looked at Tammie and noticed the white crust at the corner of her mouth. She unconsciously put her napkin up to the corner of her own mouth.

Tammie looked outside at her daughter. "I'm going to break up this backyard love affair between Kylee and Shadow."

Celia got up and called out for Shadow. He ran into the house and pounced onto Kate's knees. She bent down and put her face into his and let him lick every inch of her skin.

Tammie winced at the display of affection. "Hi, Shadow." She reached to pat his back. He ran into the other room.

Stretchie

Celia's phone buzzed, and she read the text. She rolled her eyes, rubbed her forehead, and put the phone down.

"Something wrong, Celia?" William scrolled through his email on the iPad.

"Wrong? I wouldn't say wrong is the right word. Tammie organized a meet-and-greet for the ladies in the neighborhood. She sent the attendance list of those who have accepted."

"And?"

"And I'm the only one who hasn't accepted. This is her second text about it."

"When is it?" He continued to scroll through the pages.

"Let's add insult to injury. It's Sunday afternoon. So much for relaxing, doing laundry, and hanging out in sweats all day."

"Sunday as in tomorrow? Wow, kind of short notice. Maybe it'll be fun. I'm going to watch the game anyway."

"Well, in her defense, she sent it two days ago and I haven't responded."

"Maybe some of the women will be nice." William swiped his iPad to close it and got up for a second cup of coffee.

"I have to bring a gift. Maybe I'll take a bottle of wine from your wine storage," she teased and then walked out of the room and again rolled her eyes.

"Nope. I don't think so. If you want to drink it, fine. If you want it as a gift at a party where you hardly know anyone—not fine. Not unless you can find a cheap bottle down there and I don't think there are any inexpensive bottles. I can pick something up for you when I get gas later."

❋

Celia entered Tammie's house through the side door. She was among the last to arrive. She put her bottle of wine, wrapped in a shiny foil bag, on the kitchen table. Most of the women were already sitting down in the family room.

"Celia, I'm glad you made it." Tammie gave her a quick hug. "You should have brought your friend Kate. She seems nice."

"She's great. We've been friends for years."

"Did she say anything about me?"

What? That's an odd question. "Well, she said–"

Tammie interrupted Celia and didn't let her finish answering the question. "Let me guess. She said I would be a good match for Will."

"What?"

"You know. She thinks that Will and I would look good together."

As a couple? "Nope, she didn't say that. She thinks I go perfectly with William. But she did say Kylee's adorable." *And she also said that the crusty crap in the corners of your mouth is disgusting.*

Celia looked around the room and gasped. *Did she redecorate?* "Hey, Tammie, the room looks good. Did you change it from how it was?"

"Yes, I changed it last week. Do you love it?"

Of course I love it–it's almost identical to my family room. Have you no pride? "Yes, it's lovely. We seem to have the same taste in decorating."

"Really?"

What the fuck? Yes, really. I feel as if I'm in my own house. "Don't you think this couch looks the same as my couch? This coffee table matches the one I have."

"What a coincidence. I guess great minds think alike." Tammie smiled at Celia.

Celia walked into the kitchen and took an exasperated breath.

Tammie greeted a new guest at the front door.

"Holy cow! I love this!" screamed a woman in a purple coat and white scarf as she walked into the foyer from the front door. "Where on earth did you get such a great piece?"

"Oh, that's Stretchie." Tammie walked over to the tall giraffe and touched its neck and moved away.

"And the tree next to it. Amaaaaazing! Looks like it's in the wild. Tammie, you have such great taste."

Celia heard the conversation and rushed to the foyer. Her mouth dropped. The foyer was identical to her own. Not similar–identical. Standing by the stairs was a tall giraffe, identical to her giraffe. Standing next to the identical giraffe was a green ficus, identical to her green ficus.

Are you fucking kidding me? Celia stared at the giraffe and the tree with shock.

"Tammie, where did you get this great idea?" The woman in the purple coat touched the tree and then ran her fingers down the neck of the giraffe.

"Oh, I saw it in a home magazine and had to have it."

"Tammie, that's the same tree and giraffe I have in my entryway." Celia tilted her head and squinted at Tammie.

"Really? I've only been in your house once, maybe twice. I can't even remember how it looks."

"Well, now you won't have to, because it looks like this. Exactly like this."

The woman in purple gaped at Celia, shook her head, and walked away.

Am I being punked here? Am I in an episode of the Twilight Zone? *How can she so blatantly copy me? Did she rob me? I would have noticed if my stuff was missing. Right? This is unbelievable.* Celia walked back to the kitchen and took a cupcake from the cupcake tree that sat in the middle of the table. She ate the top with the frosting and tossed the bottom in the sink. She walked over to the tree and took another cupcake; again–she ate the top. As she was about to take her third frosted delight, Tammie appeared next to her.

"So? How do you like my redecorating skills?"

First of all, they aren't YOUR *decorating skills–they're mine. Second of all, how do you have the brass ones to ask me that?* "Of course, I like your taste. It's exactly the same as mine. Don't you agree?"

"I don't remember. I think maybe I subconsciously replicated your furnishings without knowing it. It's like I saw it, it registered and then later I couldn't remember where I saw it. Hasn't that ever happened to you? You see someone who looks familiar and you can't place where you know them from, yet you know you know them. Or maybe you see something that reminds you of something you saw before, and you can't remember where it's from? I think that's what happened here. I swear it wasn't intentional. If mine is like yours, then I think I subconsciously loved your house and didn't realize these ideas were from you. You know what I mean?"

That's quite a monologue of an excuse. "I can see how that would happen." Celia lied.

"You know what they say: imitation is the highest form of flattery. Right?"

"Is that what they say?" *And who are THEY? I wonder what she paid for the tree. She probably got a better deal than I did. Figures!*

"You're home early. That was the quickest party ever." William relaxed on the couch identical to Tammie's couch and flipped through television stations.

"Are you watching the game?"

"Commercial. How was the party? I take it not good if you're home this fast. Any nice people there?"

"I have no idea. I didn't talk to anyone."

"Why?"

"William, you won't believe this. She copied our family room and foyer almost exactly. She has the same giraffe and tree and the couches and coffee table are the same. She even has the same bicycle lamp with the red seat."

"Celia. Get serious. Why didn't you talk to anyone?"

"William, I'm not kidding. Here, look." She threw him her cell phone and then jumped on the couch next to him. She took the phone and opened her picture folder and scrolled through the photographs. "Look familiar?"

"Yeah, it looks as if you took pictures in here, and now you're trying to tell me it's Tammie's house."

"It IS Tammie's house!" Celia raised her voice high. "See the kitchen in the background? That's not our kitchen. We have white cabinets–hers are dark wood."

William's eyes popped. "You're kidding me. Is this a coincidence? Do you know for sure she copied you?"

"I was there less than a month ago to bring her some mail that accidentally got in our mailbox. Trust me, I would have remembered the giraffe, if nothing else."

"Well, my dear, imitation is the highest form of flattery."

Celia screamed and walked out of the room. "I'll never have any of those women over here, because they'll think I copied HER!"

Three Minutes

William left for work earlier than usual. He'd been traveling often and needed time in his office to catch up from being on the road. Celia smashed her snooze button. The snooze feature stopped buzzing when an hour had passed. When she woke up, her hand was still positioned on the button. It was 10:00 a.m. She rolled over and fell asleep again.

At 11:20, her cell phone buzzed and interrupted a sound sleep. She opened her eyes and saw Shadow sitting by the bed. He was staring at her intently. *Shit.* She reached for her phone. "Hello?" Her voice was groggy.

"Celia, are you sick? It's me, Emma. Where are you?"

"I'm home. The phone woke me up. I have a terrible headache and I must have slept through my alarm." She remembered hitting the snooze button. "I don't think I can make it in. I must be coming down with something. I've never slept this late." Her phone beeped, and she looked at the caller ID. "I have another call coming in. Let me call you back later. I'll send an email to work."

"Don't worry about it. I'll take care of letting work know. Get some rest and call me later."

Celia's phone buzzed the second she disconnected her call with Emma.

"Hi, Kate."

"Celia, I've texted you five times. You never texted me last night when you got home."

"Sorry, I fell asleep the minute I got in."

"You sound funny. Are you at work?"

Celia pulled the covers over her head. Shadow jumped up on the bed and nuzzled his face into hers. "I'm home. I woke up a few minutes ago."

"Are you sick?"

"No, I'm tired. I shouldn't have gone out last night." Shadow attempted to bite at the phone–Celia switched it to her other hand.

"I'm coming over."

"No, you're not. I'm going to let Shadow out and then lie down again."

"I'll see you in a little while. I'll bring soup. Soup is good for sickness." Kate hung up the phone before her visit became a confrontation.

Celia fell back to sleep with Shadow still close by her side. He licked her forehead–she didn't feel it.

She would have slept longer, but Shadow barked loudly in her ear. She pushed him away and he barked again. She then heard the doorbell. When she got out of bed and looked outside, she saw Kate's car parked in the driveway.

Kate used her key to enter Celia's house. Shadow raced toward her, his tail wagging wildly. "Hey, buddy." She leaned down, and he kissed her all over her face. He followed her upstairs to the master bedroom.

"I brought you soup." She handed Celia the brown bag. "Open it up and have some now."

"I don't have any appetite." She looked into the bag. "What's this for?" Celia took the soup out and held up the pregnancy test she had removed from the bottom of the bag.

"I don't think you're sick. I think you're pregnant."

"Kate. Don't be ridiculous. I'm not pregnant. I had a headache before. Hardly the sign of pregnancy."

"That's fine and good but take the test." Kate walked to the bed and picked up Celia's cell phone. "Here. Get up. Take the phone and take the pregnancy test into the bathroom. Pee on the stick and wait. It takes three minutes. When you get the positive result, and you will, call William first and then tell me. I think you should tell me first, but in fairness to him, you can let him know before you let me know."

"Kate, you're a pain in the neck. I'm not taking the test."

"Yes, you are. Unless you want to wait until William comes home. That's the only way I'll let you off the hook. Maybe you should wait for him. But you have to promise to take it when he gets home."

Celia got a twinge of excitement and nervousness at the same time. "I think I don't want to wait. I think I want to do it now. Should I wait? I want to do it now. I'm nervous. Let's do it now."

Kate took Celia by the shoulders, turned her in the direction of the bathroom and pushed her up to the door. "There you go. Shadow and I will be sitting in the sunshine on the deck. Won't have too many more of these warm days before the cold weather arrives."

Celia shook her head. "What do I even do?"

"You pee on it. Wait three minutes and then look at it. If it has this symbol." Kate pointed to the positive symbol on the box. "If it has that symbol on it, then I'm going to be an aunt. Now one last chance. Do you want to wait for Billy Boy?"

Celia walked into the bathroom and closed the door.

Kate and Shadow sat outside while they waited for Celia to come outside with the results. "Well, Shadow, do you think you'll have a baby brother or sister? It's been more than three minutes. She must be talking to William, that's what's taking her so long. Right, Shadow?"

Celia opened the slider and walked to the lounge chairs, her face flushed, and she couldn't speak. She handed the pregnancy test to Kate.

"Auntie Katie. I love how that sounds. Is William as excited as I am?"

"Kate, no one is excited as you are."

They hugged and cried. Shadow jumped up on them.

FRIENDS

Emma answered on the second ring. "Hi there. You calling about lunch?"

"As a matter of fact, I am. But a little different today. I want you to come to lunch with my friend Kate and me. We're going across the street and I want you guys to meet."

"Sounds like fun. What time?"

"The usual. Noon. If we get there then, we won't have to wait in line. Ramona's coming too." Celia laughed out loud.

"No way!" Emma was about to renege on her acceptance of the invitation.

"No, I'm teasing. It's you, Kate, and me, no Ramona. I have something important to tell you." Celia heard a click. "Emma? Emma, are you there?"

Emma raced into Celia's office and immediately sat down.

"That's not physically possible for you to get here this fast." Celia pulled out her jar of biscotti and started the espresso maker. "We have a new flavor of biscotti today—orange chocolate, very mild and very delicious."

"Start chirping." Emma rolled her hands toward her body. "You know I can't wait until lunch when you tell me you have something important to tell me."

"Well." Celia poured the coffees and opened a biscotti.

"Come on, you're taking too long. I think you're trying to torture me." Emma rolled her hands faster.

"You're the first person I'm telling. I'm pregnant. Kate was there when I took the test, but I haven't told anyone else. Except William, of course. I told him before I showed the results to Kate."

Emma jumped up and ran around the desk to hug Celia. "How exciting. I can't believe this. I'm so excited."

"I'm excited too. I'm also freaked out and nervous. I wasn't trying to get pregnant, but I wasn't trying to not get pregnant either."

"How pregnant are you?"

"Not even two months. I'm not telling anyone else, because I don't want to jinx anything. The three of you are the only ones who know. The doctor said the end of May, but I don't count on that to be exact."

"How great is this? Thank you for sharing. I'm going to be out of the building before lunch. I'll meet you and Kate across the street at noon. I'm looking forward to meeting her."

"You guys will hit it off. I know it."

Kate and Celia arrived first and were seated when Emma walked into the restaurant—they sat on the same side of the booth and left the seat across from them for her.

"Kate, this is Emma. Emma, this is Kate." Celia motioned to Kate and then to Emma.

"Emma, I feel as if I know you. Celia's told me a lot about you." Kate got up and put her arm on Emma's shoulder and kissed her cheek.

"Has she shared all my crazy stories with you? That's how I usually monopolize our time together." Emma took her seat across from Kate and Celia.

"She's told me some. Kind of like listening to a horror story. Have you seen Celia's new house yet?"

"No, I haven't made it over there, but I will." Emma looked apologetically at Celia. "I know you've asked me a dozen times."

"It's a nice neighborhood. I hope she'll meet some nice friends there."

"I know. That would be nice for her to have friends close by. That's what's great about new developments."

"Hey, you guys. I'm right here. You're talking about me as if I'm not sitting here with you." Celia pushed into Kate's side.

"I'm sure there are many nice people in her neighborhood. A few weirdos as well." Kate unfolded her napkin and placed it on her lap.

"What's that mean, Kate? You've met only Tammie." Celia poked Kate's hand with her fork.

"Like I said, a few weirdos as well. Case closed." Kate slapped her hand on the table. "She's a weirdo and you know it. You don't have to spend a lot of time with weird people to know they're weird. She should have a tattoo on her forehead that says: *It's not you. I'm a weirdo.*"

"Why do you say that, Kate? She's nice and her daughter is adorable. Don't cloud Emma's opinion."

"Celia, what did she say to you the day after she met me?"

"What are you talking about?" Celia responded.

"Come on." Kate turned to Emma and spoke directly to her. "After Tammie met me, she asked Celia if I said anything about her. Celia told her I didn't say anything. Then Tammie asked if I thought she looked like a good match for William. You know–as if she and William would make a good-looking couple. Think about it. That's plain bizarre."

"I don't think she meant what you're saying." Celia tried to defend her new neighbor.

"I don't know, Celia. I think Kate might be right. You can never be too careful about who you make your friends these days." Emma picked up the menus at the edge of the table and handed them to Kate and Celia.

"Kate, let's talk about Celia's baby. That's the exciting news for me today. Celia, have you thought about names yet? Girl names? Boy names? Did you pick which room will be the baby's room? Oh my goodness, you'll have a lot to do. I want you to know I'm happy to help with anything. Painting. Shopping. You name it."

"Me too." Kate looked at Celia. "See, Celia." She pointed to Emma. "This is what you call a normal and real friend. I might try to steal you, Emma. I'll claim you as my friend. Yeah, Emma, we look good together. Don't you think we look good together, Celia?" Kate moved over to Emma's side of the table. "There we go."

Two-Minute Marriage

"I love Kate. I can see why you two are close." Emma walked into the office kitchen with Celia.

"I thought she was a little judgmental about my neighbor. Did you?"

"It's hard to say, but if your neighbor asked if Kate thought she and William looked good together, I would be concerned. Is there a chance you heard it wrong? Are they swingers?"

"I don't think they're swingers. I think she's insecure. She's a little strange, but I think her heart is in the right place. Her daughter is very cute and she's in love with Shadow."

"Why would she say that about her and William? What does that even mean? I'd be cautious. That's all I have to say. Be cautious." Emma briefly looked away.

"Emma, what could she have meant by that comment?" Celia's tone became concerned.

"Maybe she was fooling around. I don't have a clue why she would say that. Try to forget it. Sometimes people say crazy things."

"I guess. From the stories you've told me, I know you have a lot of experience with the crazies out there. How about you? Anything happen with your nutcase this weekend?"

"Nothing big or worth discussing. She made a nasty comment about me being just the second wife. Edie said that she felt bad that I would never have what she had."

"Did you ask her what she meant by that?"

"I didn't have to ask, because she told me. She said she felt bad because being the second wife and a stepmother, I would never know what it was like to have Fredric all to myself. She said she felt lucky she got to experience him that way. It was wonderful having him and knowing he didn't have a wife before her. No ex-wife, no kids, no one. He was devoted to only her. And now, even in divorce, they were bonded together through the love for their son."

"Is she nuts? How did you respond to that one?"

"I didn't want to respond. Honestly, I moved away from her. But she didn't let it go. She asked me if I felt bad that I had to share him with Freddy and with her."

"She's out of her mind. What did you say?" Celia pushed her cup under the water dispenser and filled it.

"Like I said, I didn't want to say anything, and I walked away. I guess walking away also gave me time to think. I should have taken more time because I'm sure I could have come up with something better."

"Better than what? Tell me. Tell me."

"It's not that good, trust me. I don't remember my exact words, but I told her that I would rather be his last wife than his first. That our twenty plus years of marriage have most certainly outweighed the sixteen months they had together. Then she said that they were sixteen wonderful and happy months. I couldn't control myself and I told her to find THAT clause in the divorce papers. I told her happy marriages don't end in divorce. I walked away from her and stayed away from her. She's delusional. They had a bad marriage from before they went to town hall."

"You said that to her?"

"Yes, I did. Celia, I shocked even myself. I can't believe she continues time and time again to pull this nonsense. She has no ability to learn from her mistakes with me. If she doesn't want me to be nasty in return, she should stop with the crap. Does she think I don't realize they were married? I had relationships longer than their marriage. For goodness' sakes, I've had stomach viruses longer than their marriage."

"You're too funny. You make such amusing analogies about that marriage. We should make a list of all the things that have lasted longer than their marriage."

"Yeah. Food poisoning, menstrual cramps, hurricanes, root canals, etc. You catching my theme here? I could go on, but I can't think of more disgusting things to associate with her and her two-minute marriage to my husband."

Celia shook her head. "I can't figure people out. Why is she so determined to constantly bring it up to you?"

"Because, pathetically, she has no life. I would have compassion for her, but she's too miserable and nasty to me. As I said, I try to stay away."

Happy Birthday

Shadow raced into the bedroom the second the door opened. William tried to stop him, but the dog was too quick—he ran in and jumped on the bed. Celia, without opening her eyes, squeezed him tight as he lay on top of the blanket next to her.

"Sorry, Celia, I tried to stop him. I wanted to let you sleep."

"Happy birthday, Billy the birthday boy."

"Thank you. Sorry he woke you up."

"It's okay. I'm pregnant, not sick. I'm glad you guys woke me up. I made a list of what we need to do today and texted it to you. Do you want to go out to dinner or do something special?"

"I'll think about it." He walked out of the room and downstairs to the kitchen.

When Celia entered the kitchen, William handed her a cup of coffee. "Hey, it's your birthday, not mine. I should have gotten up to make your coffee."

"Celia, you need your rest."

"William. I'm barely two months pregnant. Remember, I am not sick—I am in perfect health. Please stop worrying about everything. You're going to make me paranoid as well as crazy as well as nervous as well as annoyed. Do you want this list to continue?"

"I get it. I'm excited, so shoot me. Since I don't know how you feel, I need to make sure you feel good." William put the coffee pot in the sink.

"Good boy." She raised her voice to a high pitch and walked over to William. She patted his back the way she did Shadow's back when he did something good.

"I'm going to do the kitchen floor. I think that was on the list, right?"

"What are you doing with that bucket?" Celia pointed to the yellow bucket he carried in with him.

"I just told you. I thought you wanted the kitchen floor washed."

"I do, and I'll do it myself. And it's a wood floor–it doesn't get washed. I have a spray cleaner and I'll take care of it."

"Celia, it's too much work for you."

"You're going to make me crazy." She shook her head and rolled her eyes. "Please stop worrying about every little thing. I need to do what I would normally do if I weren't with child." Celia air-quoted *with child* and clicked her hands in the air, as she wiggled her butt and walked away.

"I get it. Sorry. I want to make sure you don't overdo it."

She turned around and came back into the kitchen. She moved close to William and put her arms around his neck. "Now get out of here. I'm going to do the floor. If you want to help, I have some prescriptions at the drugstore and we need a few things. You can access the grocery list on your phone."

"You want me to go to the grocery store?"

"Hey, you said you didn't want me to overdo it. Getting groceries is a way you can help me." Celia hated to grocery shop.

"I'll go in a little while. Let me finish a few things here first." He left the room and took the empty bucket with him.

Celia wrapped her coat around her, took her cell phone, and stepped into the cold garage.

"Hi, Auntie Celia. Did Uncle Bill leave yet?"

Celia whispered and cupped her hand over the microphone of her cell. "No, I want him to go later today to make sure he's out around 5:00. I'll send him to get me something at the drugstore and at the hardware store too. That will keep him out for a while. When he leaves for my errands, I'll get the cake and you guys can head over here. You know the garage combination. Right? Be sure to bring Trudy too. I'll text you when the time is right."

"Mom has the garage number. You know I'm sad that we missed Shadow's birthday. We should have had a party for him too."

"I bought him a toy and took him to the park on his birthday. He didn't like the park. It was too cold. And he ripped the toy open to get the squeaky thing out. I don't think he cared it was his birthday–he didn't even know."

As Celia pulled out of the driveway, Tammie flagged her down.

"Hi, Celia. What are you up to?"

Celia opened the window. "Running out to get a few things. William's brother and family are coming for dinner to celebrate his birthday. He's gone grocery shopping for me."

"Good-looking and he shops. You sure are lucky, Celia."

"Yes, I am. Sorry to cut you short, but I'm on a time limit, as the dinner is a little surprise for him. I have to get his cake at the bakery before 5:30." She closed the window and drove off.

With the cake securely settled in the backseat, Celia drove onto Cherry Tree Lane. She noticed a package at the front steps. She drove into the garage, hid the cake, and walked through the kitchen to the front door. She picked up the package and examined the contents. *She is a piece of work. Maybe it's clearer if I call her a piece of shit.*

"Hey, Kate. Are you coming over?" Celia spoke the second Kate answered.

"We're leaving right now. Do you need anything?"

"No, but I want to tell you a quick story. When I left to pick up William's cake, I bumped into my neighbor. I told her it's his birthday. I told her I was making a surprise dinner and was going out to get his cake. When I got back, I noticed a box on the front steps. She left a cake by the door. It's big enough for a dozen people. The cake read *Happy Birthday Wills*. Is that a little obnoxious?"

"No. it's not a little obnoxious. It's a lot obnoxious. You told her it was a surprise. What if William saw it first? Wouldn't he be a little suspicious if he saw a birthday cake on the front porch big enough to feed an army?"

"Yeah, right. I didn't think of that. First of all, she wrote *Wills*. Isn't she little Miss Doesn't-Like-Nicknames? And second, we aren't at the point of being close enough that she would bring a cake over. Maybe a bottle of wine, but not a cake. That's my job."

Celia took Tammie's cake out to the garage. She lifted the trash can cover and threw it in the trash.

William arrived home before the rest of the party guests arrived.

"Hi, honey. I'm home."

Celia walked into the kitchen and kissed him hello. *Figures you'd beat everyone else to the party, you little brat.* She looked at her watch and realized Noah and his family would arrive within the next ten minutes. "You should take a shower and relax before dinner." *Maybe we can surprise you as you walk out of the bathroom.*

"Nah, I'm good. I'm going to read the paper." William took his iPad and sat down on the couch in the family room.

Well, you'll still be surprised we're having company for dinner. Celia answered the doorbell for her guests who arrived early.

Dr. Parsons

Following her doctor's appointment, Celia returned home earlier than usual. *I didn't even need Kylee to take Shadow out this afternoon. I'll take him to the park anyway. It's too beautiful out to not enjoy this sunshine. I could use some exercise.* She patted her stomach and imagined it had gotten bigger.

The garage door slammed behind her when she entered the kitchen. "Shadow!" Celia called out. The house was clean, cool, and unusually quiet. "Shadow! I'm home!" She shouted out again when he didn't come to greet her. *Did Kylee not bring him back from his walk?*

She placed two small bags of groceries down on the counter. Her pocketbook fell from her shoulder onto the kitchen floor. Shadow's food had not been touched—his water bowl was bone-dry. *Why didn't he eat? Where is he?*

She picked up the note Kylee left on the kitchen table. *Hi, Celia. Thank you for letting me walk Shadow. I love him. We had a great time. Mom even helped me watch him. Maybe one day I'll get a dog too, but I will still want to babysit and take care of Shadow, so they can be besties. Hope it's okay, Mom gave me some treats for him. He's sooooooo cute. Luv, Kylee.*

"Shadow! Come out, come out, wherever you are!" Her voice was melodic as she called for her pet and searched the first floor.

"Shadow!" The tune in her voice had lost its friendly tone; it was now full of fear. Her next call out to Shadow was demanding. "Shadow! Come!" *Where the hell is he?* Then she remembered. *The den! He must be trapped between the couches again.* She ran upstairs and into the den. She pulled out the couch. Shadow didn't come out. She crawled into the little space—he wasn't in there.

"Shadow? Where are you?" She roamed through the bedrooms and checked each closet. *Shit. Where is he? You're becoming a little sneak. You love to hide, don't you?*

She inspected under the bed in the master bedroom and in the closet. No Shadow. As she turned to leave the room, she spotted Shadow lying listlessly on the bathroom floor next to the toilet. The water had been drained out of the bowl. His breaths were labored.

"What's wrong, baby boy? Did you drink all that pukie toilet water?" She dropped down on the floor. He whimpered as she rubbed his head. His nose was dry, and he began to shake. She dialed William. He didn't answer. Her stomach tightened into knots, but she tried to remain calm.

He stared up at her with big, sad eyes.

She raced into the bathroom, picked up a washcloth, and soaked it with water. She opened his mouth and squeezed droplets of water onto his tongue.

"What's wrong with you, Shad?" She pressed the contacts button, found the number, and dialed Dr. Parson's office. The receptionist instructed her to bring Shadow in immediately. Her panic intensified.

With all her strength, she knelt and lifted his lethargic body. Nervously and cautiously, she carried him down the flight of stairs and into her car. She backed out of the driveway and sped off to the veterinarian.

"Don't worry, Shad. You'll be all right. Dr. Parsons will make you better. Don't worry, honey." She repeated the words again and again as they drove the anxiety-filled ten-minute ride to the veterinarian's office. His condition worsened during the ride. Instead of hanging his head out the window, biting at the air, as he usually did, he lay in the backseat as he struggled to breathe. She felt helpless as her poor little dog suffered.

She contacted Dr. Parson's office when she was a minute away. Shadow's breaths were sporadic strained gasps for air. He was severely distressed. Upon their arrival, Dr. Parsons, wearing a white lab coat, ran outside to meet Celia. He took Shadow from her arms and raced him into the examination room. Celia stayed in the empty waiting room as he analyzed Shadow–it seemed like hours. She paced the room. Her heart pounded into her throat. Her mouth was dry, and her palms were sweaty. She struggled to swallow. *What's wrong with him?* She held a magazine in her hand, flipped the pages, and then tossed it on the table next to her. She picked up the magazine again, rolled it into a tight tube, and tapped it against her thigh. *He's going to get better. He's going to be okay.* The words raced through her head again and again.

Dr. Parsons came out to the waiting area–without Shadow. "Celia, can you come with me?" He didn't smile. She knew it was bad.

"What's wrong with him?" She followed Dr. Parsons into the examination room.

"I'm not sure. He seems to be having a toxic reaction. I'm not certain, but it looks as if he may have ingested antifreeze or xylitol."

Celia moved closer to Shadow and rubbed his head. "How would you know which one? Where would he have gotten that?"

"I don't know. If you have antifreeze in your pipes and he drank toilet water, he could have ingested antifreeze from the water. Certain candies, gums and sweets, especially chocolates, have xylitol. Not all the symptoms are the same, but they are extremely similar."

"He drank toilet water in our house. This is my fault."

"You don't know that. You may not even have antifreeze in your pipes. If I had to guess, I would say it was the xylitol and not antifreeze. He has tremors and a rapid heartbeat, which is more common with xylitol. Without further testing, we can't ever know for sure. Poison symptoms are similar for many types of poison. Celia." He put his hand on hers. "It could be anything. Do you want me to test for sure?"

"No. I want him to feel better. Is he going to be okay?"

"I'm sorry, Celia, there is no antidote for this type of toxicity at this point." He put his arm on her shoulder. It felt heavy.

"What do you mean? You have to do something. He's such a strong dog. He never gets sick. Never!"

"Celia, his vital signs are weak. He has too much of the toxin in his system. I've given him a shot, which would have helped him by now. I'm very sorry, but I don't believe there's much hope. I'll leave you alone with him for a while. If the medication is going to help, and I don't think it will, it will help him relatively soon."

Celia sat down on the doctor's stool and rolled over to the table. She nestled her face into the fur on Shadow's neck. He was warm and soft as she squeezed him and held him tight. His paw rested on the table; she reached for it and held it in her hand. His breaths were labored as he whimpered softly. Her face stayed buried in his fur. When she kissed his neck, she could taste the salt on his fur as it became dampened with her tears. She lifted her head and held his face in her hands. She stared into his eyes, which were half open as he blinked slowly. With her head hidden in his fur, she sobbed. *Please be okay, Shadow. I love you. Please don't go, my little sweetie.*

Her heart raced as she held him tight. His whimpers quieted, and her sobs strengthened. In a moment, only her sobs could be heard. Again, she nuzzled her head in the fur of his neck and kept it there as the warmth of his body became cold. She didn't lift her head when Dr. Parsons entered and touched her shoulder. She hugged his limp furry little body against her chest. She couldn't get up.

"I'm sorry, Shadow. I love you." Her voice was muffled as she kept her head down and her tears dripped onto Shadow's fur. She let out a loud gasp to catch her breath and then continued to cry.

Dr. Parsons pulled a chair close to her and sat down. He returned his hand to her shoulder.

"It's all my fault. If I had been home, I could have saved him."

"Celia, don't blame yourself. You have no idea what happened. These poisons act quickly. Not you or anyone could have done anything to save him. You can't blame yourself. He ingested far too much to have survived."

Her sobbing continued. She pulled a tissue from her pocket, held it under her nose, and raised her head. She glanced down at Shadow's matted wet fur. "Where did you get into that poison?" Her question was rhetorical; she didn't expect an answer.

Her anxiety heightened. She stood and paced, sat down on the stool, and then stood again and paced. Dark circles appeared beneath her eyes as mascara mixed with her tears.

"I'm very sorry, Celia. Why don't we sit here for a few moments more until you feel a little more comfortable? Perhaps you should call William and have him meet you here." He got up and walked to the cooler. Dr. Parsons returned and handed a cup of water to Celia.

"Thank you." She was calm for a moment as she sipped the water. When she put it down, she burst again into tears. Her body shook. She picked up the paper cup and gripped it with both hands. "He was fine when I left this morning. You're right. I should call William and tell him. He's going to be devastated."

She reached under the stool and searched for her bag. She panicked. "Oh no. I lost my bag!" She took a deep breath. "Can I use your phone?"

"It's right here, Celia." Dr. Parsons picked up Celia's bag from the counter and handed it to her. "Do you want privacy?"

"No! Please stay with me. If you don't mind, that is."

"Of course I don't mind." He stood next to her while she dialed the phone.

"William, we've lost Shadow!" She sobbed into the telephone when he answered. She couldn't contain herself.

"Don't worry, Celia. He's probably hiding or something."

"No, you don't understand. He's gone!" Her words were barely audible between her sobs.

"Honey, I'm sure you'll find him. Did you check that hiding place in the den?"

"William, you don't understand." She could no longer speak. She stared at Shadow's lifeless body and handed the phone to Dr. Parsons.

William arrived with swollen red eyes. Dr. Parsons took him to see Celia. Together they said good-bye to Shadow.

It was more painful than she could have imagined walking into the quiet house. Shadow's water dish sat empty on the kitchen floor while his food dish sat untouched. "Our little Shadow is gone." Brokenhearted, she sat at the kitchen table.

Noah

The chatter from the television created white noise as an exhausted Celia and William slept on the family room couches.

"What was that? Shadow?" Celia woke up, startled from a sound sleep. "I must have fallen asleep." She realized Shadow wasn't there and her heart sank to her stomach. It was a sudden rush of sadness. "William, are you sleeping?"

"No, I'm here." She had woken him up.

"We have to tell Noah. I can't tell him. I'll lose it. You have to tell him. He's going to freak out." She broke into a sob and dropped her face into the palms of her hands. "Should we call him now? It's not even 8:00. I'm sure he's still up."

"I don't know. You think we should do this now?"

"Yes, William. I don't want to deal with it tomorrow. I want to take care of it now. Please." She wiped her tear-stained face.

"Should we call him now?"

"Yes, William, we should." A look of panic came over her face.

"Celia, if you're good to go out, I think we should tell him in person. We can be there in fifteen minutes. They'll still be up. Let's go."

Melanie and Glen led William and Celia to Noah's bedroom, where he was preparing for his science test.

"Noah, it's Uncle Bill." William knocked on his bedroom door.

"WOW! What a great surprise. Is Shadow with you?" Noah sat on his bedroom floor, surrounded by papers and school work.

Celia bit the side of her cheek—her chin quivered. She motioned to William that she couldn't speak.

"Listen, Noah." William looked down, rubbed his forehead vigorously, and took a deep swallow of air. "We have some bad news about Shadow."

"What? What happened? Is he okay?" Noah's voice went up several octaves. His eyes opened wide.

"Shadow died today. I'm sorry to tell you this. He got very sick very fast and there wasn't anything the doctor could do to save him."

"WHAT?" Noah screamed.

Melanie ran into the room when she heard Noah scream.

"Not Shadow!" Noah screamed again and then began to sob.

Celia sat down on the floor next to him and put her arms around him. He leaned into her and cried out of control.

"I'll go make some tea." Melanie stepped out of the room.

"What happened to him?" Noah wiped his tears with the sleeve of his shirt.

"We don't know. Aunt Celia was with him. The doctor said he didn't know what happened. It might have been something poisonous. We don't know for sure." Tears streamed down William's cheeks as he tried to maintain his composure.

"Noah, honey, I know this doesn't make it easier, but let's remember that Shadow had a great life with us, although too short. And he loved you, Noah." Celia still held him tightly. "He got excited when he was with you and Trudy."

"I loved Shadow like he was my own dog. Maybe I shouldn't get attached to dogs. It hurts too much when they leave."

"I know it does." Celia hugged him and then got up from the floor. "I don't think Shadow would want us to sit here and be sad together. Do you? Let's go hang with Trudy."

"Do you think Trudy knows?"

"I don't know. Maybe. Dogs aren't the same as people that way, but it could be possible." Celia led Noah and William out of the room.

Game Night

Celia opened her eyes. She had fallen into a deep sleep and was momentarily unaware of her surroundings. As she lifted her head, she was confused. It took a moment to realize she had fallen to sleep on the couch and not her bed. She looked at the clock and saw it was afternoon. She felt a pang as she remembered Shadow was not in the room with her.

She heard the light knock again–it must have been the first knock that had woken her up. Without thinking, she moved from the couch and into the foyer, where she opened the door.

Standing on the porch was Kylee, her eyes swollen and red. She held a bright bouquet of flowers.

Celia knew why she was there and her own eyes filled with tears. "Oh my goodness, you're the sweetest little thing. Come in." Celia opened the door wide.

Kylee entered the foyer and turned around to look at Celia. "I'm so sad and sorry about Shadow." She burst into tears and threw her arms around Celia's waist. "I'm sorry. Mommy told me last night. I couldn't sleep all night."

Celia knelt and brushed Kylee's hair away from her face. She wiped the tears of her little pink cheeks and held her tight. "I know. I'm sad too. Why don't we go into the kitchen and talk about Shadow and the fun we had with him? He loved to play catch with you."

A soft little sound came from Kylee's lips. "Okay." She wiped her face.

"I have lemonade from the farm stand. Would you like some?" Celia smiled to ease Kylee's sadness as she felt her own sadness deep in her stomach.

"Yes, please, I would." Kylee pulled out a stool from under the counter. Unlike her mother, she didn't spin around. She watched Celia intently.

"Hey, I have an idea. Why don't I make lemonade smoothies?" Celia pulled out her blender, poured the lemonade in and filled it with ice. The whirl of the machine rattled the room. Celia filled two tall glasses and placed straws in the middle. The straws stood up straight in the thickness of the drink. "These are going to be delicious. Let's see what kind of cookies are in the cabinet."

"I loved Shadow." Kylee got up and took a tissue from the box on the counter by the refrigerator. She blew her nose, wiped her eyes, and put the tissue in her pocket. "If I ever get a dog, I want it to be exactly like Shadow." She looked sadly into Celia's eyes.

"I know. He was wonderful, wasn't he? You know, you couldn't see it, but when he heard you at the door, he would jump up and down on this side of the door. He was eager to have you visit and play with him." Celia searched through the cabinet for cookies. "These have coconut, caramel, chocolate, and a delicious cookie. Do you like coconut?" She pulled the box out and showed it to Kylee.

"Like it? Try love. I love coconut. Those look yummy good."

Celia took the box of cookies and sat on the stool next to Kylee.

"Celia, would you and William ever come over to my house and play a game? We have game night once in a while and I want you to play when we do."

"That would be nice. I enjoy playing games. William doesn't, but I think I could persuade him."

"We have a game night tonight. Would you ever want to come?"

"I can come, but William's away on business. Will that work?"

"Yes, it's perfect. It's you I want to be near. I think I'm not as sad about Shadow, now that I'm with you."

"Sweetie, I know what you mean. Having you here with me right now has made me less sad. Thank you." Celia leaned into Kylee.

"We're having pizza too. Do you like pizza?" Kylee smiled. "I'm so excited you'll have pizza and game night with me."

———— ✵ ————

With a glass of red wine in her hand, Tammie greeted Celia at the door. "Come in. Kylee is over the moon excited to have you join us. Would you care for a glass of wine or a beer?"

"Your drink looks great, but I think I'll start with a huge glass of ice water. Thank you."

The fireplace roared, and the board game was set up in the middle of the room.

"Alan went to get the pizza. We always get extra to freeze. There will be plenty. Come on in and sit down."

"Kylee is adorable. We had such a nice visit this afternoon."

"Yes, she told me about it. I think she prefers being at your house more than her own. I'm sorry about Shadow, but I see Kylee a lot more these days, now that she's not running to be with your dog."

What? Glad I could accommodate you with the death of my dog. What'd you do, kill Shadow to spend more time with Kylee? What a terrible thing to say. "I miss having Kylee around. It was always fun to look out the window and see them playing in the back. I hope our child does the same thing."

"What do you mean? Are you having a child?"

Celia's face blushed. "I wasn't going to say anything. That slipped out, but yes, I'm pregnant."

"Well, now Kylee will want to babysit all the time."

"That would be great if she ever wanted to help out. She might be too young to babysit, but I would love if she wanted to help occasionally. I'd pay her, of course."

Before Tammie could respond, Alan walked into the hallway from their garage. "Dinner's here!" He brought the pizza into the family room and set up the dinner around the game on the coffee table that matched Celia and William's.

"Guess who's having a baby?" She pointed to Celia's stomach.

Celia smiled a hesitant smile. "William and I are trying to keep it a secret. Please don't say anything. It's still too early to spread the news."

Kylee perked up and ran into the kitchen. "Can I feel your stomach?"

"There's nothing to feel yet. In a few months, we'll be able to feel the baby kick. Then it will be exciting."

Celia moved into the family room and sat on the couch identical to her own. *It's a good thing I love Kylee. I'll try not to spill tomato sauce on my couch-twin*

Spontaneous Interruption

Did u leave me flowers? B U tiful! Thx. Celia clicked Send.

Celia's phone pinged a response from Emma. *How are u? Missed u. Glad ur back*

Fine-tired-stressed. Sick 2 my stomach thinking about things. Come by.

B there in 2 min

"Emma, are you a ghost who can transport herself through walls? How do you get here so fast?" Celia watched as Emma entered the room.

"I was on my way down when I responded to your text." Emma took her usual seat in Celia's office. "How are you doing?"

"I'm sad about Shadow. I find out I'm pregnant, and then in a flash, it was consumed by Shadow's death."

"How do you feel? Physically?"

"I feel good. A little tired, and a little queasy some mornings, but I feel good. I can feel a tiny bump, but it's not visible yet." She stood and pushed her stomach out.

"How's it look when you aren't forcing your stomach out?"

"Like this." Celia stood up straight and rubbed her stomach. "Can't see much, right?" Celia scrunched up her nose and tilted her head.

"It doesn't even look as if you've overstuffed yourself on Thanksgiving. Probably a few more weeks."

Celia sat down but kept her hand on her stomach. "I know you can't see anything, but I'm excited to feel a little bump when it does appear. Is that weird?"

"I think it's normal." Emma reached over the desk and touched Celia's hand. "I was sorry to hear about Shadow. Don't know if you remember, but Jasper died almost the same way. I don't think it's uncommon."

"Whatever. I'm kicking myself over and over."

"Well, don't. Honestly, Celia, I don't think it was something you did. I think it was simply a bad thing that happened to a sweet little guy. But trust me that I know how painful it is."

"I know you know, Emma. I really do."

Emma leaned back in her chair. "Yes, I do." Her face tightened up and she appeared troubled. "Listen, Celia. I've had to tell you something for a while."

Emma was interrupted by Ramona's spontaneous interruption. "Knock. Knock. Knock." As she did with each visit, she punched her fist in the air as if knocking on a door.

Aha. You and your brother like to punch the air, don't cha. Must be a thing with your family. "Hi, Ramona. Come on in." Celia welcomed Ramona and stood to move another chair closer to her desk.

"I'm leaving. Ramona, you can have my chair." Emma pushed herself up with the arms of the chair. She winked at Celia and left the room.

"Were you guys in the middle of a meeting?"

"No, Ramona. Emma came down to talk for a minute."

THE INHALER

"What day are you coming home?" Celia peeked out from the covers. "I hate when you have to leave on a Sunday."

"I know, babe. It sucks to have the weekend cut short. You sure you're comfortable with me going out of town? It's only a four-hour drive if you need me."

"Honey, I'll be fine. I feel great. If I didn't get queasy in the morning, I'd say I feel perfect. But I'll call if I need you."

"I can even come back tonight if the dinner gets out early. Or better yet, I might be able to sneak out early. I'll come home tonight and leave at the crack of dawn."

"I'll worry about you driving back and forth at those crazy hours." She pulled the covers over her head and slid down deep into the bed. "I'd rather you stay over." Her voice was muffled by the blankets.

William walked over and then pulled the covers from her head and kissed her before he left for his conference.

"I'm here and I'm checking in," William informed Celia when she answered her phone.

"What? You're there already?" Her voice was sleepy.

"Are you still sleeping?" William sounded worried.

"Honey, it's perfectly normal to be tired. I didn't sleep well last night—I caught up this morning." Celia got out of bed and picked up her bottle of vitamins from the counter in the bathroom.

"You sure everything is good?"

"William. How many times do I have to remind you that you are driving me nuts? I'm totally fine. Now go relax and enjoy your meeting."

"I'll call later. Love you."

"Love you too." She put the phone down and picked up her toothbrush. *If I brush my teeth now, I'm going to vomit.* She turned on the water and stepped into the stall shower.

She opened the top of the shampoo bottle. The smell overpowered her, and she was instantly nauseous. She immediately covered it.

In the kitchen, Celia pressed brew on the coffee pot and filled her bowl with oatmeal. As she walked to the refrigerator for maple syrup, she felt a little tingle low in her abdomen and touched her stomach.

Natural light wood. That will go with whatever sex the baby is. At the kitchen island, she ate breakfast and used her iPad to shop for baby furniture. She stood to get juice and the room began to spin. She sat down but couldn't focus on anything. Everywhere she looked, objects rapidly shook back and forth.

She sat still for over five minutes. Her heart raced, and her body was sweaty. She called Kate's cell.

"Hi, Celia."

"Kate, I feel terrible. William's away. Is there any way you can come over?" She walked into the living room and sat down on the couch.

"Celia, I'm in Florida. Did you forget?"

"Oh no. I did forget."

"What's wrong?" Kate's worry was apparent.

"I was queasy before and now my head is spinning. I can't focus on anything." Celia closed her eyes and rested her head against the back of the couch.

"Honey, I want you to call 911. You need to get to a doctor."

"Let me think about it. I'm going to go now." She leaned forward, grabbed the pillow next to her, and held it against her stomach.

"Don't think about it. I'm going to call 911 for you."

"No. Please don't call 911. I'll call Emma as soon as we hang up."

Celia listened to Emma's phone ring. "Emma, it's Celia. I'm not feeling well and hoped you could take me to the hospital. If you get this message within the next minute, call me. In the meantime, I'm going to call Tammie."

Celia's phone rang the second she hung up.

"Did you get in touch with Emma?" Kate sounded panicked.

"No, I'm calling Tammie right now. I think she's home. She might be a pain in the ass, but at least she'll be able to take me to the hospital. I can see her car in the driveway. Don't worry. I need something to help take the spins away."

"Call her right this minute. I'm going to call you again in three minutes."

"Whose car is that?" Celia walked down the sidewalk with Tammie's assistance.

"It's Alan's uncle's. He keeps it in our garage. Hope you don't mind driving in it. It's kind of old." Tammie held Celia by the arm as she helped her into the passenger seat of the car. "Celia? Do you need to rest for a minute?"

"No, I feel a little better. I don't think I should have gotten that dizzy. Did you ever get dizzy when you were pregnant?" She bit her lip.

"I don't remember, but strange things do happen to your body." Tammie helped Celia with the seat belt.

"If I close my eyes, it's a little better. Maybe we don't have to go to the hospital." Celia touched her forehead.

"Celia, I'm here now and I think we should go. Even if it's nothing, you'll sleep better knowing it's nothing. Maybe they can give you something for dizziness, in case it happens again. I brought a fresh cool water for you." Tammie reached into her bag, took out the water, and handed it to Celia. She then tossed her bag onto the floor behind her seat. "Drink the water. You could be dehydrated."

"Thank you for helping me." Celia twisted the cap off the bottle and slowly drank the water.

"I'm glad I was home to help. Where's William today?"

"He had a conference to go to, and I told him I was fine. I was fine, until I got downstairs. Except for a drop of queasiness, I've been fine."

"Don't worry, we're almost there."

"That must be William." Celia glanced at her buzzing cell phone. It was Emma–she didn't answer.

"Was it William?"

"No, it's my friend Emma from work. I should have let her know I found someone to take me to the hospital. She must be worried. I'll text her now." *Don't worry, Em, my neighbor is taking me to hospital, don't feel as bad as I did when I called you.*

"Celia, you seem a little better. How do you feel?"

"I do feel better, a little dizzy, but better. If they can give me something for the dizziness, I will be very happy. That's all I want at this point–and to lie down."

Celia's phone pinged from an incoming text. *Celia, please call me as soon as possible. I have to tell you something about Edie.* "It's Emma again. I'll call her later when we leave."

"What did she want?"

"She must have a funny story about her ex-wife. It will have to wait. She knows I don't feel well." With a concerned look, Celia looked out the passenger window. "It's odd. She doesn't usually text me about this stuff."

"She has an ex-wife?"

"Not exactly. It's her husband's ex-wife, but she says she feels the same problems as if it were hers."

"That's funny. I never heard someone say that before."

Celia's phone pinged again. *Celia, please call me asap. It's important and about Edie.* "It's my friend Emma again. She's usually not this persistent. She's never texted me about this stuff before, which makes me a little concerned. I'm going to give her a quick call; I want to make sure everything is okay."

Tammie began to cough. She started to wheeze and gasp for air. "I think I need my inhaler. It's in the back behind me. Can you reach it?"

Celia stretched her arm behind Tammie's seat but couldn't reach the bag. "Hang on. I'll get it." She unbuckled her seat belt and reached farther into the backseat.

You're Okay

"Celia." Tammie leaned over to Celia and touched her hand that barely peeked out from the blanket. Her hand was cool, and Tammie cupped it between her own and rubbed it to warm it up. "Please wake up." She continued as tears welled in the corner of her eyes and cascaded down her cheeks. She sat beside the bed and blankly stared at Celia's bruised cheeks. "Celia, you're the nicest friend I've ever had. You have to be okay. Please wake up," she whispered as she leaned in closer to Celia.

Tammie released Celia's hand from her own long enough to rub her own drained face. Once again, she clutched Celia's hand. Tammie's face was pale, her eyes sunken and dark, and her clothes wrinkled. She had barely left Celia's side since the accident. She reached for a tissue and held it to her nose. Her shoulders shook as she cried. "This is all my fault."

"Tammie!" William was surprised to see Tammie sitting in the same chair and the same clothes he had seen her in the evening before. "Have you even been home?"

"I can't leave her." She looked up to William, then at Celia, and back again to William. "I couldn't sleep at home anyway. I'd be useless there."

"Tammie, you need a break. Why don't you go home and take a nap or something? Celia should be fine. Her doctor told me she's doing well. She's sleeping because of the sedatives."

"This is all my fault, William. It's all my fault." She turned away from him and dropped her head down, as she stared into her lap.

"Tammie, it was an accident. Her doctor has assured me she'll recover and will be fine. Her ribs will take time to heal, and she'll be sore for a few weeks, but there were no serious injuries, except–" He sighed deeply. "The medication will wear off soon, and I think it's best if I'm alone with Celia. Please go home. I'll call you when it's a good time to come back. I'll need to talk to her privately when she wakes up."

He reached for her hand and helped her out of the chair. "Come on, I'll buy you a cup of coffee and a muffin, and then you should head home."

"Wait! I'll go down and get some coffee and muffins. You stay here, in case she wakes up. I'll be right back." Tammie moved toward the door and turned around to face him. "William? How are you going to tell her?"

"I don't know." He ran his fingers through his hair and then rubbed his face vigorously. "I keep thinking about it. I thought about it all night. I must have called this hospital over forty times to see if she had woken up. I don't know what to say to her. I'm afraid to deal with it. She's going to freak out. She's got enough to deal with. She hasn't gotten over Shadow and now this. I don't want to rehearse anything; I'll wait and see."

William fell asleep in the chair next to Celia's bed. Celia opened her eyes slightly and barely moved her head as she looked around the stark room. She stared up at the ceiling. She tried to focus on a vase of flowers next to the bed. She closed her eyes. She didn't see William sleeping in the chair next to her.

William's head bobbed down and startled him awake. He looked at Celia and saw her eyes were barely open. "Celia," he whispered to his wife.

Celia closed her eyes. "William? William? I'm thirsty. Could you get me some water?" She sounded sleepy and her voice was raspy and dry.

"Honey, how do you feel?" He leaned over and tenderly kissed her forehead.

"Terrible. My head aches." She opened her eyes as much as she could. The light was too bright for her; she squinted and turned her head toward William.

"I'm going to get you some ice chips. They'll help your thirst. Would you like that?"

Celia nodded.

"Celia, do you remember what happened?" William placed the ice chips on the tray next to the bed. He removed a small chip and placed it on her lips. She ran her tongue around the ice and then squeezed it between her lips.

"Sort of. I remember being in the car this morning with Tammie. I know I was dizzy and going to the doctor."

"It was yesterday, honey. Not today."

"Yesterday?" Celia didn't expect an answer. "I reached for something and that's all I remember." She closed her eyes. She sounded groggier by the minute. With her eyes still closed, she told him what she remembered. "I think Tammie was having trouble breathing."

"Honey, you're confusing the accident with how you feel right now. You're having trouble breathing now because your ribs hurt–you cracked a couple. You could breathe perfectly before yesterday." William lifted the blanket up to her neck and tucked it around her shoulders. "Let me know if I'm hurting you by tucking in the blanket."

"I wasn't having trouble breathing. Tammie was sick. I know it. No. I mean no." She sounded groggy. "I'm confused."

"It's okay, Celia. Try to rest. I'm right here with you."

"This blanket feels kind of groovy. Don't you think it feels wicked groovy, William?"

"Yes, very groovy, Celia." He tried to not snicker. Within seconds, Celia was sound asleep again. He breathed a huge sigh of relief.

For the rest of the afternoon, Celia lay motionless on the uncomfortable hospital bed. When she awoke, William remained by her side.

"How ya doing?" William touched her forehead.

"I'm tired."

"You feeling groovy, babe?" He smiled at her.

"Groovy? What decade are you in?" Her voice was a whisper.

"The groovy decade, that's what decade."

"What?" She tried to scrunch her face but winced in pain and stopped.

"Honey, you told me you felt groovy. That's all. Kind of funny, don't you think?"

She winced again and restrained herself from smiling. "Who was it that said groovy?"

"I asked if you were comfy with the blanket and you said you were wicked groovy."

"I don't remember talking to you. Was it today?"

"Yeah. A few hours ago."

"How's Shadow?"

William got a pang in his gut. "Don't you remember? Shadow is gone. It's been over a month."

"Oh." She kept her eyes closed. A tear formed in the corner of her left eye. "I'm confused. There's something else." Her eyes opened wide. "How's my baby?"

"Do you still mean Shadow?"

"No. The baby. Our baby. How is the baby?" She slowly moved her hand to her stomach. Her voice projected panic.

Celia lay still in the bed. She closed her eyes again. Tears poured from her eyes. Her hand never moved from her stomach. She opened her eyes and stared at William. "This can't be happening." She turned her head toward the window. "NO!" She was inconsolable.

William stood and leaned over the bed. He buried his head in her shoulder. His tears dripped between her skin and her hospital nightgown.

"Honey. I'm sorry. I didn't know how to tell you." He lifted his head and embraced her face between his hands.

She didn't move as they stared into each other's eyes. "I can't believe this has happened."

"Celia, the main thing is that you're okay and you're going to heal."

"William, how can I be okay?" Tears ran down her face. "I'm never going to be okay again."

"Don't say that, sweetie. Everything will be fine. I'll make sure of it."

"I'm not okay. Not now."

"Celia, you could have been hurt much worse. I'm looking at the fact that I didn't lose you too. I'm sorry."

William slid into the bed beside her and held her. She fell back to sleep. A sleep that consumed her for the rest of the day.

Seat Belts

William helped Celia into the car and buckled the seat belt around her. She was shivering, though she wasn't cold.

"You all right?" He kissed the tip of her nose.

"I don't think so, but I guess I have to be. Right?"

"No. You don't have to be anything. The last thing you need to do is worry about being strong. I'm giving you permission to let me do all the worrying."

"All the worrying?"

"Well, for the next few weeks. Listen, Kate's waiting for us at home. She's cooked a great treat for you."

"I'm not hungry. She wasted her time."

William closed the door and walked around the car and into the driver's seat.

"Kate's been worried about you. She came over and spent the entire day cleaning the house, dusting and vacuuming. She even did some laundry and made sure everything was done for you. You won't have to do a thing except rest and recover."

Celia watched him buckle his seat belt. When the seat belt clicked, something clicked in Celia's thoughts as well.

"Ya know, it pisses me off that I could get this banged up wearing a seat belt!" William started the car but didn't respond. "William, did you hear me? If I can get this hurt, have a miscarriage and break a few ribs while wearing a seat belt, then what's the use?"

"Celia, I've been wondering about that."

"Yeah, I can see why. Why even bother buckling up? At least I wasn't thrown out of the car."

"Well, that's not exactly why I was wondering about it."

"What do you mean?" She turned and looked at him.

"Celia, I was surprised that you weren't wearing a seat belt."

"Don't be ridiculous, William. I always wear one. That's the first thing I do when I get into a car." She thought about it for a moment. "In fact, I even remember pulling the seat belt from that piece of shit Tammie was driving. It was stuck, and I had to yank it to the front."

"Celia, you weren't wearing a seat belt. Did you get out of the car, and then back in, and perhaps forget to buckle the second time?"

"No. I know that wouldn't happen. I don't remember if we stopped, but I KNOW I would not drive in a car without wearing a seat belt. Maybe someone unbuckled it when they came to help."

"The paramedics were the first ones there. They said you didn't have a seat belt on. Celia, if you had the seat belt on when the car crashed, you would have marks from the seat belt. I'm confused. That's all I'm saying."

"Now this is my fault? I'm not hurt enough with the broken ribs? Now I can feel bad that I killed our baby. Are you blaming me for not wearing a seat belt, which I was wearing? I can't believe this is happening." She began to sob.

"Celia, I'm not blaming you. I'm sure you're right. In fact, I've heard some seat belts can unlatch themselves, upon impact." He reached for her hand and held it tightly. "Please forgive me. Please forget I brought it up. I should have known you would be wearing one. I'm very sorry."

"You're making that up about unlatching, and I know you don't believe me. I hate you right now."

"I know." He moved his hand from hers and rubbed her shoulder. "Let's drop it. I'm terribly sorry. I want you to feel better and I'll do whatever I can to help you. I love you, Celia, please remember that."

"Yeah, right!" She grunted and stared out the window. Tears rolled down her cheeks the entire ride home.

Tammie's Guest Room

"Hey, what's the date of your conference in Denver?" Celia opened the calendar on her computer.

"I'm going to cancel it. I don't really want to go." William sat down on the olive-green loveseat across the room.

"No, you're not canceling. You're going to the conference. I want our life to resume some sort of normalcy. We can't tiptoe around everything now. I want it to be the way it was. Before everything happened. Tell me the date. I'm putting it in the calendar." She clicked on the month and saw the conference already recorded. Celia laughed out loud. "Oops. I see the conference is in two days."

"And that's why I'm not going." William reached over to the file cabinet next to the loveseat and picked up the candy dish. He rifled through the candy and selected five purple jelly beans.

"Ya know what, William? I want you to go. I feel strong and good. If you stay home, I'll feel as if I'm not doing well and I need help. I'm begging you to go. Please." She pushed the chair away from her desk and moved to the couch, where she sat down next to him.

William put his palm out and she placed her hand in his. "Your logic makes great sense. I'll think about it."

"No, you won't think about it. You're going. I need you to do this for me. I can't keep going in circles with this conversation. You're going. End of discussion."

"Okay. Okay. But if you feel one thing, Celia–"

She interrupted his words as she pulled the scarf from her neck and smothered his face with it. "Silence." Her tone was firm.

"What about this? See if Kate can stay here while I'm away. Then I'll feel better going to the conference."

"Let me call her right now. My cell phone is downstairs. I'll be right back." Celia stood up from the couch.

"I'll get it for you." William jumped up to beat Celia to the door.

"You better let me get that phone. Didn't I just say I want things to be normal?"

"You're right." William moved out of the way and swung his hand out as if to guide her through the door.

Celia walked into the room. "Kate can't spend the night on Monday, but she can on Tuesday and Wednesday. How's that?"

"Celia, that doesn't work for me. What if you stay at Melanie's or Emma's?" William sat on the couch and picked all the purple jelly beans from the dish. He held them in his left hand and popped them one at a time into his mouth. "What about staying at Tammie's for one night?"

Celia rolled her eyes. "Are you serious?"

"Yeah. She feels horrible about the accident. She'll be happy that you don't hate her. It was an accident."

"I know it was an accident. I get it. But it's tough to see the person who caused you to miscarry. You can't understand."

"Celia, she's our neighbor. You're going to have to see her at some point. You haven't spoken to her once the entire two weeks you been home. I'm sure she'll be wonderful to you. It's also a matter of convenience. I'm serious–I don't need to go to this meeting."

"I guess that sounds workable. I do want you to go, so I guess since I'm making you go, I should make a concession for this one night."

"Celia, I can stay home."

"Nope, I'm going to stay with Kylee; if she's there, it might be nice. Kate will come the next day and we'll have fun together." Celia sat down on the chair at the desk. "Look how far up I can move my arm without pain." Celia moved her arm up over her head–she winced.

Tammie's guest room was caringly set up for Celia's arrival. Fresh yellow and white freesia were placed in a crackled glass vase on the nightstand. Magazines were artfully strewn across the bed. Scented towels rested on the chair by the door. The room was charming with brightly colored floral curtains, matching bedspread and sheets.

Four small abstract prints were uniformly arranged above the bureau. A peaceful seascape print hung above the headboard. The bed had been turned down and petite gourmet chocolates, in gold foil, were placed on the pillows. Tammie had taken deliberate measures to make sure that the room welcomed Celia.

"Good night, Celia. I'm glad you decided to stay with me." Tammie hugged her and kissed her on the cheek. "I'm also glad you feel better."

"Thank you for having me here. I hope it isn't too much trouble."

"Can I sleep in Celia's room?" Kylee ran up the stairs with a bottle of water. "Here, Celia. I brought you water to keep by your bed. Can I stay in here with you?"

"Kylee, Celia needs her rest, and you do also. Maybe another time." Tammie looked at Celia. "I'm sorry she pesters you."

"Kylee, if my ribs weren't cracked, I would love to have your company." Celia leaned down and kissed the top of Kylee's head. "Good night, sweetie. Have funny dreams."

Celia closed the door and lay down on the bed. She opened the magazine and browsed through the pages as her eyes became more and more heavy.

The siren of a police car woke her up. *I must have fallen asleep.*

She leaned down and removed her fuzzy nightshirt from her overnight bag. She pulled her sweater over her head and winced in pain as the weave from the sweater caught her earring. The earring ripped out of her ear, landed on the rug and bounced under the bed. In frustration, she threw the sweater on the bed and rubbed her ear until the sting faded. *Shit! I lost my earring.*

She removed the diamond earring from her other ear and slowly knelt to the floor. Patting the rug, she fished around under the bed–she couldn't locate her earring. She leaned over to the chair where she had placed her bag and pulled out her phone.

Her cell phone flashlight shone under the bed. *Where the fuck is that earring?* She slid her hand along the carpeting under the bed but didn't feel the diamond. Celia glided her arm farther under the bed and stopped when she felt a thin box. Gripping the edge of the box, she wiggled it out into the room. It was shallow and appeared to be the lid of a shoe box.

My earring. Thank goodness. She screwed the silver back into the earring and placed it on the bureau with its mate. Unconsciously, she glanced inside as she pushed the cardboard lid back under the bed. There were only a few items in the box. Celia picked up the foil-wrapped candies, which were identical to the one on her pillow. *One, two, three, four, five. Did she give me a candy from under her bed? Glad I hate dark chocolate. Gross.* She tossed the candy back into the box and removed the envelope at the bottom. It wasn't sealed closed–she opened it. Celia removed the picture of a dog but couldn't tell whether it was a Golden Retriever or a mixed breed. The dog was running with a stick protruding from his mouth.

She got up from the floor, sat down on the bed, and studied the picture. *I've seen this picture before. Where have I seen this picture?* Celia couldn't remember the picture. *Maybe it's downstairs in the family room. I'll check tomorrow.* With the picture returned to the envelope, she pushed the box back under the bed.

Celia crawled under the cozy blanket and opened the magazine again. Her eyes were sleepy, and she began to nod off. Without warning, her heart fluttered and she felt a rush through her body. She got out of bed, knelt on the carpet and removed the box cover again. *What the fuck? Why do you have this picture? What's the connection?* She looked at the clock; it was almost midnight. *Screw it, I'm calling.*

A soft knock on her door interrupted her as she began to dial the phone. When she opened the door, Kylee stood in the hallway, cuddling her teddy bear. "Can I come in?"

"Of course you can." Celia followed Kylee into the room.

"I brought you my teddy bear to keep you company. I like to sleep with him and thought you might want to borrow him tonight." Kylee walked to the side of the bed and tucked her teddy bear into the bed on which Celia was to sleep.

As Kylee walked away from the bed, she kicked the box lid. "Wow, you found the candy?" She was excited to see the gold foil candy on the floor.

"Is this your candy?" Celia picked up the lid and held it out for Kylee.

"It's not my candy. It's the candy my mom gave me when I took care of Shadow. She told me dogs love it. When my big brother took care of a dog once, I gave it to that dog too. I'm so happy that I was able to give them something good before they got sick."

Stay calm. Pull an Emma. Don't react. Ask a question. "You gave this to Shadow?" She held the foil-wrapped candy in her hand. A chill ran up her spine.

"Yeah, when I took him home, my mom came with me and gave me two candies to give him. He loved them. I only had the two, but I'll bet he would have liked more. I really miss him."

Celia's heart pounded. "You're a little sweetie, aren't you? You took good care of Shadow."

"I did."

Celia rested her hands on Kylee's shoulders. "Thank you for lending me your teddy bear. You should get back to bed, honey. You're going to be exhausted tomorrow. I'll come with you and tuck you in." Celia walked across the hall with Kylee and wrapped the blankets around her. She kissed her forehead and then quietly closed the bedroom door behind her.

The number she dialed rang through her cell phone.

"Celia, what's wrong? Why are you calling so late?" It was the voice of someone who had obviously been woken up.

"Emma. I'm staying at Tammie's tonight. Tammie, my neighbor. She has a picture of your dog. I know it's the same picture that's in your office. It's exactly the same."

"What do you mean?" Emma was still groggy.

"I found a picture of your dog in a box under the bed. There were chocolate candies in the box too."

"Fuck!" Emma shrieked.

"Emma, I think Tammie gave Kylee the candy to poison Shadow. Why does she have a picture of your dog?"

"Celia, you've just confirmed my suspicions. I always believed she poisoned Jasper."

"Emma, how would she know your dog? I don't get it."

"Celia, Fredric and I are coming to get you. Stay there and get ready. We'll pull into the driveway and you come out immediately."

"Do you want the address?"

"No, I know where she lives. We'll tell you everything. Stay calm."

"Emma, tell me. How do you know Tammie?"

"I didn't want you to find out this way. I tried to tell you a few times, but every time I tried, someone interrupted us."

"Tell me what?" Celia's voice shook with panic.

"Tammie is Edie."

"What? What are you talking about?"

"My ex-wife is Tammie. The day I told you her name, I said E.D. I said the initials E and D. Then you called her Edie, and I kind of liked it and it stuck. I didn't think it mattered."

"Is that why you laughed whenever I called her Edie?"

"Yes, but I never thought it would matter that you know her real name. I never imagined you would meet her. Then you bought the house on the same street as her house. I didn't want to tell you because I didn't want to influence you. Fredric said that maybe she isn't a jerk to people she doesn't despise."

"I can't believe this."

"We're already in the car. Get your things together and you'll stay here with us."

The headlights lit up the driveway. Celia grabbed her bag and crept down the stairs to the front door. The red light flashed on the alarm panel next to the foyer closet. She held her breath, opened the door, and ran to the car. Fredric jumped out and opened the backseat door for Celia. He slammed the door shut once Celia was seated. The car sped off to the sound of the house alarm blaring.

Exposed

Emma turned around and looked at Celia in the backseat behind Fredric. "Celia, I'm sorry. I didn't know what to do. When you told me some of the things she had said, I became concerned. A couple of times I tried to tell you that my ex-wife is your neighbor, but every time I started to tell you, something interrupted us."

Celia was confused. "I don't understand. How can she be Fredric's ex-wife? Her name is Edie and my neighbor is Tammie."

"I know, it's a strange coincidence, but that's who she is. I called her Edie, but it was E.D. for egg donor. I didn't like to say her name, so I nicknamed her E.D. When you showed me the house and gave me the address, I thought I was going to pass out. And then when you told me about Shadow, I was suspicious that she had a hand in his death. No, let me rephrase that: I was sure she did. I knew she poisoned Jasper, but I couldn't prove it. She was jealous that Freddy liked my dog more than he liked her."

"I think she was jealous that her daughter loved Shadow so much. She made a couple comments about it. In fact, she sounded jealous that Kylee might want to babysit for us." Celia rubbed her head and sat silent for a few seconds. "I feel like I'm in a dream—I mean nightmare." She wiped her neck, which was clammy and cold. "Freddy is Tammie's son? That's not possible. She's too young, plus her oldest is in college—I thought Alan was his father?"

"Alan is Kylee's father and Fredric is Freddy's father. She tells people she has a son in college because she doesn't want people to know how old she is, or that she was married before. It's a huge age difference between Freddy and Kylee."

A police car sped by. Fredric laughed out loud. "Wonder where that's going?"

Emma punched his arm. "Knock it off."

Celia smiled at Fredric's comment. "I'm sorry if I sound stupid, but I'm so confused. I thought her oldest son's name is Rick."

"No, it's Fredric, same as this guy." Emma pointed to Fredric, who sat next to her. "She doesn't want to call him Freddy because it's derived from Fredric, so she split his name and took the R-I-C portion. She refers to him as Freddy only when she's around me."

"When did you try to tell me?" Celia's confusion increased.

"The day of the crash, I called and texted you, but you never got back to me. I tried other times. Once we were interrupted by Ramona and another time something else happened. I figured it was a message that I shouldn't say anything. Keep in mind, I thought that she's nasty to me because she hates me. She has no reason to hate you. I wanted to tell you when you left the hospital, but I knew you had so much other stuff on your mind. I didn't think it was the right time to add to the trauma you were dealing with. Believe me, I'm kicking myself now. Never in my wildest imagination did I ever expect something like this to happen."

"Oh my God. Oh my God. Oh my God. I remember now." Celia began to sweat profusely. "You called me, and I didn't get it. Then you texted a couple times. I told Tammie about you. I told her I was going to call you back and that you probably had an ex-wife problem." Celia stopped talking long enough to catch her breath. "Tammie had an asthma attack while we were driving. She asked me to get her inhaler. Oh my God, that's why I didn't have my seat belt on. That's why. I unbuckled it to reach for her inhaler. That's all I remember."

"She doesn't have asthma," Fredric interjected into the conversation.

"Celia, she knew you were calling me. When I wrote that I needed to tell you something about my ex-wife, she must have put it together that she was going to be exposed. That's when she crashed the car."

"I can't even believe this. Ya know, in my gut, I knew something was wrong with her. It never felt right being around her. She seemed to flirt with or talk about William a little too much. It was as though she had a crush on him or something. I thought it was odd. You know that Kate thought it was odd too. I should have gone with my gut."

"Don't blame yourself. This is an amazing coincidence. It's something you'd see in a girlie movie or a silly novel. It isn't something you could have ever imagined."

"I took these with me." Celia held out her hand for Emma.

"What are they?" Emma took one of the foil candies from Celia's hand and opened it up. She put it up to her nose and smelled it.

"It's the candy Kylee gave to Shadow. She said she gave it to a dog her big brother took care of. I assume it was Jasper."

"I knew it. Didn't I say I knew it?" She looked at Fredric.

"Tammie told her the dogs would like it. Kylee didn't know what it was. She still has no idea. I should give them to Kate. I think her husband would be able to determine how bad they are."

"I can tell you how bad they are. They're loaded with xylitol. It can kill a dog quickly, as you already know."

"I know. Kylee would feel terrible if she had any idea. I feel bad for her."

"I do too." Emma handed the candy back to Celia. "Listen, you're staying with us until William comes home."

"I'm going to call him now."

Part 4

Six Months Later

THE SMELL OF THE OCEAN

"Hi, Celia. Would you be interested in coming to the mall with us?" Emma's tone was upbeat and happy as Celia answered the call.

"Us?"

"Hi, Celia." The little voice yelled into the phone. "It's me, Kylee. I hope you can meet us at the mall."

"Kylee! I'm so excited. Of course I can meet you at the mall. What are you guys doing together?"

"I'm staying at my big brother's. I'm going to stay there for a while. My mom got a small apartment and it isn't close to my school, and my dad is moving out of the house too. Someone else is going to buy it and live there."

"Wow. How is it staying at your brother's?"

"It's fun. And guess what, Celia?"

"What's that?"

"My brother said we can get a dog. I can't believe it. I'm going to have a dog." Kylee's voice was uplifting for Celia to hear.

"I'll meet you guys at the mall entrance. Does noon work?"

"Perfect!" Kylee and Emma spoke at the exact same time.

With his face lathered in shaving cream, he leaned in to kiss Celia as she walked into the bathroom. "Hey." He stroked his neck with the razor.

She rubbed the cream off her lips. "Yuk." She rubbed her lips again. "I'm going to meet Emma and Kylee for lunch. Kylee's living with Freddy right now. I guess Tammie and Alan split up."

"What a mess. I feel bad for Kylee."

"Yeah, I do too." Celia paused and smiled at William. "How are you today?" She pulled her pink fluffy robe tight around her body.

"I'm good. Why do you ask?" He washed the residual shaving cream from his face and neck.

Celia walked up behind him and wrapped her arms around his waist. "I don't know. Just checking in on you." She kissed his back, turned away and walked toward the window. She leaned against the sill as she watched a seagull fly by. "I love this view."

"What's in your hand?" William dried his face and placed his towel on the counter.

Celia giggled. "Nothing." She moved her hand behind her back.

William reached to grab Celia's waist and pull her hand forward. "What's this for?" He laughed out loud.

"Leave. I'll be out in a minute." She closed the door as William walked out.

A minute later, Celia opened the door. "Come on, let's sit out on the deck."

William followed Celia downstairs, through the kitchen, and out to the deck.

"I love this ocean view. I never would have imagined this would be my life."

"Let me see that." He reached to take the device from her hand.

She grabbed his hand. "Nope. It takes three minutes, and we've already gone through one and a half minutes. Be patient." She kissed the knuckles of his hand.

When William saw the plus sign on the stick, he jumped up. He grabbed Celia, picked her up and swung her around. She held his hand as they walked down the steps and dipped their toes in the ocean.

"Ah. No neighbors. I love our new home. I love you." She rested her head on his shoulders.